Stockholm syndrome: the psychological tendency of a
hostage to bond with, identify with, or sympathise with
his or her captor.

The Second Captive

Maggie James

First published in 2017 by Bloodhound Books

www.bloodhoundbooks.com

Print ISBN: 978-1-912175-35-2

PROLOGUE – *Beth*

Present day

'Hey, check out that tart! Can you believe the state of her?' Sniggers erupt from the two teenage boys nearby, who nudge each other as they stare at me. I avoid eye contact with them, praying they'll find another source of amusement. Ahead is a pedestrian crossing where an elderly woman waits to cross. I shuffle towards her.

'What a nutter! The bitch has got slippers on!' The mocking hoots of the teenagers follow me, straight into the ears of the old woman. Her eyes scrape over my clothes, grimace at my footwear, before she spots my jogging bottoms, slashed and dark with my blood. Disapproval tugs the corners of her mouth. I shrink, chastened, into the doorway of the nearest shop, until she stops staring.

Not that I blame her, or the boys. The cuts to my knees must look bad. As for my feet, I don't own any shoes; the soft pink slippers are my only form of footwear. My option was to wear them or go barefoot. The rain started ten minutes after I left the cottage, rendering my feet cold and wet. Sore, too. The thin leather soles aren't suitable for walking the distance I've travelled. What must it be, two, perhaps three miles? The Clock Tower is straight ahead of me, its red brick a distinctive Kingswood landmark. Past it is The Busy Bean. The coffee shop where life as I once knew it ended two years ago, when I was eighteen.

The doorway provides shelter; I tell myself I'll move on once the rain isn't so heavy. The idea of taking an umbrella didn't occur to me before leaving the cottage; it was a soft September morning as I eased myself over the windowsill, the sky a uniform blue. Weather isn't something I've concerned myself with during the last two years. You might say I've led a sheltered life during that time.

As well as my feet being sore, my calves ache; I'm not used to walking so far. Weariness seeps through me, threatening to reduce me to tears, another humiliation I don't need. To the casual observer, I must look weird enough already, what with the fluffy slippers and the bloody knees. Not to mention the jacket I'm wearing, the sleeves of which are long enough to cover my hands. It's Dominic's jacket. Like shoes, a coat isn't something I possess. I've not ventured outside the cottage for two years; it's likely I never would have again, but the urge for freedom proved too strong. As I contemplate that urge, an image arises in my brain: a woman with long, dark hair piled on her head in messy disarray, her eyes tender with the smile they hold, the love in her expression warming me to the soles of my cold, wet feet.

The rain has eased to no more than a drizzle. I should move on, but I'm frightened. Everything's louder, bigger, brighter, than I remember. My horizons have shrunk to the confines of a damp basement, and I'm unprepared for how terrifying the outside world is. Were there always so many cars on the roads? All these people thronging the streets? A child starts screaming, the sound magnified in my ears. Panic grips me. I can't do this.

It's not too late, I tell myself. Go back to the cottage; take refuge in the familiarity of the basement. Where mouthy teenagers can't mock. Where old women don't judge.

In my head, the woman with the messy hair smiles at me again. 'Come home,' she says. My panic subsides.

I turn towards The Busy Bean, its heady coffee aroma meeting me several yards from the open door. The rich caffeine scent, a smell I've not inhaled for a long time, teases my nostrils; I close my eyes with pleasure. Dominic is a staunch Earl Grey man. And what he drinks, so do I.

I walk towards that delicious aroma, as though I intend to stride through the door and order a cappuccino, grabbing my usual table towards the back, when I stop myself. The soaked slippers, the obviously-not-mine jacket mock me, echoing the teenagers; I'm too wet, too weird, too wacky, to venture inside. The windows are wet and smeary as I peer through them. None of the baristas look familiar, but then serving in a coffee shop isn't usually a long-term job option. Nobody is likely to recognise me, but I still can't go in. They'll expect me to order something, and money, like shoes, isn't a commodity I possess. I don't have a handbag, or a purse, any coins or credit cards. I did have, once, but Dominic disposed of everything I owned.

My stomach growls, no doubt alerted by the coffee and cake smells. Since breakfast yesterday, my only food has been a hummus sandwich; I need to eat, and quickly.

I turn away, and there, opposite me, leading off Regent Street, is the road towards Downend. I cross over in its direction. Saplings are growing along the pavement, their branches sprouting new life. My fingers trail over the bark of one of them, enjoying its roughness beneath my skin, such a contrast to the soft foliage above. As I explore, reacquainting myself with the luxury of doing so, a terrier approaches, sniffing me. I bend down, allowing myself to stroke its wiry pelt, before yanking my hand away, remembering. Dogs are dirty, carry disease. Dominic said so.

I start walking again. Every step is a reminder of my sore feet, my aching calves. I ignore my body and retreat into my head, my thoughts fixed on my destination. And the reception I'm likely to face. The reason I'll give for my two-year absence. My mind spins back to my parents, to my old family home, which is where I'm heading. My mother, her dark hair perpetually messy, with whom I've always been so close. My father, with his heavy jawline, his greying hair, his jowly chin betraying the fact he's going to seed, joins her in my head. Along with Troy. My brother.

One question has always tortured me. Why did no one find me? Troy must have told my parents what he saw that night. Why wasn't it enough for the police – because of course my mother would have called them – to track me down?

By now, I'm almost home.

I turn into Draper Street. My eyes fall on the house where I grew up, where I lived until the age of eighteen. Before I went missing. Tears mist my vision. My chest grows tight.

I walk towards the door. My fingers rub against what's in the pocket of my jogging bottoms, its small yet solid coolness hard against my touch.

'Wish me luck,' I tell its former owner.

My hand moves towards the bell, before stopping. To press my finger against it is an irrevocable action, bringing the inevitable question: *Where have you been for the last two years?*

Whatever my answer, it won't sound convincing. My best bet is to tell them I've been staying with friends, provoked into leaving by my father's constant nagging. *Either get a job or go to university, Beth, for God's sake!* The two choices he saw as a fit path for my future. My mother will be hurt, disappointed by my apparent selfishness, but better that than revealing the truth. How would I ever find the words?

My wet feet, my aching legs, the desperate hollow in my stomach, leave me no choice. What's more, the yearning to have my mother's arms wrap around me, the warmth of her body pressed against mine, sweeps through me with tornado-like force. 'Beth,' she'll murmur against my hair. 'You've come home. At last.'

My finger pushes the doorbell, releasing the familiar one-two ding-dong chimes deep into the belly of the house.

I wait.

Nobody comes.

Anxiety invades my brain, conjuring up unthinkable scenarios. My family have moved away, abandoned me, leaving me standing here with my ice-cold toes and my empty stomach. Then reason asserts itself; my mother's car is in the driveway, the familiar faded red of the Fiat's bodywork proof that she, at least, hasn't exited from my life. I press the bell again.

Footsteps sound out, moving towards the door. It's solid wood, so I can't see who's behind it until it opens.

Teak gives way to the hallway, and to my mother.

I'm home. At last.

PART ONE
Two years ago

CHAPTER 1 – *Beth*

I visit The Busy Bean most lunchtimes, keen for an hour away from the charity shop where I do voluntary work. The cappuccinos there are sublime, and the range of sandwiches is good too. I have another reason to eat there, though. A man. Hard to miss him, with those dark curls cut close to his head. Soft whorls my hand itches to touch. Every time he comes in, my eyes swivel his way. After a few weeks of covert glances, we get to talk at last.

It's a Monday, and I'm peeved because he's not here yet. As I extract a bottle of mineral water from the chiller cabinet, my elbow collides with someone's belly. An automatic apology slips from my mouth.

'Sorry—' The word hangs in mid-air as recognition hits me. *Him.* He smiles, revealing one front tooth slightly out of line, but every bit as white as the rest. My stare, coupled with my inability to form words, is embarrassing. A subtle waft of aftershave floats into my nostrils, a clean scent that doesn't surprise me, given the sugar-white of his T-shirt, the just-bought crispness of his jeans. What renders me incapable of speech, though, are his eyes, which are different colours. The left one blue as a bruise, the right mocha-hued. I've heard of such a thing, but I never realised it would be so unusual, so striking.

I guess he's used to people reacting the way I have. He doesn't reply, just smiles, and I notice the chicken sandwich he's taken from the chiller. 'My favourite,' I say, even though it's not, and it's a relief to find my mouth does work after all.

'Here.' He thrusts the sandwich at me. 'Have it.' The first time he tells me what to do. In hindsight, it's a landmark moment.

'Looks like I grabbed the last one.' His right hand pulls open the chiller again, extracting an egg mayo on wholemeal. His left shoves the chicken sandwich my way again as he closes the door. I take it, lost in the blueberry and chocolate of his eyes.

He gestures towards his usual table. 'Want to join me?'

I do, very much. His fingers twist open his bottle of water, its bubbles hissing as they swarm to the surface. He fills his glass. My hands echo his, except my fingers shake and I spill a few drops. 'I'm Beth,' I say, keen to cover my awkwardness.

He smiles again, the skin around his eyes creasing. I'm guessing he's in his early twenties. No more than twenty-five. Seven years isn't so much of a gap. Besides, he's a man, not a boy. Not someone who'll fumble his way through sex, like my one and only previous boyfriend. Steady on, I tell myself. You met this guy all of two minutes ago. Sex isn't on the agenda. Yet.

'Good to meet you, Beth. My name's Dominic.' With the sound of his voice, so velvety in my ear, I'm hooked. I turn his name over in my head, liking it. Do. Min. Ic. The three syllables are firm, decisive, like shots from a gun.

'I've seen you in here before,' he says.

'I do shifts in the charity shop.' My hand gestures towards Homeless Concern across the road. 'Four days a week.'

'That's good.' He doesn't ask me why I don't have a proper job. I'm grateful; such a question is too reminiscent of my father.

'What about you?' From his appearance, I can't place what he does for a living. He's not a manual worker, that's for sure. His hands, raised as he takes a sip of water, don't dig, mix concrete or slap paint on walls; the nails are too neat, too square. Something to do with computers, I guess, or the music business.

'Day trader,' he replies, a small grin tugging at his mouth when he notes my blank expression. 'I work from home. Buying and selling stocks, futures, currencies.'

I'm none the wiser, but I don't let on. 'You enjoy what you do?'

The grin disappears. 'It's hard at times. Doesn't always pan out.' He doesn't elaborate, so I don't press the issue.

We chat some more. I find out he's an only child, both parents dead. 'You live alone?' I enquire. My mind is spiralling forward. The prospect of dating someone with his own place, without a family, where I can escape the pressures of mine, holds vast appeal. Too late, I realise that the question reveals my interest in him, makes it sound as if I'm sniffing out a girlfriend, or a wife. He doesn't wear a wedding ring, but not all married men do.

He grins again. 'Ever since Dad died. What is it now, six years ago?' Something I can't decipher edges into his eyes as his gaze burns into me. 'Maybe I've become a bit set in my ways. Need a woman to sort me out.'

He's straight, then. Not that I ever thought otherwise.

'How old are you?' I can be direct at times.

'Twenty-eight.'

Older than he looks. Not that it deters me. Ten years between us isn't a huge gap, not really, and he'll be a refreshing change from the boys from school.

'I'm eighteen.' Best to find out now if I'm too young for him.

'Thought so.' Dominic doesn't say it as though it's an issue.

He finishes his sandwich. Mine lies uneaten on its plate, despite the rumblings in my stomach. Impossible to talk to this man with food in my mouth. His eyes, that weird yet wonderful juxtaposition of blue and brown, hold mine and I sense he's itching to say something, but isn't sure how. Up to now, he's been so self-assured, and his sudden reticence charms me.

'Would you like to go out with me sometime?' he asks.

Oh, God. He's interested in me, despite my lack of job, the fact I'm fresh out of school, all the things I've been imagining would deter him. Later, after I'm shut in the basement, with time to reflect, I realise they're what render me vulnerable to Dominic, turning me into a fly, him a spider.

Dad won't approve; I'm supposed to be sorting out university courses, not dating older men. The thought of my father's disapproval adds fuel to the attraction this man holds for me. I still hesitate, though.

'Might be a bit difficult,' I say. 'What with still living at home.'

The eyebrow over the brown iris quirks upwards. 'You're not allowed out?' Again, later on, when I'm in the basement, I grasp how manipulative he is. How the nuances in his voice goad me into proving I'm an independent female, capable of making her own decisions.

'Of course I am.' My tone betrays my irritation. 'How about tonight?'

A satisfied grin appears on his face. 'Fine,' he says. 'I'll decide where's best for us to go.'

I approve of the way he determines the course of our date. A precursor to how he decides everything when we're at the cottage. So much for my professed independence.

'Can you give me a lift? I don't drive.' Another factor rendering me more vulnerable. Right now, though, I want and need to trust Dominic, and so I do.

We make arrangements. He'll pick me up at seven at the end of my road, promising to have me home by eleven.

'Don't be late,' he tells me.

***

I'm standing on the corner of my road five minutes before seven. The evening is chilly, and I shiver as I wait. My jeans, fresh from the laundry basket, are too tight, the material compressing my stomach. Always quick to react to nervous tension, it's swollen. For that reason, I've not eaten, unwilling to risk a full-on bloat party in my guts. Besides, Dominic might be taking me for a meal, and I pray the pressure against my waistband will ease soon. Atop the jeans, I'm wearing a mulberry silk shirt, a bargain from the Homeless Concern shop, its softness caressing my skin under my linen jacket. Smart casual is the way to go, especially as I don't even know where we're heading. My eyes are ringed with kohl, a soft brown that matches both them and the small mole underneath the right one. My mouth is slick with mulberry lip-gloss, my cheeks are brushed with colour and my dark hair is loose around my shoulders. For those few moments while I wait, I'm the spider, not the fly.

Bang on seven o'clock, a car approaches. It's sleek and silver, its windows darkened, the BMW insignia cresting its bonnet. A whiff of money accompanies the car, the scent of its owner's financial deals wafting my way. The driver eases the BMW alongside me. A window lowers, revealing Dominic.

He looks good, all dark curls and entrancing eyes. A tiny frown creases his forehead, just for a second, as his gaze sweeps over me. It's disapproval, although what's initiated it baffles me. His censure wrong-foots me, rendering me nervous.

When he speaks, though, his tone is warm, the frown gone. 'Get in,' he tells me.

We drive for a while, heading towards Hanham. Cradled in the leathery comfort of the BMW, I allow its smooth motion to steer me wherever Dominic has decided we're going. He doesn't say much, the occasional snippet of small talk. I respond in kind, thankful to be where I am, beside this man with the mismatched eyes and enticing hair. Maybe tonight I'll get to experience those curls under my fingers. My crotch twitches at the thought.

We turn down a side road, where Dominic parks up. 'We're here,' he says, getting out and opening the boot. I stay in the car, staring across the grassy area ahead. In the distance, a large brick-built chimney tower lurches against the evening sky, its angle several degrees off-kilter as though it's drunk.

Dominic strides round to my side of the car, pulling open the door for me, an old-fashioned gesture that's touching. In his other hand, he holds a blue chill-bag, and my empty stomach, its bloat now eased, anticipates food. A blanket is tucked under his arm.

I swing my legs from the car. 'What is this place?'

'Troopers Hill,' Dominic replies. We walk across the grass, heading towards the chimney, the heels of my sandals sinking into the soft ground, still tacky from yesterday's rain. The grass is cold and ticklish against my bare toes. We're nearing the top of a hill; the chimney is in front of us, and I can't see anything beyond it, not now, anyway.

He swings round to smile at me. 'Thought we'd have ourselves a bit of a picnic. The view's great from up here.'

And it is, once we get closer to the chimney. We're high up, and my home city of Bristol stretches before me, its roads elongating into the distance. Two hot-air balloons, riding the evening air, float towards us, the faint hiss of their gas jets reaching my ears. I'm entranced. Why have I never been here before? The shame of my insularity, the narrowness of my fresh-out-of-school focus, overwhelms me, and I promise myself things will be different from now on. I'll explore, learn, and travel. With Dominic, of course.

Oh, the irony.

'Old copper smelting works,' he says, gesturing towards the chimney. 'A good place to sit, check out the city.' The balloons drift closer, their jets hissing louder, and I picture myself one day, floating through the air, Dominic beside me, the Pyramids below us reduced to children's play shapes. Or perhaps it's the Australian outback – hot, red and fiery – underneath us. The details don't matter.

Dominic spreads the blanket on the ground and sets down the chill-bag. He unzips it, extracting a bottle of white wine and two glasses, thick and heavy with gold rims. He's clearly a man who values quality. I'm unused to alcohol but I don't intend to admit the fact.

'Here.' He hands me a glass of wine, misted from the cold of the liquid. I take a sip, and suppress a cough; the taste is acidic yet sweet, a promise of things to come. A smear of my mulberry lip-gloss stains the glass.

Dominic unpacks French sticks, Camembert, knives, plates. I break open my bread, slice off a chunk of the gooey cheese and slather it inside. We eat in silence. The dusty rind of the cheese, its sour creaminess, tastes good against the crustiness of the French stick. I'm conscious that my bites are too large, that crumbs are sticking to the corners of my mouth. When I drink the wine, it's in gulps now, Dominic providing regular refills. To me, the evening is perfect, as we sit on the blanket, the chimney tower listing to one side behind us. The balloons are long past; the light is fading from the sky, the cool of dusk spreading across the city. My head, unused to the alcohol, is heavy, fuzzy. I'm aware I'm drinking faster than Dominic, but I remind myself he has to drive. Besides, my first experience of being tipsy is pleasant. I prepare to float away on the evening air, in the wake of the balloons.

Dominic reaches out a hand, and his fingers against my skin are electrifying. Something inside me flares into life, a firecracker of desire sending a storm of twitches through my crotch. He touches the corner of my right eye, his thumb caressing the mole underneath. 'You're too pretty to need make-up,' he tells me. The reason for his disapproval when he saw me earlier clicks into place.

A smear of kohl is on his thumb as he retracts his hand. He rubs it away with a finger. 'Come on,' he says. 'We'll walk through the trees.' He takes my plate, knife and glass, packing them along with his own in the chill-bag. The wine bottle is now empty, at least two-thirds of its contents in my stomach. My legs don't work well when I stand up.

We walk along a narrow path and down a flight of steps into the woods. The light has almost gone; pale moonlight filtering through the trees is our guide. The wine has lulled me into a sensation of safety, despite the fact that I'm half-drunk, alone in a dark place with a man who's an unknown quantity. So far, the evening has been perfect, a sublime mix of food and balloons and, oh my God, the brush of his fingers against my face. Tonight I'm invincible, inviolate, the world at my feet. Our feet.

The path twists round, up more steps, before emerging near the grassy area I saw before. Dominic eases me through the wooden gate. 'Car's back that way,' he says, gesturing towards the thick hedge skirting the grass. I'm both relieved and disappointed he didn't try anything on while we were alone amongst the trees.

He doesn't when we're back in the car, either. I'm expecting him to reach over from the driver's seat, pull me towards him, his mouth seeking mine, but he doesn't. Instead, he drives me back to the corner of my road.

'Can we do this again?' he asks. I nod, and he smiles.

Later, in the basement, I realise how well Dominic played me that night. Establishing trust with the wine, the walk through the woods. So I'll have faith in him, be reassured he's a man who'll treat me with respect. No getting me drunk for a quick fumble on the ground beneath the trees. In my naiveté, I'm ripe for Dominic Perdue, a spider whose web, sticky as flypaper, consists of wine, cheese and charm.

***

We go out again at the weekend, a Sunday afternoon stroll through Castle Park, ending at the Harbourside. Dominic buys fat falafels that we eat, tahini running down our fingers, as we walk across the cobbles. Boats bob on the water to our right, the yellow and blue of a harbour ferry purring past us. The sun is hot on my arms; the noise of people around us buzzes in my ears. Outside the Arnolfini, Dominic stops.

'I'll get us some drinks,' he says. 'A cold cider will do nicely, what with it being so warm.' He doesn't ask whether I like cider, not that I know. He disappears inside.

I discover that I do like it. The sharp apple tang hits the back of my throat as we sit, side by side, on the cobbles. Again, with hindsight I realise Dominic's working to a precise plan. We're in public, on a hot Sunday afternoon; nothing about our date can possibly spook me. All part of his design: taking me to places where either nobody is around or else blending us into a crowd. I have no doubts, no prods from my intuition alerting me to what lies behind the blue and brown of his eyes. Instead I fall, a plum ripe from the tree, into Dominic's grasp. I want this man, and by now, I'm desperate to experience passion, abandonment, everything missing from my previous sexual encounters. I'm convinced this man holds the key to erotic nirvana. So far, my experience has been limited to a few unsatisfying fumbles, all hard shoves and fast orgasms, neither on my part. When I was seventeen, Darren Rogers, a classmate, convinced me to lose my virginity in the back of his beat-up Fiesta. Subsequent replays didn't improve my view of sex.

'Want to come to my place for dinner sometime this week?' Dominic asks.

I don't hesitate. 'I'd love to,' I reply.

CHAPTER 2 – *Dominic*

Whenen the idea to kidnap a woman first comes to me, I'm not too fussy about whom to take. Someone young, pliable, whom I can mould into the perfect companion, but other than that, I've few criteria. I search, but somehow no woman strikes the right note with me. One day, driven by an impulse I don't fully understand, I retrieve from my spare bedroom an old photo, one I've not looked at since my father died. As I stare at it, I realise what's missing from my plan. Restitution.

Beth Sutton's the one who'll help me achieve it. At eighteen, she barely qualifies as a woman. She fits the bill, though; her resemblance to her predecessor is striking, given they're not related. I've chosen well. I've discerned from our conversations that tension exists at home. Issues with her father, apparently. She yearns to cut loose, without knowing what she wants from life. It'll be my pleasure to teach her. If I break her in right, all she'll want will be me.

I dress with care for our dinner date tonight, taking pains to preserve the image she's formed of me. The successful financial risk-taker with the flash BMW; the man who'll wine her, dine her, show her a good time. Such foolish, schoolgirl fantasies. What I have to offer Beth Sutton is more solid, more real, a permanence that'll force her to grow up. In time, she'll come to love me, accept the security I'll give her, thank me for it. Sex isn't the reason I chose her. Rutting like animals holds no appeal for me. What I want is more complex. A companion, yes, but a mother figure as well, and for that her age is an obvious disadvantage. I'm prepared to wait, though. In my head, she's my companion first, and then, when she's earned a few privileges, she can take care of me. Beth being so young is good, really. With her glowing skin, her shiny hair, she's clearly healthy, not destined for an early grave like Mum. The woman who was dead by fifty, a mere seven years after my birth. A miracle she ever conceived, given the thirty kilos of surplus flesh she carried, not to mention her stratospheric blood pressure. She did, though, and refused to contemplate abortion.

'Told her to get shot of you, but the bitch wouldn't have it.' Oh, blunt was my father's middle name. I was seven years old when he laid that one on me, right after his hand cracked against my face, knocking me backwards. We'd just returned from Mum's funeral. She'd been my shield against this man. Always there, my protection when he lashed out at me. Now my safeguard was gone.

Her voice echoes in my head, a memory from long ago.

'I'm going upstairs for a bit of a sleep.' My seven-year-old self, absorbed with my Lego, didn't respond. Something for which I've always blamed myself. I never got to hear her voice again. Instead I carried on playing, grateful for the fact it was a weekend, my father at a football match. He wouldn't come home for hours. When he did, he'd stink of booze.

At six o'clock, I realised I was hungry. The house was silent. Normally at this time, Mum would be in the kitchen, cooking our evening meal, plating up my father's food for whenever he decided he'd had enough alcohol. I ran upstairs, intending to ask her to cook fish fingers tonight, unaware of what awaited me.

Her door was open. Mum lay on top of the duvet, fully clothed, her head turned towards the window. A tiny flash of awareness sparked in my brain that something was very wrong, but at seven I lacked the ability to process the thought. I stood by the side of her bed.

'Mum? Mum, I'm hungry.' When she didn't respond, I shook her shoulder, wobbling the flesh on her arm. Then I walked to the other side of the bed.

Realisation hit me the minute I saw her face. Her mouth hung slack, a line of spittle running from one corner. Her eyes were wide and staring. At seven years of age, her death struck me hard with a cruel reality check. A brain aneurysm, swift and lethal, had snatched my mother from me.

I crawled onto the bed beside her, pushing myself into her arms one last time. When my father stormed upstairs, hours later, demanding food, that was how he found us.

Memories that over two decades later are fuzzy around the edges. Her face has faded to a blur in my head. All I have is the recollection of her voice, the squeeze of her arms around me, her scent in my nostrils. Dad slung all her possessions in the bin after her death. Her clothes, all the photos of her – everything was destroyed. Just the memory of her embrace, along with the scent of Samsara, remains. An evocation that fades over the years, as any perfume will, leaving only a faint trace at the back of my skull. When I go into department stores, I head for the fragrance counters and breathe in my mother. A bottle of Samsara sits in my bedside cabinet, a constant reminder of her.

So Beth Sutton has big shoes to fill. It'll take time for her to grow into them, adapt to what I'm asking of her, but she will. I've been waiting twenty-one years for her to keep me company. Tonight her new life will begin.

***

I'm supposed to be cooking for Beth, but the kitchen is cold, unused. My stomach, knotted at what I'm intending, rebels at the idea of food. I'll eat later, when Beth's safely stowed in the basement. I've picked well, choosing a girl so confused, so mixed-up. When I first saw her in The Busy Bean, something about her called to me. Was it her air of vulnerability, the way her shoulders spoke of unhappiness as she drank her coffee, unaware of me watching through the window? Oblivious of the fact I already knew her name and where she lived?

Not a soul knows she's coming here tonight. 'You're my guilty secret,' she told me at the Harbourside when I probed, veiled questions designed to dig out who, if anyone, she'd told about us. I'm reassured.

'Easier that way.' She shrugged. 'Otherwise I'll get the "while you're under my roof" lecture from Dad.' A smile. 'Nobody knows about you, Dominic.'

That's good. Very good. So far, Beth Sutton has proved an easy catch. I smiled back, reeling her in further. Oh, I'm adept at the gestures that crack open a female's defences, my teachers the DVDs I watch. I take my cues from the masters of the art: Brad Pitt, Colin Firth, Johnny Depp. In real life, I've never had a girlfriend, never wined and dined a female apart from at Troopers Hill. It's been a good many years since any woman set foot in this cottage.

A memory stirs within me, deep and primeval. I clamp down on it, hard. Tonight's not the time to remember such things. This evening is about Beth. What I can offer her. And what she'll give me in return once I've broken her in. The relationship we'll forge will be good. Strong, enduring.

Not like my parents' marriage, its pendulum swinging between bitter rows and angry silences. They married late in life. Past forty, my mother's health wasn't good; keen to produce a child before the menopause claimed her, she settled for Lincoln Perdue as her best bet. As for him, I'm guessing he wanted a live-in maid service: his meals cooked and his laundry done, with sex on tap to boot. He must have figured a wife to be cheaper than a combination of housekeepers and whores. Being a father didn't come as part of the package, though. Small wonder he loathed me from my birth. Especially my eyes, which entrance some people and repulse others. One a soft brown, warm, with faint gold flecks, inherited from my mother. The other blue, chilly, with hints of green, straight from his genes. People's eyes can change colour during childhood, from what I've read. Had my mother lived, I believe my blue iris might have darkened under her influence to match its sibling. I'd have ended up with her eyes. Instead, I'm a weird hybrid.

'The child's a damn freak,' I heard Dad shout at Mum once, when I was supposed to be asleep. Instead, I was crouched on the landing outside my bedroom, listening to yet another argument, my mother's words ricocheting off the walls downstairs like bullets.

'He's your son, for God's sake. I'll take Dominic and leave you, Lincoln, if you don't shape up, treat him better. As well as quit the drinking. The other women.' My father merely snorted in reply.

My life would have been different had she followed through with her threat. Instead, the aneurysm claimed her three months later. At seven years old, life abandoned me to Lincoln Perdue, and the rest of my childhood was spent tiptoeing around the cottage, in constant fear of his rages. Mostly he ignored me. After Mum's death, my father, wealthy from his building business, hired a local woman to clean, do the laundry and prepare our meals. To the outside world, I presented an acceptable face: smart clothes, enough food to eat, nothing to spark alarm from the teachers at school. Inside, I withered, starving emotionally. The pendulum swung in favour of my blue eye, and the gradual warping of whatever genes my mother gave me commenced. Her influence still lingers a little, though. Despite my plans for Beth Sutton, I'm a better man than my father was. His views on women were evidenced by his porn stash.

I discovered it when I was ten years old. Dad was downstairs, watching sport. The muted voice of the television commentator reached me as I lay on my bed, together with my father's shouts of derision. Bored, I wandered across the landing into his room, careful to avoid any squeaky boards. The cottage where we lived consisted of two old miners' residences, converted years before into one, its eighteenth-century floors prone to creaking. If he caught me in his room, it would mean the back of his hand cracking across my face, but I sometimes stole in here anyway. The room always had a stale odour from his frequent belching and farting.

I slumped against the wardrobe, hugging my knees, my cheek resting on my arm. My gaze travelled across the floor, spotting something under the bed. I unravelled, going over to peer underneath. A pile of magazines nestled against the skirting board over the far side of the bed; the one I'd seen had slipped from the top. My fingers reached in, pulling the magazine towards me.

After so many years, my memory of the woman on the cover is still sharp. She was naked, on her hands and knees, facing the camera. My eyes skimmed over the curves of her waist, her heavy breasts, towards her mouth. In it was a red ball, the woman's lips stretched around the plastic, leather straps securing it in place. Repulsion hit me, the image being beyond my ten years of age. My fingers reached out to trace the O-shape of the woman's mouth as it embraced the sphere that was gagging her.

Later on, I did understand. While it's not a path I'll ever follow, the photo calls to something buried deep in my psyche. The need to control, inherited from my father.

***

I never knew much about Dad's other women. He didn't bring brought any of them to the cottage, but sometimes he arrived home, belching alcohol, his shirt buttoned up in the wrong holes. When he did, the perfume of his latest whore came with him, mixed with the whisky on his breath. I used to wish he'd do it more often; he was mellow afterwards, his urges slaked, meaning I got shouted at less. Over time, as I transitioned towards manhood, Dad's visits to the whores declined, along with his health. Years of booze and burgers had taken their toll. His waist ballooned, stretching his trousers around his belly like the woman's mouth around the ball-gag. Red veins scribbled themselves across his nose and through the whites of his eyes. Sometimes he'd clutch at his chest, pain slashing deep lines into his forehead, beads of sweat dotting his skin. His legs often swelled and turned an ugly crimson.

By the time I turned eighteen, my father had started to wheeze, his breath sounding like air dribbling from a balloon. An inhaler joined the prescriptions for angina and cellulitis in the bathroom cabinet. As his asthma worsened, it was never far from his side, either in his pocket or next to the television remote as he slumped in front of the weekend football. The visits to the whores were rare by then, declining in inverse proportion to the height of the stack of magazines under his bed.

***

I was sixteen when I first contemplated suicide. The idea came to me as I lay on my bed, listening to my father curse at the television downstairs. Earlier on, he'd hit me. His cellulitis had flared up again, and his mood was foul as we eat dinner. As a result, I was nervous, my fingers clumsy, knocking my glass of water across the table. My father hauled himself to his feet, his face ruddy with rage.

'Stupid bastard!' His right hand swiped my cheek, knocking me from my chair. He was panting, sweating, and utterly repulsive. I grasped the table to prevent myself falling further, the jolt as I did so spilling his beer. I didn't wait around, heading straight for the door, but even with his bulk, he managed to grab me. His arm lashed out, once, twice, spreading fiery pain though my face. As soon as I recovered, I bounded up the stairs and out of his reach, his curses following me to my room.

As I lay on my bed, I realised my existence was meaningless and had been from the moment Mum died. The world would be better off without me, and vice versa. What stopped me was the inability to decide how best to kill myself. I had no access to sleeping tablets, and I was too much of a coward to slash my wrists. Drowning held no appeal either. Too likely to be ruled an accident; if I was to commit suicide, then I wanted the world to know I chose to end my own life. With a note, explaining why.

The solution came to me eventually. The basement. I'd hammer a hook into the wooden rafter that ran across the ceiling, and I'd hang myself. Release from the hell I live every day was possible; I savoured the thought, knowing it was available if my father got truly unbearable. Instead of a noose, I slid into my first episode of depression. A dark beast that's stalked me ever since, eager to sink its fangs into my flesh.

Beth will rescue me from its bite.

***

As I head downstairs, ready to collect my girl, the twin smells of disinfectant and air freshener assault my nostrils. Such odours were banned when my father was alive; he claimed they triggered his asthma. Since his death, I've kept the cottage as clean, as neat, as Mum always did. It'll impress Beth, when I bring her through the front door, when she realises this is no squalid bachelor pad, stale with old pizza and cigarettes. The pine freshness will also prevent her from realising I've not cooked any food.

The keys to the BMW are where they always are, together with my house keys, on a hook behind the front door. I'm nothing if not neat. My fingers reach up to grab them, this morning's threatening letter from the bank shoved to the back of my mind. OK, so I've been on a losing streak. A few lucky deals and I'll be on top again. I'm Dominic Perdue. The markets never beat me for long.

As my hand takes the keys from the hook, an urge to check the basement stops me. One last look, to ensure everything's ready for my guest.

I replace the keys and backtrack to a door on the right, opposite the staircase. My hands reach out and pull it outward, revealing steps leading downward. The basement isn't large, occupying the space under one cottage out of the pair, before some previous owner knocked both houses into one. For some reason, he or she didn't do the same with the basements, keeping them as two separate rooms accessible from opposite sides of the cottage. It was my father who blocked off one of them, its entrance now walled up and papered over. Across the ceiling of the remaining one is the wooden rafter from my suicidal fantasies. Three things are in the basement, the bare minimum she'll require. My father would say I've been generous in what I've provided. Beth Sutton will have to earn whatever privileges I choose to grant her. Her first few months in here will teach her that.

I remind myself I'm granting her the most precious privilege of all. The right to life. The last occupant of the basement didn't enjoy such a luxury.

Enough. I'm as ready as I'll ever be. Time to collect Beth Sutton and introduce her to her new life.

CHAPTER 3 – *Beth*

At the Harbourside, Dominic informs me he makes a mean bouillabaisse. 'Great,' I say, although I have to Google it later to find out what I'll be eating, and when I do I persuade myself I'll enjoy it, despite the fact I've always disliked the taste of fish. We agree to get together the next night.

When the time comes, I dress with care, sex on my mind. I'm going to Dominic's house, after all, and he's not mentioned driving me home afterwards. Easy on the make-up, I remind myself. I fringe my eyes with a hint of kohl, floating the lightest brush of rose across my cheeks, painting gloss onto my lips. My dress is new, the pink and white pattern hugging my breasts and ending just above my knees. Classy but understated. I pull a denim jacket around my shoulders and grab my pink duffel bag, packed with a toothbrush, my cosmetics bag and fresh underwear. Everything I'll need to stay the night with Dominic. I assume he'll provide the condoms.

'Won't be back tonight, Mum. Going to stay with a friend,' I call into the kitchen as I head down the hall.

My mother stands in the doorway, tiredness in her eyes. She's worried about the lack of clients for her language tutoring business, from what I've overheard her telling Dad. I hoist my duffel bag over my shoulder and smile at her. Hers in return is strained.

As I wait on the corner of the road, Troy leaves the house, walking towards me. A few seconds after he's passed by without a word, I spot Dominic's car approaching. My soon-to-be boyfriend slides the BMW against the kerb, and then gets out of the car. 'Hey there,' he greets me.

In the distance, I see Troy staring back at us, before he saunters down the road and out of my thoughts. I ease myself into the BMW's passenger seat. A moment of panic slaps me in the face; I know so little about this man. I've no idea where he lives, what his house is like. He's mentioned his job, told me he's single, but we've never discussed his past relationships, how his parents died, whether he's lonely at night. I remind myself we drank wine together on Troopers Hill, with him the perfect gentleman, never pressing his advantage as we strolled through the trees. You can trust this man, I tell myself. Everything will be fine.

Dominic starts the car. We head through Kingswood, past the charity shop and The Busy Bean, out through Warmley on the A420. 'I don't know where you live,' I say.

Dominic smiles. 'Not far from here. An old mining cottage. You'll like it.'

We turn left at the signpost to Siston. After a few hundred yards, Dominic swings the car into a narrow entrance hidden by trees. The BMW bumps its way along a lane before twisting left and pulling up in front of a house. It's old, all right, the roof bowed; I realise the cottage must have been two at one time. I can see the scars where a second front door must once have been. No sounds greet me as I exit the car. We're so close to the city and yet we're worlds away. From other houses, too.

'It's so quiet here. You have neighbours nearby?'

'None close.' Dominic locks the BMW with a click of his key fob. 'That's good. Nobody to poke around in my business.'

My heels sink into the stone chippings as Dominic leads me towards the front door. I'm hungry; the idea of fish stew, off-putting initially, now appeals. All part of the changed, try-anything-once, Beth. We'll eat, we'll talk, and I'll discover new things about this man who's been filling my head all day with his dark curls and strange yet wonderful eyes. Sex will follow. It'll be good, I'm sure. My eyes run over his chest and I picture my hands removing his T-shirt, before sliding lower.

Dominic leads me through the door into the lounge, flicking on the lights as he does so. The open-plan space is period-quaint; an inglenook fireplace dominates the room, a wood-burning stove nestled in its depths. A doorway leads off one end; through the gap, I spot a fridge-freezer. His kitchen, I presume. Wooden stairs, matched by the beams traversing the ceiling, lead up to the first floor. The furniture's dated, a sharp contrast to Mum's penchant for Ikea. Dominic favours heavy pieces, mostly mahogany, the most solid of which is the dining table and chairs to my left. The neatness in here is a stark contrast to my bedroom at home. 'Tidiness is for people who don't have lives,' is Mum's creed, and I'm with her on that one. The room is devoid of flowers or candles; no romance greets me from its depths. Nothing indicates food will be served soon. I can't detect any cooking smells, no lingering odours to suggest Dominic has already prepared our meal and is about to warm it through. Surely he doesn't intend to cook it from scratch while I wait? My culinary knowledge is hazy, but even I know that a complicated dish such as bouillabaisse can't be rustled up in half an hour.

'Will it be long before we eat?'

Dominic smiles. 'Let me take your jacket, Beth.' He moves behind me, pulling down my sleeves as I shrug myself free. 'Glass of wine?'

'A dry white would be lovely.'

'Coming right up.' As Dominic moves into the kitchen, I follow him. It's small, functional and, like the lounge, devoid of any indications of food preparation. Immaculately clean, too. I stare at the oven, wondering whether it holds a casserole dish, ready for Dominic to heat up. An explanation comes to me; his penchant for order has made him clear the kitchen before he left. Yes, that must be it. I relax, my fingers reaching to accept the glass of chilled white Dominic hands me.

'French,' he says. 'Chablis. Cheers.' We chink glasses, drink our wine. For me, it's more of a gulp. I realise I'm nervous.

'To us,' I say, emboldened by the alcohol.

'I'll drink to that.' Dominic sets down his empty glass, and then takes mine. His strange eyes transfix me. 'We can finish those later. Come with me. I want to show you the cottage.'

***

As I follow Dominic, I have no warning of what's about to happen. My mind's running on fish stew; I picture Dominic serving up steaming bowlfuls, with crusty baguettes on the side. We'll drink more wine, and there'll be afters; I rack my brains for a typical French dessert. Fruit tart, perhaps, or crème brûlée. Dominic stops at a door I'd not noticed before, set opposite the stairs, low and concealed. It's old, made of tranches of wood held together by planks nailed across the top, middle and bottom. An antique metal lock, painted black, fastens it shut. The cellar, maybe? Or another flight of stairs to the upstairs rooms? Yes, that explains it. A second staircase from when the two cottages were separate.

Dominic opens the door towards us, forcing me to step back. Even at this point, no premonition stirs within me; I'm enshrouded in my naiveté, cocooned by my fantasies about Dominic. His aftershave tickles my nostrils, and my fingers itch to touch his neck where curls of hair overlap onto pale skin. Later, when I'm in the basement, I realise that even if my gut had screamed a warning at me, it would have been futile. My imprisonment was guaranteed from the moment I stepped into the BMW.

He flicks on a light, and I see that the steps leading away from the door point downward, not up. A cellar, then. What's down there, I can't guess, but I doubt it stores junk. If it does, why show me? My mind returns to the wine; perhaps he's a connoisseur. That would fit in with the BMW, the flash life as a financial trader. Racks of bottles must be what await me. Dominic moves past me, placing one hand over my eyes. I giggle; his touch is soft, a feathery pressure from his palms darkening my sight. I picture the same hand, later when we're in bed, how it'll caress me, and I tingle between my legs.

'I have something to show you,' he says. Laughter echoes in his voice, his breath warm against my ear, provoking further tingling. Still no hint of danger warns me. All that exists in my world is Dominic, the faint soap smell emanating from his palm, the press of his body against mine. He moves forward, inching me towards the wooden steps.

'Don't worry,' he says against my ear. 'I'll guide you.' I lower my right foot onto the next step, conscious of the firm pressure of his other hand against my left arm. We descend until the wood changes to concrete under my feet.

The room is cold, a hint of damp in the air, and I cross my arms to brace myself against the chill. Dominic steps away from me, but with his hand still covering my eyes. In that moment, I'm aware, in a flood of intuition that arrives way too late, of a shift in the atmosphere, as though he's unleashing something deep within. A shiver runs through me.

The pressure against my eyelids eases as Dominic removes his palms. 'Open your eyes,' he instructs. I do.

The wine racks from my imagination aren't here. Not much is. A grey plastic cube, large enough to sit on, is in one corner. I stare at it, its familiarity teasing me. Then the answer clicks into place. Mum's friend Donna has one in her camper van. It's a chemical toilet. To my left is a metal filing cabinet with three drawers. At its side is a fold-up single bed, the blue of the mattress showing through the slats of the base, the wooden headboard that's horizontal across the top keeping the whole thing closed. Nothing else is in the room. A thick rafter runs across the ceiling. Up high, on the wall opposite me, a tiny window holds my reflection, flattened and distorted.

I crush the panic sweeping upwards into my chest, threatening to seal my throat. He's just being thorough in showing me the cottage, I tell myself.

When I turn around, Dominic is at the foot of the stairs, blocking my exit.

'Why did you bring me down here?' My voice is too high, too shrill, and I fight for control.

Dominic smiles. 'Do you like it, Beth?' His expression is alive with something – purpose? Excitement? I drop my gaze as I move towards the stairs. He's still blocking my path.

'Can we eat now? I'm starving.' My voice betrays the fear pounding through my brain, urging me to leave now, get out somehow, anyhow, away from this man who I don't recognise, not any longer. Dominic doesn't reply, but continues to bar my exit. I step backwards, forcing myself to meet his eyes, those weird irises that no longer attract me, but terrify me instead.

'Please, Dominic. This isn't funny. I need to eat. You said you'd make bouillabaisse.' I cringe at the whine in my tone.

'Not tonight, Beth.'

I lunge at him then, trying to force my way past, but he has the advantage in height and weight, and his hand, no longer gentle, crushes my upper arm. Blackness lurks in his expression, his mouth hard and unsmiling. It's as though a puppy has peeled off its skin to reveal a rattlesnake, and my mouth parches into a desert, rendering me incapable of speech. My head bangs against the wall as he pushes me backwards. Terror hammers in my chest. Blood pounds in my ears.

When he speaks, his tone is calm, measured. 'You'll be staying here.'

I twist my head from side to side, tortured syllables emerging as I attempt to form the word *no*. What the hell does he mean? I can't stay here, not in this damp basement. This isn't a place to live. Except that it is. There's a bed. A toilet. What purpose the filing cabinet might serve an occupant of this dank room, I'm not sure.

Dominic's eyes never leave mine. 'This is your new home, Beth. You'll live down here, at least for now, until you're ready to come upstairs. I've chosen you, you see.'

Chosen me? I stare at him, still incapable of speech.

'To be my companion. There'll be rules, though. You'll start with the basics, with what you have here, and you'll earn more privileges, providing you behave. If you do what you're told, you'll be fine.'

Horror clenches my stomach. Then he releases his grip on my arm, stepping backwards towards the stairs. I stay frozen against the wall.

'Open the top drawer of the filing cabinet,' Dominic says. 'Take out what's inside.'

I don't move, not a muscle, not an inch.

'Do it.' Steel is in his voice. I edge towards the filing cabinet, my eyes never leaving his face. We're snake and rabbit, deer and hunter. My fingers hook around the handle to the top drawer. I'm struggling to remain calm, but the message hasn't reached my trembling hands. I pull open the drawer.

Inside, neatly folded, are clothes. I pick up a pair of blue jogging bottoms, a white T-shirt and sweatshirt, before dropping them back in the drawer. I stare at him, stupefied.

'Underwear's in the next one down,' Dominic says. 'I didn't know your size, so I had to guess. Everything might be a bit big. I erred on the side of caution.'

'You're insane!' The saliva drains from my mouth again, leaving my lips stuck to my teeth, as I clock the way his expression darkens at my words. He takes a step towards me, and not a shred of pity exists in either of his strange eyes. I shrink against the filing cabinet, the chill of the metal pressing into my hip.

'Take off your clothes. Put these on instead.' He's so close I can smell the wine on his breath. 'I'll turn my back to give you some privacy.' He's as good as his word, but he still blocks the stairway.

'Do it, Beth.'

Fury boils through me, replacing the fear, and I launch myself at him, hammering on his shoulder blades with my fists. He turns; with one move, my wrists are held tight in his hands, and I'm struggling, useless against the strength of his grip.

'Told you,' he says. 'You have to earn privileges. You've already lost your first one. Like I said, I was prepared to turn my back. Now I won't.' He releases my wrists, pushing me towards the filing cabinet. 'Do it. Put the clothes on. Toss your old ones over here. You won't need them anymore.'

I don't move.

'I'm not leaving this room until you change clothes, Beth.' He smiles, viper-like. 'I've waited years to find you. A few hours won't make any difference.'

My mind spins, thoughts tumbling like dice through my head. He said I have to live here. He's no ordinary run-of-the-mill psycho, then; he's not planning to kill me. Not a rapist, either. He's had sufficient opportunity if that was his thing. My best bet is to comply. Do what he wants, change clothes. I need to buy myself time, keep him sweet. Then work out how to escape. Stay calm, Beth, I tell myself.

I pick up the jogging bottoms, T-shirt and sweatshirt, placing them on the floor. I pull open the second drawer and take out the top layer of what's in there: pale blue knickers, a matching bra, along with socks. Everything looks my size. Also in the drawer is a pair of slippers, pink and fluffy. I take those out as well.

'Put the clothes on, Beth,' Dominic repeats. As good as his word, he doesn't turn away. I do, though.

I slip off my shoes, toeing them to one side, before pulling my dress up and over my head, leaving me exposed in my underwear. Off come my knickers, yanked off as quickly as my fumbling fingers allow. Heat warms my face at the thought of my bottom under his gaze, but it's better than presenting him with my front view. My hands can't tug the fresh panties on fast enough; clumsiness makes me catch them on my knees. The blue jogging bottoms go on next. My fingers fumble with my bra clasp, and I don't breathe until I've clipped the new one into place, making me decent again. Within another minute, I'm wearing the white T-shirt and sweatshirt, my own clothes piled on top of my shoes on the floor. Then I face Dominic.

'Slide your things over here,' he tells me. My right foot inches out to push the shoes and clothes towards him. His gaze never leaves my face as he stoops to pick them up.

'I'll bring down a plate of food in a bit,' he says. 'If you behave, that is. No screaming or any nonsense like that. It won't be bouillabaisse, I'm afraid. Sandwiches will have to do.' He gestures towards the filing cabinet. 'Loo rolls are in the bottom drawer, along with tampons.'

I'm too stunned to reply. 'You'll be happy here, Beth,' he says. He smiles at me as he backs towards the stairs. 'When you've learned the rules. I've lost two women from my life. I don't intend you to be the third.'

I stare at him.

'You should be grateful,' he says. 'The last occupant of this room didn't make it out alive. Things will be different with you.'

***

After he's gone, I stand in the middle of the floor, listening, as the sound of a key locking the door reaches my ears. Once I hear the latch click into place, I hold my breath, alert for further noises, but after Dominic's footsteps move away only silence surrounds me. No sounds reach my ears through the tiny window, either. My reflection stares back at me from the glass as I berate myself. How could I have been so gullible? Fooled by wine and a fancy car?

The basement is chilly, devoid of heating, and I shiver, not entirely from the temperature. My arms clasp around my body, as much for comfort as for warmth, as I close my eyes, expelling the breath I've been holding. Then the tears start, hot and stinging, self-pity choking my throat. Oh, God, dear God, I chant in my head. Ironic that I'm begging a deity for help when religion has never featured in my life. Pascal's wager in a different form, although I can't bring myself to smile at the irony. God's not here in this basement with me, I'm sure of that.

But there has to be hope. I'm alive, aren't I? I pace the floor, from the window to the opposite wall and back, the cold of the concrete striking up through the soles of my slippers. It takes eight strides. My rhythm established, I walk, my arms still clutching my body. Think, Beth, I urge myself.

Nothing in the room presents itself as a method of escape, not at first sight. Exiting via the window is impossible; it can't measure more than a foot in width, less in height. No way can I squeeze through, even if I manage to break the glass without alerting Dominic. The door is locked and my captor is upstairs. I can't imagine myself overpowering him.

My thoughts turn to my parents. They haven't a clue where I am, and calling my mobile will prove useless. The only solution, although the thought of Mum's distress wounds me, will be for her or Dad to realise something's wrong. Troy will tell them he saw me getting into a BMW with a man. He'll be able to describe Dominic to the police. Not to mention the car; my brother's an aficionado. He'll probably have glanced at the registration plate, clocked the year of manufacture, remembered that even if he doesn't recall the whole number. The police will do an Identikit likeness of Dominic. Someone must know him, although when I consider how solitary his life is, my confidence deflates. Don't go there, I tell myself. You'll be found. It might take a few days, a week even, but it'll happen. In the meantime, I'll do whatever it takes to survive. If that means doing what this weirdo wants, following his rules, then I will.

Despite my attempts at self-reassurance, the notion, unwanted and terrible, persists: what if I'm not found so easily? My gut clenches, but this time it's very real, accompanied by an urgency that's impossible to ignore. I rush to the chemical toilet, flipping up the lid, yanking at my knickers and jogging bottoms. I make it just in time as my bowels open, the foul splatter hitting the plastic below. The stench of my fear wafts into my nostrils. I sit on the hard seat for a long time before I haul myself off, heading for the toilet roll in the filing cabinet.

When I'm done, I drag open the folding bed, locking the metal struts into place. I lie on the bare mattress, bereft of sheets, pillow or duvet. I guess they're part of the privileges he expects me to earn. I force myself to breathe with slow, deep inhalations, despite my lungs having grown too large for my chest.

When I'm halfway towards calm, I allow myself to examine my prospects if I'm not found. My only chance is to outwit my captor. I have no handle on what drives this man or how deep his psychosis goes, though. If he doesn't intend to rape or murder me, his game plan's a mystery.

Or is it? Dominic's words float back to me. *This is your new home, Beth. I've chosen you, you see. You'll be happy here.*

Tears slide down my face. How the hell do I escape this nightmare?

***

An hour later, the door unlocks. Dominic walks down the stairs, carrying a tray. On it is a plate with a sandwich and a bottle of water.

Before he can speak, I stand up, facing him. 'You fucking bastard. Let me go, do you hear me? Right now.'

Dominic places the tray of food on the bed. My words hang in the air between us. Not that they have any effect. Instead, he grasps my wrists in his left hand and with the other strikes a ferocious back-hander across my cheek. My neck whips sideways as the blow knocks the breath from my lungs. Blood from my nostrils mingles with snot as an insistent throbbing pounds through my nose. We stare at each other. His gaze is unwavering, pitiless.

Dominic releases my wrists, gesturing towards the filing cabinet. 'Get yourself some loo roll. Clean yourself up.'

I obey, while a mantra hammers in my head: *I hate you, I hate you, I hate you.* I drop the bloodied paper into the chemical toilet.

He moves closer. 'You will speak to me with respect at all times. No swearing, no back-chat, not ever.'

'Fuck you!' Within seconds, I'm regretting my words. Another merciless blow swipes my cheek, sending me crashing to the floor. My face is flaming, a burning testimony to my hatred of Dominic Perdue. Were it possible to kill the bastard, I'd do so in a heartbeat.

'Guess you need to clean yourself up again,' he says. I don't respond, my breathing ragged, choked with snot. When I fail to move, he grabs the toilet roll, thrusting it at me.

'Do as you're told. Or you'll regret it.'

I don't doubt him. I tear off more sheets, the paper coming away red as I dab at my nose. At least it doesn't feel broken. Small mercies.

'Are you going to use foul language towards me again?'

Only one response is possible. 'No.'

'Apologise for your behaviour. Now.'

I gulp in air, loathing what he's forcing me to say. 'I'm sorry.'

Dominic draws in a long breath, releasing it slowly. From my crumpled position on the floor, I wait.

'You have so much to learn,' he says. 'About how your new life will be.'

So calm, his voice, such a contrast to the violence of a moment ago. Soft whimpers escape me as I struggle to breathe, my nose still clogged and bleeding. I don't respond, unwilling to provoke him further.

'Understand this, Beth,' he says. 'Anything less than total obedience on your part will not be tolerated.'

CHAPTER 4 – *Dominic*

All quiet below. No sound from Beth. I walk into the kitchen to heat some soup. I'm almost too hyped-up to eat; elation and apprehension lie side by side in my stomach, making weird bedfellows. It's unfortunate I've had to use force to gain Beth's respect, but a little discipline isn't a bad thing. She needs to learn from the outset what I expect of her. A philosophy my father would have approved of. As I stir the pan of soup, I remember the face of the first woman who occupied, albeit briefly, one of the basements under the cottage.

In my head, it's fourteen years ago, and I've returned two days early from a school camping trip, thanks to one of our teachers suffering a burst appendix. It's late evening, and dark; I hoist my rucksack onto my shoulders, dredging up the courage to walk inside the cottage. No lights are on; perhaps my father's gone to sleep already. Then I notice his car's missing from the driveway. Probably visiting one of his whores, I decide. That's good. With any luck, I'll be in bed before he arrives home.

Wrong. As I move towards the front door, headlights sweep through the trees and I shrink back among them. My father's Lexus appears in the driveway and the gravel crunches as he pulls up and kills the engine. Dad steps out. He yanks open the boot and reaches in. Then a head emerges, my father's hands hauling someone from the vehicle.

'Stand up, bitch.' His voice is a low bark. Instinct, honed by years of living with him, warns me to stay where I am, concealed by the darkness. The woman holds her hands in front of her, wrists tied together. Her feet stumble across the gravel towards the cottage, her body propelled by my father's grasp on her jacket.

They disappear inside, leaving me pressed into the protective cover of the trees, unsure as to what I've just seen.

I don't dare go in, not when I've no idea what he's up to. If my father, believing me elsewhere, has brought one of his prostitutes back home, then my life will be worth less than a shovelful of shit if I disturb him. I'm chilled, and I'm hungry, yet I stay put, my feet shuffling from side to side as I debate what to do. Muffled sounds reach me from the cottage, but I'm unable to identify them. Then a light goes on, but not in Dad's bedroom. Instead, it's coming from the side of the cottage, from the tiny basement window.

Despite my fear of my father, I'm intrigued. I tiptoe over to the window, squatting next to it, the rough stone of the wall against my back. Dad's voice, anger swelling its volume, reaches me through the glass.

'A whore like you deserves whatever she gets.' Then I hear a hand striking flesh, followed by a stifled scream. The terror inside me thickens, its grip relentless.

'Fucking bitch.' My father's voice grows fainter as his shoes clump against the wood of the basement stairs. I hear the door bang, but not the latch clicking into place. He's gone to get something then, intending to return; I don't have much time. I edge closer to the window and peer through the glass.

The woman lies on the concrete floor, her eyes closed, her wrists bound held together with thin cords. Not as old as Dad, maybe mid-thirties, but it's hard to tell. She's wearing a jacket over a cream-coloured top, teamed with jeans. Dark hair. Duct tape seals her mouth. I can almost smell her fear as she twists her forearms back and forth, seeking escape from the tight knots. Her head bucks to and fro, as though she's convulsing, and I realise she's talking to herself, despite the tape. I stare at the dark stain that spreads over her groin as she pisses herself, a puddle of her terror seeping across the floor.

Then I hear the basement door being opened, and the clump of feet on the wooden stairs, and I pull back, breathing hard, my own fear ratcheting up several gears. My eyes squeeze shut as my head touches the frigid stone, the pounding of my heart deafening my ears. What the hell is going on here?

One thing's for sure. No way can I reveal I've come home early, pretending I'm unaware of the woman in the basement. He's planned this, whatever this is, using my camping trip as the ideal time to carry out his perverted scheme. Who the woman is, I haven't a clue, but the cords, the tape, my father's anger – none of it bodes well for her as she lies soaked in her own urine and terror. The excitement in Dad's voice I noted earlier floats back to me, the stash of porn under his bed coming into my head.

I need to find a place to spend the night; it doesn't matter where. I consider calling one of my friends, asking if I can stay overnight, but reject the idea. What reason can I give? None that I can think of, and besides the last thing I want is anyone coming to the cottage to collect me, spotting something they shouldn't.

In the end, I walk across the fields, finding a sheltered spot under some trees, hidden from view, and I unpack my sleeping bag. I don't sleep, just snatches of a light doze. Whenever I close my eyes, the woman's wet crotch flashes before me.

***

When I awake, I'm chilled and soaked from the morning dew. I towel myself dry, and then repack my sleeping bag, before eating the last energy bar from my rucksack. I need to discover what's happened to the woman. She's a lure so powerful I don't even try to resist.

An hour goes by before I dredge up the courage to walk back to the cottage, skirting round to the basement window. It's still early, just after seven, the air fresh and cool as I pad over the gravel. I crouch to one side of the window, breathing long and hard, summoning up every inch of nerve to peer through the window.

When I do, I see the woman's eyes are closed, but she's awake. She's lying on the old Z-bed, rocking back and forth, her movements intended for self-comfort. The duct tape still seals her mouth, but her lips move against the material as though in prayer. Besides the fact her wrists are now unbound, something else about her is different; I can't pinpoint what, though. Too preoccupied last night by the fact she'd wet herself, I didn't take in many details. She's still terrified, that's for sure; her fear is so tangible it all but permeates the glass dividing us.

I pull back from the window, ideas hurtling through my brain. If I walk in now, tell my father I've returned early, no harm will come to the woman, not if Dad knows I'm back. I'll no doubt cop one of his backhanders; he'll shout, make my life hell, but I'll have saved the woman. I know, deep in my brain, that she needs rescuing from whatever horrors Lincoln Perdue has already inflicted and those he's planning.

Then I hear sounds through the window. My father has returned to the basement. I squat against the wall once more. Too afraid of being seen, I daren't peer through the glass.

Muffled protests from the woman reach my ears, sounds stifled by the duct tape. They grow louder and more desperate, and I pick up scuffing noises, telling me her shoes are scraping against the concrete floor. Maybe he's taking her home then, but I don't hear two pairs of feet on the wooden stairs. Instead, I detect the buzz of a zip being pulled down, then another, the rustle of clothing being adjusted, as the muted pleas increase. Then my father's porcine grunts sound out, his breathing harsh and raspy, and understanding slams into me.

I deduce from the quality of the noises that he's facing away from the window, and when I edge my face towards the glass, my breath steamy against it, I'm proved correct. He's dragged the woman off the bed and onto the floor. My father's trousers hang around his knees as he pumps into her from behind, his buttocks pale and flabby as they bounce back and forth. Little of the woman is visible, obscured as she is by her aggressor's bulk. Her neck is under my father's hand, her cropped hair against his palm as he presses her right cheek into the floor. Her mouth is still moving against the duct tape.

My father thrusts and pumps his way to sexual nirvana, trickles of sweat running down his arse, wet patches appearing on his shirt back to match the ones in his armpits, and I'm unable to drag my gaze away. It's ugly, repulsive, disgusting beyond words, but the scene holds an incredible fascination, a compelling something I'm unable to identify, that glues my eyes to the glass. My breathing synchronises with my father's rapid grunts. Then he pulls out his cock; I can't help but stare at it, the way it's all slick and glistening, the head a purple mushroom. He hauls the woman onto her back and shoves himself inside her once more, his hands trapping her against the floor, her throat his captive. Panic has forced the woman's eyes wide, thick tranches of white visible under her irises. Her short hair is damp with sweat as she jerks her head from side to side in a futile attempt to break free. At first my father's hands appear to be holding her in place so he can fuck her. Then realisation dawns on me. As his climax builds, he's choking the life out of her.

The two bodies on the basement floor buck and thrust and struggle against each other, and then the woman's head shifts so her gaze aligns with the window, and she spots me through the glass. Her body jerks with shock. As our eyes meet, my father throws back his head. He comes in a noisy, sweaty, rutting splendour, the shudders of his orgasm clenching his damp arse cheeks. As the last few spasms course through him, all remnants of life leave the woman's eyes, still fixed on my own. His hands release her throat as his breathing slows.

At fourteen years of age, I stare into a woman's face as she dies. The experience marks me like indelible ink. It's the tipping point in my life, an event leading me to depression and thoughts of a noose strung from the basement rafter.

I twist away from the window. Then I grab my rucksack and tiptoe across the gravel, before my feet hit grass and I take flight, desperate to put distance between the cottage and myself.

***

After an hour or so, I return, fear and curiosity jockeying for position in my skull. Once there, I position myself under the oak at the top of the driveway. My father's car has gone. I wait. Ten minutes later, he returns, hauling various sacks from the boot, carrying them into the cottage. Building supplies, from what I can make out. Cement. Lime. A tarpaulin. Later, muffled sounds reach me: banging, a saw hewing through wood, the wet slap of mixing cement. Hours pass while I wait. Then he leaves again.

The sun has nearly vanished from the sky. Unable to face another night sleeping rough, I walk towards the cottage. Silence greets me as I open the front door, my fingers trembling. I make straight for the basement. It's empty. A faint stain marks where the woman's urine flooded from her bladder the previous night. I trace its edges with the toe of my shoe, as I relive the scenes once more in my head, before pounding up the stairs to my bedroom.

Hours later, I hear gravel crunching under the wheels of a car. My father has returned. I force myself to go downstairs, so he realises I'm home. He reeks of booze, his eyes bloodshot.

'What the hell are you doing back early?' Spit flies from his mouth as he stares at me, hatred in his face. I explain about our teacher's burst appendix, before skirting past him, eager for the sanctuary of my bedroom. My father offers no explanation as to why he's bricked up one of the basements, but I guess his reason. He's obviously chosen to keep the woman's body close by, presumably as a trophy. Why move her into the other basement, though? Why not keep her where he killed her, in the room containing the Z-bed?

It takes me a while before I figure it out. Lincoln Perdue's nothing if not practical. Where he entombed her lacks a power supply. That part of the cottage is simply less useful.

The lime puzzles me, until I do some research online. Turns out it's used to mask the odour of decomposition. I'm guessing the woman's now wrapped in a tarpaulin shroud, itself encased in lime and cement. Something else also makes sense: why, just before I left for the camping trip, he fired the woman who did our cooking and cleaning. Impossible to carry out his plan with her coming in each day.

At the weekend, I find his victim's handbag, hidden in a suitcase stuffed at the back of his wardrobe. It's large, fashioned from purple leather, held shut by a gold clasp. I open it, taking out her purse, fingering the jewellery stashed inside the bag. As is something else. I draw it out, fascinated, repulsed. Too late, I realise what was different about the woman the second time I saw her in the basement.

***

Some responsibility for the woman's death is mine, of course. I chose to watch her die, when I could have banged on the glass, run into the cottage, saved her life. Terror of Lincoln Perdue rendered me impotent, however. Later, I think back to what happened, and I understand why the thought of going to the police never crossed my mind, not even after he'd bricked up the basement. My father had bullied me into submission too effectively, meaning thoughts of rebellion didn't enter my head. If I'd acted differently, then perhaps… But I didn't, and now a different captive is imprisoned here. Beth's not gagged, her hair is long instead of short, she's younger, but otherwise they're similar. With her, I'll repeat the experience, but endow it with a different ending. The girl in the basement will live. In time, she'll love me.

My plan for restitution, made good.

CHAPTER 5 – *Beth*

S leep is impossible my first night in the basement. Without a blanket or duvet, the chilly air seeps into my body, leaving me stiff and exhausted by the time light penetrates the tiny window. He didn't take my watch, so I know it's two minutes after six. I've spent the night with his words in my head, about not intending to kill me, how this damp, dark place will be my home. They offer a small measure of comfort, as does his apparent disinclination towards sex. Dawn sees me renewed with hope on two levels. I'm certain I'll be found soon, and if I'm not, then I'll discover a way to break free from this hellhole.

'Get your act together, Beth,' I admonish myself. 'One way or another, you'll survive this. You have to.'

No sounds reach me from above. I'm guessing I have time before Dominic puts in an appearance. Preferably with breakfast. The sandwich he brought me last night barely dented my hunger and after the chilly night on the fold-up bed, I'm ravenous. I need to use the toilet, too. So far, I've held on, but both my bladder and bowels are desperate for relief.

I cross the floor, pull up the lid of the chemical toilet, push down my jogging bottoms, and squat my butt on the hard plastic. When I'm done, I sit there, contemplating my prison.

The window doesn't offer any options for escape. Too tiny, too high up. The toilet might, although it's too bulky to use as a weapon. It offers other possibilities, though. I stand up, staring at the blue liquid in the pan. Some strong chemicals down there, for sure. A possibility, if I can scoop the stuff out. Throw it in the bastard's eyes – that's got to at least blind him for a while – and then up the stairs and away before he can recover.

Next, I scrutinise the filing cabinet. It's metal, so it could be useful if I'm able to prise something loose from it. I cross to it, pulling out the drawers. My arms reach inside, hoping to find a strut I can work loose, but without success. The handles don't budge when I tug at them. They're fixed too tightly to undo one with my nails.

Lastly, the bed. My fingers twist at the nuts, but they don't move. Even if I managed to unscrew any of them, I can't see what I could use as a weapon. Sure, the headboard's an option, but I doubt I'm capable of exerting enough force to do more than deliver a hard blow with it, which would provoke rather than stun my captor.

No, the toilet chemicals are my best chance. I'll need to be quick, as well as accurate, waiting until he's away from the stairs to allow me my exit, and facing me so I can blind the bastard. How to conceal what I'm intending to do, though? I stare at the water bottle he brought me last night, now empty. The blue chemicals will be obvious through the clear plastic, so once I've filled it I'll have to stash it somewhere until my chance arrives. The bed offers few options, which leaves the filing cabinet. Concealed behind it for quick access, perhaps. I push against the grey metal. It moves easily once the castors engage.

Something else occurs to me. I'm concerned it'll be his word against mine once I'm free; I need to circumvent that. At first, I'm at a loss how to achieve this, before the brickwork gives me an idea. I slide the filing cabinet further from the wall. Then I remove one of my earrings.

It's a ruby stud, part of a pair given to me by Mum for my seventeenth birthday. I press a finger against the gold post. Strong enough to scratch a message on the wall. The plaster is old, no match for the hard metal. I crouch next to the wall, and carve letters onto its surface.

'Beth Sutton. Abducted by Dominic Perdue on…' As I scratch yesterday's date on the wall, sounds alert me. My captor is descending the main staircase of the cottage. I scramble upright, my breath catching in my chest, then I push the filing cabinet back into place before rubbing the earring free from dirt. To my relief, his feet bypass the basement and head into the kitchen, but I don't dare do any more scratching. I'll finish the message later, after he's gone. Right now, I long for breakfast.

Ten minutes later, a key turns in the lock, and Dominic walks down the stairs. I'm lying on the bed again, arms wrapped around my knees, although it's less chilly now the sun's up. He carries a tray in his hands and I'm beyond grateful. No coffee, but he's probably considered the risk of me throwing the scalding liquid into his face. Instead, he's brought more bottled water, a bowl of muesli with milk, and a round of toast.

'You behaved well last night after I left,' he says, as though I'm a child. 'No shouting or silly stuff. You've earned yourself a shower. Once you've had breakfast.'

I stare at him. A shower. Right now, it's the most wonderful idea in the world; a chance to warm up, scrub the chill of the basement from my pores. It means getting naked, though. Will he insist on watching me? Then my mind runs over what I might find in his bathroom: a razor or an electric toothbrush, perhaps, something I can use as a weapon.

He gestures at the food. 'Eat, Beth. Then you can shower.'

You bastard, I say in my head. Not aloud, though. I daren't risk another crack across my nose. Instead, I adopt a wheedling tone.

'Could I get a blanket and extra clothes? It's freezing down here.' I maintain eye contact, widening them, giving him the full wounded-fawn effect.

He nods. 'I'll bring you a pillow and a duvet for tonight. Meanwhile, if you're cold, put on another sweatshirt. Plenty in the filing cabinet.' Hardness sets into his face. 'Understand this, Beth. I'll get you some bedding, but I can take it away whenever I choose. How comfortable you are depends on your behaviour. Including shower privileges. Step out of line, and you'll wash in cold water from a bucket. Or not at all.'

His words, and the steel behind them, chill me. I stare at him.

'I can remove the bed, too. The toilet. You decide, Beth. Now eat.'

Our eyes meet for a few more seconds before I nod. I'm too terrified of what I've seen in those weird blue and brown irises to do otherwise.

An oval pill sits on the tray beside the water bottle. My first thought is that Dominic intends to drug me, to keep me acquiescent. I pick it up, rubbing my fingers over the smooth surface.

'Multivitamin and mineral,' Dominic says. 'For vitamin D. You won't be getting any direct sunlight, not down here.' At that, I start to cry, hot tears stinging my eyeballs and splashing onto my sweatshirt. More than anything, this gets to me: the idea he's planned this in every detail, even my health care needs, and that he intends my stay in this foul basement to be permanent. Sobs wrench from my chest, rendering me incapable of eating, but have no effect on the man standing before me. After a while, they subside into tiny hiccups.

'Eat your breakfast.' His tone delivers ice to my ears. 'Now, or forget the shower.'

I dig in and eat, my throat closing against the food. When I'm done, I pick up the tablet and swallow it with a gulp of water.

'Good girl,' he says. 'You can shower now.'

Dominic waits while I fetch clean underwear from the filing cabinet. Then he marches me up the stairs, his right hand gripping my arm, his body close behind me. We walk through the kitchen and into a small lobby, with a door to one side. Dominic nods in its direction. 'In there,' he says. 'You'll find everything you need. Five minutes, Beth. After that, if you're not done, I'll come in and get you. Understand?'

I nod. Then I open the door.

Inside is a shower, along with a small washbasin. Shampoo, soap and conditioner sit in a plastic tray attached to the wall of the cubicle. Mirror tiles above the basin reflect my nose, bruised and encrusted with dried blood. The kohl around my eyes is a smeared mess. A bath towel hangs from a hook on the wall. Toothpaste and a toothbrush, a new one, are by the sink. The brush is a manual one, not electric, so less effective as a potential weapon. No razor. I undress and turn on the water, allowing the heat and steam to take me away from this place, waft me back home to the power shower in our family bathroom. Far better than the weak flow under which I'm standing. I soap myself, before rinsing, towelling myself dry and pulling on the clean clothes. Then I brush my teeth.

Dominic's as good as his word. As I wash out my mouth, the door opens, and he's there before me. 'Time's up,' he says. His gaze sweeps around the room, checking everything's as it was. Tears prick at me again. I'm sensing I'll get little chance to outwit this man.

His hand clamped to my arm, he escorts me back to the basement, before picking up the tray, including both water bottles. If that's to be the norm, my plan with the toilet chemicals is shafted. Chin up, Beth, I remind myself. He'll slip up, get complacent, and then you'll get your chance.

'No noise. I have to work,' he tells me. He gestures around the basement. 'One more thing. This is your home now. I expect you to keep it tidy.'

Then he locks me in my prison again.

I spend the morning attempting to calm myself, telling myself I'll be found before long. Mum will expect me back by lunchtime, so she'll be getting worried soon. By evening, she'll have persuaded Dad to inform the police. A day, two at most, and they'll be hammering on the cottage door. In my head, I picture my reunion with Mum. The desire to see her face, her wayward hair and her lop-sided smile, to sink into the warmth of her arms, brings a physical pain to my heart. Have faith, Beth, I reassure myself. Do whatever the bastard wants. Keep him sweet, and you'll come through this.

Meanwhile, I take out my earring and complete the message on the wall.

***

And that's how I play things, at least at first. I make my bed every morning. Dominic brings food three times a day, and I eat while he watches me. Afterwards, he clears everything away, so I'm never left with a knife, not that blunt dinner cutlery makes an effective weapon. He doesn't speak much, but his gaze hovers over me, ensuring my compliance. As for me, I avoid looking at him whenever possible; eye contact between us means forging a connection, something unthinkable for me.

In between meals, I lie on the bed, planning what I'll do after I escape. I'll travel first, I decide. I picture myself sipping wine on a Greek island, the houses white sugar cubes with sky-blue domes. Or I'm atop Sydney's Harbour Bridge, panting and sweaty after the climb, the sun on the water blinding me. I spend hours this way. Why not? I've nothing else to occupy my time while in this shit-hole. Besides, despair is waiting to claim me if I'm not vigilant. Once I surrender to it, I'm lost.

***

Three nights have now passed. I persuade myself I'm doing well at staying positive. It's early days, I reassure myself. Is there a margin of time before a missing-persons investigation gets underway? In which case, the police might not have launched their search until yesterday, so it's not surprising they've not found me yet. They'll have protocols to adhere to, procedures to follow. They'll need to track down male BMW owners in Bristol with cars matching the make, model and colour of Dominic's. Their photo-fit artist will work with Troy to get a description of my abductor. When the police do arrive at the cottage, I'll scream like crazy, bang on the window, and my time in this foul basement will be over.

***

Positive thinking is growing harder. Five nights I've spent on this thin mattress, the wooden slats pressing into my spine as I try to sleep, although at least I have a pillow and duvet now. Small comforts, along with my five-minute shower every morning. The tiny room's for my sole use, Dominic's informed me; he uses the main bathroom upstairs. Today I lost track of time in there, the hot water washing away the tension in my belly. True to his word, Dominic bangs on the door after my allotted time span.

'Time's up,' he shouts through the door. When I don't come out quickly enough, he barges in as I'm fastening my bra, giving him an unplanned eyeful of my breasts. My body twists away, as far from him as I can get in the tiny space, but not before I've seen the expression on his face. Distaste, which delivers a small measure of reassurance. Not once has Dominic ever tried anything sexual with me. No kisses, no furtive gropes of my bottom or boobs, not even any allusions to sex. He's had plenty of opportunity to rape me and he hasn't. To my mind, that means he won't in the future.

The future? What the hell am I saying? My positive thinking plummets into a swallow dive. It's the morning of the sixth day. Why haven't I been found? What are the police playing at? However hard I try to stay focused, reassure myself it's only a matter of time, the endless hours of inactivity grind away at me. The hands on my watch move with agonising slowness, the four walls of my prison becoming my coffin, despite what Dominic said about me not dying. If my life is to consist of this dark basement, if I'm never to see the sun again, then I may as well kill myself. Not that my options are extensive. I could drink the chemicals from the toilet, or starve myself, but the first might not kill me and the second is an end so horrible I can't go there, not yet. It gives me an idea, though. Time to test the bastard's boundaries; discover how far I can push him. I'll stage a hunger strike.

When Dominic next brings me food, chicken soup and a cheese baguette for lunch, I shake my head. 'I don't want anything,' I tell him.

'You have to eat.' He pushes the tray closer. 'I'll stay until you do.'

He can't force me. I keep my head turned, refusing to engage with him.

'Either you eat, or you won't shower for a week. Your choice.' I glance up at him, and his face is harder than the walls of my prison. We're locked in a crazy battle of wills but I've come too far to back down.

I lose, of course. After one shake of my head too many after he continues to order me to eat, Dominic storms up the stairs, cursing under his breath. The door bangs behind him and I'm left alone. The tray of food sits on the floor, the smell of the soup a cruel temptation. I huddle, foetus-like, on the bed and stare at the wall.

Dominic doesn't appear again that day. The soup grows a paper-like skin; the baguette becomes hard. My fingers stray to it often; its golden crustiness sings a siren song to my stomach. It's ten o'clock at night when I cave in, seizing the stick with both hands, forcing it into my mouth, tearing into it, the sharp edges gouging my gums. Oh, God, it's so good, so fucking good. The stale cheese is nirvana, the soggy salad a delight, the hard bread filling and satisfying. The desperation in my stomach has stilled for now.

The night is a cold one. I put on extra trousers and another sweatshirt so I can sleep, and I'm still frozen. At six, I drag myself off the mattress to use the toilet, my eyes heavy after only three hours of rest. Dominic will bring my breakfast soon, I tell myself. Hot buttered toast, maybe scrambled eggs, a slice or two of bacon. My stomach is so, so empty, and I realise I'll never be able to starve myself to death, not ever. When Dominic comes, I'll eat every bite he brings me, and then I'll apologise. I hear my own voice in my head. I'm sorry, I'll tell him. I'll behave from now on. Just allow me my food.

Seven o'clock comes, bringing Dominic. He's a man of habit, my mealtimes predictable in their regularity. I scramble off the bed, eager for breakfast, as he unlocks the door.

His hands are empty. No tray of food, and despair drags tears into my eyes.

He stands there, at the top of the stairs, looking at me. 'You've not had your soup,' he says.

What? I've done what he asked, eaten what he brought me, well most of it, and I stare at him in disbelief. He can't expect me to eat stone-cold soup. Can he?

'Eat it. When you have, then, and only then, will you get anything else.' He bangs the door shut. The steel in his voice doesn't allow me to hope he'll change his mind. It's another hour or so, though, before the hunger in my belly forces me to eat the soup. Its congealed surface resists the spoon at first, before allowing me to scoop up a mouthful. My throat gags as my lips close around the cold liquid, and I tell myself not to be so fussy. Despite the fact that chicken soup should be hot, not this frigid mess, it's not as awful as I'd feared. It's soup, just at the wrong temperature. I finish the lot within two minutes.

Bang on one o'clock, my captor returns and removes the tray. Five minutes later, he's back with my lunch, a couple of bacon rolls. 'I'm pleased you've decided to be sensible,' he informs me. I don't reply, too intent on wolfing the food. He watches me eat, then leaves.

When he returns in the evening, bearing chicken curry and rice, I mutter a 'thank you'. A smile is beyond me, but having so little food the last two days has hammered something home to me: I depend on this man for my survival. He brings my food, my water, empties the chemical toilet. My life depends on playing whatever sick game he has in mind. He harbours a dark something I've no desire to provoke.

After I've eaten the curry – home-made and excellent – he makes as if to collect the tray. 'Wait,' I say.

'What?'

'Can I take a shower now? I really need one. I promise I'll eat all my food from now on.' I sound like a kid agreeing to taste her broccoli.

'No.'

'Please?'

He shakes his head. 'Rules are rules. The sooner you understand that, the easier you'll adapt. I said no showers for a week, and that's what I meant. Don't think you can play me for a mug. Because if you do…' He bends closer, his mismatched eyes never leaving my own, and I flinch as his breath fans my face. 'You'll be disappointed.' He picks up the tray.

'You fucking bastard!' A wild sweep of my hand sends the tray, plate and cutlery crashing onto the concrete. I stoop to grab the fork, all thoughts of placating my captor gone from my head. Instead, feral fury engulfs me, rage at the way he's brought me here, his presumption that I'll be his plaything, his pet. My anger makes me lash out, intent on jabbing the fork into the first soft flesh of his I can find, but he's too quick, too big. His fingers clamp around my wrist as I lunge forwards. The pressure is unbearable; I cry out, sinking to my knees, still in his grip. Then his hand releases me. Next second it swipes across my face, delivering a blow so hard it knocks the breath from my lungs and my body to the floor. He steps over me, ignoring my frantic gasps, and picks up the tray, handing me the bottle of water.

'No food tomorrow,' he says. Then he leaves.

I haul myself onto the bed, wiping my face with the back of my hand, snot oozing from my nostrils, tears running from my eyes. I stagger to the filing cabinet and pull out a wad of toilet paper, dabbing my cheeks and blowing my nose. The terror inside me has grown extra heads.

It's my fault for provoking him. Whatever I do, I mustn't lose my cool again.

***

Dominic's as good as his word. No food arrives the next day and by the time I try to sleep, all I can think of is my stomach, which growls with emptiness. Thirst leaches the saliva from my mouth, but I need to eke out the water I have. Fear bites into me as I chop and change positions during the night, an occasional light doze being all I manage.

No breakfast arrives the next morning, either. I'm desperate for a shower as well. I debate with myself whether to ask for one, but decide against it, reluctant to provoke him further. Given the events of yesterday, I've no reason to think he'll relent, although the thought of not showering for a week is loathsome. Play the game, Beth, I remind myself. Your mission is to survive, not fret about when you'll next enjoy soap and water.

I sit on the bed, eyeing my watch as the time creeps onwards. Please God, let him appear with my lunch in due course. Until the police rescue me, I'll toe the line, just to get food.

The door is unlocked at exactly one o'clock. Dominic walks down the stairs. 'I hope you intend to behave from now on,' he says.

'I'm sorry about before.' I force myself to meet his eyes. 'Please. Can I have something to eat?'

He cocks his head to one side, his gaze appraising. 'You reckon you deserve food? After the way you behaved?'

'Yes.' His expression darkens. 'No.'

'You swore at me. I've already told you that's unacceptable.'

I bite my lip, unnerved by the steel in his gaze. 'I shouldn't have done that.'

'You were going to stab me.'

'That was wrong of me. It won't happen again.'

'It had better not.' Do I imagine it, or does his face soften?

'Please. I'm so hungry. I'll behave from now on. I promise.'

He nods. 'I'll bring your lunch.'

When the tray arrives, I notice the cutlery is now plastic. I'm guessing that'll be the norm from now on, and I'm annoyed with myself for losing a possible weapon. No more outbursts, I resolve. The smell of the beef stew tantalises me and I can't shovel the food into my mouth fast enough, grains of rice falling on the tray as I eat. Whatever else he may be, the bastard's a good cook.

When I've finished, he leaves without a word, tray in hand.

My brain's working better now that my stomach's full. Time to consider my options. A shaft of sunlight piercing the dirty pane draws my attention to the window. A thought blossoms in my head. I was wrong to think the tiny aperture held no possibilities for escape.

I sit on my bed, considering how best to put into action my new idea.

I can't act on what I've decided right now, though. He'll be down those stairs the minute the sound of breaking glass reaches his ears, making it far too rushed for what I'm planning. He needs to be unsuspecting, moving at his usual pace, as he comes through the door. It opens outward, on the left side. I'll be waiting for him, behind and on the right, with a shard of glass in hand. I stroke my throat, my fingers gauging where the pulse beats, the optimum place to aim for when I strike at him.

I'll wait until he leaves the cottage, and then seize my chance. What with the window being so small, and round one side of the house, he'll never notice the broken pane of glass when he returns.

***

My chance comes the next day. It's mid-morning, and I'm lying on my bed, fighting the panic that's growing within me. I'm losing track of time. I've been here eight nights now, or is it nine? Ten, even? When you've nothing with which to occupy your time, the minutes, hours and days merge into one, and if I'm to stay sane, I need to get out of here as soon as possible. Right when desperation threatens to engulf me, I hear the jangle of keys, followed by the slam of the front door. The gravel crunches under my captor's feet as he walks towards his car. The engine of the BMW purrs into life, and then he drives away.

Silence envelops me in the empty cottage. My brain whirs. He won't risk leaving me for long. I'm surmising a grocery trip. Ten minutes to get to Kingswood and park. Half an hour to shop, ten minutes to drive back. Fifty minutes before he returns.

I put on my remaining clean socks as padding against the thin soles of the slippers, ready for when I need to run. I use the toilet. Then I grab my pillow, pressing my fist deep into it, my fingers tightening in its cotton case. The sides dangle against my forearms, but I don't have anything with which to bind the material to my hands. It's not ideal, but it'll suffice.

I drag the chemical toilet across the floor and position it under the window. It's sturdy enough to take my weight when the lid's closed, and once I stand on it I can more or less reach. The putty looks old, the glass cracked across one corner. I'm hoping it'll break on the first blow, but my first punch proves me wrong. My fist in its protective pillow bounces off, a dull throb of pain spreading across my knuckles. I aim another blow at the window.

On the third try, the glass shatters, pieces slicing through the pillowcase, narrowly missing my hand. Because I punched outward, that's where most of the shards lie, outside on the ground. I discard the pillow, stretching on tiptoe to collect them, edging my hand through the broken window, my fingers exposed to the sharp edges of the glass. I shiver at the unaccustomed sensation of air against my skin. The first two shards are too small for my purposes; I toss them on the basement floor. Number three proves perfect. Six inches long and two wide, one edge curved like a cutlass, a narrow triangle ending in a sharp point. A bead of blood blossoms when I test the tip against my thumb.

Tension clenches my bladder, compelling me to pee again. Then I walk to the top of the stairs and position myself behind the door.

CHAPTER 6 – *Beth*

'**M**ove away from the door, Beth.' Fuck. He knows. He's aware I'm waiting for him, shard of glass in hand, poised to strike. Realisation hits me. Between when I heard the BMW pull up, and Dominic slamming its door, the time that passed until he entered the cottage was too long for getting groceries from the boot. I picture him, tiptoeing across the gravel so as not to alert me. Then squatting by the window, picking up the glass, deciding how he'll play things.

His voice is calm. From Dominic, it's more chilling than anger.

'I know you're there.' Again, no rage. I can't call out to deny it, not when we're inches from each other, only the rough oak of the door separating us.

'Walk down the stairs. Stop at the bottom.' I obey, my body thankful to be moving after its self-imposed stillness, inching down the steps until my feet touch concrete. The jagged hole left in the window mocks my failure. My fingers still clutch the shard of glass.

The door opens. Dominic descends into the basement, a hank of rope over one arm, his face an inscrutable mask as his eyes spot my makeshift weapon. 'Drop it,' he orders.

I don't comply. Instead, I lunge forward, aiming for the sweet spot on his neck. As I go in for the kill, a grip of steel encircles my wrist, the pressure on my veins relentless. Dominic's eyes are ice-chips that freeze my soul, his face so close to mine we're almost touching.

'Drop the glass,' he commands. This time, I comply. He releases his hold on me, so he can crack his hand across my face, once, twice, in a replay of my first night here. Knocked to the ground by the force of the blows, I gasp for breath as I wipe blood from my nose.

I'm not given any respite. Dominic yanks me up by my arm, pushing me onto the bed. He twists the rope around my wrists, far too tight, and I wince as he loops the ends around the metal frame of the bed. The coarse fibres bite into my skin, chafing it, and I squirm, but asking him to loosen it is pointless.

'I need to make sure you don't try any funny business while I clean up this mess,' he says.

After he's disabled me, Dominic walks up the stairs, returning with a dustpan and brush, sweeping up the shards of glass. Then he leaves. Panic swells inside me as his feet hit the stairs. I can't even access the toilet, although my bladder is screaming for relief. Strange noises assault my ears; I realise I'm whimpering. Then other sounds intrude on my terror. Rhythmic ones, the back and forth of a saw. He's planning to board up the window.

Sure enough, minutes later he returns, an oblong of plywood in one hand, hammer and nails in the other. He strides past me. With quick precision, he bangs the wood into place against the window frame, cutting off the blessed sunlight. My connection to the outside world vanishes.

Dominic yanks the waste tray from the chemical toilet and leaves the basement again. When he returns, he's carrying a bucket, several newspapers and a bottle of water. 'No,' I plead. 'Please. Do anything else, but leave the toilet.'

He doesn't reply, but instead tugs at the knots binding me, tearing the skin as he releases my wrists. Angry welts circle the skin on them.

'Water only. No food for three days,' Dominic announces. 'No showers either. You shit, you piss, in that bucket. Afterwards, you use the newspapers.' He crosses to the filing cabinet, removing the remaining toilet paper. Then he leaves. I'm alone, shivering on the bed, and within seconds, I've disintegrated. Dominic has sloughed off the top layer of my humanity, leaving me raw and primal, as whimpers tear from my throat, a rhythmic chant of *no, no, no*, as I rock back and forth, to and fro, my arms around my knees. Tears course down my cheeks and snot slides, unchecked, from my nose. It's a long time before I'm all cried out.

I stay in my foetal huddle all day and throughout the night. My mind is blank. To think is to exist, and right now, I'd prefer annihilation. At seven a.m., my ears detect sounds from above. Dominic is up and moving around. My stomach is growling in desperation, but all I have is water, which has to last me three days. My mouth is dry, my tongue tacky with thirst. The catatonic state I've been in has denied my body water for hours. The need to drink becomes overwhelming, and I uncurl, muscles shrieking with stiffness as I plant my feet on the floor. My legs wobble under my weight as I grab the bottle of water from the filing cabinet. So satisfying, that first gulp sliding down my throat.

Then I sleep at last.

***

When I awake, my watch tells me it's four in the afternoon. I eye the bucket, the newspapers. Then I sob again as I pull down my jogging bottoms and squat. It's the most undignified thing I've ever done.

Degrading it might be, but it's what saves my sanity. Not the bucket, but the newspapers. As I tear a page off one of them, I stop, my hand halfway towards my bottom. Words. News. The outside world. I've had no mental stimulation since my abduction. After I clean myself, I seize the pile of newspapers and I swear I read every word in them over the next two days. From the *Evening Post* I learn about Bristol City Council's plans for budget cutbacks. The *Financial Times* pontificates about the boom in the housing market. I doubt its pink pages have ever been used to wipe an arse before. Whatever I read, it reminds me life exists beyond this basement, a world in which people buy property, get married, find jobs and live their lives. I may be trapped in a basement, held prisoner by a psycho, but I'm Beth Sutton, I'm eighteen years old; escaping this hellhole becomes every bit as imperative as that gulp of water earlier. A primitive survival mechanism clicks into place in my brain, and with it comes my mother's face. My reason to cling to sanity.

'I'll get out of here,' I promise her. 'Soon.'

But three days without food exact their toll on my body. Not just the constant reminders from my stomach, so bad that I become obsessed with food, torturing myself with images of Mum's roast lunches, her weekend power breakfasts, the baguettes at The Busy Bean. My breath turns stinky, its foulness unrelieved by water or toothpaste. By the evening of the second day, my head is pounding, forcing me to abandon my newspaper reading and curl into a ball of exhaustion. I calculate I've another twenty-four hours to endure.

***

Food is coming, I'm sure; I hear noises from the kitchen as I squat over the brimming bucket. By now, the smell is beyond disgusting. A nugget of satisfaction comes my way as I imagine the bastard emptying it, as well as collecting the screwed-up balls of newspaper on the floor. As I add another to the collection and stand up, woozy from lack of food, the basement door opens.

Dominic strides down the stairs. His nostrils flare as they detect the stench, disgust etching itself across his face. He holds a plate, on which is the most wonderful sight. A thin cheese sandwich, plain, no salad, on wholemeal rather than the white I prefer, but right now it's food heaven. He thrusts it towards me, setting a fresh bottle of water on the mattress. I react at once, shoving the sandwich into my mouth, chewing furiously, my dry gums struggling with the bread. I cough and splutter, but it's still the most delicious food I've ever tasted. Huge swigs of water join the mess in my mouth as I cram nourishment into my starving body. I've turned feral, a bear emerging from hibernation, primeval and wild. I'm past caring, though. I have food at last.

When I'm done, I force myself to look at my abductor. 'Thank you,' I say, human again. My overwhelming gratitude towards him shocks me. As does the knowledge that I'll do anything and everything he wants, if he continues to bring me food.

Dominic doesn't reply. He takes the plate upstairs, returning with a plastic bag, fresh newspapers and a clean bucket. Out of the bag, he extracts rubber gloves, snapping them on before transferring the soiled balls of newspaper into the bag. He leaves the replacement bucket and newspapers and carries the brimming pail up the stairs.

'Shower,' he says when he returns, and I can't get up the stairs fast enough.

***

At six o'clock, Dominic brings my evening meal, a small bowl of tomato soup and half a French stick.

'Minimal food,' he announces. 'Until you learn to behave. The bucket stays, too.'

I smile and thank him. Once more, I'm grateful. When he's gone, I devour the food within a minute.

It's another three days before I get anything other than basic rations. I've lost weight, when I didn't have any to spare, and I'm tired all the time. Worse, a low-grade headache pulses behind my eyes. Still, I get to shower and brush my teeth every day, the smell of lemon shampoo and the taste of spearmint beyond wonderful. Every time my brain battles the black moments that threaten to engulf it, I picture Mum's face, and I promise myself I'll kiss her again one day.

Depression is insidious, though. It snaps at my heels, dogs my thoughts, and sniffs out the weakness in me. It's my companion when I awake, my lover as I sleep. Something in me breaks during those six days of minimal food, making it hard to maintain even a semblance of positivity. Where the hell are the police? Why haven't I been found?

***

Proper meals eventually resume. After the third day of soup and bread, Dominic brings me chicken casserole, engendering an instant surge of gratitude. Stronger this time, too. Weird. As I thank him, I'm shocked by how beholden I feel towards this man. My abduction, starvation, life in this foul basement – none of that matters, not set beside the fact he's brought me this wonderful meal.

Afterwards, he delivers apple crumble, heaven in a bowl. 'Take your vitamin pill,' he instructs. Something else signalling the return to whatever passes for normality in my world.

I swallow it, eager to comply. 'Thank you,' I tell him again.

He shrugs. 'Give me your tray. Then I'll fix the toilet for you, take away the bucket. As long as you behave, remember.'

I can't lose the newspapers. Unthinkable. 'Please? Leave the bucket. I don't want the toilet.'

'Don't mess with me.' His tone is sharp. 'You can't possibly prefer the bucket. What are you playing at?'

'The newspapers,' I say. 'I... I need something to occupy my brain. I'm begging you. The bucket's vile, but it means I get to read. Don't take that away. Anything else, but not the newspapers.'

'You'll use the chemical toilet. No buts, Beth.' He eyes the pail with disgust.

'I'll do whatever you say. But please, Dominic. Allow me something to read.' He doesn't reply, but takes my tray and walks up the stairs.

When he returns, he's holding the usual carrier bag and rubber gloves, along with loo paper and the waste unit for the chemical toilet. No newspapers. Despair hits me hard. Reading material is a privilege I need to earn, I guess.

I ask as much.

'Yes.'

'How?'

'Told you. Do everything I say. No tricks. When I judge you've earned the right, I'll bring you books.' He inserts the waste unit into the grey cube, and then leaves with the bucket and soiled newspaper.

***

Not long afterwards, I resurrect my plan to use the chemicals from the toilet, the idea enticing enough to rouse me from my depression. After I make my decision, I behave impeccably. I do whatever Dominic says, thank him for my meals, eat my food. Outwardly, I'm submissive, accepting of my fate, everything he desires of me. Inwardly, I build up my hatred of my captor, reminding myself of how he's starved me, hit me, denied me showers and meals. How he's killed at least one other woman, judging by what he told me the first night I was here. I suppress all thoughts of the weird gratitude I experienced when he brought me food. My loathing burns fiercely, keeping me halfway sane, as does my desire to see Mum. Not to mention Dad and Troy. Jake Wilding, my best mate. Whenever despair threatens to engulf me, I indulge in my mental travels, and wait for an opportunity to carry out my plan.

Over time, I detect Dominic's wariness around me lessening, as I continue to comply with whatever he wants. When I judge the moment is right, I strike.

It's morning, and he's brought me my breakfast tray. 'I don't feel well,' I tell him after I've eaten, doing my best to make my voice sound hoarse.

His eyes narrow, scrutinising me. 'You look fine.'

'Woke up with a sore throat. Headache, too.'

Dominic frowns. 'I'll bring you a paracetamol.'

'Thank you.' I smile at him. 'That should do the trick.'

He goes upstairs, returning with a foil packet, popping me a tablet from one of the blisters. I wash it down, smiling at him again.

'Think I'll go back to bed. Please, could you leave me the water? Until my throat's better?'

He nods, and I do an inner fist pump – *yes!* I eat my breakfast under his scrutiny, before climbing into bed. Dominic picks up my tray, taking the bottle of Evian and handing it to me before leaving. Ignorant of what I have in mind, he won't consider its thin plastic a threat. He'll be back at one o'clock with my lunch. I'll be waiting for the bastard.

***

I'm ready way ahead of time. The water bottle, three-quarters full of liquid scooped from the toilet, is concealed under my pillow. I'm wearing an extra sweatshirt and two pairs of jogging bottoms, ready for when I'm outside. Don't fuck this up, Beth, I tell myself. My palms sweaty with nerves, I perch on my pillow, feet on the floor. That way, when Dominic bends to put my lunch tray on the bed, I'll have a clear line of exit to the door after I've blinded him. He doesn't lock it behind him when he brings my meals, only after he leaves.

The wait is agonising. The minutes tick by as the morning crawls on.

At one o'clock precisely, Dominic unlocks the door, walking down the stairs with my lunch. Chicken soup. Shame I won't be around to eat it. Confidence surges high in me. You can do this, I tell myself.

'You're better?' he enquires.

'Much.' I smile at him. He turns towards the bed, intending to place the tray on it, and I stand up. Time to blind the bastard.

One hand draws the bottle of chemicals from under my pillow, seconds before the other twists off the top. As I do so, my right foot lashes out, landing a powerful kick on his left ankle, intended to unbalance him. A yelp of pain escapes him as he staggers to one side, then my hand flings the toilet chemicals towards his face. He's too quick, though, bigger and faster than me, and his arm rises up, connecting with mine, knocking my aim off course. Dark blue liquid, thick and strong smelling, streams past Dominic to land on the floor. In an instant, I'm on the bed, pinned underneath him, my wrists held tight against the duvet by the iron grip of his hands.

He stares at me, those weird eyes boring into mine, his body heavy against my own. His face is mere inches away, his breath fanning my cheeks. Panic prevents the air from leaving my lungs. Still keeping me trapped, he removes his hands from my wrists, placing them around my neck, one above the other, so that my throat is completely under his control. His gaze never leaves my face. The world reduces to this moment. Nothing else exists. We're suspended in time, my heart hammering against my ribs, his fingers tight against my flesh. I wait for them to squeeze the life from me.

They don't, though. Dominic keeps them on my neck, but the rage drains from his eyes, to be replaced by an icy calmness.

'That was stupid of you,' he says.

I don't respond. Any chance I have of survival depends on my complete compliance, of that I'm sure.

'You know the rules. And you deliberately broke them.'

His grasp's slack enough to allow me to breathe; only terror prevented me before. I manage a nod.

'I've given you everything. A home, the food you eat, the clothes on your back. All I ask in return is a little respect. Do I get it? No.'

His hands relinquish their grip on my neck. With brutal strength, they slap my face, each side, hard; one, two. Fire flames through my cheeks.

Dominic stands up. 'Told you when you arrived. Your life, how comfortable you are, what privileges you enjoy, depends on your behaviour. A simple principle. Looks like you've not grasped it yet.'

I stare at him, my breathing laboured, my chest tight.

'No food for three days. Water only. No bedding, either. The bucket's coming back, too.' He hooks his fingers into my sweatshirt, dragging me off the bed. Suspended from his grasp, I hold my breath as he brings his face up close and personal with mine. Not a shred of pity lurks in his expression. 'Get this into your head, Beth. One way or another, I'll break you.'

CHAPTER 7 – *Dominic*

I meant it when I said I'd break Beth. Fury pounds through me when I consider how she could have blinded me. Gratitude is a lesson she needs to learn, and soon.

The following evening I put my plan into action. Beth must be desperate with hunger by now; I'll turn that to my advantage. First I take from the fridge the four chicken drumsticks I defrosted earlier, and pick potatoes from the vegetable rack. I coat the drumsticks with beaten egg, then dip them in flour seasoned with herbs and spices, my own special recipe. Next I peel the potatoes, then slice them into generous wedges while the oil is heating in the deep-fat fryer. I set a tray with everything I need: plate, salt cellar, plastic bottle of vinegar, mug.

Before long everything is ready. I take the tray and walk towards the basement door, unlocking it. As I pad down the steps, Beth sits up on the bed, her expression wary. I lock my gaze on her as I sit on the bottom step, the tray perched on my lap. Her attention isn't on me, however. Instead it's focused on the plate of food.

I shake salt over the chips and add a splash of vinegar. Beth's nostrils twitch as the enticing odours from my meal reach them. The scrambled eggs I cooked for her yesterday morning must be a distant memory now. I pick up a chip between my fingers, pretending to study it before placing it in my mouth. Then I select one of the drumsticks and bite deep into the flesh, my eyes never leaving Beth's. Grease runs down my chin and I wipe it away, licking my fingers afterwards, and then my lips.

I smile at her. 'Cooked to perfection, even if I say so myself.'

A strangled moan escapes her. I take a mouthful of tea, preparing myself for what's to come.

'The thing is, Beth,' I say. 'What you tried to do yesterday was bad. It shows you're not thinking straight. What did you hope to achieve? Assuming you managed to escape, what did you imagine you'd do after that?'

I wait for her reply. When it doesn't come, I pick up another drumstick, pointing it Beth's way, almost as though I'm offering it to her. Her gaze devours its trajectory as I bring it back to my mouth, tear off a chunk of flesh. Torturing her this way is such sweet pleasure, and besides, it's no more than she deserves.

'Did you really believe you could go back to your parents' house?' I'm careful not to call it home.

Still she doesn't reply.

'If that's what you were thinking, you'd be wrong.'

She moistens her lips. When she speaks, the word is barely a whisper. 'Why?'

I take another bite of chicken. 'You really think they'd want you back?' Shock flashes into her expression.

'Want to know what would happen if you turn up, claiming to have been abducted?' She doesn't respond, but her eyes are wells of misery.

'You wouldn't be believed.'

Beth bites her lip, her gaze falling away. 'You're wrong.' Her tone lacks conviction, however.

I smile, enjoying the moment. Another chip finds its way into my mouth. I wasn't joking when I told Beth they were cooked to perfection.

'Your father,' I say. 'He'll tell you you're just seeking attention.'

She shakes her head. 'He's not like that,' she whispers.

'Oh, he is, Beth, believe me. Didn't you tell me he's always on your case about something or other?'

'Yes, but -'

'The way he'll see it, you'll have run off to spite him. Then made up some absurd cover story. You reckon you'll be welcomed back with open arms? Think again.'

Her expression is stricken. I've clearly hit a sore spot, so I continue to probe it.

'Don't think your mother will be any different,' I say.

At that, Beth's head jerks up, her face mutinous. 'Mum loves me. She'd never believe I'd deliberately hurt her.'

I pick up another drumstick and take a mouthful, playing for time while I consider my response. Have I overplayed my hand?

'We're just speculating here,' I say. 'None of this will actually happen.'

Her eyes fill with tears. One escapes, a solitary trickle sliding down her cheek.

'The sooner you accept this is your home now, the easier it'll be for you.'

'No,' she says, so low I can hardly hear her.

I set my tray on the ground. All that's left of my meal is a few cold chips and the remaining drumstick. 'I'll never let you leave, Beth. As far as the outside world is concerned, you're dead.'

A low moan escapes her. She shakes her head.

'In time, you'll accept this as your home. You'll understand the advantages of what I'm offering you. Safety, security. As well as -' My brain baulks at saying the word 'love', although it's what I mean. As I struggle for an alternative, the mutiny I witnessed earlier in Beth's face flares into life again. Anger sparks in her eyes.

'Safety?' She spits the word at me as though it's poison. 'How can you say that? When you hit me, starve me, treat me like shit -'

My hand cracking across her face stops her from saying more. The force of the blow sends her backwards as her hand flies up to nurse her cheek, her eyes never leaving mine.

I nudge the tray to one side as I stand over her. She needs to understand what's at stake here.

'You need to learn some manners,' I say. 'As well as gratitude.'

She lowers her hand, revealing a red hand print. Rebellion still lurks in her expression.

'You have a bed to sleep in,' I tell her. 'Clothes to wear, a toilet, the use of a shower. Compared to many people in the world, you enjoy privileges they only dream of.' I step closer to the bed, noting how Beth flinches. 'So don't you dare whine about how I punish you, how I deny you food. Had you behaved yourself, I wouldn't have needed to hit you. Had you shown more respect, you'd have a stomach full of food.'

She's silent, but her mouth has a sulky twist that irks me.

'Can you deny the truth of what I'm saying?'

Still she doesn't reply.

'You have a choice, Beth,' I say. 'When I ask you a question, I expect an answer.'

I lean over the bed, placing my fists either side of her knees, my face inches from hers. 'Whether you comply decides whether you eat tonight or not.'

I've caught her attention with the hint at food. The defiance in her face isn't so pronounced now. I'm making progress here. So I plough on.

'Did you expect to throw caustic chemicals at me and not suffer the repercussions?'

'No,' she whispers.

'Do you think you can defy me without incurring the consequences?'

She shakes her head.

Not good enough. 'Answer me.'

'No. I was stupid to think that.'

I reach down to the tray, select the smallest chip and offer it to her. She devours it in a millisecond.

'See?' I smile at her. 'Good behaviour gets rewarded.' Her eyes flick to what remains on the plate, a desperate plea in them. I ignore it. I need to strike hard, now, while she's receptive.

'Do you think I won't kill you, Beth?'

'I...' She moistens her lips, clearly unsure how to respond. It's a reply, though, of sorts, and at least she's trying. She's earned herself another chip. Like the first, it's gone straight away. I'm saving the drumstick as my main bargaining tool.

'It wouldn't be the first time.' Terror flares in her eyes. I smile.

'I am my father's son, after all,' I say. She doesn't understand, I can tell.

'She was a couple of year older than you.'

Fear creeps across Beth's expression. 'Who?' she whispers.

'Her name doesn't matter.'

'It's true, then? I'm not the only girl you've brought here?'

I shake my head. 'No.' I let that information sink in before I continue.

'At first she seemed everything I'd been searching for,' I say. 'Before I brought her here, I mean. I thought she'd make the perfect companion. But she disappointed me, Beth. Badly.'

'How?'

'She didn't appreciate what I did for her. Just like you don't.'

'What -' She wets her lips again, and when she speaks, her voice is hoarse. 'What happened to her?'

'I killed her.'

'How?'

'You don't need to know. But you should take care you don't end up the same way. No more attempts at escaping.'

'I won't.' She's lying, I can tell, but we'll work on that. Together. We have time, after all.

'Good girl.' I scoop up the remaining chips, all four of them, and present them to Beth. Is it my imagination, or does gratitude flicker across her face? If so, we're making progress, and faster than I'd hoped.

'Let's recap,' I say. 'You're better off here, Beth. Do you agree?'

She nods. 'Yes.'

'If you pull any more stunts like the one yesterday, you'll end up dead. Same as the first girl I took.'

'I understand.'

'Your family have moved on. Like I said, they wouldn't welcome you back.'

Right when I think we're getting somewhere, mutiny tightens her mouth.

'You're wrong.' Beth's tone is one of defiance. 'You're a liar. My mother will always want me back.'

My hand flies out, grips her throat. I squeeze my fingers against her flesh, just enough to elicit a gasp of terror.

'You've used up all your chances, Beth,' I tell her. 'This is your last warning. If you want to stay alive, you'll learn to toe the line.' I release her to step away from the bed, bending down to pick up the food tray. Beth's eyes hover over the drumstick, but she's smart, despite the bad attitude; she must realise she's lost all chance of further food tonight. I turn my back on her and walk up the steps without a further word.

Upstairs again, I mull over what just transpired. Despite the obstinate clinging to her past, the petty rebellion, I'm encouraged. Food is proving an effective tool in retraining Beth, one I can employ as often as necessary. Along with the revelation I've already killed another woman. Fear will keep her in line, of that I'm sure.

One way or another, I'll break Beth. And when I have, I'll rebuild her into my perfect companion.

CHAPTER 8 – *Beth*

Dominic, true to his word, denies me food, bedding and the toilet for the rest of the three days, forcing me to use the bucket. At night, I brace myself against the cold, my stomach pleading for sustenance. My mind runs through the possibilities, looping around the basement in a hopeless effort to discover a way to secure my escape. By the time my captor brings me food again, I've faced up to the obvious: I'm all out of options.

The blackness of depression descends with full force then, cloaking me in its depths. I sleep as much as possible, thankful for the oblivion it provides. With Dominic, I go through the motions: eating the meals he cooks with passive acceptance, careful not to provoke him in any way. The memory of his hands around my neck is too recent, too potent; the knowledge he could kill me whenever he chooses forced deep into my awareness. Piss him off, and I'll be the second female who's not made it out of this basement alive. I'm not sure I care any longer. Death might offer a welcome release.

One night I dream of Mum. After I awake, her face slips back into the realms of the insubstantial, but the essence of her remains. My desire to kiss her again surfaces from the blackness, and it's what saves me. Spurred on by the thought of seeing her, I decide on a way to beat the depression. In place of my usual foetal huddle, I devise an exercise regime. Bunny hops, push-ups, walking. Stretches, too. At first, my body, unaccustomed to activity, protests; my muscles scream for mercy, resulting in fierce aches and spasms the next morning. I persevere, urging myself on: five more push-ups, ten extra laps of the basement. On the third day, I notice the doorframe, and administer a mental head slap for not spotting its possibilities before. Then I'm up the steps, my arms grasping the top of the door, hauling myself up and down until I'm exhausted. As the days slip by, I force the depression into retreat, honing my determination to be reunited with Mum.

***

By my reckoning, I've been a prisoner for eight weeks when I find the silver charm.

Dominic allows me fresh bedding every Monday. Each week he waits while I strip off my duvet cover, pillowcase and the sheet covering the mattress, before giving me new ones, folded and smelling of lilac-scented laundry powder. Today he hands me the blue cotton set, my favourite. After he's gone with the used bed linen, I take the bottom sheet from the bundle and ease it over the mattress. I stretch it towards the corners, tucking in the left edge and then the right, the one nearest the wall. As I do so, my fingers detect something beneath the rough surface of the mattress. Whatever it is, it's small and hard, and I can't determine the shape. I flip back the sheet, exposing the mattress again, and I spot a rip in the fabric. I ease my index finger into the slit, and fish out what's inside.

It's a tiny silver boot, with a loop where it once hooked onto a woman's charm bracelet. The metal is cool and smooth under my exploring fingers. I trace the heel, the toe, the miniature laces. All this time I've slept on this mattress, the charm hidden beneath my feet without me realising it was there. Was I restless last night? Have my movements worked the charm closer to the surface, ready for me to discover? The boot lies in my palm, its weight barely registering against my skin. So tiny, so perfect. Whose was it?

Only one answer fits, and my breath catches hard against my ribcage.

'The last occupant of this room didn't make it out alive.' His words when he brought me here. My question to him later: *What happened to her?* His response: *I killed her.*

The weird gratitude I've experienced towards him sometimes has made me forget what this man is. A kidnapper and murderer. I'm not the first female to occupy this basement. Proof of that lies in my hand, confirmed by Dominic's words. I scratched a message on the wall behind the filing cabinet as evidence of my captivity. This woman secreted a charm from her bracelet into the mattress.

How did he kill her? Strangulation, I suspect, given his reaction after the incident with the toilet chemicals. She'll have done something to provoke a dark rage in him. What he did with her body, I can only speculate. I can guess, though. He's a control freak; he'll want to keep her close by, even after her death. I've worked out that this basement extends underneath half the cottage; the other part must be sealed up. Although I've no evidence to confirm that's where she is, my instincts tell me I'm right. An image arises in my mind of her corpse, desiccated and shrivelled, on the other side of the wall, and I run to the chemical toilet and flip open its lid, heaving up my breakfast toast and porridge.

My guts continue to cramp as I huddle once more on the bed, the silver charm clutched in my sweating palm. He intended the other woman to be his companion, but instead he killed her. Now I've taken her place, the second captive of the basement, and I need to ensure I don't end up dead as well. I can survive this, I persuade myself. For Mum's sake, as well as my own. In an attempt at self-comfort, I rock myself to and fro, but my predecessor's decayed corpse the other side of the wall intrudes. I picture her spine arching as she struggles against her killer, then her bones yellowing in the damp of the other basement. In seconds, I'm heaving over the toilet again.

Amy. I decide to give the first captive of the basement a name, because now she's real. She looks like me too, this Amy, victim number one of a warped mind. Hair toffee-brown, eyes dark and large, skin pale and clear. My new companion. Dominic Perdue's not alone in needing a friend; Jake Wilding, my best mate, seems very far away right now. The thought of her body on the other side of the wall doesn't strike horror into me any longer. Murdered Amy becomes my ally. The one person who understands the horror I'm enduring.

'How long did he keep you here? Before...' I realise I've spoken my thoughts aloud. The first signs of insanity? Maybe. Now I've met her though, Amy comforts me, inspires me, her voice whispering in my head at night, while my fingers caress the silver boot. 'Stay alive, Beth,' she admonishes.

'I will,' I reply into the darkness. Her charm soothes me, lulls me to sleep. When I awake, I stuff it back into the mattress, so it'll be safe from my captor. To lose it would be to lose Amy. If that happens, I'll tip over into madness.

***

Christmas comes and goes. I get a card, depicting a reindeer decked in tinsel, the greeting inside a hollow one. *Wishing you festive fun that's overflowing with love and laughter!* The words mock me with the images they invoke. My family around the kitchen table. Dad carving a turkey, Mum pulling crackers with Troy, me hogging the cranberry sauce. In contrast, I eat my Christmas lunch perched on my bed, no tinsel, no holly, no tree. For my Christmas present, Dominic fits an electric blanket over my mattress, a welcome antidote to the chilly nights in the basement. I'm terrified he'll discover the tiny silver charm as he tugs the corners into place, but he doesn't.

***

I'm crying one night as I talk to Amy. 'I've been incarcerated in this hole for six months now, maybe seven,' I tell her with a sob. Without the newspapers to give me the date, I'm fuzzy about time. Nearly two hundred days, most of them lacking sunlight, thanks to the window board.

'You need to be careful,' she replies. 'Or you'll slip into depression. It's a tough hole to climb out of.'

'I'm already there,' I tell her. Not surprisingly, the dark moods continue to hover, enshrouding me, more so in the mornings, when I awake to another day as Dominic Perdue's captive. Each one is a mind-numbing mirror of its predecessor. I'm exercising less and less, preferring the oblivion of sleep. Inside, I'm deteriorating, my only activities each day being to eat and shower. The possibility of being reunited with Mum seems increasingly remote.

I'm careful never to do or say anything that might anger Dominic, leading to his hands grasping my throat again. *One way or another, I'll break you.* He's not managed it yet, but he's close. I'm not sure how much longer I can stay sane.

***

One evening Dominic surprises me by returning after he's cleared away my meal tray. I'm startled, thrown by this change in our routine.

'You've been behaving well,' he comments. I stare at him, uncertain as to where he's going with this. He smiles at me, and then leaves.

And returns with a stack of books. He tosses them on the bed, and I fall on them in the same way I did that thin cheese sandwich months ago. A Jodi Picoult, a couple of romances and two historical novels. They're reassuringly fat, stuffed with delicious words that will soak into the desert of my brain, resuscitating it. For a second, I'm so grateful that the urge to hug Dominic overwhelms me, and then I remember. The bastard's the reason I'm here.

'Told you before,' he says. 'That I'd bring you books. When you'd earned the right to them.'

I decide to chance my luck. 'Any chance of a newspaper every day as well? Please?'

He nods. That's good. I'll be able to keep track of the date now, and with what's happening in the world. I push further.

'Would you...' I swallow. After months in a windowless room, my next words matter like hell. 'Could you take down the window board? Allow me some sunlight?'

To my despair, he shakes his head.

'I won't break it again, I promise. Put bars over it, if you must. But I need natural light. I can't bear being down here with nothing but a dim light bulb.'

'No.'

'Please.' I'm close to dropping to my knees in front of him. I want this so, so badly. My pride has fled, defeated by the glorious prospect of seeing the sun's rays through that tiny window.

'Get shatterproof glass,' I beg. 'I won't cause you any trouble, I promise. I've learned my lesson. I'll be what you want me to be. You'll see.'

My pleading works. Dominic nods, and again I restrain myself from hugging him, so overwhelming is my gratitude. He's brought me books, he'll allow me my newspapers, and he'll remove the board at the window. An emotion akin to happiness washes over me. Once he's gone, I drop to the floor, intent on resuming my long-neglected exercise routine.

The next day, the board comes down, and shatterproof glass replaces it, clean where the old pane was grubby, and I cry as the sun pierces the dark basement for the first time in months. By now, I've read half the Jodi Picoult, and a copy of Bristol's *Evening Post* sits on the bed beside it. My world has shrunk to the dimensions of this room; so have my expectations. I have food, reading material and sunlight, and I won't ask for more. Not yet.

***

A week later – I'm keeping track of the days now, thanks to my daily copy of the *Evening Post* – Dominic returns after removing my evening meal tray. I'm apprehensive, but he doesn't appear angry. Why would he? I've taken pains to do everything he wants. No lingering in the shower. Eating all my food. Saying please and thank you, even giving him the odd smile. Things are going well between us.

'Do you remember what I told you the first night you were here?' His expression betrays nothing. My memory from back then is hazy, thanks to my overwrought emotions. I'm struggling to grasp his meaning. At least I don't sense anything bad in what he's saying. Instead, Dominic seems almost excited.

'That this is your home now. How you'd be happy here. How I chose you.'

His words come back to me now. 'To be your companion, right?'

'Yes. For us to be together.'

I stare at him. For whatever weird reason, Dominic Perdue has fixated on me as his salvation from loneliness. Which means so long as I provide what he needs, I'll live. With that, I shiver. This man is a killer, I remind myself.

I grope for the right response. All I manage is a high-pitched, 'Really?'

He nods. 'That can't happen just yet. You need more time to get accustomed to your new life. But you're learning. Doing well. I think, eventually…' His smile, when it comes, reminds me of our lunch together, aeons ago at The Busy Bean, when I fantasised about a relationship with this man. A tug of the old attraction squeezes me; I clamp down on it, annoyed. Remember where you are, I remind myself. What he's capable of.

'What?' A privilege, holding the power to transform my world awaits me. So close I can almost taste it. Why else would he smile at me that way?

And I'm right. Dominic's next words are amazing, incredible, beyond all my dreams.

'In time, I'll allow you upstairs. Give you the run of the lounge and kitchen.'

I don't hesitate. My arms fling themselves around him as I press my head against his chest, tears sliding down my face. 'Thank you,' I murmur before I pull away. Shock reigns in his face, but he doesn't appear angry. He steps back a pace, clearing his throat, and when he speaks, his voice is thick.

'Under certain conditions. I'll need to know where you are at all times. I'll search you if I have to. If I go out, you'll return to the basement. You'll still sleep down here. But you'll be able to watch television, take a shower whenever you want.'

I swallow hard. I crave this; what's more, I need it. The blackness is always lurking in this basement, waiting to claim me, despite the novels, the newspapers, the exercise. What he's offering is a golden carrot I'll do anything to obtain. He wants a companion. Well, I'll give him one. I'll be the best fucking companion anyone's ever had if he'll allow me upstairs.

'I'd like that,' I tell him. Right now, I don't trust myself to say more.

***

Once he's gone, tears run into my mouth, as I laugh and cry and beat my fists against the wall in triumph. Possibilities pour through my head. His kitchen, complete with knives. Doors, front and back, to the outside world. I'll establish his trust and watch for opportunities. Yes, oh God, yes. I'm inching closer to freedom and it beckons me so tantalisingly, sweeter than forbidden fruit.

The thing is, Amy's not enough for me. Dominic Perdue's lonely, but so am I. In the same way I crave sunlight, I'm desperate for companionship. Even if it's with my abductor, I need to connect with another human being. A real one, not the fantasy that's Amy.

Calculations flash through my brain. Months of good behaviour earned me my books. How long before I can go upstairs? Several months more, I reckon, and the balloon of my ecstasy deflates somewhat.

Guilt, dark, unexpected and unwelcome, rushes in to replace it. The kitchen knives. Am I really contemplating using them against the man who feeds me, clothes me, brings me books, on whom my life depends? How ungrateful is that?

It takes an effort to remind myself how I got here.

***

I don't press Dominic about being allowed upstairs. I hint, though.

'It's my birthday next week,' I inform him one day. 'Next Tuesday. The fifteenth.' Will he allow me upstairs for the occasion?

Dominic smiles at me. 'I'll remember that,' he says. I'm filled with hope.

I turn nineteen on a day indistinguishable from all the others, apart from some new clothes and a card. Cartoon flowers on the front, a large yellow sun behind them. Inside, a cheesy message greets me. *May your birthday be filled with sunshine and smiles!* The pale light struggling through the grimy basement window reminds me the sentiment is hollow. I take care not to betray my disappointment. From its place on the filing cabinet, the card mocks me.

While I'm waiting for him to allow me upstairs, I read, do push-ups, and fight to keep depression at bay. It's hard going. As well as the physical exercise, I need mental stimulation. The Jodi Picoults are fine, but don't provide brain food. An idea forms, one that'll bring me closer to Mum in my head. As a language tutor, she's our family linguist.

The next day, I accost Dominic after breakfast. 'Can you buy me a beginner's book on learning Italian? When you next go to the shops?'

Dominic looks surprised, but nods.

'And one about the country. Lots of pictures.'

Suspicion crosses his face. 'Why? It's not as if you'll ever travel there. Your place is here with me. Don't forget that, Beth.'

'I won't. But I can go in my head, can't I? And I've always wanted to learn Italian.' A lie, but who cares? Language studies will be my mental equivalent of push-ups. 'Please. What harm can it do?'

Dominic goes shopping that afternoon, returning with a beginner's Italian course and a guidebook to the country. Happiness sparks in me. 'Thank you,' I tell him, my gratitude sincere.

The ensuing weeks aren't so bad. I'm in a firm routine now. Exercise in the morning, an hour after breakfast. Then affirmations, a source of amusement for me whenever Mum's friend Donna Keating banged on about them, but which now become essential. *I am free. I am calm, strong and resilient. I escape this basement.* The content varies, but the essence – freedom – never wavers. I chant the words repeatedly, until desperation cracks my voice.

After lunch, I grapple with my studies. My mind, deprived for so long of nourishment, soaks up the Italian language. *Letto, toilette, classificatore.* Bed, toilet, filing cabinet. I practise aloud, my words bouncing off the walls. Twenty new ones each day, I promise myself. In the evenings, I read the novels Dominic brings me. He's somewhat stereotypical in his choices, usually chick-lit and romances; I decide to put in a few requests for when he next goes to the library. Thomas Hardy, maybe a Hemingway or two. Stephen King, Lee Child. Hope rises within me, a glimmer of a wider life, one that includes upstairs, and I repeat to myself: *I am free. I escape this basement.*

CHAPTER 9 – *Beth*

ad I known then how long I'd be in the basement before Dominic allowed me upstairs, my sanity would have shattered for good. He's cautious, this man, realising my access to the rest of the cottage poses numerous possibilities for escape. All of which I've discussed with Amy.

'He can't be careful all the time,' I tell her. 'Maybe he'll slip up, leave the door unlocked after he's been to the rubbish bins. Did he ever do that with you?'

When she doesn't reply, I continue anyway. 'Perhaps I'll find something I can use as a weapon, or a tool. I'll hide it in my mattress, and he won't realise it's missing.'

Another night I discuss the cottage's windows with her. 'They might not be double-glazed, not in a place as old as this. Easy to smash.'

Weeks go by, though, without any mention of Dominic permitting me to go upstairs. Panic sets in. What if it's enough to keep me locked in the basement, a few minutes of daily conversation sufficient for him? Jesus, no, no, no. I need to get upstairs; I must, despite my books, Italian studies and Amy's company. I'm nineteen years old; the idea of decades spent in captivity is intolerable.

'Find a way, Beth,' Amy urges, every night before we go to sleep.

'I will,' I promise her.

I remain patient. I never ask Dominic when I'll be allowed upstairs, afraid he'll believe my sole motive is escape. Then I grow restless, desperate. Dominic wants something from me; he's waiting, but for what? I mull it over at nights, discussing it with Amy.

'Tell me how to get out of this hellhole,' I beg her.

'You're too passive,' she replies. Perhaps she has a point. Does my captor think that by existing down here on his terms, without any real interaction between us, I prefer the role of abductee rather than kindred spirit?

'Talk to him,' Amy advises. 'Draw him out. Remember, knowledge is power. Know thy enemy, and all that.'

I guess I've nothing to lose by changing my game plan. Hard to do, though. What can we discuss? Day trading, the financial markets? No way. His bullshit detector will sound the alarm if I feign interest in such topics. Better to start with the safe stuff, like what he watched on television last night. Ease my way in, working up to more personal matters, questions that might scrape over raw nerves. Such as: what was his childhood like? What happened to his mother? How did his father die?

I start the next day. My question takes him by surprise as he picks up my breakfast tray.

'Anything good on television last night?'

'Wildlife programme. Then a horror flick.' His gaze is penetrating, curious, as his eyes sweep over my face. I smile back.

'Which one? I've always enjoyed scary movies.'

And so it begins. Dominic does most of the talking, which fits in with my plan. I interject with comments when appropriate. *Interesting! Really?* and *I didn't know that.* I think I'm on the right path; in front of me is a man desperate for companionship. He doesn't spend long with me that first time, but his expression as he leaves holds satisfaction. This is what he's been seeking from me, what I've not provided so far. I'll prove I can be his companion, that I'm worthy of being allowed upstairs. I'm more pumped than I've been since I arrived, and the black shroud of depression recedes.

I establish a pattern. After breakfast, I ask about the previous evening's television. After lunch, I enquire about his work, confining myself to asking whether things are going well. He always shrugs in response. I sense business isn't great these days; the BMW must be the result of a previous lucky streak. In the evenings, television rescues me again as we discuss what he intends to watch later. It's too soon to edge towards personal stuff, but my efforts yield results. One evening, when he arrives with a fresh stack of books from the library, a cardboard tube is tucked under his arm.

'Do you like it?' he asks, as he Blu-tacks a poster of the Colosseum onto the wall. A boyish need for approval lurks in his tone.

'It's wonderful,' I assure him.

'I thought, what with you being so interested in all things Italian...' A minute thread of communication forges itself between us. I smile at him, forgetting for a moment that he's my kidnapper.

After that, I get more presents. One in particular catapults my gratitude levels skyward. Dominic comes to the basement one evening, a package in one hand. He thrusts it towards me.

'A little something to keep you company,' he says. His expression is expectant, hopeful. I stare at the gift he's brought, and tears fill my eyes.

It's a radio. I rip open the box, delight hammering in my brain. Nothing fancy, just a basic model, but, oh God, I now own a radio. A wonderful, incredible, amazing radio, and I'm so grateful I can't find the words to thank Dominic. I have to hope my smile, along with the tears running down my face, are enough. It appears they are, because he smiles back, his hand patting my shoulder for a second before he leaves.

I'm alone with my treasure, and yet not alone anymore. I'll have other people with me in the basement, even if it's their disembodied voices. I make plans. I'll find some broadcasts in Italian. Listen to the news daily. Check out local music stations to accompany my morning exercises. The radio will hold the depression at bay. I'm buoyant, optimistic.

Amy often whispers in my head when I tell her, every night, it won't be long before I escape.

'But *when?*' she asks, and I'm reminded that I've been a prisoner for over a year now.

***

When Dominic brings me my breakfast one morning, a week or so after I get my radio, I don't enquire about last night's television. Instead, it's time to take action. Amy's right. I've been passive for too long.

'Can I ask something?'

He nods.

'I'd like to be allowed upstairs,' I say. 'Just once. A trial run, if you like.'

Dominic is silent, and panic claws at me.

'We could watch television. Eat a meal together.'

Still no response.

'Please.' I'm reduced to the level of a five-year-old, begging for treats, but this has mammoth significance for me.

Right when I'm on the verge of tears, he gives me my answer. 'OK.'

I'm stunned. Oh, my God. He's agreed. At last I'll get to leave my prison. OK is the most beautiful word in the English language.

'You mean it?' I whisper, my voice hoarse with emotion. He nods.

'When?'

'Soon.'

'This evening?'

He bites his lip, not answering again, and terror clutches me. Have I been too pushed too hard? I stay silent, awaiting my fate.

'OK,' he says eventually.

***

Tonight Dominic is allowing me out of the basement for five hours. He'll bring me out of here at six, and return me at eleven. He's nothing if not precise.

'Just the once,' he's told me. 'For now, anyway.' It's enough, and I'm determined not to waste this opportunity. When I'm upstairs, I'll be observing, taking mental notes, eyeing up my chances for escape. The day passes in a blur of exercise, Italian and Jodi Picoult. Six o'clock comes, bringing with it Dominic, but no meal tray this time. Instead, he stands at the top of the stairs, the door ajar behind him. 'Up you come,' he instructs. I don't need telling twice.

I step past him, and close my eyes with the joy of the moment. The air is different up here. Warmer, less damp. 'What's that smell?' I ask.

Dominic guides me towards the kitchen. 'Bouillabaisse,' he says. 'I decided it was time I cooked it for you.' A large pan sits on top of the stove, the aroma tantalising. He takes a bottle of white wine from the fridge. Chablis, same as we had at Troopers Hill, a hundred lifetimes ago.

Dominic twists off the top and pours a generous measure for me. For a second, I'm back at that weirdly angled chimney, amid my girlish fantasises of a future with this man. Be careful what you wish for, as they say.

He raises his glass. 'To us.'

'To us,' I echo. The first wine I've tasted in over a year slips down my throat, cool as a stream in winter, and I close my eyes again. Right now, my world almost passes for normal.

Dominic takes a fragrant tray from the oven. I open my eyes. Foil-wrapped logs of garlic bread sit on it, their smell entrancing. He ladles bouillabaisse into bowls and gathers cutlery. Then we move into the dining area, where he's set two places at the table. A single rose, dusky red, stands in a vase besides mine. My fingers inch towards it and I pull it out, Dominic's gaze on me all the while. The petals are velvet-smooth beneath my touch, the overtones of romance impossible to ignore. The scent is beyond wonderful, its rich notes reminding me of a time, a place, outside these four walls.

'It's beautiful,' I tell him.

The fish stew is excellent, an aromatic concoction of cod, plaice and shellfish. The bread runs thick with garlic butter, which oozes over my fingers as I mop up the juices from the stew. I drink, I eat, and I savour the bliss of freedom. Dominic doesn't speak much, merely nodding when I compliment him on the food. It needs more salt, so I sprinkle on a smidgen, before digging in again.

'Cruet set in the middle of the table, please, Beth.' Dominic's tone is sharp.

I pause, staring at the salt pot to the left of my plate, where I put it.

'A place for everything and everything in its place, as the saying goes.' Dominic pairs the salt with the pepper, slap bang in the centre between us. 'Remember that.'

I learn more rules as our meal progresses. No food to be left on the plates. Stack them to the right afterwards. Knives and forks on top, ready for the dishwasher. My fingers slip as I comply, and I grab a knife before it slides off, conscious of his eyes watching my every move.

For dessert, we eat chocolate and orange mousse, delicious beyond measure, and when I push my plate away, I'm happy. When I thank Dominic, I'm sincere, my earlier disquiet over the salt pot forgotten. It's seven o'clock. Four more hours of freedom. I'm guessing we'll watch television. Dominic gestures me towards the sofa, handing me a TV guide. 'Whatever you want is fine by me,' he says. I choose a rerun of *Pride and Prejudice*, the film version with Keira Knightley. Ah, simple pleasures.

Dominic's clearly uninterested in what unfolds between Elizabeth Bennett and Mr Darcy. No, he's enduring it because he wants tonight to be special for me, and I appreciate that, I really do. At times, it's as though we're like any other couple; Mr and Mrs Normal, and the realisation shocks me. I recall my fantasies about Dominic from long ago; guilt stabs me as I remember how my fingers itched to stroke his hair. Surprised at the turn my thoughts are taking, I dig them out of the recesses of my brain, examining them in my head. The images are seductive, enticing.

Eleven o'clock comes far too soon.

***

The next day, I awake, my head fuzzy from the wine, stale garlic souring my breath. I'm euphoric at having escaped the confines of the basement, even if only for a while. Dominic granted me normality for a few hours, and I'm beyond thankful to him; reluctant though I am to admit it, last night I did more than escape the claustrophobic confines of the basement. With the poster, the radio, the books, this man has managed to connect with me, meaning I respond to him when it's the last thing I should do. I'm angry with myself for not hating Dominic, but the truth is – I don't.

I'm confused, though. This is the man who abducted me, who once had his hands around my throat, who told me he killed my predecessor. I should hate him, and I did, at first, but the nature of my emotions towards him now defies definition. If it weren't for the fact that every night I sleep locked in his basement, I might forget what's keeping me from Mum. I'm aware I don't think of her so often anymore. Oh, she's always there, in my head, but she's fading, a little every day, and I've no idea how to claw her back.

'Focus, Beth. Find how to escape, before he kills you too,' Amy reminds me. She's right, I tell myself.

***

What I end up doing is withdrawing, unsure how to relate to Dominic anymore. I'm aware I may scupper my chances of further evenings upstairs, but Amy has a point. I'll never escape if I empathise with him. Instead, I pull back to regroup, re-evaluate. To do my best to kick into touch my weird feelings towards the man who abducted me. I change tack. I don't smile at him. No more questions concerning his day, what he'll watch later on television. I still thank him for everything, taking care to stay polite, not give him a reason to starve or hit me again. But I sever the growing connection between us, hack it clean through, although it proves harder than I imagine.

Puzzlement lurks in his eyes the first time I take my food tray from him, a muted 'thank you' my only interaction with him. Tension tightens my muscles as I eat the mushroom tagliatelle he's prepared, aware he's scrutinising my every move.

'That was good,' I say after I finish, keen not to appear too withdrawn. I don't interact further, though, and after a while, he leaves. Once he's gone, I berate myself; why I am finding this so difficult? How come I'm fighting the urge to call him back, re-establish the fragile bond I've decided to break?

Dominic hovers as I eat breakfast the following morning, expectancy in his face; presumably he's waiting for my usual enquiries about last night's television. Instead, I focus on my food.

'Did you sleep well?' he asks after I finish eating.

'Fine, thank you,' I reply, my tone robotic, my gaze on the floor.

The pattern repeats itself for one more meal before Dominic strikes. After my continuing reticence at lunch, he grabs my Italian grammar, along with the Sophie Kinsella novel I'm reading and my other books, placing them on the food tray.

'You won't be needing these,' he informs me, ice in his voice. Fear floods me. I've pushed him too far.

'Please.' He walks up the stairs, ignoring me. 'Don't take my books.' The basement door bangs shut behind Dominic, before he twists the key in the lock.

I'm silent, terrified, when he brings my food that evening. Short rations, just soup and bread. His expression is granite-hard. When he speaks, his voice is curt. 'You need to understand something.'

'What?'

He squats in front of me as I perch on the bed, his mismatched eyes level with mine. We lock gazes. I await my fate.

'I'll tell you again. Your life is completely in my hands. What you eat, what you wear, whether you shower or read. I can return those books. Or, if I choose, you'll never read anything again. The choice is yours, Beth.'

I nod, my mouth drained of saliva.

'I've told you what I want. A companion.'

I nod again.

'The evening we were upstairs. It went well, I thought. But afterwards…' A shake of his head. 'You blanked me. Why?'

Lying's not an option; he'll spot deceit straight away. 'I'm confused.'

'Why?'

'Because I enjoyed our time together.'

'That's a problem?'

'Yes. No. I'm all muddled up in my head. I shouldn't have liked being with you.'

He nods. 'I understand. It's early days still. Always knew it would take time.'

Early days? I've been here well over a year. I'm reminded, forcibly, of how Dominic Perdue has planned a long-term arrangement for me right from the start.

'This isn't a normal situation. It's not surprising you're mixed-up. But it's also good.'

'How?' I force the word past dry lips.

'It proves you're starting to love me. Exactly how it should be.'

Oh, fuck. Fuck, fuck, fuck. Love him? The man's insane. Yes, my emotions towards him are all over the place, but I can't love him. My shock must have registered in my face, because he smiles at me, the skin around his eyes crinkling, luring me against my will into his brown and blue irises.

'Only natural,' he says. 'Oh, you might be fighting it now, but it'll happen, in time. You'll love me, and once you do, you can come upstairs every evening. We'll talk, eat together, watch television, like a regular couple, only we won't need anyone else.

We'll be enough for each other, you and me, and it'll be good. You'll see.'

***

My books arrive back with next day's breakfast tray.

'Thank you,' I say, and my gratitude is genuine, unforced.

Dominic shrugs, but his expression belies his supposed nonchalance. I press ahead while I have the advantage. 'Anything good on television last night?' And so we slip back into our former routine of smiles and small talk.

I'm aware I've a world of lost ground to regain. Dominic's guarded at first, but he gradually eases back into our old way of interacting. Within a day or two, the awkwardness has gone between us.

Meanwhile, I ponder his words. Love him? No. Whatever my emotions towards him may be, they'll never be love, not the way I've always imagined I'll one day experience it with my soul mate. I guess love can take many forms, though, so maybe it's not a bad way to describe how Dominic affects me. His loneliness touches me, sparking something akin to affection. He's a man cut off from human contact, so warped he believes the only way he can get a woman is to kidnap her. Were he to rape me, I'd loathe him forever, but he appears to lack any sign of a sex drive. Instead he's created this weird life where he controls me utterly, while being kind as well. Take the presents he's given me: the radio, my books. He's only ever hit me when I've deserved it by breaking the rules. Beth Sutton has become a dog eager to please its owner, and the thought both appals and soothes me. It's much easier to go along with what Dominic wants. All he craves is companionship; isn't that what everyone needs? To experience warmth, a sense of connection?

Hell, I need it too. Life's better this way.

CHAPTER 10 – *Dominic*

Beth is coming along nicely. I never expected any of this to happen quickly; I have to make allowances, expect the odd hiccup. She says she's confused; well, of course she is. Overall, she's doing well, given that I've only had her for fourteen months. The human mind requires time to adapt, but it's an infinitely malleable organ. A little sensory deprivation: the boarded-up window, a few sparse meals, a bucket for her toilet needs. Enough to crack her bravado. Force her to earn her privileges, teach her what I expect from her. The punishments have been hard on both of us. The measures she's forced me to adopt, such as denying her food, haven't sat well with me. Neither has the way she's provoked me into hitting her. A necessary evil, though, like breaking in a horse. Part of making her understand how things must be, shaping her the way I want her. In that respect, I have my father's genes. The need to control runs deep in both parent and son, and I intend to police Beth very carefully indeed.

Our evening together was a success, despite the petty rebellion that followed. Easily crushed, of course. Beth's words come into my head. *I enjoyed our time together.* Followed by: *I shouldn't have liked being with you.*

But she did, though. It's as I told her: she's starting to love me. In a few months, I'll allow her upstairs again, depending on how she shapes up. It's too soon right now. The part of me that's been lonely too long baulks at the delay, but I remind myself to be strong, stick to the plan.

That's where my father went wrong. Warped by his sexual urges, those base instincts I'm proud not to have. He never wanted a companion, the way I need Beth; the only thing he craved was a quick fuck. And his motives were darker, more complicated. He could have bought sex from a whore the night he killed that woman, but his victim fulfilled a different function. I recall how she rocked back and forth, her attempt at self-comfort futile. The way her piss spread across the basement floor as her terror flooded from her bladder. My father's hands around her throat, squeezing, choking. And the definitive moment for me, as her eyes met mine while Lincoln Perdue strangled the light from them.

I've never experienced sex. I don't read or watch porn. I don't masturbate. When he killed that woman, my father also murdered my libido. I don't miss what I never had, though. Life's simpler, easier, without being ruled by one's prick.

Tomorrow I'll cut another rose from the garden to put on her breakfast tray. Little things matter. All the small gestures my father never made with Mum. Beth's softening towards me, I can tell. Before, when she smiled at me as I brought her food, the expression in her eyes never matched the curve of her mouth. Slowly, imperceptibly, the two eventually met, and Beth's smiles aren't faked anymore. They fuel my conviction that she'll love me one day. The thought causes something akin to happiness to steal into my heart, my chest tightening with the unfamiliar emotion. And when she realises how she feels, she'll want to be with me, which means bringing her here wasn't wrong, not at all. How could it be? I knew what was right for her before she did, and acted accordingly. Once she starts to care for me, I'll never be lonely again.

***

Time passes. Day after day, Beth smiles and we talk, but I don't mention bringing her upstairs again. Instead, I do my best to keep her happy. Books as fast as she can read them. More posters for her walls. With every new thing, she thanks me, a question lurking in her eyes: when will you allow me out of here?

One day, after she's eaten the lasagne I've brought her, a voice inside whispers to me. *Talk to her.*

'Beth,' I say, as I take her tray. 'You want to come upstairs again, right?'

Hope flares in her mocha eyes. 'Yes.' Her eagerness fills the basement, so strong I can almost taste it. 'More than anything. Can I? When?'

'Soon. When you're ready.'

'I'm ready now.' She stands up. We're close, our bodies mere inches from each other, her heat meshing with mine. It's intimate, and way too intense. I step backwards. Her gaze falters; she nibbles her lower lip as she clocks my withdrawal.

'Not quite.' This will be a test. Will she understand what's required of her, the key that'll unlock the basement door?

Tears wet her eyes. 'Please, Dominic.' How seldom she uses my name. Something in me yearns to reassure her, tell her it'll be OK, but my inhibitions still my tongue. Instead, I step further backwards, cursing the fact I'm my father's son in so many ways.

'I've been good, haven't I? Done everything the way you want?' A wheedling tone, one I don't care for, lurks in her voice.

'Not everything.' The curtness in my words matches the manipulation in hers. I pick up her food tray and move towards the stairs. Behind me, the slam of the basement door cuts off her pleas. Afterwards, watching television alone, I alternate between annoyance at myself and certainty I've done the right thing. If Beth is to share my life, I need to be firm, establish the rules. The lonely part of me berates me for being a fool. The room seems empty and lacking, the sofa too big without her beside me. I remind myself I need to stay strong, but why is it so damn hard?

The next morning, when I take Beth her breakfast, I see she's been crying, and my heart twists with guilt. My girl gazes at me, her soul naked in her eyes, no trace of manipulation in those dark irises.

'Tell me,' she says, brushing away a tear. She drops her eyes, placing her hands in her lap, her fingers twisting around each other. The urge to comfort her grows stronger, but I quash it.

'I have to know. What you want from me.' Beth's eyes meet mine, and our connection is real, electric, popping and buzzing with glorious promise. I sit beside her on the bed, close enough to absorb her body heat.

'I've already told you. I want your love.' There, I've said it. To my disappointment, she drops her gaze, breaking the bond between us. For a second, I'm minded to hit her, slap her across her stupid, ungrateful face, teach her some respect.

'I—' Her voice is cracked, uncertain. My impatience surges. Is it too much to expect her to love me? After everything I've done for her? Perhaps she needs one or two privileges docked. Maybe I'll remove all of them. Starve her for a few days. See how she likes *that*.

'I will try.' Another tear inches down her pale cheek. 'But you have to understand, Dominic. This is hard for me.'

No, it's simple, I tell her in my head. Just love me. Then I'll be complete.

'You, keeping me locked in here. It's been nearly fifteen months now, in which time I've never seen the sun, or gone for a walk. All this time, shut in a basement. I'm dying here, withering into dust because *you*—' She gulps in air, and when her eyes meet mine again, desperation stares from them. 'You have to allow me upstairs again.'

She's right. We're circling each other here with our expectations. For me to allow her upstairs, she has to love me. For that to happen, she needs time away from the basement. Chicken, egg. I remind myself who's in control here.

'Say it,' I command. 'Tell me you love me.'

'I—'

'Even if you don't mean it. In time, you will.'

She takes another gulp of air. 'I don't understand.'

'It's simple enough. Say the words.'

Beth stares at me, but remains silent.

'Tell me you love me. Do it.' Steel in my tone.

She swallows. Is what I'm asking so hard?

'Don't piss me around, Beth.'

'I love you.' The lie is obvious, but we're making progress.

'Again.'

'I love you.'

'Again. More feeling this time.'

'I love you.'

'Better.' Enough for today, I decide. Beth's aware of how to unlock her prison. It's up to her now.

Later, upstairs, I reflect on the twist our mutual dance has taken, and I'm pleased. Happy, even, especially when I think of what's to come.

We're making real progress.

***

The next evening, I cook Beth bouillabaisse again for her supper. Another red rose, this time from a florist, tiny sprigs of baby's breath poking forth from the wrapping, lies on her tray. So does a glass of chilled Chablis. A message to her, loud and clear. See, Beth, it says. This is how things can be. If only you'll love me.

I notice her eyes taking in the tray's contents, its significance. 'Fish stew,' she says. 'Been wondering when we'd have that again.' The connection between us ignites once more. In that moment, I know, I absolutely *know*, we're back in time, ages ago, upstairs. I'm enduring *Pride and Prejudice*, because it's what my girl wants to watch.

Beth eats the bouillabaisse, mopping up the last of the fishy juices with her bread. I refill her glass with wine and she drains it, giggling. She's unused to alcohol, and the glass is a large one.

'Thank you,' she says, a hint of a slur in her voice. 'To what do I owe this honour?'

Is she mocking me? Irritation ignites in my belly, before I remind myself she's had too much to drink.

'Nothing. Just thought I'd treat you to a special meal.'

Another giggle. Say it, the voice in my head urges her. She doesn't, though. Instead, her body flops back on the bed, one arm behind her head, her gaze fixed on the ceiling. 'I could get used to this,' she says. Then she starts to sing, her voice whiny and breathy, annoying as hell. 'Don't worry, be happy…' A tiny belch erupts from her, along with a laugh. 'Any idea who sang that?'

I yank her upright, my anger fierce and hot. She yelps as my fingers dig into the soft flesh of her upper arm. 'Ow! What have I done wrong?'

'Drink this.' I shove the open bottle of mineral water, untouched on her tray, towards her. My hand forces it between her lips, liquid soaking her T-shirt. Crude sounds emit from her throat as she chokes it down, before her frantic gasps tell me I've gone too far. I pull back, leaving her panting, wiping her chin. I've been rough, but she deserved it. A little discipline won't go amiss.

She's sober now, her eyes on mine, fear dark in them. Part of me curses myself for putting it there. What the hell did I expect? I gave her the wine, refilled her glass.

'I don't like you getting drunk.' It's the closest I can manage to admitting fault. 'No more booze. Not if you can't handle it.'

'I'm sorry.' Her response betrays her contrition. 'I've spoilt everything.'

'Do you love me?' I have to ask, even though I'm aware she doesn't. Not yet.

'Yes.' The response is too quick, too automatic, to convince.

'Say it.'

'I love you.' It's enough. For now.

The next day, I cook a special meal, an apology in culinary form. Duck breast with plum sauce, steamed broccoli and wild rice. No wine this time. Strawberry cheesecake for dessert. Another rose on her tray.

'Is it good? You like it?' I need her praise, even if her love lies tantalisingly out of reach.

She nods. 'It's excellent. Not eaten duck before. You made the sauce yourself?'

'Yes.' No lie, that. My father may have been as much use in a kitchen as a chocolate kettle, but Dominic Perdue's a different animal.

She forks the last mouthful past her lips. They're greasy, glistening with juices from the meat. A tiny spot of plum sauce sits beside them. Before I realise what I'm doing, my fingers reach out and wipe it away. Beth jerks back like a scared puppy. Electricity sparks between us again, proclaiming, loudly and beyond doubt, that our connection is real. She swallows, dropping her gaze, slicing her fork into the cheesecake I made earlier. It's damned good, I must admit. She clearly enjoys it, because the slice disappears within a few minutes.

Beth returns her plate to the tray. 'I'm sorry I upset you yesterday.' So eager to please, my girl. She's come a long way.

'It's OK.' Time for her lesson. 'Say it.'

'What?'

'Don't mess with me, Beth.'

'You mean—' She swallows.

'Yes. Tell me you love me.'

Only a slight hesitation before she complies. 'I love you.' The moment is golden.

***

Beth's been with me for fifteen months now. Next week, it'll be our second Christmas together. It's too soon to allow her upstairs again, but I'll make the occasion special for both of us. Turkey with all the trimmings, a bottle of expensive wine, one of those artificial trees to brighten up the basement. Tinsel for the walls. She'll appreciate my efforts, realise how good her life with me is.

Memories of my last Christmas with Mum float into my head. My mother's laughing, handing me my present: the Lego I played with as she died, oblivious to the fact the woman I adored was leaving me. I clamp down on my grief. This year, with Beth, I'll create happier memories.

***

Two days before Christmas. Beth's decorated the basement with tinsel, bedecked the tree with baubles, perched a plastic fairy on top. This afternoon, I'll drive into town and buy her present. Something more personal than the electric blanket I gave her last year. Right now, it's time to serve her lunch: cream of mushroom soup with a baguette. I unlock the door and carry the tray downstairs.

Something's very wrong. Beth's huddled on her bed, her legs drawn up tight to her chest, her back to me. Sobs rack her body as she rocks to and fro. The moans of despair escaping her confound me. She seemed so happy when I brought her breakfast. Asked if I could get her more tinsel, maybe a set of lights for the tree. I stare at her, thrusting the memory of the first occupant of the basement from my head, unwilling to dwell on how much Beth resembles her right now.

I'm unused to sobbing females. Incapable of hugging Beth, I opt for sternness.

'What's the matter with you? Pull yourself together, for God's sake.'

Beth uncurls, turning towards me. Her face is reddened with crying, her cheeks mottled, the rims of her eyes pink and swollen. A rope of snot hangs from her right nostril. Her hair is a tangled mess. When she speaks, sobs choke her throat.

'I was listening to one of the local stations,' she says.

I become aware of music tinkling from the radio on top of the filing cabinet. Irritated, I stride over and switch it off.

'I heard my mother's voice.' Beth's sitting upright on the bed now, her gaze on the floor. She's stopped crying. Her abrupt switch from despair to calm unnerves me. I wait, aware this won't be good.

'On the radio. An appeal, begging for information about my whereabouts. Asking me to get in touch, if I'm alive. So I can be home for Christmas.' Beth wipes the snot from her nose with the back of her hand. She raises her eyes to meet mine. I'm rendered uncomfortable by how hard it is to hold her gaze.

'This is your home now.'

Beth shakes her head. 'No.'

Anger rises within me, hot and acidic. Just when I thought we were making progress, she springs this crap on me. Well, I won't stand for it.

Beth gets up, only a few inches now separating us. 'Do you have any idea what it was like to hear her voice? Begging for my return? Do you, Dominic?'

I hold my breath. I sense we're at a tipping point here.

'I'll tell you,' Beth continues. 'Hell, that's what it was like. No different to the rest of my life here.'

Every man has his breaking point. My anger erupts into a volcanic fury that engulfs me, driving reason from my mind. The ungrateful bitch. She describes the home I've created for her as hell, does she? After everything I've done to make her happy? Doesn't she realise how thankful she should be? For her food, her clothes, the light from the window? For the fact she's still alive?

Rage drives my hands towards her throat. The calm flees from her face, to be replaced by terror. My fingers squeeze her windpipe, cutting off her air, as my arms haul her feet off the floor, her body a rag doll as I shake her back and forth. Dominic Perdue has disappeared. In his place, my father arises, his dominion supreme over the woman beneath him. In my hands, Beth becomes Lincoln Perdue's victim, and I'm back in time all those years ago, except this time I've switched roles with her killer.

My fingers continue to squeeze. The woman whose throat they're choking flails helplessly in my grip. I throw back my head, reminiscent of my father as he fucked the life from his victim. As I do so, the stench of piss, sharp and rank, hits my nostrils.

Dominic Perdue snaps back into my head in an instant. I'm dragged into the here and now, to this basement, to the fact Beth's suspended above the floor, held by my hands. My gaze travels down her body. A dark stain is spreading over her crotch as her urine floods onto the floor. Ashamed, I release my grip on her. She collapses, gasping for air, into the puddle of piss.

Oh God. Dear God. Beth nearly died just now, the same way her predecessor did. So terrified she wet herself, no different from the other woman all those years ago.

I stand over Beth as she lies there, soaked and stinking, and I make a silent vow. I'll prove I'm a better man than my father.

***

Later we talk, after I've removed the radio. The last thing I need is another appeal from her mother when her twentieth birthday rolls around. I've allowed Beth to shower; she's wearing fresh clothes, and I've cleaned the basement floor. The scent of lemon disinfectant fills my nostrils as we sit side by side on her bed. She's not crying, but the remoteness in her expression is unnerving. I don't look at the livid bruises on her throat. Instead, I stare at my feet.

'I'm not a monster,' I say. Beth doesn't respond.

'But you have to understand you'll never leave here. If you can accept that, we can be happy.'

'Can we?' Her voice is dull, drained.

'Yes.' Time to dangle a carrot. 'Remember what I once told you?'

'What? That the last occupant of this room didn't make it out alive? Yes, I remember. You said she disappointed you, wouldn't do what you wanted. So you killed her.'

'Not that.' I wish I'd never told her I'd brought a woman here before her. Some things should remain unsaid. *I killed her. How? You don't need to know.* Not surprisingly, she's terrified she'll end up the same way, but she won't. In future, I'll exercise iron self-control.

'I meant about allowing you upstairs again.'

Beth's head jerks up, twisting so our eyes meet. I've hit home, I can tell. She's taking the bait.

'I need that,' she says. 'I can't spend the rest of my life in this basement. Please. I'm begging you. Let me out of here.'

'I'll consider it. If you tell me you love me.'

She swallows, dropping her gaze. 'I love you.'

For now, I'll take what I can get. I won't ask for more, not when she's so raw emotionally. Instead, I stand up, eager to make amends. 'When you're ready, I'll allow you upstairs again. Not just the once, either.' Sweet relief floods me. At last, I'll get my companion. Why have I denied myself so long? 'You'll need to behave. At all times.'

'I will. I won't let you down, I promise.'

'That's my girl.'

CHAPTER 11 – *Beth*

*O*ne way or another, I'll break you. Dominic's words, after the incident with the toilet chemicals, circle through my head as I lie in bed that night. Sleep is impossible, not with the memory of his hands around my throat, squeezing, denying me oxygen, their pressure relentless. The terror that pounded through my brain as he did so refuses to leave. The marks of his fingers, his thumbs, are livid on my flesh. After I showered earlier on, they mocked me as I inspected my neck in the mirror tiles. My windpipe is sore, bruised, as is my soul. If this is my life, it's not worth living. The humiliation of flooding the floor with my own piss is a degradation too far.

'What's the point of going on?' I ask Amy, her charm clutched in my palm.

'Do you have a choice?' she responds. I'm not sure I do. Suicide doesn't appear an option; I'd already discounted death by starvation during the first weeks here. If I don't die, though, how can I endure the days, the minutes, the seconds, without the hope I'll escape this place?

'Help me.' I've no idea whether I'm begging Amy or the God I don't believe in. My words become a mantra, my lips chanting a ceaseless plea: *help me, help me, help me*. My arms around my shins, my head tucked against my knees, I rock my body back and forth, seeking comfort that doesn't come.

In the silence of the basement, a voice interrupts my litany.

'Come home, Beth. Please, darling.'

'Help me,' I reply, before the breath seizes in my chest. Because the plea in my head isn't from Amy, but from my mother. Her radio appeal for me to make contact, to come home for Christmas.

Tears scratch the backs of my eyes. I pull myself up in bed, my spine against the headboard, replaying the broadcast in my mind.

'My name is Ursula Sutton. Fifteen months ago, my daughter, Elizabeth Ella Sutton, disappeared after saying she was going to spend the night with a friend,' Mum's beloved voice says. I'd not been paying attention to the radio, intent on my morning exercise routine, my arms aching after fifty press-ups. The shock when her familiar tones sound into the basement, so imploring, so desperate, is immense. I freeze, every atom of my being attuned to her voice.

'Since that time, we have not seen or heard from her. Beth, if you're listening, please get in touch. Let us know you're safe, at least. We've been so worried, sweetheart. All we want is to see you again. To have you back for Christmas.' Tears burst through the dam of my mother's self-control, morphing into all-out sobbing. 'Come home, Beth. Please, darling.'

Anguish erupts through my body, despair filling my soul, blurring the rest of the broadcast. Vague details reach me as the presenter takes over, giving a helpline number people can call if they have information concerning my whereabouts. Mum, oh Mum. Dad, Troy. Dominic told me my family would forget me, not welcome me back, but he was wrong. I'm the one guilty of forgetting them, and I loathe myself for my treachery. I sob out every minute of the last fifteen months as I huddle on the basement floor, until I'm exhausted, then I drag myself onto the bed and cry some more. I don't stop until Dominic unlocks the door to bring my lunch tray.

Now, hours later, deep in the silence of the basement, the memory of my mother's voice in my head, I ask myself a question. Has Dominic Perdue been as good as his word? Has he broken me?

***

Sometime towards dawn, I drift into a restless sleep. I dream of Mum. The sequence is chaotic, muddled, the way dreams often are. I'm seventeen again, back in our garden at home, barbeque tongs in hand, smoke rising from the grill. The wind whips my hair around my face as I laugh into the camera, Dad telling me to stop squinting so he can take the shot. The sun's in my eyes, though, so I can't. Mum shouts something at me from the kitchen doorway.

'What did you say?' I yell, the breeze ripping my words from my mouth.

'This is your home now, Beth,' she replies. 'I expect you to obey the rules.' Her voice deepens, to that of a man, and I realise it's Dominic talking, not my mother. Terror drags me awake; I'm sweating with fear. Memories wash over me. A lifetime ago, the first part of my dream was reality. The proof sits on the windowsill at our house in Downend: a photo of me, keen to show Dad my barbequing skills. It's encased in a silver frame, one of my gifts to Mum the Christmas before I disappeared. Tears prick my eyes as I reunite with my family, in my head if nowhere else. I cry, because I doubt it'll ever happen. My life is here now, with Dominic. Escape seems such a remote possibility. Haven't I exhausted all avenues?

'Not upstairs, you haven't.' Amy's voice startles me. 'And you're not broken, Beth. You never were.'

She's right. Damaged, yes. Broken, no. My desire to see Mum's face returns, strong and fierce, its flame burning high. To be held in her arms again as her frizzy hair tickles my cheek. Fuck Dominic Perdue. If I play him correctly, he'll allow me upstairs before long, I'm sure.

'Don't waste the opportunity when it comes,' Amy warns. 'Escape might not be as impossible as you think.'

**

On Christmas Day, Dominic hands me my present, encased in thick silver paper, a bow on top. 'Got it in an antiques shop in Clifton,' he announces. 'Cost a small fortune.'

'Thank you.' I unwrap it carefully, aware Dominic won't approve of me carelessly ripping off the expensive packaging. It's a wooden box, clearly old, its lid intricately decorated with birds, flowers, trees. The workmanship is exquisite.

'From Sorrento. Seems marquetry's a big thing there.' Dominic's voice betrays the fact he's anxious to curry favour. 'Do you like it?

'I love it.' Have I injected enough enthusiasm into my voice? Whatever I do, I mustn't antagonise him. My fingers slide over the box, touching its plants, their leaves, the trees, things I may never see again. I marvel at Dominic's lack of awareness. Eager to give me a gift in line with my interest in Italy, he's overlooked the fact I have no possessions to keep in it.

'It's beautiful,' I tell him. I'm not lying. The box means nothing to me, though. His keenness to please me does. I make a decision. In future, I'll watch every word that comes from my mouth. I'll be meekness personified, ready to exploit Dominic's newfound contrition. Amy has a point. Upstairs may hold new possibilities, and if I play my cards right, Dominic will allow me out of the basement before long.

My emotions where he's concerned continue to defy logic. I've no idea what's made him so fucked-up, but his childhood can't have been normal. Dominic's not a bad man, not really. When he wants, he can be so kind. Take the Italian box. He meant well, I guess. As he did with the artificial Christmas tree, the tinsel, his attempt to make the basement more festive. Concentrate on the good in him, I tell myself. All the things he does for you. Don't dwell on the way his hands felt as they squeezed your windpipe. Because if I do, I'll slide into the blackness again, losing my newfound connection with Mum.

Her voice echoes in my head. 'Come home, Beth. Please, darling.'

***

Today is New Year's Eve. 'Tomorrow,' Dominic tells me when he brings my evening meal.

'What?'

'Upstairs.'

'Really? You'll allow me out at last?'

'Yes.'

'Oh, my God.' Pleasure infuses my every syllable. 'All day?'

'No. Just the evening. You'll come upstairs, and we'll eat, watch television, talk. Like a normal couple.'

My hands brush away tears. 'You've no idea what this means.'

'I'll check where you are at all times, mind. No funny stuff, Beth. Not like—' He gestures towards the window, the toilet. 'Otherwise— '

'You mean—' He's referring to when he tried to strangle me. 'I'll be good, I swear. I won't cause any trouble.'

'If you love me, you'll find it easy to behave.'

'I will.'

'Do you? Love me?'

'Yes.'

'That's my girl.'

'So tomorrow...?'

'Yes. We'll spend the evening upstairs.'

'Thank you. I won't let you down. I promise.'

***

Six o'clock the next day can't come soon enough. A new year, a new start. I skate through my Italian practice; verbs, tenses and vocabulary jumbling together in my head, my mind elsewhere. Reading doesn't help; I pick up the latest James Patterson novel, but the sentences tumble and skip over each other, and by the time I concede defeat, I can't recall a single word. Faint cooking smells tantalise my nostrils: onions, garlic, the aroma of sizzling meat. I inhale with pleasure, and as my lungs fill, so does my heart. With glorious hope.

At six on the dot, Dominic unlocks the basement door. I'm off my bed straight away, my feet pounding hard on the stairs as I race up them, awaiting his permission to step through into freedom.

'Supper's ready, Beth,' he says. I walk past him and gratitude swells in my chest, jockeying with hope for first place. The smile I give Dominic is wide and genuine, my appreciation sincere. His lips turn upwards, the skin around his eyes crinkling, and the connection between us fizzes with promise. He gets it, the thankfulness I feel; how, unlike my fake smiles from before, this one's real. Our evening together will go well.

And it does. 'Sit down,' Dominic instructs. A red rose sits beside my plate, as does a wine glass. An open bottle of Cabernet Sauvignon, too. No more than half a glass, I tell myself. Dominic disappears into the kitchen and part of me takes note. He can't watch me all the time. There'll be moments when I'll be alone, and I avail myself of the current one, my eyes sweeping the room. The paint around the nearest window is peeling, the wood rotting. No lock, just a simple metal clasp. The gap, when the sash is raised, should be large enough to permit escape. It'll be noisy, though, the wooden frame creaking and groaning its way up, alerting Dominic to my plans.

My hopes deflate. He'll have considered every angle before allowing me up here. Look at my place setting, for example. No cutlery, nothing I can use as a weapon.

Dominic returns, bearing a steaming casserole dish, a fragrant meaty aroma escaping its depths. 'Beef bourguignon,' he announces as he places the food on the table. He disappears again, back seconds later with plates heaped with rice. His final trip produces a ladle and cutlery. He spoons out generous portions, before pouring an inch of red wine into my glass and a full measure into his. Steam swirls upwards from my plate, from baby onions, button mushrooms, chunks of beef coated in a rich sauce. My mouth waters, but I don't dare dig in. Dominic hasn't given me permission.

'Eat, Beth,' he says.

I do, and it's beyond sublime, our first proper meal together. Yes, we've eaten up here before, once, but I don't count that. Such resentment I held in my heart towards him back then. A lifetime ago. Tonight I won't allow discontent to prick the bubble of my happiness, even if I'm still planning to escape. For this evening, and the others that follow, I'll be content to savour what passes for freedom for me.

I'm careful to do everything right. When I use the salt, I replace it where it was, next to the pepper in the centre of the table, making sure to look to him for approval. Our eyes meet, a message broadcasting from mine. *See? I remember the rules.* His smile informs me he understands what I'm telling him. I eat, sip my wine, praise his cooking, and say yes to seconds. Dessert, too. While Dominic's fetching apple pie from the kitchen, I inspect the nearest window. It's painted shut. I get up, checking the others. Same result. Escape via the windows is impossible. I make it back to my seat, the bubble of my pleasure pricked, a second before Dominic returns, pie dish in hand.

After our meal, he opts for a rerun of *The Shining* on television. I've already seen it, but I'm happy to let him control the agenda. Besides, he tells me I can choose next time, and happiness clutches me as I contemplate the idea of *next time*. I enjoy every minute of the film, and before long, eleven o'clock rolls around. Time to return to the basement.

'Say you love me,' he commands, as he steers me towards my prison.

'I love you.' The taste of apple pie and red wine in my mouth reminds me that, for a few hours, I came close.

***

I'm unable to sleep, too excited, euphoria flowing through my veins. The prospect of spending every evening the way we did earlier is beyond comprehension. Five hours a night of glorious freedom, despite the fact he'll watch me all the time. I don't care, though. For a few hours every day, I'll have a semblance of normality in my world.

I turn my pillow over, resting my cheek against its cool surface, my mind racing through possibilities. I'm wondering if he'll permit me more privileges, given time. Allow me to cook for him, even. When I lived at home, I never bothered, but now I want to learn. My opportunities for stimulation aren't great, so I'll take what I can get. Besides, it might please Dominic if I adopt a nurturing role. Whether he'll ever trust me around knives is debatable, though.

Slow and sure, I tell myself. My captor is not someone to be hurried. One small slip and I might end up confined to the basement for good – a thought so terrible panic squeezes my chest. No, no, no. Whatever happens, I need to cling to my newfound freedom. If I do what he asks, I'll be fine.

Apart from the fact he wants me to love him. I can't, I won't, do that.

There's no denying it, though. I don't hate him anymore. Did I once smash a window then lie in wait for Dominic, violence in my heart? Given the opportunity now, I'd be incapable of thrusting a shard of glass into his neck, and the change confuses me. I'm not sure I can label my emotions for this man. They should be hatred, but they're not. I remind myself how kind he can be. The radio, the Italian books, the wooden box. The red roses.

My mind hovers over the roses. A symbol of romance. I consider Dominic's daily requests for me to say that I love him. Not once has he ever said it back. What his emotions are towards me, I have no idea. It's as though he can manage the roses, but putting his feelings into words is clearly a step too far. He wants to receive love, not give it. As though he's parched, desperate to soak up the pseudo-affection he forces me to offer. Too needy to give in return.

Behind the basement wall, I sense Amy's presence. She doesn't speak, but she doesn't have to. Her warning penetrates the bricks, reminding me I can never underestimate Dominic Perdue, not if I'm ever to escape my prison.

Escape. How can I pull it off when Amy didn't? The idea requires more energy than I possess, and anyway it's such a remote possibility. Too much effort, the likelihood of success too remote. I recall the lounge windows, painted shut. Besides, what opportunity do I get? Dominic watches my every move. If I'm to avoid the blackness of depression, I mustn't torture myself with thoughts of escape.

Except I can't help thinking of Mum. 'Come home, Beth. Please, darling.'

CHAPTER 12– *Beth*

We establish a routine, every evening much the same. Food, wine, television. I'm putting on weight, my former food deprivation long in the past. I'm almost happy now I have my five hours of freedom a day.

'You're making progress, Beth. But don't ever forget the kind of man he is,' Amy warns me.

'I won't.' My reassurance sounds hollow to my ears. To remind me of my promise, I fall asleep each night with her silver boot in my grip, replacing it each morning in its hidey-hole in the mattress. I'm finding it harder and harder to remember my abduction, to brandish it as a shield against my kidnapper. The recollection of his hand striking my face, forcing me to shit in a bucket, starving me, is elusive in my brain, fading into the past along with Mum's beloved face. Did he really tell me he killed a woman, because she didn't conform to his expectations? Perhaps he just said that, to keep me afraid, exert more power over me. He may be disturbed, unbalanced, but the idea of him having the capacity to murder doesn't ring true anymore. After all, he didn't strangle me when he had the chance. What's more real is his need for my company, the way he cooks my favourite dishes, the roses he gives me. Besides, I need him too.

Our life together is quiet, settled. Sometimes I feel I'm a hundred years old, not almost twenty. What happened to the naive eighteen-year-old who dreamt of foreign travel and working with children, I haven't a clue, but I suspect Dominic's iron control strangled her a long time ago. It's too much effort to contemplate what I'd be doing had he not taken me. I don't even consider escape anymore, now I've decided the possibility's too remote.

After a few months, Dominic permits me to leave the basement on Saturday and Sunday afternoons as well. I'm in heaven. He unlocks the door at one o'clock at weekends, ready for lunch. We eat, and then I dust and polish the living room while Dominic clears up in the kitchen. I revel in our cosy domesticity, the pleasure I derive from such simple tasks, although I'm careful; he's very particular about me replacing everything exactly where it was. One time I forget, and an ornament ends up facing to the left rather than to the right. As a punishment, Dominic denies me dessert for a week. I don't complain. My fault for not following the rules.

After lunch, we usually read together, curled up in separate armchairs, our books on our laps. I favour novels, Dominic prefers biographies. We're a cosy couple, him and me.

One day he surprises me. 'You've saved my life, you know.'

'How?'

He doesn't reply. My mind seeks answers. What does he mean? In the future, when I'm in a confident mood, I'll tackle him. I'll probe beneath the surface of the man who holds me captive, by mind control rather than with locked doors these days.

'Tell me you love me,' he commands every night before returning me to the basement.

'I love you.' Over time, the lie gets easier.

Perhaps it's the truth.

***

One evening, my courage high, I decide to delve deeper into my captor. Hunt for clues, discover what drives the man, what's warped his psyche, moulded him this way. We've just finished supper. Dominic gets up to clear the table, but my words stop him. 'Can we talk?'

Surprise crosses his face. Me moving the goalposts has thrown him, I can tell. 'What about?'

'You.'

Dominic's expression shutters within a heartbeat. 'No.'

'Please. We never discuss anything important.'

He sinks back into his chair. 'What's brought this on, Beth?'

My mouth is dry. Tread carefully, I remind myself. 'We live together. We share meals. Yet I know so little about you.'

A shrug. 'Not much to tell. What you see is what you get.'

'I don't think so.' Risky, to contradict him, but I have to test the waters. 'You said once I saved your life.'

His mouth tightens. 'It's like I told you. I needed a companion.'

'You were lonely.'

'Loneliness is for wimps.' His tone is harsh.

I back-pedal, trying a different tack. 'Tell me about your childhood.'

He shifts in his seat. 'Why are you asking me these questions? I told you in the coffee shop about my family.'

'You said your mum died when you were seven. Your father a few years ago. That doesn't tell me about you.'

'Yes. It does.' His tone is forceful, direct. For a moment, I'm uncertain whether I've pushed too far, if I should leave it for now. I don't, though.

'Please.' I make my voice soft, without threat. 'I'd like to know. Your mum, for example. Did you love her? Did you miss her after her death?' I hold my breath, waiting for the thin ice beneath my feet to shatter, plummeting me into the depths of Dominic's anger, his reprisals, but instead his face softens.

'Yes,' he replies. 'To both questions.'

It's not his mother, then, who's warped him. He plainly adored her, and I'm guessing she loved him too. The knowledge makes me happy. At least he's experienced love at some stage in his life, this man who's so needy he demands declarations of affection every night. Pity and compassion snake through me in equal measures. My fingers reach across the table and touch his forearm, lingering on his bare skin, before I pull them away. Surprise crosses his face, but he's not angry, I can tell. So far, so good.

'What about your father?'

Dominic's face shutters. 'I've already told you. He died several years ago. Enough questions, Beth. Turn on the television. I'll clear the table.'

I obey, conscious I've ventured into forbidden territory, unsure whether I dare risk broaching Perdue Senior again. I'm positive his father must have abused him. Why else would Dominic blank me like that?

As we watch television later, I agonise over the way his skin made my fingers tingle as I touched his arm. How in that moment the only emotion I held in my heart was empathy. Is that a precursor of love? I have no idea, but later, when Dominic commands me to say the familiar words, they ring true in my ears.

***

I leave it a few days before I ask any more questions. This time, I try a different tack. A risky one, but I need to find out, once and for all, whether Dominic's a murderer. He confessed to killing a woman, sure, but how can I square such an admission with the man I know?

It's a Saturday afternoon, almost time for him to start making supper. I've long since lost interest in my book, content to sit, legs curled beside me, in one of the old Chesterfield armchairs. My bare feet leave sweaty marks on the green leather of the seat. Instead of reading, I watch Dominic, noting his intense concentration on his book, another biography. The top of his head is inclined towards me, and I notice he's thinning around the crown. I remember how once I itched to run my fingers through his dark hair.

At last, he shuts the book with a snap. Then he looks up, sees me gazing at him, and his eyes narrow.

'What?' he says.

'There's something I want to ask you.'

At once, he's wary. 'I'm not fond of questions, Beth.'

'I get that. But I need to know.'

He's silent. No doubt dreading me mentioning his father. 'It's about the other woman,' I say.

His gaze hovers over me, appraising, searching for clues as to my motives. Is he about to blank me again? He clears his throat. 'You mean the one I killed.'

'What was her name?' In my head, she's Amy, so anything different will be weird.

He draws in a breath. 'Julia,' he says. 'Her name was Julia.'

'Did she look like me?'

'Yes.'

'How old was she?'

'Twenty when I took her.' He's lost in his memories now, his gaze averted, his mind elsewhere, back with the woman he murdered in the basement. 'And twenty when she died. We were together for two months, no more.'

I've done well to survive this long, then. I moisten my dry lips. 'How did you kill her?'

'Strangulation. Like I once told you, I'm my father's son.' He looks at me then, and his fingers reach over to caress my neck, briefly, before his hand drops away. 'You're different, though. She disappointed me. You don't.'

It's true, then. The same as when he tried to choke me. Did Amy - no, Julia - piss herself as his fingers squeezed her throat, the way I did? I gaze at Dominic's nails, at the dark hair on his knuckles. I picture his hands around her neck, his fingers squeezing the life from her, and panic engulfs me. Too much, by far. I've probed too hard, and I only have myself to blame for the terror now swamping me. Pure instinct drives my response. With one smooth movement, I leap from the Chesterfield, but Dominic's too quick. He stands up, blocking my way, his hands gripping my upper arms. The pressure of his fingers reminds me of my predecessor's fate, as the dread hammering through my chest multiplies.

'Beth.' Dominic's tone is commanding, but I can't meet his eyes. Those mismatched irises have witnessed a woman choke to death.

'It's good that you're afraid. It shows you understand how things must be. You'll be OK, though. You're not Julia. This time, it's different.'

***

Over time, I realise something's wrong with Dominic. Our cosy life together continues, but for the last three months, he's been moody. Uncharacteristically so. Apart from the times I've stepped out of line, he's rarely been angry. Not so now. These days, his frame of mind fluctuates wildly, making me uneasy. If he's having a breakdown, I'm screwed. The thought of an unhinged Dominic is terrifying. If that dark part of him forces its way to the surface, it won't bode well for me.

The first time I notice anything is wrong is after breakfast one day.

'Could you buy me some new pyjamas?' I ask. 'The elastic is broken in one of my pairs.'

To my alarm, annoyance creeps into his expression. 'No.'

I'm knocked off balance by his abrupt tone. My throat grows dry.

His mouth curls with irritation. 'You'll have to make do. It's not as if it matters, not when you're asleep.' He grabs my breakfast tray and leaves without another word.

I'm confused by his refusal. I tell myself it's a one-off, but it's not; the pattern continues. One evening he snaps at me over dinner.

'No wine?' I ask, noting the absence of our usual bottle of French. A simple question; I'm used to a glass with our evening meal. Perhaps Dominic forgot to buy any when he went shopping earlier.

His face is pale, closed. When he speaks, his tone is curt. 'No. Water tonight.'

'OK.' I daren't risk saying more.

'I've spoiled you, that's the problem. You're not grateful anymore.'

I'm silent, turning his words over in my head. 'I'm sorry,' I say, and I am. For demanding new pyjamas, wine at dinner, not showing enough gratitude.

He doesn't reply, and I fall silent, unwilling to provoke him further. We don't speak again throughout our meal, and when he returns me to the basement, he doesn't ask whether I love him.

After that, I take careful note of Dominic's moods. In one respect, I'm reassured; I don't think his grouchiness heralds mental illness. Stress appears to be the trigger. I've noted when he's worse, and it's always after the post arrives. Dominic receives very little mail, but occasionally he gets a letter, and they're becoming more frequent. Afterwards he's snappy, distant, his expression closed. The first time it happens, I'm in the basement, doing my morning push-ups. Above me, the letterbox rattles and the sound of mail plopping onto the mat reaches me. As do curses, minutes later. Dominic's not one for swearing, so when I hear a fist pounding on something, the words *Fucking bastards!* accompanying the thud of flesh on wood, I'm scared. A door bangs upstairs. I distract myself with more exercise. Lunch is late that day, Dominic silent as he brings my food. I sense my concern won't be welcome.

The scenario repeats itself a couple of times more. Am I imagining it, or does his anger swell with each episode? Every time it happens, I take care to stay quiet and subdued. Whatever's bugging him, I pray it blows over; he's made me realise how vulnerable I am. How dependent on him. Once I considered my forays out of the basement the pinnacle of my aspirations. Now I'd be happy to spend more time confined to these four walls, if Dominic reverted to the way he was. These days, his mood can change within a nanosecond.

***

One evening, we're upstairs, eating our supper. A mixture of leftovers I recognise from meals we had earlier in the week, stir-fried with white rice. That's new. Normally Dominic buys brown basmati, the expensive stuff. I stare at the pale grains, aware they're significant in some way.

Dominic's silent, brooding. Another letter arrived this morning. When he escorts me to the basement later, he surprises me by accompanying me down the stairs. He doesn't speak but goes to my bed, yanking back the duvet, tugging at the bottom sheet. His hands pull at the electric blanket.

'Remember my silver charm in the mattress, Beth,' Amy warns. I'm petrified he'll discover it, take away my link to her, be angry I concealed it from him. My throat is closed, my mouth dry, but I force myself to speak.

'What are you doing?'

'Isn't it obvious? I'm removing your electric blanket.' His hands are close, frighteningly so, to the rip in the mattress.

'Why? Have I made you angry?'

He straightens up, facing me. 'No. But you don't need it now summer's here.'

'But—' I don't dare remind him the basement's chilly at night whatever the time of year. Once he's gone, I huddle, shivering, on the bed, the silver boot clutched in my palm. The leftovers at mealtimes, the removal of the blanket – everything points to Dominic being on an economy drive. Up to when the moodiness started, we lived well. The best fillet steak, smoked salmon, organic vegetables. Branded toiletries in the shower. Now we eat white rice with yesterday's leftover pork, and I brush my teeth with Tesco Value paste. My twentieth birthday came and went with no present, just a card. What this means for me, or for us, I'm not sure, but I sense it's nothing good.

***

A week later, I discover what the problem is. Another letter arrived this morning, followed by the now familiar cursing from upstairs. Later, Dominic's expression is shuttered, brooding, as he serves our evening meal. Chicken casserole, the proportion of meat to vegetables skewed in favour of peas and carrots. Wine with our meals is now a distant memory. We eat in silence.

The main course finished, I stack our plates, ready for Dominic to carry into the kitchen. When he does, I notice a torn envelope, tossed into the nearby waste basket.

'Ice cream for dessert.' Dominic's voice from the other room makes me jump as I stare at the discarded letter. 'We'll have vanilla tonight.'

'Fine,' I shout back, as I hear the freezer opening. My feet pad over to the waste bin. I extract the two halves of the envelope, folding them over and shoving them in the pocket of my jogging bottoms. By the time Dominic returns with dessert, I'm back at the table, my expression neutral.

Once he goes into the kitchen to load the dishwasher, I extract the two halves from the torn envelope, hold them together, and read.

It's from Lloyds Bank. Dominic is six months in arrears with the mortgage on the cottage. Thousands of pounds are owing, and the tone of the letter is unsympathetic. Seems they're not receiving any response to their previous correspondence. They mention the possibility of a court order. Repossession, even. Patience is obviously running out at Lloyds.

I'm puzzled. Dominic rarely mentions his father, but I swear he told me, back at The Busy Bean, that he'd inherited outright possession of the cottage after Lincoln Perdue died intestate. No mention of a mortgage.

The BMW. His expensive clothes, the organic food. Dominic's work as a day trader clearly doesn't support the way he likes to live. I suspect his finances have been operating in overdrive for several years now, probably since his father's death.

Repossession. Dominic will never allow that to happen, surely?

'He'll kill you first,' Amy whispers in my head. 'How would he ever explain you away?'

She's right. Impossible for Dominic to ensure my compliance through a move into alternative accommodation, should repossession take place. He doesn't trust me enough, not yet. For him, the easiest option is to murder me, then dispose of both my body and Amy's.

Terror drains the saliva from my mouth. I'll be nicer to him, I tell myself. Anticipate his every need, talk to him, make him see how much he needs me. If I can do that, then he won't kill me. He won't be able to.

'We'll watch that Bruce Willis film later,' Dominic shouts from the kitchen. Startled, I drop the letter. Before he comes back in, I replace it in the two halves of the torn envelope, and then return them to the waste basket.

***

Today's a Saturday. It's twelve thirty, and we're having an early lunch, a simple affair of hummus and salad sandwiches. Dominic's relaxed, less jumpy, mentioning the Robert De Niro film we'll watch later on television. I slather hummus onto bread, piling on lettuce, the aroma of garlic wafting from my food. Then the sound of feet crunching over gravel reaches me, and the letterbox opens. The day's mail, late this morning, falls on the mat.

Dominic's up and off his chair faster than a runner from the starting blocks, his expression morphing in an instant from relaxed to harried. Dread clutches me tight. So far, I've been shielded from the anger the letters provoke, safe in the cocoon of the basement, but now I'm vulnerable, exposed. I pray whatever's on the mat is junk mail.

It's not. Dominic's shout of *For fuck's sake!* crashes off the walls as he returns, his face striking terror into me, and I shrink into my chair, wishing myself invisible. He paces in front of me, his hand raking his hair in frenzied swipes.

'The bastards. The greedy money-grabbing pricks.' He clutches the letter tight in his hand, so hard it's bent in half. One sheet of white A4, its back to me. Dominic's feet pound the carpet as he walks, his fury almost palpable.

He looks at his watch. Then at me. He grabs my right arm, the plate it's holding tilting, so that salad drops on the floor. His other hand closes around my left wrist, the pressure making me wince. His tone is impatient. 'Back to the basement. You can take that with you.' He means my lunch, I presume. I struggle to keep my sandwich on the plate, the fingers that still hold my knife pressing against the bread. I'm dragged towards the basement door. Dominic yanks it open. Seconds later, I'm on my bed, my prison door locked, the sound of tyres spinning on gravel reaching me as Dominic drives away.

CHAPTER 13 – *Dominic*

B ankers. Scum of the earth. Who the hell do they think they are? Losing the cottage is unthinkable. I was born within its walls, grew up in them. Now, at last, it's a proper home for Beth and me. I won't, I can't, allow a faceless bank to steal it. OK, so I'm behind with the mortgage repayments. Nothing I can't make up once the markets swing my way.

I've been a fool to ignore the letters from Lloyds, though. No more. I'll take a firm stance. Go to the Kingswood branch, tell them to lay off me, give me more time. Nothing's left of my inheritance from Dad, but I won't let that worry me. His money set me up while I was learning the ropes as a day trader, has kept me afloat these last few years. It's not been enough, though; the financial markets can be brutal. I was forced to mortgage the cottage shortly before Beth came to live with me. She doesn't know that I'm in financial shit, but why should I tell her? Such matters are none of her business.

I brake hard, not having seen the red light. Five past one. The Kingswood branch will be closed. The one in Broadmead opens later on a Saturday. When the lights turn green, I ease the car forward, heading along the A420 towards the city centre.

Eager to thrust those bastard bankers from my mind, my thoughts return to Beth. Things are moving towards love with her, just as I predicted. Our relationship is warm, cosy, the way I pictured it. The road to where we are now hasn't been easy, but it's been smoother than I'd dared hope.

I hear Beth in my head now, see her face. 'I love you,' she says, her eyes downcast. My girl's shy when it comes to expressing emotion. Yeah, we're good together. Over time, our dinners, the television programmes we watch, will obliterate her memory of the abduction. One day, I'll believe her every time she says the words. Perhaps I'll even say them back. It's been a long time since the dark beast of depression stalked me. I've not considered hammering a hook into the basement rafter to hang myself since Beth arrived at the cottage.

Yes, I'm happy with my life. I have a home and a woman with whom to share it. I've proved I'm a better man than my father was. I deserve what I have.

I drive into the NCP at Broadmead and park the car. Time to sort out the bastards at the bank.

Beth stays in my head as I walk away from the BMW. Her dark eyes fill my thoughts as I exit into the street, and I never see the car heading my way.

***

The blow shocks through me, knocking me sideways. I'm shunted towards the pavement, a crack sounding as I crumple to the kerb, banging my head as I fall. My mind struggles to comprehend what's happened, disbelief hammering in my brain. No pain, not at first. Instead, I'm suspended in denial while the world carries on around me in slow motion. Then I ease myself up, supporting my weight on my arms, and catch sight of my right leg.

Agony hits me then, so intense it's white-hot, roiling up through me from my shattered limb. A scream bursts from my mouth, followed by another, as I stare at my bloodied trousers. A woman stands beside me, shouting into her mobile over the roar of the traffic. Words reach me through the haze of pain. 'Help is on its way… you'll be all right… hospital…' but I don't respond. I can't, incapable of anything other than riding the excruciating torment from my leg. Along with the lesser hurt in my head. Fuck. Why the hell couldn't I have been knocked unconscious? I bite my lower lip hard, the coppery taste of blood oozing into my mouth.

'Beth, Beth,' I mutter, and whoever is kneeling next to my head speaks, his breath fanning my face.

'Is Beth your wife? Can I call her for you?'

Dear God, no. Not that anyone can contact her at the cottage. I shake my head, clenching my teeth, sweat dappling my forehead.

'Is she your girlfriend?'

'Don't have one.' With any luck, the man will assume he misheard me when I said Beth's name. Too much effort to explain the lack of a landline at home, how I disposed of Beth's mobile along with the rest of her stuff after she arrived. Or did I? I'm struggling to remember.

After an interminable wait, the wail of sirens hits my ears. Thank God. The paramedics are brisk and efficient, but it's still too long before they strap a mask over my face and I drag in the first delicious lungful of gas, dulling the pain, rubbing off its sharp edges. A soft blanket of mental bubble-wrap cocoons me. I drift into a soothing torpor, aware I have cause for concern, but I can't remember what.

I'm loaded onto a stretcher, a female paramedic speaking in soothing tones as her colleagues shift me into the ambulance. We reach the Bristol Royal Infirmary within minutes, where I'm X-rayed, although any fool can see what's wrong with my leg. I'm lucky, I'm told. A clean break, no pins required, just a plaster cast.

'Anyone I should call?' a nurse asks me.

'Beth,' I manage. 'My girlfriend. She'll be worried.' I'm puzzled. Why does my voice sound as though I'm speaking through treacle?

The male paramedic shakes his head. 'He said he didn't have a girlfriend.'

The nurse bends over me. Such beautiful dark eyes she has. Such lovely skin. Her hair entrances me. Mahogany brown, long and shiny, pinned in a silver clip. I'm confused. Since when has Beth worn her hair like that? She's saying something, but I can't make out the words.

I know what I want her to say, though.

'Tell me,' I manage, although the two syllables are a drain on me. I dredge up the last of my energy. 'Tell me you love me.'

Above me, Beth's image blurs. Her lips move, though. Forming words of love. That's my girl.

Other words float through the haze in my brain. *Confused... struck head on pavement... possible concussion.* I don't understand what they mean.

***

Later, after my leg's set in plaster and I'm ensconced on a hospital ward, I manage to sleep for a while. When I awake, my head's clearer; it's easier to think, despite the headache that throbs deep in my skull. From the window opposite my bed, darkness stares back at me. What time is it? I spot a clock on the wall near the double swing doors. It's nine o'clock at night, apparently. I'm desperate to get back to Beth, and as her name sounds in my head, I realise what I need to concern myself with. An image arises in my mind of me, back at home and on crutches, unable to stop Beth should she grab my house keys, escape in mind.

As I debate my options, a doctor comes to talk with me. Seems the hospital wants to keep me in overnight.

'Why can't you send me home?' I ask.

The woman shakes her head.

'You've sustained a mild concussion as well as breaking your leg, Mr Perdue,' she says. 'You were confused when we admitted you. How does your head feel now?'

'It hurts. I'm not confused, though. I just need to go home.'

'Do you live alone?'

I nod. 'Yes. No family.' The flash of sympathy in the woman's eyes angers me. She hasn't a clue.

'It's important you have someone with you following a concussion. You're best off here. We'll keep you in overnight, and with any luck you'll be able to return home tomorrow.'

I acquiesce, because what else can I do? Beth is safely locked in the basement, I tell myself. She'll be fine. I'll follow the doctor's orders. For now, anyway. I'll rest, sort out the headache, and tomorrow I'll get the fuck out of here.

***

When I awake, the clock on the wall says five a.m. My head no longer feels as though it's stuffed with cotton wool, and the pain in it has gone. It's still dark, but going back to sleep's impossible, not with the man in the next bed snoring like a pig. Now my head's better, I need to face facts. The reality is that Beth's locked in a basement, miles away, with no way of knowing what's happened. What thoughts have gone through her head, as the hours pass, when I don't return? The scene from yesterday haunts me, when I dragged her towards the basement door, fury at the harsh letter I'd received spreading a red mist through my brain. Her yelp, the way she winced as my fingers closed around her wrist, the fear in her face.

'I'm sorry,' I whisper into the darkness.

At least she's safe. She has a toilet, her books. I force myself to think. Food, water? I allowed her to take her sandwich with her. No water, though; she'd been drinking orange juice, which she left at the table. She'll be thirsty, then, as well as hungry, and I make a decision. No matter what that goddamn doctor says, I'm out of here today.

I form a plan. I'll take a cab to the cottage, let Beth out, allow her food and water. Until my leg heals, I'll sleep downstairs, the sofa cushions and a duvet providing a temporary bed. Beth will care for me. She's well trained enough by now. Besides, looking after me might help her to love me more. I tell myself not to worry. It'll be a test, in a way, of how far she's come.

CHAPTER 14 – *Beth*

I curl up on the bed, no longer hungry, waiting for Dominic's return. The silence in the cottage disturbs me almost as much as his rage earlier. I doze, my eyes closing for a few minutes of respite before they jerk open again. Time crawls by. Half one. Two o'clock. Three. He's never been gone this long before.

Five o'clock. My stomach is growling now, so I eat the remains of the sandwich, its bread now stale. I've nothing to drink and the beginnings of thirst are making themselves known. Then I curl back up again, watching the time count upwards on my watch.

Six o'clock comes, and no Dominic. Normally, at this time, he'd be preparing our supper, with me inhaling the heady aromas emanating from the kitchen.

Seven o'clock, and I'm even hungrier. Scenarios run through my head. Dominic angry, confronting the sender of the letter. A row that culminates in him drinking himself into oblivion. No. The image doesn't fit; he's always controlled around alcohol. A car problem, then. The BMW's developed a fault, and the breakdown service has been slow to arrive. To delay him over six hours, though? A voice inside me says no. I drown it out. It's possible, I tell myself.

Eight o'clock. Definitely not a breakdown, then.

Nine o'clock. If he doesn't come back, I'll die of dehydration in here.

Sometime after ten, I drift into an uneasy sleep, from which I wake often, hunger in my belly, but what's worse is the thirst. My mouth is dry, my brain obsessed with water, blessed water, cool, sweet, refreshing. I had orange juice with lunch, before Dominic's meltdown, but no liquid since. Memories of my early days in here, when he left me without enough to drink, press in on me, and my desperation doubles.

***

By morning, I'm beyond desperate. My body is stiff from tension and lack of rest. The hunger in my belly has doubled, and my tongue is dry and bloated, a hideous monster in my mouth. I'm dizzy, my brain addled with dehydration and the need for sleep. Purple bruises have bloomed on my wrists from when Dominic yanked me towards the basement. My mind runs over the options for escape but draws a blank. I cycle through the possibilities I've previously rejected; the window, the door, and they're useless, every one. It's hopeless; I'm trapped, no way out. I'll die in here, never seeing my mother's face again.

Huge gasps of despair rack me. 'I'm sorry, Mum,' I say.

***

My guts are what save me. I've been too preoccupied to sort out the fullness in my bowels, but the need to do so is becoming urgent. I uncurl myself from the bed, staggering to the toilet, my legs stiff.

When I'm done, I sit for a moment, and that's when I spot my empty plate, complete with the table knife, on top of the filing cabinet. The sunlight filtering through the window catches the metal blade, which glints into my eyes. I go over, picking it up, my fingers testing the blunt tip, playing over the smooth surface. In his haste to leave, Dominic didn't notice I'd taken it with me, and if he had, he'd have discounted it as a weapon. Its rounded end is useless for stabbing anyone.

Not completely without practical applications, though. Not where the basement door is concerned.

I walk up the stairs. The door is ancient, its lock darkened with age; I slide the knife between it and the jamb. A tight squeeze, but it fits. I ease the blade downward, until it rests on top of the latch, metal against metal.

I hesitate. Part of my brain insists I should wait for Dominic's return. He'll be furious if he gets back and discovers I've left the basement; I'll lose my privileges, be condemned to reduced food rations again. Better not to risk it, I decide, but then I run my tongue over my chapped lips. The temptation of water in the kitchen tortures my dry mouth, urging me to use the opportunity I've been granted. I pull the knife free from its wooden groove and reposition it.

This time I slide it forward, against the metal of the latch, wiggling the knife from side to side, up and down, testing for leeway. The wood of the door jamb splinters with the pressure, granting me extra space. As well as an idea. I pull the knife out and chip away at the jamb. It's soft, old, damp, and I don't need much effort to prise a few shards free. I continue to push metal against wood, gouging deeper, widening the gap near where the latch sits. After five minutes or so, my wrists ache, but a small pile of wood chips lies at my feet. More room exists now to insert the knife, and I reposition it, this time against the metal, and press. Hard. I'm rewarded with a slight give towards the right, away from the door jamb, igniting hope. I draw the knife out, pushing it back in deeper, angling it toward my left, hoping to edge it between the latch and the wood. With the knife gripped in both hands, I angle the pressure toward the right and the latch yields a little more.

I stand back, wiping my forehead, tiny bits of wood on my arm scraping against my skin. My breath comes in harsh rasps, but I'm close, so close. When my breathing slows, I chip at the doorjamb again, and this time a bigger chunk splits away. My intuition tells me it's enough. With a deep inhalation, I thrust the blade into the hole and tug towards the right. The latch springs away from its home, all the way, causing me to release the knife. As I do so, the mechanism clicks back into place, but I now know escape is possible. I reposition the knife, shoving hard as the blade presses the latch back, and the door gives way. I stumble into the hallway, then run to the kitchen. I twist open the taps, sticking my head into the sink, my gulps frantic, water spraying everywhere. The flow comes straight from heaven and I can't get enough. When I eventually raise my head, I swear I'll never take lack of water for granted again.

Next I wrench open the fridge in search of food. I drag out cheese, a half-used bag of salad, a jar of mayo, before snatching what remains of a sliced loaf from the bread bin. Minutes later, the makeshift sandwich sits in my stomach, and for the first time in hours, I can think straight.

***

After I've eaten, I sink to the kitchen floor, my arms hugging my knees. What to do, what to do? I can return to the basement, of course, wait for Dominic, but the thought terrifies me. He'll be so angry at me for not staying put. He might never trust me again. Perhaps he'll even kill me, the way he did with Julia. Or Amy, as I still think of her.

Another option, equally frightening, exists. Escape. The freedom for which I've longed the last two years is within my grasp, but I'm not sure whether I can take it. Maybe I'm better off staying put. If he does return and discovers me trying to leave, I'm dead, for sure. Like Julia.

In the end, escape wins. It's the less terrifying choice.

I run through my options. Both the front and back doors are locked. I'll need to find a way to break out. Then run, and fast. I struggle to remember the road layout outside the cottage. Turn right at the top of the driveway. A mile or so to the main road. Where I'll be safe, where there's traffic, noise, people. Through Kingswood, then head towards Downend. Home to my family. At the thought of Mum, my resolve strengthens.

***

The first thing I do is explore upstairs, the one part of the cottage I've never been. I'm searching for anything to help me, from money to a spare set of keys to the outside doors. As well as something more substantial than my slippers to wear on my feet. I enter

Dominic's bedroom, my senses alert for sounds from below. The room is bare and impersonal; no pictures on the walls, no clothes on the floor, no books on the cabinet. No phone, either.

I stare at Dominic's bed, at the masculine navy-blue duvet cover. Without thinking what I'm doing, I lie down on it, curling myself into a ball before burying my face in one of his pillows. I breathe in the scent of the man with whom I've lived for two years, and it's as though he's beside me, so strong is his presence in my head. I drift through the memories we've made together, and time slips from my grasp. When I open my eyes and check his alarm clock, a good hour has passed.

With a start, I haul myself off the bed to resume my search, starting with the wardrobe. Jackets, shirts, trousers, colour-coordinated and facing to the left, greet me, and I bury my face in the soft cotton of the nearest shirt. Beneath me, shoes line up in precise pairs. I align my pink-slippered foot alongside one. Too large, by far.

Next I tug open drawers in his bedside cabinet, hunting for something I don't find. No spare keys, no money. What I discover is the exact opposite. Credit card demands. Stern letters from his bank, demanding the arrears on the mortgage. Statements revealing an alarming increase in his overdraft.

The bathroom, his office and the spare bedroom prove equally fruitless. The latter, clearly used as a storeroom, is stacked with boxes. Beside them sits an old suitcase. I don't bother investigating any of it. Nothing up here can help me.

Wait, I'm wrong. I walk back into Dominic's bedroom and reopen the wardrobe, taking out a leather jacket, a soft black one. The label says Forzieri, the quality shouts expensive. I pull it on, although it's way too big; the sleeves hang beyond my wrists, the hem skirts the backs of my thighs. Then I return downstairs.

***

My original intention to escape through either the front or back door is soon thwarted. I examine the wood around the main entrance. Not a chance. The frame's too thick for me to force, even though I now command a whole array of possible tools from the kitchen. The door itself is solid wood, stout and unyielding when I press against it. Besides, it sports two locks, a stout Chubb sitting beneath the older, weaker-looking Yale. Impossible to break out this way. The back door's equally impassable, being of new construction, uPVC and double-glazed.

Time for a rethink, and fast. I reconsider the windows. Painted shut they may be, but they're still wood containing a single pane of glass. Which I can break.

I grab towels from the downstairs shower room, before returning to the kitchen. My gaze settles on the knife block, nestled in a corner on the worktop. It's brushed aluminium, weighty in my hand as I lift it. I take it, along with the towels, to the window at the rear of the cottage. Even now, with freedom minutes away, the possibility that Dominic will arrive back as I step through to freedom terrifies me. No, I'll make my escape through the back, enabling me to hide in the garden if I hear the BMW pull up. Stupid, but his control over me still grips tightly.

I shrug off the over-sized jacket, and then pull out the knives, placing everything underneath the window. I rip down the net curtain. Then I pick up the empty block, and with one swift movement, I heave it through the air. The noise as the glass breaks shatters the silence in the cottage. A hole, jagged cracks running from it, sits in the middle of the pane, not big enough to climb through, but easy enough to enlarge. I cover my fist with swathes of thick bath towel, punching at the glass around the opening. The glass is old, the putty weak, and the final barrier to freedom doesn't take long to remove. By the time I've finished, all that remains of the original window pane is a few shards clinging to the frame. I unwind my makeshift gloves, dropping the towels on the floor. The gap is now large enough to step through.

I don't, though. Doubt prevents me, along with fear of what lies beyond the smashed window. After being a prisoner for so long, the thought of the outside world is frightening. The enormity of what I'm contemplating sweeps over me, drying my mouth with terror. Barely conscious of what I'm doing, I walk towards the basement and down the steps into the familiarity of my prison. Defeated, I sit on my bed.

My mother's beloved voice echoes in my head, here where I last heard it.

'Come home, Beth. Please, darling.'

In that moment, all doubt falls away, to be replaced by new resolve. I walk towards the steps, then stop. One last thing before I leave this place. If I'm to be free at last, a memento from my time here is coming with me. My fingers reach under the sheet to pry into the hole in the mattress. From it, I extract the tiny silver shoe, placing it in the pocket of my jogging bottoms. Then I go back upstairs.

I place the towels along the windowsill, covering the sharp edges of glass that remain. On goes Dominic's jacket, my arms swallowed by swathes of Italian leather. I swing one leg through the window, my hands steadying myself on the windowsill. My other leg rises up and over, as my body eases through the gap, before I drop onto the gravel below.

I sink to my knees, oblivious to the shards of glass slicing into them. I pull pure, clean air into my chest, and nothing in my life can ever trump this moment. First I laugh, then I cry as the sweet sunshine bathes my face. After two years of captivity, I'm free.

CHAPTER 15 – *Dominic*

I discharge myself later that morning, despite the reservations of the hospital staff. I lie about my pain levels; they're high enough to soak my shirt with sweat, despite my medication, but what the hell. A porter will deliver the BMW later, after I've sorted out Beth. I'm careful to stipulate I'm not in any hurry to get my car back.

Traffic is heavy on the way home. Even worse, the taxi driver chatters incessantly, when I need to be alone in my head with Beth. We grind along the A420, inching closer to my girl, the delay grating on me until I barely repress my inner screams.

Overall, though, I'm buoyed up, optimistic. She'll be so grateful, so pleased to see me. We won't speak of it, but the message is clear. Her life and her well-being depend on me, her benefactor, the man who's moulded her into what she is today, the perfect companion. My Beth. I picture her, waiting on me, nursing me, doing everything a companion should, and I smile.

Eager as I am to get back to my girl, I forget my leg as I exit the taxi, jarring it against the door. The shock sends waves of pain through me; sweat breaks out on my forehead as I struggle to calm my breathing. I promise myself I'll pop another painkiller after my reunion with Beth.

My fingers fumble as I turn my keys in the front door. I nudge it open with my shoulder. Then a fireball of fury surges through me, slamming my emotions hard against a brick wall. Denial and disbelief add themselves to the mix. The basement door is open.

I pound my crutches over the floor so I can stare through the doorway, down the stairs, into Beth's empty prison cell. The atmosphere in the cottage is silent, devoid of human presence. She's gone.

'Beth!' Her name bounces off the cottage walls as I scream it. It strikes me how chilly the room is, and then I notice the towel on the windowsill at the back of the lounge, the broken glass, her escape route.

The damaged wood around the basement door tells its own story. A tale of negligence on my part. She must have hidden a knife on her, the one she used with lunch, the last time I shut her in the basement. Watching me, biding her time, taking advantage as soon as she spotted her chance. The bitch. The cunning, conniving, cheating little cow. Whatever dreams I harboured of a life together have splintered into a million pieces, and my rage cools. A chilly determination replaces it. The details can come later, but I'm certain of one thing. Beth Sutton will pay for her treachery.

I'm a reasonable man; I could forgive her breaking out of the basement. Understandable. I'd been gone too long; she needed food, water. I'd even have been prepared to gloss over the knife she hid from me, if only she'd been here when I got back. If she'd shown she was worried about me, that she did love me, despite the way we began. Impossible, though, to forgive the betrayal the broken window represents.

***

My body needs food, water, but such matters will have to wait. I ease myself onto the sofa, thoughts thudding through my brain. Images of Beth at a police station, sitting opposite the officers who'll come to arrest me. The words 'tricked me… kept me prisoner' fall from her mouth. Bitch. In my mind, I'm there in the room, an invisible witness to her treachery, and then I become real, solid, as my hand cracks across her face, smacking retribution into her as the blow sends her crashing from her chair.

The problem is, I've no clue as to when she escaped. How much time she's had to spill her story to her parents, the police.

How long before the interviewing officers decide they have enough reasons to knock at my door? I don't doubt she'll involve the police; it's simply a question of when. I've been a fool, a blind, deluded idiot, to believe she'd ever love me, that I could mould her into my companion. Take the incident with the basement window. Cunning, right from the start. Not to mention her declarations of love, all of them false. Me stupidly taking pleasure in making her say the words whenever I wanted, as if she were a talking doll. Why did I never admit to myself that she always needed prompting?

Anger surges through me before I give myself a mental head slap. It won't be long before the police knock on the door; I need to think fast. When it comes to it, it's Beth's word against mine. Nobody will have witnessed her escape through the window, what with the cottage being so isolated. I haul myself to my feet, wincing as pain burns through my plastered leg. I have work to do. I remind myself to call a glazier tomorrow.

I head to the kitchen, where I locate several carrier bags. Time to tackle the basement. I survey the stairs. Remember how they showed you to do it in hospital, I tell myself. I position my crutches on the first step, breathing deeply, relying on my upper body strength to propel myself, my right leg dangling in the air. Slowly, each movement carefully considered, I ease my way downwards. Once I gain in confidence, it's not so hard, although I'm panting by the time I reach the bottom.

It takes four journeys, back and forth, as sweat beads my face and soaks my clothes. Using the crutches on the stairs gets easier each time, but it's still no picnic, especially when carrying things. Eventually, Beth's stuff, everything I was kind enough to allow her, is upstairs. Her books – man, they were heavy to lift – her clothes, the wooden box. I allow myself five minutes of rest, no more. When I return to the basement, I tear the posters from the walls and drag the waste container from the toilet. Finally, I strip the bed, folding it back up before dragging the duvet up the stairs. At the top, I survey the basement. A Z-bed, a metal filing cabinet, a toilet that's not even usable, thanks to the tray being upstairs. No clue a woman has ever been here.

Beth's DNA is an issue, of course, one which I haven't a hope of eliminating. Her hairs will be in my shower drain, flakes from her skin everywhere. Not a problem; it's in my interest to admit she's been here. We've been dating, I'll say. That's how she can describe the basement so accurately, because she's been to the cottage. It was I who finished it; she was too young, too clingy, too unstable. She didn't take well to me ending the relationship. The classic scorned woman syndrome. Out for revenge. Held her captive? Utter nonsense. You understand, don't you, officer?

Although I won't show any understanding, not when I catch up with her. Has she forgotten I know where she lives?

I'll bide my time, though. If she goes missing shortly after accusing me of kidnap, mine will be the first door the police knock on. Besides, my leg is a problem. It won't heal overnight, and I'll need to be capable of overpowering her. Might be several weeks before I'm able to give Beth what she deserves. Revenge is a dish best served cold, as the saying goes. A delay will prove beneficial, lull her into a false sense of security. I'll need to keep track of her whereabouts, make sure she doesn't move away. Regular taxis to and from Downend won't come cheap, but they're a means to an end.

'I'm coming for you, Beth,' I promise her.

My work's not done, though. I drag her bedding to the sofa where I'll be sleeping for the time being. Then I sort out Beth's possessions. The wooden box, her Christmas present that cost me a fortune – not that the bitch was grateful – goes on top of the dresser. Her Italian books and the classics disappear into the bookcase; the Jodi Picoults are tossed into the bag containing her clothes. Her toiletries – I eye the tampons with distaste – join them. When I'm done, Beth's things fit into two carrier bags. I pull out my mobile and call a cab.

It's night-time now. A light drizzle falls as I'm driven up the A420. Once I've exited the taxi in Kingswood, Beth's toiletries go straight in the nearest rubbish bin. Her clothes, along with the novels, are next for disposal. I wipe sweat and rain from my face, hauling myself across the road, the bag dangling from one finger as I manoeuvre the crutches. The Homeless Concern shop is my destination. It's fitting her stuff will end up back where she once volunteered, despite the sign asking people not to leave donations in the doorway. If a homeless person finds the clothes, well and good; they'll disappear below the radar that way. If they're still there by morning, the charity will wash them, ready for sale, removing her DNA.

When I'm done, exhaustion claims me. I'm tired and angry, not to mention cold and wet. Pain flares through my leg, reminding me that my medication is back at the cottage, possibly with the police as well. Opposite, The Royal Oak beckons. Screw everything. I need a drink.

***

A pint of Theakston XB, welcome yet unfamiliar, slides into my stomach. I'm a wine man by choice, but tonight I need something different. It's noisy in The Royal Oak, too crowded and stuffy after the quiet of the cottage, the sheer number of people overwhelming. It's good, though. Despite the cast on my leg, I'm just an ordinary guy who blends into the background, a man enjoying a pint the same as all the other customers.

I sip my beer, Beth's betrayal biting hard. She said she loved me. Yet she abandoned me as soon as she got the chance. Her, the rat. Me, the sinking ship. Bitch. My father was right to murder that woman all those years ago. I understand that now. Women aren't to be trusted.

I recall my warning to Beth a while back. *Her name was Julia. Twenty when I took her. And twenty when she died.*

When I find the treacherous cow, I'll bring her back to the basement; this time, she'll never leave. I intend to kill her. After I'm done, I'll seal her body up in there, to keep company with the corpse the other side of the wall.

'I love you.' The memory of her voice mocks me. In the image, my hands rise to her throat, squeezing, choking and her face transforms, her hair shortens, and I'm looking at the woman Dad strangled. In my brain, my fingers continue to press, until Beth or the other female, whoever it is, goes limp, her weight sagging against me.

I'm my father's son when it comes to murder, for sure. A fact he found out before he gasped his last breath.

In my head, I'm twenty-two again. Still living with the prick, unable to afford my own place, my hatred of him increasing daily. One day, after he'd been particularly obnoxious, something snapped inside me. My father's ill health, his worsening angina, along with the increasingly frequent asthma attacks, became my ally. My plan was simple, once I conceived the idea.

One Saturday afternoon, he settled on the sofa for his television football fix. 'Where's the bleeding remote?' he bellowed, his breath laboured.

I stood before him, legs wide and firmly planted, my grin cocky. All the years of kow-towing to him melted away, leaving me the proud possessor of the upper hand. I waved the remote in the air.

'Come and get it, you bastard.' The first time I'd ever challenged him.

My father's face darkened, his breathing harsher than ever. His eyes were in danger of popping clean from his head if they bulged any further.

'What the hell are you playing at?' He spat the words at me.

'They'll be kicking off round about now,' I said. 'Bristol Rovers need to win to avoid relegation, don't they? Important match, this. You won't want to miss it.'

'Give me that fucking remote.' My father struggled to shift his bulk off the sofa. Once on his feet, he lunged toward my hand, but I evaded him with ease, one fluid movement placing me beyond his reach. He tried to speak, and the onset of asthma became evident, so strenuous were his efforts to drag air into his lungs. Into passageways that were steadily narrowing.

'Come and get it, dick-head.' I didn't need to dodge him this time. It was plain he wouldn't be moving far, except to retrieve his asthma inhaler. Right now, it was in the front pocket of my jeans.

He turned towards the coffee table, where he expected it to be, only to find it gone. Panic rendered his breathing even more laboured. Sweat ran down his cheeks. His hands checked his trouser pockets, urgent, questing. The rattle from his airways grew louder. He glanced at me then, and my fingers, hooked into my waistband, drummed a tell-tale beat against the inhaler. A sweet moment, the instant understanding bloomed in his mottled face. When my father realised I intended to kill him.

Strangled noises issued from his throat. I pictured it, swelling, closing over, as the sounds grew ever more panicked. His face had never been redder. Or more ugly. I watched, fascinated, as my father crumpled to the floor, clutching his chest.

He didn't take long to die. Without his inhaler, the prick was doomed. I savoured every second as he choked to death before me, vanquished at last. Eight years on, the memory's as compelling as ever.

Once he was dead, I called 999, playing the panic-stricken son, the one who didn't hear his father's dying struggles because he was upstairs, listening to music through his headphones. I placed the inhaler under the sofa, out of sight.

'Must have fallen there, got kicked out of the way,' I told the paramedics, fake grief in my voice, after they arrived. I played my part so well; everyone believed me to be a distraught son. Given Dad's medical history, his death was declared a natural one, no suspicious circumstances. I was free of the bastard at last.

***

Back at The Royal Oak, I return to reality to discover last orders sounded ten minutes ago. Time to leave, take a taxi home, get my head straight in case the police are waiting for me.

Thank God, the cottage is deserted when I arrive. Once inside, I decide to brave getting to my bedroom on crutches. It's late, I'm exhausted, and I need to sleep in my own bed, not the sofa. After I've successfully managed the stairs, I pause on the landing, my thoughts with Beth. She's either not told anyone or else is taking her time in doing so. Or the police are sceptical of her story. Good options, and in my favour. I've done as much as I can to shield myself against the bitch.

No, I haven't. As my eyes fall on the contents of my spare room, I spot the suitcase on the floor. And remember its contents.

Difficult to explain, if the police come knocking.

They'll need a warrant to search the cottage. Whether Beth's statement will be sufficient to enable them to obtain one, I've no idea. The contents of the suitcase need burning or burying, but I'm reluctant to do so. They're significant in making me the man I am today. I can't get rid of them. Same reason I kept the other basement blocked up. If the police search the cottage and open the suitcase, though, they'll discover evidence of the murder my father committed. In it are the woman's possessions, taken by him as trophies. After I killed the bastard, I bundled up his stuff, shoved it in the spare room, the boxes long overlooked and forgotten along with the suitcase.

I should be safe, though. If the police question me, they'll find I was a school kid at the time, away camping when the woman disappeared. Once they find her body in the second basement, Dad will cop the blame for her death, albeit posthumously. Sweet pleasure fills me in contemplating the prick being fingered for murder after so long. 'Nothing to do with me,' I'll say, if the police open the suitcase. 'Everything in that room belonged to my father.'

My shoulders relax, the tightness in my chest loosens. Whatever happens, I'll deal with it.

'I'm coming for you, Beth,' I say. 'As soon as my leg heals. And when I do, you're dead. You can count on it.'

PART TWO
Present Day

CHAPTER 16 – *Ursula*

My hands swoosh the duster over the lounge furniture, my mind occupied with my daughter, as always. Cleaning is a ritual I perform daily: vacuuming, polishing, wiping throughout the house, surprising my former self, the woman who once scorned housework. Now the routine of swish and swipe helps keep me sane until my husband and son return home.

Tears prick my eyes, and I slump in an armchair, unsure whether my legs will support me for much longer. The pain of Beth's disappearance is as sharp as it's ever been and I don't kid myself it'll get better.

I reach towards the sideboard, my hands grasping the silver photo frame, a present from Beth the Christmas before she disappeared. In the picture, my daughter laughs into the camera, her dark hair blowing around her face. Her eyes are squinting against the late afternoon sun, giving no hint of their soft mocha hue. She's in our back garden, barbeque tongs in her hand, smoke rising from the grill in front of her. Happier times, before she vanished from our lives.

Since then I've split my life into two parts, before and after, making Beth's disappearance the equivalent of BC and AD in my head. Not that I've ever been religious. Any leanings in that direction have been extinguished by a loathing for a God capable of snatching my daughter from me. Beth's my firstborn, the child I've always loved the most, not that a mother is supposed to admit such things. She's always been my darling, the one I've fretted over. The spectre of her faddy eating phase during her teenage years, when I had to coax her at every meal, gnaws at my mind.

My husband never mentions our girl anymore. When I do, he dispenses well-meaning advice, its subtext being how I should move on, as though my emotions have stalled at a green light. 'We need to face facts, Ursula,' he tells me, his tone patronising. 'The statistics show...' I suppress the urge to tell him to shove his damn statistics up his arse.

Oh, Chris isn't a bad man. It's just that, to him, emotions exist to be controlled, not expressed. He believes our daughter is dead; it's what he means by quoting 'the statistics'. For someone who's been missing as long as Beth has, the odds of her being alive aren't good. I know the figures by heart. I visit the Missing People website daily, often hourly, scouring the reported sightings page. I'm one of the most prolific posters in the forums, seeking reassurance from parents more fortunate than we've been, ones who've had their children restored to them.

I remember a fight Chris and I had, a couple of weeks after Beth vanished. We were in our kitchen; I was unloading the dishwasher, handing plates to him.

'She'll come home,' I told him. 'She's taking time out, that's all. You shouldn't have pushed her so hard about going to university.'

My husband's hand stopped in mid-air, frustration rolling off him in waves. 'Christ Almighty, Ursula! Beth's disappearing act is *my* fault now?'

Yes, I replied inside my head. You were always on her case. *Why haven't you filled in those university applications, Beth? Why don't you get a proper job instead of volunteering for that charity? You can't mooch around forever.* Every time he started on her, I'd see a hunted look creep into her eyes. Leave her alone, for God's sake, I'd tell him later when we were in bed. Give her room to breathe. She's only just finished school.

Anyway, that time in the kitchen, the desperation of the last two weeks boiled into one volcanic outburst of frustration. I whipped round and smacked the plate against Chris's head, his goddamn head, and the delicate bone china shattered with an almighty crack. His mouth sagged open with disbelief as I slumped onto the floor, hot tears on my cheeks. Nothing he could say pacified me; we hurled accusations like daggers at each other, batting insults back and forth across the dishwasher.

So every time Chris drags up those damn statistics, I want to yell at him the fact that'll hurt the most. That thirty per cent of adults who go missing do so because of family issues. Beth, eighteen when I last saw her, is classed as a missing adult, even though I find it impossible to think of her other than as my baby girl, my firstborn. Family issues, I snarl at him in my head. You piled too much pressure on her. That's why she left.

I'll forgive her anything, if she comes back. I won't believe my daughter is dead. She's out there somewhere. When she's ready, she'll call me, return home, end my time in limbo.

The alternative is unthinkable.

***

I hear voices at the front door, a key in the lock. Chris and Troy are home. I walk into the hall to greet them, duster in hand.

My son pushes past me to hang up his school blazer. One hand shoves his untidy fringe out of his eyes. At sixteen, he's prone to teenage sullenness, and he's tired, no doubt, after a long day of calculus and chemistry. Beth and Troy were never close; he always regarded her as intellectual bindweed, her brains a challenge to his preference for football, and I acknowledge with a pang that my son, fourteen at the time of Beth's disappearance, has blossomed since then in a way that can't be explained by maturation alone.

Chris gives me his customary peck on my right cheek, his eyes not meeting mine. 'Had many students today?' he enquires. My husband has always regarded my part-time language tutoring as a hobby job, reinforcing his disinterest when he doesn't wait for my reply.

'Saw Troy at the bus stop. Gave him a lift home.' He sniffs the air, failing to detect any cooking aromas. 'What are we eating tonight? I fancy bangers and mash.'

'Coming right up.' I head for the kitchen as Chris and Troy chatter away in the lounge, their voices loud. I tune them out as I extract sausages and peas from the freezer. Then I peel potatoes and set water to boil. My thoughts steer back to Beth. The day she disappeared. I replay her voice in my head, as she tells me she's going out.

'Won't be back tonight, Mum. Going to stay with a friend.' Her eyes didn't meet mine as she said the words. Distracted at the time by worries over my business, I failed to detect the obvious lie. Why didn't I pick up on the fact she planned to spend the night with a boyfriend? Press her for details? Find out where she'd be?

Instead, conscious of not wanting to pressurise her the way Chris did, I hugged my daughter. Unaware I wouldn't hold her in my arms again for another two years.

***

The day after Beth's disappearance, still unknown to me at that point, I was up early to spend the day with Donna. We'd planned shopping and lunch at Cabot Circus. After her divorce, we'd grown even closer, seeing each other several times a week. She's the sister I never had. Once there were three of us – me, Donna and Anna – locked in a friendship so solid our husbands referred to us as Macbeth's witches. We often talked of Anna when we were together, sadness winding through our voices like a maggot in our friendship's apple.

So I met Donna in town, and we had lunch, we chatted and then at four o'clock I went home, expecting to see Beth; for her to enquire about Donna, how my day had been, and I'd show her the new jacket I'd bought. My mood was light, buoyant, as I arrived home. I walked into the lounge to find Chris and Troy sprawled on the twin sofas, their eyes on the TV sports channel.

'Where's Beth?' I asked. I was met with shrugs.

I tried again. 'When did she get home?'

'Not seen her today.' Chris addressed Troy. 'Is Beth in her room?'
Troy shrugged again. 'Dunno.'

Eager to show her the jacket, I climbed the stairs and knocked
on her bedroom door. When there was no reply, I turned the
knob and entered. She wasn't there. No sign of her pink duffel
bag either. The first icy fingers of worry tugged at my stomach.

I checked my mobile. Nothing from Beth. Fear now had every
inch of me in its clutches. I left frantic messages for her. When
she didn't respond, I got on the phone. Jake Wilding, Anna's son
and long-time friend of Beth, hadn't heard from her. Neither had
anyone else.

It was mid-evening before I persuaded Chris we needed to
phone the police.

***

After the police got involved, everything blurred in my world. As
an adult, her disappearance ranked as less worrying than that of a
child, or an Alzheimer patient. I explained that she'd never done
anything like this before, we'd always been so close, she always
called me if she was going to be late, and no, there weren't any
problems at home, not major ones anyway. I became aware of
my voice rising into hysteria, of how Chris was stifling the urge
to say that Beth had been rather - how could he put it? - difficult
recently.

'Did she have a boyfriend, Mrs Sutton? Anyone other than a
friend she might have stayed with?' the investigating officer asked.

Maternal protectiveness boiled in me, anger at what I saw as
delay in finding my daughter forcing me into uncharacteristic
terseness.

'No,' I snapped. The memory of Beth's evasiveness the previous
night stabbed me with guilt. Why didn't I twig she was lying?
How come I didn't confront her?

'Ursula.' Chris laid a hand on my thigh, in a gesture meant
to reassure but instead patronised. 'The police are just doing their
job.'

I ignored my husband. I fixed my gaze on the officer, whose face betrayed he'd seen the worst of human nature. 'Find her,' I hissed. 'Get my daughter back.'

***

He didn't, though. Beth remained missing. Frustrated with the lack of progress, I obsessed over the Missing People website, devouring every one of Chris's beloved statistics. Three hundred thousand missing persons reports were filed each year in the UK; my daughter had been sucked into a morass of unexplained disappearances, her face joining the other photographs of absent people, her details filed in the charity's database. Jake Wilding organised Twitter and Facebook campaigns to find Beth; they produced nothing but dead ends. As for Troy, my son retreated into a shell of teenage silence. Me, I haunted the charity's helpline, sobbing my grief and frustration into the ear of whoever answered; my distress was a tidal wave that any second might hurl me into oblivion. Was it this way for Marcus Wilding, I wondered, after Anna disappeared? The statistics flooded over me again; eleven per cent of missing people vanished through mental health issues. Depression had stalked Anna for years before she walked out on her life. Somehow, I doubted Marcus suffered too much, unlike his son Jake. Anna's husband is a cold fish, my friend's marriage a constant source of unhappiness to her back then.

This is different, I told myself. Beth may have had her issues, sure. Who doesn't? She wasn't depressed, though. My daughter will come back. She has to.

Chris and I descended into a maelstrom of arguments, our marriage, previously rock-solid, cracking under the strain. At night, we pulled ourselves to opposite sides of our bed, him afraid my despair was contagious, me furious at his emotional constipation. In a replay of the dishwasher incident, during one row I accused him of driving our daughter away.

'She didn't want to be a bloody paediatrician, for God's sake. OK, so she said she wanted to work with kids. Next thing she knew, you had her pegged to head up a children's cancer unit.'

'Is that so wrong? To want the best for her?' Chris's tone was clipped.

'Couldn't you just let her be? No wonder she ran away.'

It was then my husband spoke the words that led to me moving into the spare bedroom the next day. I've slept there ever since.

'She's dead, Ursula.' My breath froze in my throat, my body stilled. I was incapable of reply.

The bed undulated as my husband turned to face my back, which I held rigid in silent accusation. His hand touched my shoulder, before I shrugged it off.

'You have to face facts. A few arguments over what she does at university aren't enough to make her leave home. Why has she never called, texted, emailed? God knows I don't want to say this, Ursula, but somebody got to our daughter. Somebody bad, I mean. She's dead. Has to be.' A crack in his voice betrayed the fact that despite his stick-up-the-arse attitude, Chris is a good father. Beth's disappearance has torn him up too, but unlike me, he bottles it inside.

I swung my feet out of bed, pulled on my dressing gown and walked out of our bedroom without a word.

***

Back in the present day, I mash potatoes, pour boiling water on gravy granules, slap two fat sausages onto each of our plates. I ladle peas alongside, and place the meals on the kitchen table. The air is heavy with meaty smells, and I'm sweating, perspiration dampening my forehead. My hair is impossible thanks to the steam. I push it off my face, smoothing my palms against my T-shirt.

'Food's ready,' I shout. The sofa springs squeak as my husband and son get up and lumber towards the kitchen. Chris and I have forged a truce over the past two years by ceasing most of our communication. Our marriage has been reduced to polite pleasantries over meals and conversations conducted through our son. When I focus on Troy, I can almost overlook the fourth chair at the table, the one that's been empty for too long.

So I'm unaware of how my day will soon be ripped from its roots, tossed into the air tornado-style. I eat, the sausages peppery in my mouth, the peas popping from their skins as I chew. I study my son. Troy, once past the awkwardness of puberty, will be a heart-stopper in the looks department. His skin is breaking free from acne and the tops of his arms strain against the fabric of his T-shirt. He joined a gym last month; I suspect a girl is involved somewhere.

I smile at the thought as I scrape the remains of my meal into the bin. Chris is loading his and Troy's plates into the dishwasher. My mind is on the evening ahead. I'm debating whether to watch television or carry on with the novel I'm reading, when the ding-dong of the doorbell cuts through my thoughts. Chris pauses in mid-stoop over the dishwasher.

'Not expecting anyone, are we?' he asks, irritation ploughing furrows into his brow. Not one for surprises, my husband. I shake my head.

'Another bloody salesman, I expect,' he mutters. 'Best ignored.'

Troy's already left the kitchen, his footsteps heavy as he goes upstairs. I slide my plate into the dishwasher, shove in my cutlery and top up the rinse aid. The ding-dong sounds again. Is it my imagination or does it sound more urgent?

Chris tut-tuts with annoyance.

'I'll get it,' I say.

I move towards the front door, still unaware of how these seconds, as my feet pad along the carpet, mark a defining moment in my life. I pull the chain from its hole, twist the latch and tug open the door.

A second later, my world shatters into pieces.

No, that's not correct. My life disintegrated two years ago; what happens now is that the bits fly upwards, glue themselves together, reuniting into one glorious whole, into something so wonderful, so momentous, that I'm rendered speechless.

Beth, my darling girl, the love of my life, stands before me.

She's put on weight, her skin is pasty-pale and her hair has lost its former sheen, but it's her all right, come home at last. Beth's eyes pierce my own, their soft brown depths veiled in tears. I'm frozen in time, drinking her in, but alarm bells shriek in my head. Her clothes, for one thing. They're weird; a large man's leather jacket hangs from her shoulders and my mind back-flips with concern as I take in the filthy soaked slippers under the jogging bottoms she's wearing. The cuts, fringed with blood, slashed into the fabric over her knees.

None of that matters though, not now.

I reach out and pull my daughter into my arms, where she slots as though she's never left.

'Beth,' I murmur against her hair. 'You've come home.'

CHAPTER 17 – *Beth*

Safe in my mother's arms, I'm positive I did the right thing in leaving the cottage. Dominic is still in my head – he always is – but for once I force him to the back of my skull, my mind focused on how good Mum smells. The familiar scent of Chanel promises to make everything better, the way it did when my five-year-old self fell off my bike. Relief sweeps through me, scouring away the last two years. I'd happily spend the rest of my life in Mum's embrace, but she pushes me gently away.

'Are you all right, my love?' she asks. Incapable of speech, I nod. It's enough, it seems. Her arm around me, she draws me inside my childhood home.

So familiar, yet different. The hall has been re-carpeted in pale mint. My mother's framed embroidery, riots of lazy-daisy stitches, still hangs on the wall. Pungent potato and sausage odours hit my nose as we move down the hallway; Mum's arm is tight around me, fierce and protective. We walk into the kitchen.

My eyes meet my father's. Shock, disbelief, and then delight cross his face. Dad loves me. He's a good man. It's just that he always expects so much of me.

'Beth!' My name explodes from his lips as Mum releases me, allowing Dad to crush me to his chest. The lub-dub of his heartbeat thrums in my ear as his shirt rubs my cheek; I bask in the moment. Behind us, Mum's calling up the stairs, her voice loud, urgent. 'Troy! Can you come down here, please? Now.'

Dad lets go of me, holding me at arm's length, his gaze penetrating. He's aged, I realise. The fleshy padding around his neck has thickened. His hair's more grey than dark now, the lines in his forehead deep grooves. More red veins in his cheeks, across his nose, through the whites of his eyes. He appears closer to sixty than fifty-two. It's a shock.

'Beth,' he says. 'Where have you been? Why didn't you—' At that, Mum steps in, literally, between Dad and me.

'Not now, Chris. Can't you see she's exhausted? Soaked to the skin? Darling, can I get you something to eat?'

I nod, hunger by now a wild beast in my stomach. I sit at the table, shrugging off Dominic's jacket, draping it over the back of my chair. My father watches as Mum butters bread, piles on slices of ham, spreads pickle and salad on top. Her hands draw a knife through the finished sandwich, neatly bisecting it into two triangles.

'It's wonderful you're home, sweetheart.' My father sits down opposite me. 'We've been so worried—'

'I've already told you. Leave her be.' Mum places my food in front of me, and I seize it, stuffing a corner of the sandwich into my mouth. As I raise my hands, I realise she's staring at my wrists, her expression shuttered. The bruises Dominic put there yesterday are in full bloom now, angry welts of blue and purple circling them in livid bracelets. My mind runs through possible explanations, none of them plausible. Because Mum will ask, of course she will. Not with Dad here. She'll wait until we're alone. Pain slaps me hard at the thought of lying to her.

Footsteps sound on the stairs, then in the hallway. My brother walks into the kitchen. For an instant, shock renders his face a mask. I take in how tall he's grown, how his hair's longer now, his frame more solid. He stares at me, this brother of mine, as shock morphs into something else – what, I'm not sure, but for a second, guilt lurks in his eyes.

'Look, Troy! Your sister's back. Safe and home at last. Isn't that the best thing ever?' Delight overflows from Mum's voice.

Troy's gaze flickers between her and me. 'I guess.' He hovers in the doorway, uncertainty in his face. Then he comes forward and squeezes me in an awkward hug, his eyes not meeting mine as he steps back afterwards. 'Thank fuck you're safe,' he mutters, so low only I can hear.

Dad clears his throat. 'We need to know what happened, Beth. Why you never got in touch – not once – in two years.'

Mum rounds on my father. 'Plenty of time for questions later,' she tells him. 'Beth's cold, and she's soaked, in need of a bath and clean clothes. Can you at least allow her that?' An edge exists in her tone towards Dad I don't remember hearing before. I wonder how much things have changed in my absence.

I finish the sandwich, pushing the plate away. 'I'd love a bath.' The need for hot, soothing water in which to soak my sore feet has grown imperative. Mum nods. I hug her briefly before hurrying upstairs, pushing past Troy. Behind me, I hear my father's voice, although I can't distinguish the words.

I walk across the landing towards my old bedroom. I pause with my hand on the brass knob, before I step back in time two years. Inside, nothing's changed. My swimming certificates still line the walls. My childhood teddy bear gazes at me from my bed. The air holds the scent of lemons, and I realise the room's uncharacteristically clean. Mum, of course. My heart squeezes at how she's kept everything ready for my return. In my trouser pocket, my fingers turn over Amy's tiny silver boot, before depositing it in the top drawer of my bedside cabinet. Then I rummage under my pillows, locating my pyjamas in their customary spot. I grab my dressing gown, achingly familiar from before, from its peg. Into the bathroom I go.

Once the bath is full, I sink into the foam, the heat soaking the pain from my feet. I can make out the occasional word from downstairs. My father's voice, always louder than Mum's, his tone curt. 'Demand answers... make her tell us...' I tune him out, sliding further into the strawberry-scented womb of the bath.

Dominic reigns supreme in my head again, now Mum's not around to oust him. Panic grips my throat, my chest, my stomach. Is he alive or dead? Something bad has happened, for sure. He'd never abandon me, or desert the cottage, so abruptly otherwise.

My dilemma is this. What do I tell my parents? The truth isn't an option. They'll insist on the police being told and if Dominic's in trouble, if he's hurt, I can't bear to think of him being arrested thanks to my betrayal. Besides, bringing a court case against him will destroy me. I'm reminded of the TV dramas I've seen, in which vulnerable women get torn to shreds in the witness box by sharp-tongued lawyers. My options condense into one. I'll lie; say I've been staying with friends. It's weak, and doesn't explain why I never got in touch, but its simplicity suits me. I'm too mentally washed-up to fabricate a complex lie. Mum will be hurt, but it's better she thinks me selfish and uncaring than she discovers the truth.

***

Eventually I haul myself from the sanctuary of my bath. I'll have to face the inquisition below sometime; it may as well be now. I towel myself off, before climbing into the pyjamas, loose enough to still fit me despite the extra kilos I've gained. I belt the dressing gown around my body, then go downstairs, walking towards the kitchen. Through the open doorway to the lounge, I see Troy draped over an armchair, his legs dangling, his fingers tapping his mobile. He doesn't glance up, but he's aware of me. Why doesn't he speak, say something? Earlier, in his awkward adolescent way, he seemed glad to see me. Now he's ignoring me. Well, two can play at that game. I head into the kitchen. My parents are still sitting at the table.

'Can I get another sandwich, Mum?'

'I'll make it.' But my mother doesn't move towards the bread bin. Instead, she pulls me into her arms, her hug so tight I can barely breathe. Sobs rack her chest as she holds me close.

'My darling Beth.' Her words are muffled against my hair. 'I always hoped... always believed you'd come back one day. And now you have.'

Dad comes to stand behind me, his hands on my shoulders. Mum's clearly hammered home the point to lay off me tonight. 'Welcome home, sweetheart,' he says. 'We've missed you so much.'

***

I don't sleep well that night, Dominic on my mind throughout the long hours. Besides, my mattress is too soft, too comfortable; I'm used to the hard, thin Z-bed in the basement. I toss around, desperate for oblivion, but sleep proves elusive, even though tiredness infuses every cell of my body.

As I lie awake, I notice something weird. When Mum comes up to bed, I hear her footsteps go into the spare room at the end of the landing. Not into the master bedroom next to mine, where she's always slept with Dad.

Once morning comes, I sneak in after she's gone downstairs for breakfast. Everything indicates Mum sleeps here permanently. Her clothes are in the wardrobe, her hairbrush and toiletries on the dressing table. Books and an alarm clock are on the bedside chest of drawers. This room is very much occupied, I realise. At what stage in the last two years did my parents' marriage began to unravel? Guilt pricks me. Was my disappearance the catalyst?

I pad down to breakfast, still in my dressing gown, conscious I'll need new clothes. Nothing in my wardrobe fits anymore. Mum and Dad are at the kitchen table; Troy's nowhere in sight. Dad's shovelling scrambled eggs into his mouth, a small fleck of yolk nestling on his upper lip. Mum cradles a mug between her hands, a slice of toast half-eaten on her plate.

My mother sets down her coffee, coming to hug me. My nose is against her hair, the apple scent of her shampoo drifting into my nostrils. 'Sleep well?' she asks.

'Like a log,' I lie. I'm conscious Dad hasn't spoken to me yet. He's always been a loving father; I don't doubt he's overjoyed at having his little girl home. But he's angry too, and I can hardly blame him. Nervous, my teeth chewing at my lower lip, I glance at him as I extract myself from Mum's arms. He meets my eyes, but doesn't smile.

I gesture towards his scrambled eggs. 'Can I get some of those?'

'For God's sake, Beth.' The annoyance in my father's voice slaps me hard. He stands up, clearly dredging up his self-control before continuing. 'You waltz in here, without having phoned, texted, emailed, anything at all to reassure us you weren't lying dead in a ditch, and you demand bloody scrambled eggs? Don't you think you owe us an explanation?'

Mum steps between Dad and me, breaking the tension. 'Don't, Chris. Please.'

Dad steps away, the anger draining from his face. 'You're right. I'm sorry, Beth. I didn't mean to lay into you like that. But we do need to talk.'

'Let me handle this.' Mum's hands press on my shoulders, pushing me into the nearest chair, before sitting down herself. I lean my arms on the table, forcing myself to regain control. 'Darling, you need to tell us where you've been, why you never got in touch. We won't be angry, I promise. We're all delighted you're home, that you're safe. But Dad's right. We're your family. We have a right to know. Please, Beth. Please tell me.' Her eyes, the edges more deeply creased than I remember, never leave mine. I swallow hard. Here it comes. The moment when I disappoint the woman I love so much.

Impossible to do. I break eye contact, my gaze falling on my hands, the nails of which pick at each other. 'I can't tell you,' I say.

My father's anger explodes from him, his self-control clearly exhausted.

'Did you run off with some boy? Been shacked up with a guy? Is that what happened?' Has he always shouted so loudly? Unknowingly, he's hit the bullseye. I shake my head, unable to look at him. My nails gouge deeper into the skin of my left thumb.

Mum leans across the table, her eyes pleading. 'Please tell us, Beth,' she says, and the entreaty in her voice twists my heart. I burrow deep into my misery, as if it's my shell and I'm a tortoise. Her fingers reach up to stroke my hair.

Silence for a minute. I can do this, I tell myself. How ironic that I have to lie to protect the truth. I force the rock in my throat downwards as I address Dad. 'I stayed with a friend. In London.'

'And you didn't consider calling us? To tell us you were safe?'

'No.' I pick at my index finger. 'I meant to, but then...' I shrug. 'Time went on, and it got more difficult. I'm sorry. Not sure what else to say.' Weak, not an explanation at all, and right now, I'm glad I'm not looking at Mum. Better not to witness her disappointment.

'We called the police. You're officially listed as a missing person. Jake Wilding – he took it badly. After – well, you know. What happened with his mother. We – I, that is – believed you must be dead. So you see...' Dad's hands grasp mine, stalling my restless assault on my cuticles. The man who read me a bedtime story every night when I was a child is back. His anger's gone, at least for now. Like I said, he's a good father, one who only wants the best for me, even if he pushes too hard sometimes. 'You have to tell us where you've been.'

Images of a courtroom, of those sharp-tongued lawyers, swarm into my head. I stay silent.

'Why were you wearing slippers, Beth?' Mum asks.

When I don't reply, she tries again. 'You had no money with you. No purse, no handbag. Were you running away from someone? Did you leave in a hurry?'

My throat closes over again, but I manage to speak. 'I was with a friend. Really. She's at college in London.'

'What's her name?' Mistrust tinges my father's tone.

'Dominique.'

Exhaustion sweeps over me in one gigantic wave, my bedroom upstairs calling me, away from the questions, the anger, from my mother's inevitable disappointment.

'Can I go back to bed?' I ask.

'What about your breakfast? I'll make you scrambled eggs.' Mum takes bread from the bin, opens the fridge.

'Beth's not a child,' Dad growls. 'She can get her own breakfast.' Behind his gruff tone lurks relief I'm home, but he's too much for me to handle right now. With any luck, he'll be off soon to work, to the firm of surveyors he runs. As for Troy, he'll go to school, and Mum and I can be alone. Her language tutoring has never taken up much of her day and even though I'll have to carry on the lie I've started, I'll find a way to mitigate the hurt I've caused her.

Mum ignores my father, her hands whisking eggs. 'One or two pieces of toast?' she asks.

'Ursula.' Dad stands up, moving round to take the bowl from her. 'We need to be practical. Inform the police. As well as the Missing People charity.'

I'm puzzled. What does he mean?

Dad spots my confusion. 'They provide help when someone disappears. Your mother's constantly on their website. As for the police, we reported you missing straight away, of course we did. But you didn't want to be found, remember?' The anger is back in his voice. 'You were in London, or so you said. With this friend of yours, this Dominique, who up until yesterday none of us had ever heard of.'

Guilt stabs me hard, scoring a direct hit in my gut. I'm unable to look him in the eye. Instead, I swallow remorse, a bitter pill so early in the day. I'm bewildered as well. Once Troy provided a description of Dominic and the BMW, the police should have been able to track me down. Fury surges through me then, unreasonable, sure, but then I've spent two years locked in a basement. I'm entitled to resentment, even if my incarceration was due to my own stupidity. Between the police and the Missing People charity, I should have been found. Why wasn't I?

CHAPTER 18 – *Ursula*

In the end, it's left to me to contact both the police and the Missing People organisation. Chris storms from the kitchen, shouting how he's going to work, how I can damn well sort the whole ridiculous mess without him. His exit leaves Beth drained of colour, darkness haunting her eyes. The door slams behind Chris, leaving me with my daughter.

'I'm sorry, Mum.' Her words are a whisper, no more. My heart cracks open. Something bad has happened to my girl, I'm sure of it.

I won't press her, though. Beth's like a timid puppy right now; she needs time, coaxing, gentleness. Requirements Chris, with his anger, his impatience, his gruff masculinity, can't comprehend. She's home now; I'll love her, I'll cherish her, and one day she'll tell me the truth.

'You can borrow my clothes for now,' I tell her. 'They'll be big on you, but we'll go shopping for new ones.' I smile at her, but her strained expression doesn't ease.

'Don't make me go to the police, Mum.'

'I won't.'

'I can't face them. I'm sorry.'

'It's OK.' I'll drive into town this afternoon, talk to someone at the main Bridewell station. They'll send the family liaison officer to see Beth, but I'm guessing once they're certain she's home and well, all they'll do is update their database. One of Chris's beloved statistics resolved. When they come, it'll be just the two of us; no Chris, I'll make sure of that. As for Missing People, I'll contact them tomorrow.

'Go back to bed, love,' I say. 'I'll sort everything out.'

She doesn't move. Her gaze is fixed on the salt and pepper pots; two china cats, black for pepper, white for salt, a present from Anna Wilding years ago. They sit to Beth's left, next to the rack of toast she's not eaten. Something in her expression disturbs me.

Quick as a snakebite, her hands grab the two cats. She slams them in the centre of the table, her mouth a grim line of determination.

'Condiments go in the middle of the table!' The darkness behind her eyes freezes my core to ice. 'A place for everything and everything in its place!' She storms from the kitchen, leaving me dry-mouthed with shock.

***

It's five thirty, and Chris has arrived home from work. 'Sorry I lost my temper this morning,' he says, his lips pressing briefly against my cheek. 'Where is she?'

'Upstairs. In her room.'

Chris slumps onto the sofa. Tiredness hangs under his eyes; the lines scored down his face appear deeper than they did yesterday. He rubs his jaw, as if by doing so he can erase the tension between us.

'How is she?'

I tell him about the salt and pepper pots.

Chris merely shrugs. 'She was probably cranky, what with me going off at her the way I did.'

'I went to the police.'

'What did they say? Do they want to see Beth?'

'Yes. They'll send someone to the house.'

'We need to discover what happened, Ursula.'

'Leave her to me. I'll get it out of her. But she's fragile, Chris. She doesn't need you shouting at her.' Too late, I regret my words.

'Yeah, take her side, why don't you? Bloody typical. You've always been quick to make excuses for her.'

My hackles shoot upwards to match his. 'For God's sake! She's home, she's safe, she's…' I'm about to say she's well, before I remember she's far from being that. 'Don't you care?'

Chris's irritation deflates. 'Of course I do. I love our daughter. When she went missing, I was out of my mind with worry. It's only natural I'm keen to find out what happened. If Beth's in some kind of trouble, if she needs our help, then she'll get it. But we have to know what we're dealing with here. If she won't be honest with us, our hands are tied. You've been with her today. Has she said anything to you?'

'Not much. But I think Beth's been the victim of abuse.'

'That's ridiculous. What makes you say such a thing?'

'She was wearing slippers,' I reply. 'Slippers, Chris. Why not shoes? What about the man's jacket? Where was her handbag, her money?' He tries to butt in, but I forestall him. 'And don't forget the bruises. Didn't you see them? On her wrists.'

A huff of exasperation escapes my husband. 'Has she put you up to this? Made up this story to avoid explaining her whereabouts for the last two years?' Chris's voice rises higher, his tone louder; Beth will hear, and I have to protect her. Besides, I realise what lies behind my husband's seemingly unfeeling words: guilt. He'd prefer to label our daughter selfish and a liar, rather than entertain the idea of anyone hurting her. Chris can't bear to admit he failed as a father to protect her. I lay my hand on his arm, the gesture stemming his torrent of words.

'She stayed in her room most of the day. Told me she was tired.'

'Typical.'

'Don't be so hard on her. How do you explain the bruises?'

'An accident. She probably banged into something.'

'They look like someone's gripped her wrists. Tight enough to leave marks. What does that tell you?'

He shrugs. 'You tell me. Sounds like you've got it all figured out in your head.'

'You don't think it's weird that she's supposed to have been in London, and yet somehow she turns up here, with no money? How, exactly? I went through the pockets of that jacket, Chris.

When she went to the bathroom. No train or coach tickets. No cash, either.'

Another shrug. 'She probably used the last of her funds to buy a ticket. Then binned it when she got to Bristol.'

'How did she get from the bus or the train station to here? You're telling me she walked all the way? In slippers?'

Chris spreads his hands wide, defensively. 'She might still have had cash on her when she arrived. For a bus, taxi, whatever. Jesus, Ursula, I don't know. How the hell am I supposed to, if she won't be straight with us?'

'What about the jacket? It was a man's one. Why didn't she wear her own?'

My husband merely shakes his head.

'As well as the fact she never phoned, never called. Oh, I know what you think.' My voice rises higher. 'The great Chris Sutton, who's so wise, says she's young, selfish. But Beth and me, we've always been pretty solid. She'd have got in touch, if she could.' My throat cracks on the last syllable.

'Ursula.' Chris's tone is calm, measured. 'I love my daughter. I do. But I'm not blind to her faults, like you are.'

***

Six-thirty, and Troy's not back from school yet. I can't hold off serving up the evening meal any longer. We're having Thai green curry, not that Beth eats much of it. Her face is devoid of colour, her hair a mess, and her silence imbues the atmosphere with heaviness. One good thing, though: Chris has promised to lay off her, at least for tonight, and for now, he's holding true to his promise.

The black and white china cats sit plumb in the centre of the table. I've made very sure of that.

I plate up Troy's meal and stick it in the microwave. At that moment, I hear the front door open. Seconds later, my son breezes into the kitchen.

'You're late,' I say.

'Went round to a mate's. Lost track of time.'

The microwave dings. Troy sits at the table and I place his food in front of him. He digs in straight away, shovelling chicken into his mouth, rice falling from his lips.

'Isn't it wonderful your sister's home?' I ask him.

My son doesn't reply.

'Troy?'

He bites his lip, avoiding my gaze. 'Yeah, it's great.' His tone belies his words, though.

I frown, uncertain as to what's going on here. My children have never been close, sure, but I realise that since Beth's return, her brother has barely spoken to her. Not when I've been around, anyway. Even allowing for teenage sullenness, I can't account for his behaviour. Now's not the time to tackle him, though. I'm jaded from the argument with Chris and aware of the tension emanating from Beth across the table. Her gaze is on Troy as he scrapes the last of the green curry sauce from his plate. He blanks her completely.

'I saw Marcus Wilding today,' Chris says. 'Told him Beth's back. Which means Jake will know by now.'

Beth pushes her plate away. She chews the skin on her bottom lip. The mention of Jake Wilding has clearly unsettled her. They were always close. She ought to go and see him. I doubt she will, though, not yet. Too soon.

***

Next day, I'm sitting opposite Donna in The Bluebell Cafe, waiting for our orders to arrive. We've both plumped for salad, conscious of our thickening waistlines. Donna knows Beth's home. She's the first person I called, that same evening, while Beth was taking her bath. This woman, my friend for four decades, realises better than anyone how Beth's disappearance nearly destroyed me. Donna listened every time I needed her to; endless hours when I'd cry, rage, and pronounce there couldn't be a God, if my beloved daughter could be wrenched from me so abruptly.

So here she is, Donna Keating, her delight about Beth's return crinkling the skin around her eyes. Her hair is loose today, a maelstrom of copper curls cascading from her scalp and tickling her elbows as they rest on our table. True to her colouring, she's pale and freckled, but Donna's turned being a redhead into an art form. It's as though she's got in the way of a paintbrush when it's being flicked. Minuscule splodges of burnt umber dust her nose, her cheeks and her chin. I trace them with my eyes as they disappear into her cleavage. We've often swum together, taken saunas. There isn't an inch of my friend that isn't freckled.

'So,' Donna says. She sips her mineral water. 'Beth's home at last. I'm delighted for you, babe. Can't tell you how much.' Her hand squeezes mine across the table.

'It's a miracle come true, Donna. She's back. Home where she belongs.'

Our food arrives. Chicken salad for Donna, ham for me. I gather lettuce, cucumber and meat on my fork, uncertain of how to proceed. How best to air what's on my mind. I've been loath to leave my daughter to come here, but I need Donna's input, away from Beth's ears. She'll realise trouble is brewing in the Sutton household. Forty years of friendship have honed her instincts around me.

She eases her way in gently. 'How does she seem? You didn't say much on the phone.'

I bite my lip, setting down my fork. 'She's... she's strange. Withdrawn.'

'Did she say where she's been? Why she left?'

'Yes. But she's lying.'

'About what? All of it? Or just part of it?'

I shrug. I tell Donna the story of Beth's reappearance at our front door, the soaked slippers, the man's leather jacket, the way her eyes don't meet mine when she says she's been in London. I leave out the salt and pepper pots for now.

'She met with the police family liaison officer this morning,' I tell Donna. 'Spun her the same crap she did with us, about staying with a friend called Dominique. She seemed tense, on edge, relieved when the woman left. Why won't she tell the truth? I don't get it.'

Donna leans towards me, her salad as neglected as mine. 'Chances are she's embarrassed. Guilty at the way she upped and left, so she's on the defensive now she's back. Odds are she shacked up with a guy. Doesn't want to admit it to her father. I bet Chris hasn't been easy on her.'

'Is he ever?'

'The slippers are weird, though.'

I tell Donna about Beth's bruises, the finger-sized ones on her wrists.

'Have you asked her how she got them?'

'She wouldn't tell me the truth even if I did. I'm sure of that. Something's very wrong with her, Donna.' I push my plate away. 'Look, can we get out of here? I need some fresh air.'

We grab our jackets, settle the bill and head towards Castle Park. The breeze is a soft caress against my cheeks as we make for the wall overlooking the river. Beneath us, a lone canoeist paddles under Bristol Bridge. I perch on the cold stone, Donna next to me. Even though we're so close, right now I can't deal with eye contact, not when I need to give voice to the terror inside me.

I tell Donna about the salt and pepper pots. 'Thing is, I've noticed she's like it in other ways too. I caught her this morning, in the lounge, straightening all the photos on the windowsill. When she'd finished, they were all the same distance apart, all turned at an identical angle.'

I hear Donna blow out a breath beside me. I picture her expression: two vertical grooves parting the freckles on her forehead as her eyebrows lace together. Her hand squeezes mine.

'Talk to me, Donna. You know about this stuff.'

'Babe, that was years ago. Before my divorce.' The trauma of her marriage breakdown led to her abandoning her master's degree in psychotherapy.

'Even so. You've studied these things.'

'It's hard to say without knowing more. The obsession with neatness, though – it's a coping mechanism. People create order in their physical surroundings because they lack it emotionally.'

'I'm concerned she may have been with someone abusive, Donna.'

'Because of the bruises?'

'Yes. Not to mention the slippers, the lack of money. She left somewhere in a rush. Maybe she was running away.' My stomach tightens at the thought of Beth being hurt.

'Could be. But you'll have to let her tell you in her own time, when she's ready. Don't push her, or else she might take off again.'

'You're right. She's so withdrawn, though. Hasn't contacted any of her friends, not even Jake. Spends a lot of time in her room. I've got her back in body, but not in spirit.'

'She may be scared as hell, remember. If she's run away from an abusive relationship, that is. Like I say, give her space. You two were always close. She'll talk to you, in time.'

'I'd want to kill anyone who's hurt her.' Fury spikes my voice with venom.

'You're her mother. That's natural. But, Ursula…'

'What?'

'It may not be the same for Beth.'

'What do you mean?'

Donna's silent for a while, clearly measuring her answer. When it comes, it shocks me. 'She may have feelings for whoever's abused her. Even though she's managed to break free from him.'

I don't reply. My brain can't compute how Beth – or anyone – can care about someone who's violent towards them. My mind pictures her delicate wrists, bruising under a man's cruel hands, and I wince.

'It happens, Ursula. Explains why battered women stay with brutal men. It's not just the terror keeping them where they are.'

'I don't get it.'

'These men, they're not aggressive all the time. Afterwards, they plead remorse. Ask for forgiveness, although they've just beaten their partner black and blue. They swear they'll change. Claim it'll never happen again. The women believe them.'

'Why? I still don't understand.'

'Violence mixed with pseudo-loving behaviour is a potent and dangerous combination. Like a drug. Keeps the woman hooked, in the hope the loving part will win out.'

I stand up. 'I wish Anna was here.'

***

I arrive home. It's too early to start preparing tonight's stir-fry. Caffeine first, and then I'll be able to think. Process what Donna told me, square it up with the livid marks on my daughter's wrists. Did Beth leave home for a guy, fancying herself in love? Say she did. Life's peachy at first. Then things turn sour. She tries to leave, lover boy turns violent, hits her for the first time. The next day, he cries as he looks at her blackened eye, then swears it'll never happen again. Beth believes him. After all, she's burned her boats; pride forbids her to up and leave, crawl home chastened and repentant. So she stays.

The next time, the man changes tack. She provoked him. It's her fault he hit her. And so, in my head, Beth turns into a statistic of a different sort from those on the Missing People website. Now she's a battered woman, a victim of domestic abuse. What led to her breaking free doesn't figure in my mental scenario. One day she'll tell me.

The memory of her the last time I saw her, her dress, the kohl-rimmed eyes, her new jacket, pierces me though. So young, so vulnerable, clueless as to how the wrong man might suck up those come-hither vibes oozing from every pore. Marking my Beth as a possible punch bag.

What I said to Donna, about wanting to kill anyone who hurt her, is true. Chris's words, that Beth may have fallen victim to an opportunist killer, gnawed away at me, however much I wanted to reject them. While she was gone, I'd imagined myself the avenging angel, hunting her murderer. When I found him, he died in a variety of ways, some protracted and painful, others swift and satisfying.

What I'd do in reality is another matter. I've never been able to answer the question – would I kill for Beth?

CHAPTER 19 – *Beth*

When I surface for breakfast the next day, Mum tells me Jake Wilding's phoned.

Guilt swamps me because I've not contacted him yet. 'How did he sound?'

Mum shrugs. 'He's not angry, if that's what's bothering you. Just wants to catch up.'

'I'll call him.' I head into the hallway, making for the landline. I've not got a mobile anymore and a limit exists to how much I can ask Mum to buy for me. God knows what Dominic did with mine. Without it, I don't have Jake's number. Instead, I reach for Mum's old-fashioned book, flipping through to the W's. Marcus and Anna Wilding, the 'and Anna' long ago scored through in black biro.

'It's me,' I say when Jake answers the phone. The silence stretches between us before he speaks again.

'Beth.' A wealth of emotion in his voice.

'I'm back.' Such a stupid thing to say.

'Yeah. Dad told me.' A pause. 'You OK?'

'Can I come over?' I need to see him. The two of us go back forever; we were best mates before my disappearance. I'm not ready for the third degree from him, though. If I can't tell Mum about Dominic, I sure as hell won't be telling Jake.

We arrange that I'll go to his house tomorrow afternoon, once he's finished work. Seems he's now a personal trainer at a local gym. No surprise there; he always was a fitness fanatic.

The next day, I'm strangely nervous as I ring the doorbell. The door opens, and Jake stands before me. 'Hi, Beth,' he says, his expression uncertain.

It's Jake, and yet it's not. Two years, plus the job at the gym, have bulked out his frame. His biceps strain against his sweatshirt. What strikes me most is the stubble; a bristly darkness stains his chin and upper lip. A man has replaced the boy I once knew. Other than that, he's more or less the same. Dark hair, as wayward as Mum's, his fringe falling in his eyes. His eyes, aquamarine chips set either side of a ski-slope nose, survey me. I'm uncomfortably aware of the extra kilos I've gained.

Jake smiles at last. 'It's good to see you, Beth.' He steps forward to hug me and our bodies meet, awkward and tense. So much has happened since we last met, and it's like embracing a stranger.

He stands aside to let me enter, and I make for the lounge, the house already familiar from countless previous visits.

'Dad won't be home from work for a while,' he says. 'Thank God.' Jake has long since labelled his father a prick. I'm inclined to agree, despite the lustful thoughts I used to entertain about Marcus Wilding.

'You've not thought about moving out?' I ask.

'All the time. I only live here because I can't afford my own place. Soon, though.'

We sit on the sofa, the atmosphere strangely formal, strained by our two-year hiatus.

Jake clears his throat. 'Am I allowed to ask where you've been?'

'No. I can't go there, Jake. I'm sorry.'

'OK. If that's how you want to play things.'

'It is.' Time to turn the conversation. 'What are you up to? Besides the personal training?' My voice is too shrill, too full of false gaiety, in my effort to lighten the mood.

Jake shrugs. 'This and that.' He gestures towards the windowsill. 'As you can see.'

Arrayed before me are various photographs, shot in close-up, their colours rich and gorgeous. I pick up the closest one. A flower. The brilliant blue hues, the silky sheen of the outer petals as they burst forth from the purple centre, the thick spider-like stamens, entrance me.

'What is it?'

'A cornflower.' He's embarrassed, and I'm guessing it's because photographing the inner life of plants is at odds with the sports-mad Jake I used to know. 'Micro-photography, it's called. Been doing it for a while now. You can imagine what Dad has to say about it.'

I can. Marcus Wilding's relationship with Jake mirrors in many ways mine with my father, although Chris Sutton's a far better man. The two of them go way back, bonded over Rotary Club meetings and rounds of golf. Jake's father, ever Mr Macho Man, won't have taken well to his son's penchant for flowers.

I set the photo on the windowsill. As I do, I catch sight of one that's familiar from my visits over the years. Anna Wilding, Jake's mother, whose mental health problems led her to walk out on her life, leaving her son to be raised by a succession of nannies. Her disappearance has always been a raw wound for him.

Jake catches me eyeing her picture. 'I'll make coffee,' he announces.

***

As Jake busies himself in the kitchen, I pick up the photo. Anna Wilding, Mum's childhood friend, stares back at me. I don't remember her; aged four at the time she left, I was more concerned with dolls than with Mum's friends. I trace my fingers over the glass, following the curve of Anna's hair as it sweeps over her shoulders, falling to her waist in a thick cascade. Physically, we're alike, Anna's dark eyes mirroring mine, as do her full lips. She'd be in her early fifties now, her luxuriant hair streaked with grey, her ripe mouth thinning with age. I remind myself Anna Wilding is almost certainly dead, however much Jake might wish otherwise.

My thoughts turn to Jake's father. Marcus Wilding was often there when I spent time with Jake before my disappearance. I'd stare at him, observing what good shape he was in for a man in his fifties, his hair still thick, his nose lacking the spider veins scribbled across that of my father. Once or twice, I caught his eyes straying in my direction, their expression holding something feral, but he never acted on it. How weird would that have been, anyway? Jake and I have been mates since primary school. Shagging his father might have crossed my mind, but as for doing it? No way.

Jake lumbers in, clutching two mugs of coffee. 'Milk, one sugar. I remembered.' Pride laces his voice.

'I don't—' I stop myself. Dominic never allowed me coffee at the cottage; he only ever drank tea. 'Thanks.' The aroma of freshly perked java hits my nostrils as I imagine cocaine might, and I recall how particular both Jake and Marcus are over coffee.

Jake sets my mug in front of me, eyeing the photograph I'm still clutching. He sits beside me, and a waft of aftershave joins the java in my nostrils. Something else that's new.

He takes the photo from my hands, and his expression tells me the hurt of Anna's departure is as painful as ever. Jake has always been obsessive where his mother's concerned; I remind myself to tread carefully.

'When you disappeared, it stirred it all up for me again. Mum leaving, I mean.' His eyes are fixed on Anna's face.

'I'm sorry.' More than he'll ever know.

'Still no news of her,' he says, his voice flat.

I'm silent, unsure how to respond.

'I don't remember much about her,' he says. 'I was only four when she left. But I know she loved me.'

'Mum's always said how much Anna adored you.'

'She'll come back.' I stare at Jake. He can't believe that, not seriously. Anna Wilding is surely dead, either by her own hand or from a life lived rough on the streets.

'You did, Beth. She might, too.'

'That's different.' The words are out before I can suppress them. I pray his absorption in his mother will prevent him from probing the distinctions.

Jake sets the photo back on the windowsill. 'There's no evidence to suggest she's dead.'

Only common sense, I think, but don't say.

'No suicide note. She was depressed, her brain chemicals out of sync. She'd never have abandoned me otherwise.'

I'm at a loss how to respond. Jake's hair is flopping in his eyes, as usual; he pushes it aside impatiently. 'You don't agree.'

I choose my words carefully. 'She's been gone a long time, Jake.'

'She loved me. Dad might have written her off, wiped her out of his life, but I won't. I can't.' For a second, the four-year-old Jake is sitting beside me, a world of hurt in his voice.

'Surely she'd have called. At least once.' Too late, I realise my mistake.

Fury flies into Jake's eyes. 'You didn't.'

I'm incapable of replying. I turn aside. Jake won't have it. He grasps my arms, forcing me to face him again.

'Not once, Beth. No phone calls, no emails, in two years. You got any idea what your mother went through? I thought you two were close. Obviously not.' Contempt joins the anger in his voice. 'You selfish bitch.'

Shock hits me, hard, as well as hurt. Jake's never spoken so harshly to me before.

At that moment, the sound of a key being turned in the front door reaches my ears. Jake's father is home.

***

Marcus Wilding is still a good-looking guy. He's kept himself in shape, his belly flat, not straining against the waistband of his trousers like Dad's does. Pale blue eyes, chilly as an ice-block. Sandy hair, more pepper and salt than I remember. Still thick, though. The old tug of attraction returns, before I suppress it.

He's surprised to see me, I can tell, and his eyes widen a fraction, his body stopping in mid-stride as he enters the room. Nobody speaks. His gaze sweeps over me as I stand up.

'Hi, Mr Wilding,' I say. To my ears, my voice sounds gauche, like the schoolgirl he must remember.

I've put on weight and my hair's longer now. What must he see as his eyes appraise me, his expression a mask? I remember the way he used to glance at me before, and my cheeks flush with heat.

'Beth.' His voice is deep, direct, self-assurance in every syllable. 'Your father told me you were back.' Do I detect censure in his tone? Perhaps. Marcus Wilding can be, as Jake puts it, a prick at times, and with that comes the tendency to judge.

'Jake and I were just catching up.'

Marcus's nod is curt. 'Any coffee left?' He stalks from the room without waiting for a reply, leaving an invisible fingerprint of his presence. Compared to his father, Jake appears faded, insubstantial. I sit on the sofa again. We don't look at each other, or speak. The sting of his words – *you selfish bitch* – hovers between us, along with the hurt they provoked. For a second I'm tempted to tell him the truth, before I quash the impulse.

Jake shifts beside me, and I'm aware once again of the tension between us. Contrition washes over me. 'I'm sorry,' I say.

He huffs out a breath, but his anger appears to have gone. 'Like I said. You could have called.'

Marcus strides back in, mug of coffee in hand. I'd forgotten how commanding the man is, how he sweeps into a room and takes over, untroubled by doubts people will fall in line. The arrogance that's led Jake to label his father a prick. He sits opposite me, his scrutiny intense. It's as though his son isn't even in the room, and heat warms my cheeks again. Something's different in the way he's staring at me. At eighteen, my body was still childish, my breasts mere patties, my hips and thighs thin from faddy eating. Two years on, my chest has burgeoned; my bottom has transformed into twin melons. Now it's not potential Marcus is seeing, but fulfilment, and I sense he approves. His eyes caress my boobs before he lifts his gaze to my face.

'You've changed. Grown up.'

I'm uncertain how to respond. 'I guess so.'

A half-grin twists Marcus's mouth. I fantasise, fleetingly, about him kissing me. Something about this man both scares and excites me, and I can't deny I'm drawn to him. I suppress the thought, memories of Dominic stabbing me with guilt. Beside me, Jake shifts, clearly uneasy at the way his father is staring at me.

'You'll have to come round again soon,' Marcus says. 'I'm sure Jake's missed you.'

***

Afterwards, I walk home, lost in thoughts of Jake's father. A slight drizzle is falling, the air cold as the evening dims around me. I pull my jacket tighter, keen for the warmth of my bedroom. As I turn the corner into my street, I spot someone at the other end, off in the distance, in my peripheral vision. A man, tall, dark-haired, one leg in plaster, his arms hooked over crutches. For a second the resemblance to Dominic is so strong, I freeze, my gaze rooted to the ground, too afraid to raise my eyes in case my abductor appears before them.

When I do, the man has gone.

I release the breath I've been holding. It can't have been him, I tell myself.

Nevertheless, I don't sleep that night. I replay that split second over and over, in an attempt to grasp it, but the details remain elusive. Was it Dominic or not?

By morning, I've persuaded myself I over-reacted. Get a grip, I tell myself. It wasn't him.

CHAPTER 20 – *Beth*

O ver the next week, Marcus Wilding takes up residence in my head. I can't stop thinking about him. Jake and I meet for coffee, walks in the park, and all the while I'm eager for news of Marcus, what he's doing, whether he's mentioned me. When I ask about going to his house, however, Jake seems non-committal, and I'm reluctant to antagonise him again. I don't understand the pull his father exerts on me, why seeing him the other day has sparked this obsession. Before Dominic took me, I'd viewed Marcus as fuel for my teenage fantasies, but not a serious sexual prospect. Now I'm on fire for him. Something strange lies behind my compulsion, however, and it takes me a while to understand what it all means.

One night, unable to sleep, my hands between my legs as an imaginary Marcus rides my body, I decide to force a meeting between us. When I do, I'll discern whether the spark between us holds the potential to ignite into a fire. I persuade myself my motives are purely sexual, still unaware what's driving my behaviour.

Once I've chosen a day to visit him, I prepare myself mentally. I tell myself Marcus and I have a date and that I'm going to his place because he's cooking us a romantic meal. The memory of Dominic's fictional bouillabaisse from the night he captured me slams into my head, before I eject it.

On the chosen evening, I dress carefully. Since my return, my wardrobe is limited to what Mum's bought me. Just the basics, nothing dressy. I plump for my new jeans, which fit snugly, and a cream V-neck top that clings to my breasts. I stroke blusher into the groove between them, enhancing my cleavage. A hint of rose on each cheek. A swipe of lip-gloss on my mouth, a flick of mascara on each eye, and I'm done. Something tells me Marcus, like Dominic, doesn't approve of women wearing too much make-up. I survey myself in the mirror, breathing deeply to calm my nerves. Marcus will be in control tonight. I'll send the smoke signals his way, and it'll be his decision whether he fans them into a blaze or not.

My mother's waiting for me as I descend the stairs.

'Are you OK, love? You're very pale.'

'I'm fine.' She doesn't appear convinced. 'Just off to see Jake.'

Mum manages a small smile. 'Don't be late back, will you?' The memory of two years ago must haunt her, torment her with the worry I might disappear again. How can I blame her, when I've led her to believe me capable of such selfishness?

***

A grey Lexus sits on Marcus's driveway, proof he's home. I press the doorbell. My palms are damp, my stomach clenched.

The door opens. Marcus stands in front of me, and cords entwine around my lungs, crushing out the air.

'Beth.' His voice contains a dark timbre that sends frissons pit-a-patting up my spine. 'Jake's not here.' He frowns. 'Band practice. Didn't he tell you?'

'He might have done,' I lie. 'I must have forgotten.'

Marcus doesn't invite me in, and my palms grow damper. I wipe them surreptitiously against my thighs.

'Can I use your bathroom? I need to pee.' Wow, Beth, I chide myself. Great way to let him know he lights your fire.

Marcus stands aside, allowing me to enter. When I come downstairs again, he's in the hallway, gazing up at me, and I register the way his stare grows more appraising, sliding away from my face and over my body. His eyes hover on my breasts, and then glide to my legs before shifting to my boobs again. The same damp heat that reddens my cheeks invades my crotch. For a second, I break eye contact.

When I manage to look at him, he's frowning once more. 'I'll tell Jake you were here. Any message?'

I shake my head. 'I'll come back tomorrow.'

'You'd best phone first. I'm pretty certain he'll be working an evening shift at the gym.'

'Will you be in?' Too late, the words tumble from my mouth, revealing my hand too soon.

His frown deepens. 'Yes, but I don't see—'

'How are things going with your business?' I stumble on, aware my voice is unnaturally high. 'I've not seen you for so long. It would be good to catch up.' I pull myself taller, moving closer. 'Do you have time for a coffee?'

For a moment, my humiliation appears inevitable. Then his eyes flicker south to my breasts. He nods.

In the kitchen, Marcus gestures towards the coffee grinder. 'Make yourself useful. I take mine white, no sugar.' The old Beth, pre-abduction, would have resented being ordered around this way. Now I like it.

As I tip beans into the grinder, get milk from the fridge and mugs from the cupboard, he stands behind me, his presence tingling my skin, shivering my spine.

'Why are you here, Beth?' He's rumbled me, but he's puzzled too. As to why a girl – no, a woman – so much younger, a mere school kid when he last knew her, might be interested in him. His ego's at war with his common sense; his brain telling him he's misinterpreting the signals, while his crotch is encouraging him to go for it.

I continue the lie. 'Didn't remember Jake's band practice.'

The connection between us shatters. Marcus grabs my arm, forcing me to face him.

'Forget the coffee.' He makes a point of glancing at his watch, and I'm crushed, his dismissal obvious. 'You should leave.'

Heat flushes my face again. I grab my bag. 'It was good to see you again, Mr Wilding.' His nod is curt. Embarrassed beyond words, I make my escape.

Back home, in my bedroom, I hunt for scraps of reassurance. He's definitely noticed you, I tell myself. Remember how he stared at your boobs?

Marcus possesses more self-control than I do, though. He'll have been considering all the reasons why he shouldn't fuck me. His cold, analytical side will remind him he's a business associate of my father. His accountant, no less. Not to mention Jake, my long-time mate, being his son. To top it all, over thirty years' difference in age separates us.

***

I wait a few more days before I chance my luck again. It's Saturday night, and Jake will be out with his mates, or the new girlfriend I suspect he has, whereas I'm guessing Marcus will be at home.

This time, I wear a dress. Mum's been giving me money, and earlier on, I raided the charity shops in Downend, finally bagging myself a bargain. Pure silk, V-necked, tight under my breasts and sheer to below the knee, in a pale shade of blueberry. Soft ruching around the neck and hem. Classy, making me appear older than twenty. I root out shoes and a leather clutch to go with the dress and top it off with a cream linen jacket. I'm all set to seduce Marcus Wilding. I don't allow myself to consider too deeply what I'm doing here.

The reception Marcus gives me when I arrive is cool, bordering on hostile.

'Jake's out.' He doesn't invite me in, and I can't pull the bathroom trick twice in a row.

'I'll tell him you were here. Phone first if you plan on coming round again. It'll save you a wasted journey.' His words sting, but before he closes the door his eyes suck me in, sweeping over my bare legs, the silk dress hugging my breasts. His words convey rejection, but his stare tells a different story. I'm deflated and encouraged, rolled into one.

The next day, I phone Jake. Seems I was right. He's seeing someone called Sophie.

'Just casual, for now,' he says. 'Early days yet.'

He tells me he's going to a gig at the Bierkeller with Sophie tomorrow night. I'm happy for him. No jealousy; we've only ever been mates, and I'm glad we're regaining our old closeness. I'm pleased for other reasons too. Jake having a girlfriend, along with his job, means he'll be out most evenings. Giving me the chance to see Marcus. I don't recognise the person I'm becoming, and it's because, in many ways, I'm no longer Beth Sutton. She doesn't exist anymore.

'Mum,' I say later on, when we're alone in the kitchen after supper. 'Can I ask you something?' I'm curious as to whether she's noticed a difference in me.

'Anything, my love. You know that.'

'Have I changed? From how I was before I went away?'

Mum doesn't reply at once. She draws in a breath, holding it as she studies my face for clues. 'Yes. A lot.'

'How? In what way?'

'It's not just that you're older.'

'What do you mean?'

'There's a big gap between eighteen and twenty for everyone. A lot can happen. People go to university. Start their first job. Maybe get married. So I'd expect you to be different.'

'But I've not done any of those things.'

'Well, that's a start. At least I know that much about what you've been doing. Or not doing.' Mum's tone holds no obvious hint of rebuke, and yet my guilt flares into life.

'I can't tell you where I've been.' My voice is a whisper, no more.

Mum's hand reaches across the table. She places it firmly on top of mine; her skin is cool, dry, as her fingers stroke my own. Her words, when they come, are a further caress. 'What is it you're so afraid of?'

My eighteen-year-old self, so easily fooled, rises up before me. The girl who allowed Dominic Perdue to abduct her. 'That you'll be disappointed in me.'

'Never.' Mum shakes her head in emphasis. 'Not in my Beth. When you trust me enough, you'll talk. I'll say it again. If you're frightened of somebody—'

'I'm not.' How can I tell my mother I miss the man who held me captive? That, in my way, I'm mourning him, because I'm scared he might be dead? Impossible to make her understand what I can't fathom myself.

For a second, an insane idea flashes across my mind. Should I return to the cottage, attempt to find out what happened? I clamp down on it instantly. Impossible to even consider such madness.

I pull my hand from hers, signalling the conversation is finished. Disappointment sparks in her eyes.

***

The next day, I awake to the realisation my old enemy, depression, has returned. As I stare out of my bedroom window; it's a day like any other, dew still beading the grass, a promise of sun infusing the sky. Why Dominic's loss has chosen today to attack me, I've no idea, but right now, the pain of missing him is a knife in my belly. My talk with Mum last night has stirred everything up in my head. I return to bed, unsure how I'll get through the day, let alone the rest of my life.

My desperation leads to the inevitable. That evening, I'm back at Marcus's house.

He appears tired when he opens the door, shadows under his eyes, hair rumpled, feet bare. Clearly I've come at a bad time. I hold a DVD, one of Troy's ninja flicks he'll never miss, before me like a shield. 'Brought this for Jake.'

Marcus's gaze appraises me. I'm wearing jeans and a plain top, my make-up minimal, hair clipped off my face. Playing safe after overreaching myself with the silk dress. Tonight I look younger than my age. Am I imagining it, or do his pupils dilate?

He stands aside to let me pass, still not speaking. I follow him into the lounge. His breath, tinged with alcohol, floats into my nostrils. A glass of whisky, one finger left, sits on the coffee table, a half-full bottle beside it.

'What's your game, Beth?'

I place the DVD next to the bottle. 'I thought Jake might like—'

'Don't lie.' His curtness cuts like a whip. 'I've no idea what you're up to, but whatever it is, you need to stop. Right now.'

'Not up to anything.' My eyes are incapable of meeting his.

Marcus gulps his whisky. Only a few millimetres are now left. 'You come round here, all dolled up, when Jake's out. You make doe eyes at me. Now you pretend I've imagined it? Give me some credit, for Christ's sake.' He drains his glass.

Tears hover behind my eyes and I blink them back, aware a crying female will irritate Marcus beyond endurance.

'I play golf with your father. He's one of my clients, remember.'

I nod, my gaze on the soft cream of the carpet.

'You're Jake's friend. How would he react if he knew you've been coming here all dressed-up, wanting God knows what?'

'I want you.' I'm surprised how firm my voice sounds. My eyes meet his at last. All I see is weariness.

'Why? That's what I can't fathom. I'm over thirty years older than you.'

I shrug. No way can I explain the desperation inside me. 'I just do.'

'Not going to happen.' He slams down his glass, making me flinch. 'You need to leave. Now.'

***

I do my best to eject Marcus from my head, without success. Ever so slowly, I'm coming to understand my fascination with him. Marcus Wilding, so cocky, so arrogant, evokes in me the same response as Dominic Perdue. The need to comply, because that way I'll survive. It's what's been missing since my return home. Someone to direct me, tell me what to do, so I have no room for doubt. Without direction, I can't function anymore. That's why Marcus, who's Dominic's double in many ways, is a flame to my moth. In my head, the two men fuse into one and I can't always tell them apart.

Two weeks go by before I visit again. This time it's different; his son will be there. Jake and I continue to rekindle our friendship, with calls, texts and walks in the park. Seems he's been recording some new songs with his band; he's asked me over tonight so he can play them for me. He'll think it weird if I say no. My stomach knots as I press the doorbell, but it's Jake, not Marcus, who answers. Complete with rumpled hair and bare feet, achingly reminiscent of his father.

I check the lounge as we head upstairs. Marcus is watching television, hitting the whisky again. He doesn't glance my way.

In his bedroom, Jake's fingers fly over his guitar. His style's changed; the notes are darker, earthier, than I remember. I absorb myself in the music, my mind pulled away only when I hear Marcus moving around downstairs.

Later, he's coming out of the kitchen as I descend the stairs, ready to go home. Our eyes connect. He nods at me. I manage a half smile, but I'm relieved. Our meeting hasn't been as awkward as I'd feared.

After that, I'm more relaxed about visiting Jake, my interactions with Marcus always polite but distant. I run into him about once a week when Jake and I get together, and I'm careful to appear detached, neutral, while sending the occasional flirtatious glance his way. His curtness rebuffs me, but his pupils, engorged with desire, don't.

***

One evening, as the light fades from the day, I arrive on his doorstep. I have a valid reason to be here; Jake asked me to come over. Seems things with Sophie are more off than on. 'Need a female perspective,' he tells me on the phone.

'Jake's not here,' Marcus informs me when I arrive. 'He had to go out. Some trouble with that girl he's been seeing. Gone over to her place. He said he'd text you.'

I pull my mobile, bought for me by Mum, from my bag. One new notification. 'Sorry, I didn't get it in time.'

He nods. Then he stands back, pulling the door open wider. 'Come in,' he says. In that instant, I'm certain I'll soon be in his bed, with him fucking my brains out.

We sit opposite each other in the lounge. 'I still think you're too young,' he tells me.

'I'm not.'

'No idea what you want from me.'

'Isn't it obvious?'

'Or why.'

'I can't explain. Does there have to be a reason?'

'No. But there is, with you. I just can't fathom what it might be.'

'Does it matter?' I wince at the whine in my voice.

'Don't be ridiculous. Of course it does. Other people are involved. Your father. Jake.'

'They won't find out.'

Marcus snorts out a breath. 'You're so naive.' His brusqueness cuts deep, but I push the pain aside.

'We're both adults. I'll be off to university soon,' I lie. 'Don't worry. I'm not making this something it can't be.'

His gaze strips me bare, his appraisal brutal. What he sees, I've no idea, but he gets up, walking to where I'm sitting, pulling me up by my arm. 'Make sure you don't. This is sex, Beth. Nothing more.'

'I get that.' For me, it's more, but I'm not going to let on.

'Until you leave for university. Then we're finished.'

'Suits me.'

'Enough talking. On your knees, now. Suck me off.'

***

Afterwards, he sits with his back against the sofa, his expression closed. 'You need more practice,' he remarks, and the comment stings with its casual cruelty.

'It's been a while,' I say.

He shrugs. 'Get me a coffee. White, no sugar, in case you've forgotten.'

His recovery time is short, it seems. Once he's drained his coffee, he pushes me to the carpet, entering me from behind. His fingers reach round to rub my clitoris, roughly but effectively, and we're fucking at last, oh God, yes we are, hard and so good, different from anything I've experienced before. All my thoughts are concentrated on Marcus, as his are on me, because neither one of us hears the sound of a key in the front door.

The door to the lounge opens. Jake stands in the gap, horror in his face as he takes in the scene before him. Our eyes meet, and shame steals over me, before he stalks from the room, fury in his face.

**

We're in Marcus's kitchen one morning two weeks later. Last night, without planning it, I stayed over for the first time. Jake's in his room upstairs, probably waiting for me to leave. Since he discovered his father fucking me in the lounge, he's refused to speak to either of us, although I refuse to dwell on the shame I felt. Marcus and I are both free agents, both adults, I tell myself. Jake needs to grow up, accept our relationship.

Marcus hasn't offered me breakfast or even coffee. I've clearly outstayed my welcome, despite the fact the taste of his semen is still salty in my mouth.

'Twice a week, Beth. That's the deal. Take it or leave it.'

'Please.' I have no pride where Marcus Wilding is concerned. 'Why can't I come over tonight?'

'I'm busy.'

'Doing what?'

'None of your concern. Now get out of here. I need to go to work.'

I'm pressing Marcus too hard, I'm aware of that. I'm pushy, too talkative – traits he despises in women. What we have will end one day, but with any luck not yet. Without him, I'll collapse; he's the trellis, I'm the vine. His spine as he stands at the sink sends an unambiguous message: *leave*. I push back my chair.

'Bye, then.' I keep my tone light, unconcerned. He doesn't respond, but his back stiffens. Not a good sign.

After I've left, I remember – too late – that Mum will have expected me back last night.

CHAPTER 21 – *Ursula*

I'm unable to shake off my fury, no matter how many times Chris tells me I'm overreacting. He's shocked when I swear, something I never do normally.

'For fuck's sake! Beth didn't come home last night, and you accuse me of blowing things out of proportion? What the hell am I supposed to think?' I run my hands through the tangled mess that's my hair. I've not brushed it today; it bears witness to my sleepless night. Meanwhile, our daughter is upstairs, having sauntered in this morning after I dozed off sometime after dawn. The first thing I do when I wake up is check her room, and there she is, in bed asleep. Hair flopping across her face, the duvet moving as she breathes, unaware she put me through hell last night.

My husband shrugs, his eyes on his mug of tea. 'Told you. Beth is selfish. Not to mention immature.'

'I thought—' I drop my toast on my plate. 'That she'd gone missing again.'

When Chris doesn't reply, I pose the question that's been bothering me. 'What's happened? To the Beth I used to know? She's like a stranger since she's come home.' I choke back a sob. 'I can't get through to her. I don't recognise her anymore.'

'You need to back off, Ursula. Stop mollycoddling her. No wonder she can't stand on her own two feet.'

'This is *my* fault?' I stifle the urge to slap my husband.

'You've tried to be her friend rather than her mother. Failed to set her boundaries. That's the issue, as I see it.'

'You should get to work.' The ice in my voice leaves my husband under no illusion as to my opinion of his words. We don't speak again before the slamming of the front door announces his departure.

Arsehole, I tell myself, before my thoughts turn to my daughter. Chris is right. She's selfish and thoughtless; while she's living under this roof, she'll toe the line. Wow. When did I turn into my mother?

I spend the morning in a frenzy of cleaning, not caring if I wake Beth. Serve her right, I decide. When the little madam surfaces, we'll be having words.

Twelve o'clock comes and goes before I hear movement from upstairs. Ten minutes later, my daughter walks downstairs. I'm in the lounge, pretending to read one of my Spanish texts; she tries to slip past the doorway without me noticing.

'Where the hell have you been?' I'm aware of the tightness in my lips, matched by my voice. By now, my anger's percolating nicely. When I don't get a reply, I discard the book, marching into the kitchen.

Beth has her back to me, tension written into the way she wears her shoulders as earrings. She's still in her pyjamas, slotting bread into the toaster.

'Answer me when I speak to you.' My mother speaking again, but I'm as pissed off as it's possible to be.

'Sorry. I should have called.'

'Not good enough.'

She shrugs. 'Something cropped up.' She faces me now, pretending to be oh so casual, but I'm not fooled. Her eyes won't meet mine. The memory of the bruises on her wrists flashes into my head, abating my anger somewhat. Has she been with her abuser again?

I sit down, forcing myself to stay calm. 'Do you have any idea how worried I was? When you didn't come home? What went through my mind?'

Guilt edges into her lovely eyes and for a second the old Beth stares at me before she looks away. 'Like I said, I'm sorry.'

'Where were you?'

'With a friend. Had a bit to drink, decided to stay the night. By then it was too late to call.' She still won't return my gaze and I'm certain she's lying. She always was piss-poor at it. My suspicion that she's been with the bastard who gave her those bruises grows, as does my determination to unearth what's going on.

'Who's the friend?'

'Nobody you know.' Another lie. Beth must have seen my reaction. 'An old mate from school.'

'You've pulled that one before. Remember? Before you disappeared for two long, lonely bloody years.' My voice is as exhausted as the rest of me. I'm drained by the emotion engendered by her reappearance, the constant rows with Chris, the whole blasted shebang of life that's smacking me in the face right now. I get up and fill the kettle to distract myself. When I turn around, Beth has gone.

***

Thank God, Troy and Chris are out. It's a good hour or so before I finish crying and head upstairs to Beth's room. I've debated whether I should call Donna, ask her advice, but I decide I need a better handle on what I'm dealing with here. So far, I have nothing but suppositions.

I knock on Beth's door. When she doesn't reply, I push it open.

Beth is asleep on the bed, her knees tucked into her chest, her mouth slack. She looks as vulnerable as the day she was placed in my arms as a new-born. My anger melts; I move forward, stepping on a creaky floorboard. Her eyes fly awake, terror peeking from them, until she recognises me. Her fear reinforces my suspicions. My daughter has been abused, and if it takes forever, I'll prise the truth out of her.

'Talk to me, love.' I reach out a hand, stroking her cheek. 'I was worried, that's all.'

She sits up, pushing back her hair. 'I'm sorry I didn't call.'

'Tell me who you were with.'

'I did. An old friend.'

'I don't believe you.'

'Why would I lie?' She swings her legs onto the floor, as if to stand up, but my hand darts out, grasping her arm.

'Has someone hurt you? Whoever you were with the last two years? If some man's abused you—' I drop my grip, aware that I'm holding her too tightly. 'Tell me. We can sort it out. Make sure he never harms you again.'

'Nobody's hurt me.' Beth stands up, stretches, giving a fake yawn for my benefit. 'Look, Mum, I need to take a shower, get dressed—'

'So you can disappear again?' Icicles hang from my words, her evasiveness sparking my anger back into life.

'No. Because it's nearly two o'clock, that's why.'

'Do you plan on going out again tonight?'

'Is that any of your business?'

'Out of courtesy to your father and me—'

Beth laughs. A nasty snicker. 'Will you listen to yourself? Give it a rest, Mum.'

'What's his name?'

'Not been with any guy.'

'Don't lie to me, Beth.' I take her hand again, but she snatches it away.

'I'm not lying to you!' I'm shocked; Beth never shouts at me. I stare at her. She's angry, and yet scared. That's what I'm picking up here. Fear.

'OK, I was with a guy. Happy now? It's allowed, remember. For a twenty-year-old to be seeing someone. To have sex.'

'Who is he?' I inject a calm I don't possess into my voice.

'Why should I tell you?'

'It's not Jake, then?' I'm positive it can't be, given the fraternal nature of their relationship, so her reply comes as a shock.

'Spot on, Mum. I was at Jake's house. Can I go take a shower now? I need—'

'You and Jake?' I'm stunned. A lot's changed, I remind myself. Maybe being apart has led to them seeing each other in a new light. No bad thing. Jake is a sound lad, unlike his obnoxious father. I'm puzzled, though, as to why Jake didn't insist on Beth phoning me. He's always been the responsible sort.

Beth's expression is evasive once more. 'There's no me and Jake, Mum.'

'Then why did you say…?'

'It's his father, OK? I was with Marcus Wilding last night. Now will you get off my case?' She barges past me, heading for the bathroom, rendering me speechless. Beth's words slam into me, knocking the breath from my lungs. Marcus Wilding? The man I endured for Anna's sake when she was still around, but whom I've always loathed? He's old enough to be her father, not to mention being Chris's accountant.

I force air into my lungs, trying to unscramble my brain. At least I can be sure Beth wasn't with Marcus Wilding during the last two years. Impossible with Jake still living at home. Why she's turned to him now, I can't fathom, although Donna doubtless will have her own pet theory. Her words about abusive relationships sound in my head. 'Violence mixed with loving behaviour… a dangerous combination… keeps the woman hooked.' Does that explain Beth choosing a control freak like Marcus Wilding? Is male mistreatment some kind of drug for her?

She needs help, and fast, but how do I convince her? I'm out of my depth here, sinking in the murky waters of Marcus Wilding.

'He makes me feel secure, Mum.' I've been so absorbed I don't hear Beth padding back into the room.

I stare at her, stupefied. 'What?'

'I need to feel that, Mum. Secure, I mean.'

'And you can't get that here? From your family?'

'Not like that. Not the way Dom—' She bites off her sentence. When I press her as to her meaning, she crawls into bed and drags the duvet over her head, shutting me out.

***

190

Beth heads straight to her room after supper that evening. We've not spoken since our conversation earlier.

Troy pushes his chair back. 'Going out?' I ask.

'Yeah. With some mates.'

'Call me if you stay out late.'

Chris cocks an eyebrow at me after Troy's left.

'What's with you? You never usually say stuff like that to Troy.'

'He's male. Not so vulnerable.'

'As who?' Chris blows out an exasperated breath. 'You mean Beth. Last night. We've come back to her again. As always.'

'Do you know where she was?' I swear, if Chris is aware our daughter is sleeping with Marcus Wilding and didn't tell me, our marriage is finished.

'I haven't a clue.'

'She stayed with Marcus Wilding last night.'

'*What?*' My husband's voice reveals he's been in the dark about this too.

'They're having sex.'

'You can't be serious. She told you this?'

'Yes. Says he makes her feel—' It's hard to utter the word. 'Secure.'

'I don't believe it.' Chris's tone is firm, assured. 'No way, Ursula. He's old enough to be her father, for Christ's sake.'

'Doesn't seem to stop her.'

'She's seeking attention. Jesus, don't you understand? It's not enough for her to disappear for two years and refuse to say where she's been. No, now she makes up crap like this. Stuff I can't, I won't, believe. Marcus Wilding? He's my accountant! He's in the bloody Chamber of Commerce with me, for God's sake!' Chris's face is red with anger, his forehead shiny, the veins on his nose purple.

'Keep your voice down, please.' My words are icicles. 'Can't we discuss this like rational adults?'

'Which our daughter, apparently, is not.'

'I still think…' I hesitate, sure Chris will pooh-pooh what I'm about to say. Hasn't he already? 'That she's been abused.' I plough on, despite the contempt in Chris's expression. 'She's been with some man, who's controlled her. Hurt her. Then she managed to break away. But she still needs this guy. Donna says—'

'Oh, for Christ's sake. Donna Keating is not the source of all knowledge on psychological issues, just because she started a master's degree she never finished. Face facts. Beth needs to grow up. Fast.'

'She's never had the chance.' I force myself to stay calm, despite the urge to slap my husband. 'She was eighteen when she left, fresh out of school. Then she spends two years in an abusive relationship. How the hell can she become the mature individual you expect her to be?'

'We're the ones being abused. By her. You have no evidence for this, Ursula. Just a couple of bruises.'

I'm too tired to remind him of Beth's clothes when she arrived, her lack of money or phone. Instead, I try a different tack. 'She's changed. She fusses over how things are arranged. The cruet set, for example. There's other stuff too. Yesterday I found her reading one of my Italian books.'

'So?'

'She took French at school. She's never studied Italian.'

'Obviously she has. While she's been away. Doesn't gel with your theory about her being abused, does it?'

I'm done here. Discussing our daughter with Chris is harder than swimming through treacle.

***

The next evening, I catch Beth as she's heading out the door, wearing a clingy top that hugs her breasts, hauling them skyward. Her outfit is far too tarty for my liking.

'I won't be home tonight,' she informs me. 'So no need for you to worry, OK?' She pretends to rummage in her bag to avoid eye contact.

'Is it him again? Marcus Wilding? Beth, for God's sake—'

'I'm not a child, Mum. I can do whatever I choose.' She pulls open the door and slips through it, too quick for me to stop her.

I stalk back into the kitchen to confront Chris. 'You have to talk to Marcus Wilding. She's staying over with him again tonight. This can't go on.'

My husband has never courted conflict. I watch as his expression betrays how he's working through the reasons why he shouldn't do what I've asked. 'We only have her word for this. I still think it's all a fantasy.'

'Tackle Marcus about what's going on. You've not spoken to Beth about it?' Stupid question. Of course he hasn't.

Chris's eyes roll. 'As if. Listen, I'm meeting Marcus tomorrow. Business lunch. I'll broach the subject, if you insist. He'll confirm it's all a lie, something we're probably best off ignoring. Wherever she's going tonight, it won't be to see Marcus Wilding.'

***

Beth slinks home the next morning as Chris is leaving for work. She heads upstairs without a word to either of us. 'Remember what you promised. Ask the dickhead,' I hiss at my husband.

That evening, it's Chris's turn to hiss as he strides through the front door. 'Where is she?' he demands.

'In her room. What did Marcus say?'

'He denied it.'

'And you believed him?'

'No. The bastard was lying. It was in his face, for a split second after I confronted him. Arsehole. He's over thirty years older than her.' He pushes past me, heading up the stairs, with me following.

Chris barges into Beth's room without bothering to knock. My daughter is on the bed, staring at the ceiling, chewing the fingernails of one hand.

'What the hell are you playing at?' he says, his voice low yet filled with anger. 'You're sleeping with Marcus Wilding? Can't you find someone your own age?'

Shock flies into Beth's face. 'Leave me alone, Dad, can't you?'

'He's old enough to be your father!'

'Don't, Chris. Please.' It's as though my husband doesn't hear me.

Mutiny replaces Beth's initial shock. She scrambles off the bed, defiance in her expression. 'It's none of your business who I sleep with. I'm an adult, aren't I?'

'Then behave like one, for God's sake!'

Beth's mouth tightens, before she grabs a jacket off the back of a chair. Then my daughter storms down the stairs. The front door bangs. She doesn't come home that night.

***

When she arrives back the next morning, her face betrays that she's bracing herself for a fight. Me, I'm too weary, too bone-exhausted, for an argument. Instead, I crave an inkling of the closeness we used to share. 'Coffee?' I enquire.

Beth shakes her head, her face parchment-pale, her hair unbrushed. She doesn't look well, and love squeezes my heart.

'Tea, then,' I say, steering her to a seat at the kitchen table. 'And toast.' As I dump bags into mugs and fill the kettle, she plays with a teaspoon, threading it through her fingers, her expression vacant.

I set her breakfast before her. 'You told me you need to feel secure. That you couldn't get that here,' I say.

The teaspoon moves faster, a whirl of silver, back and forth.

'Then you said something else. Something I didn't quite catch.'

Flashes of sunlight hit the spoon as both of us stare at it. 'Tell me. When you were away. Were you with someone?'

Beth shifts restlessly in her seat. Her top teeth tug at her bottom lip, worrying it, chewing at the skin.

'Please, sweetheart. I won't ask anything else, I promise. Did you stay with a man?'

She drops the teaspoon. 'I guess,' she says, and my heart squeezes again. The closeness I crave inches closer.

'Thank you,' I say. I meant what I said. No more questions, not for now.

'I miss him, Mum.' I stare at her. 'I don't understand why, though.' Then she pushes her chair back, leaving her tea and toast untouched.

***

I'm ready for a dose of Donna's particular brand of common sense. 'Can I come over?' I say when she answers her phone. She catches the nugget of worry in my tone.

'Beth?' she asks.

'Yes.'

'Get your butt over here. I'll cook us both some lunch.'

The morning is bright, crisp, although chilly. As I leave the house, I pause before unlocking my car, gazing up at the house. Beth's curtains are drawn; I'm guessing she's gone back to bed.

As I drive away, I notice a man, standing on the pavement close to our house, staring in its direction. He's tall, dark-haired, with one leg in plaster, his weight borne on crutches. I'm tempted to stop the car, demand to know who he is, rattled by the way his gaze is fixed on my home. Before I can, though, he hobbles away, heading in the other direction.

Once he's out of sight, I rebuke myself for letting concern for Beth override common sense. I'm being paranoid; the poor guy was probably just grabbing a respite from his crutches. Nothing for me to worry about.

***

'You need to rein Chris in.' Donna can be direct at times. We're at her house, on her sofa, our feet tucked up behind us as we sip our coffee. We've just eaten Donna's signature dish, peri-peri chicken.

'He's always so damn confrontational with Beth,' I tell her.

'That's why he needs to butt out. If you're right, and she's been abused, has endured a co-dependent relationship, then she needs a safe environment in which to deal with her emotions. Sounds like you're making progress. A little, anyway.'

I grimace. My recent conversations with Beth have inflicted wounds in my soul. 'She's beautiful. Smart. She could have any man she wanted. Why pick Marcus bloody Wilding? The archetypal arsehole?'

'I suspect the fact he's a control freak is exactly why she chose him.'

'What do you mean?'

'When we spoke before about Beth, we touched on domestic abuse. But did I mention Stockholm syndrome?'

I stare at her. 'What's that?'

'A psychological condition in which hostages express empathy with their captors, often defending their actions. It's a survival mechanism. When a victim identifies with their abuser, the bad guy no longer seems a threat. It's not confined to hostage situations, though.'

'No? What else?'

'It can explain domestic abuse, as well as animals staying with cruel owners. Stockholm syndrome can arise in any situation where an inequality exists in the power balance, and one person's well-being, possibly their life, depends on the goodwill of their abuser.'

'So if Beth has been in a controlling relationship—'

'She may be suffering a form of Stockholm syndrome. Marked by guilt, confusion, you name it. Even love for this man.'

'Love?'

'Yes, weird as it seems.'

'"I miss him. But I don't understand why." That's what she said.'

'That tends to confirm my theory. She needs help, Ursula.'

'I know.' I swing my feet off the sofa and stand up. 'I just don't have a clue how to give it to her.'

CHAPTER 22 – *Beth*

I can hear Mum downstairs, fixing coffee. We didn't speak over breakfast; an uncomfortable silence infusing the atmosphere. Well, it's my life, and I'll do what I want. I didn't spend two years banged up in a basement for her to tell me how to behave, especially now I'm twenty.

The irony doesn't escape me; I sleep with Marcus Wilding precisely because he *does* tell me what to do. He's a controlling bastard, but a good-looking one who enjoys pulling my strings. He knows what his dick wants and he makes damn sure I give it to him. I'm not complaining. He's not into kinky stuff, thank goodness, and he always ensures I come. I don't doubt the reason, for Marcus, is ego-based. A woman in his bed who didn't orgasm would be an affront to his sexual prowess.

One of Mum's Italian grammar books lies unread in my lap as I stare out of the window. I've made half-hearted efforts to maintain my language studies, but my motivation is fading now Dominic's no longer in my life. Despite my relationship with Marcus, I miss my captor. What the hell happened that day he disappeared? Some kind of a breakdown? He was clearly angry, no doubt frantic about his debts. Not impossible for him to have crashed mentally. Vanished into the murky depths of life on the streets, like Mum's friend Anna probably did. My stomach contracts at the notion of Dominic, always so fastidious, grimy and unshaven in a filthy sleeping bag. Whatever he's done, he doesn't deserve that.

'Beth? Can I come in?' Mum's knuckles rapping on my door shake me from the fog of my thoughts.

'If you must.' I'm bracing myself for an argument. I remind myself I love my mother, even though right now that love seems very distant.

Mum enters my bedroom. She perches on the end of the bed, her posture awkward, as if squaring up for a fight. She doesn't speak at first, just looks at me; I turn away, unable to bear the love in her eyes.

'He's too old for you, sweetheart.'

I don't reply. I can't deny it; besides, I'm postponing the moment when we start to argue.

'He's a friend of your father. Don't you understand how embarrassing this is for him?'

I bristle. 'Is that important? If Marcus makes me happy?'

'You don't look happy. Or sound it. Happiness doesn't consist of moping all day in your bedroom.'

'I'm OK.'

Mum shakes her head. I've never been able to fool her for long. She picks up the Italian grammar. 'Why the interest in learning Italian?'

I shrug. 'Thought about exploring Italy one day. Seemed a good idea to learn the language.'

'And you decided this while you were gone?'

I nod.

'Will you ever tell me where you've been?' Tears hover in Mum's voice.

'I can't,' I whisper.

'Was it so very bad?'

'No. Yes, parts of it. I can't talk about it. I'm sorry.'

'Why not? Can you at least tell me that?'

'I'm sorry,' I repeat.

Silence for a while. My fingers pluck at a loose thread at the edge of my duvet.

Mum draws herself closer, and I observe with a pang how deep the creases by her eyes have become. Her skin appears drier than I remember, her hair frizzier. When did I last take any notice of her? I've been too self-absorbed, too selfish. The urge for her to rock me in her arms, as she did when I was a child, to make everything better, overwhelms me. Then, like a wave on the shore, it recedes, leaving the chasm between us wider than ever.

'He's never been what you'd call a nice man, you know.'

We're back to Marcus. I'm grateful for the diversion from Dominic Perdue.

'Anna wasn't happy with him. Often complained how difficult he was to please. I've always thought he contributed to her mental health issues, what with trying to control her all the damn time.' Mum's voice grows louder. 'One day, you'll realise what he's like, but by then he'll have hurt you. He's that type of man.'

She's right, but how can I explain I need Marcus Wilding's peculiar brand of supervision to hold me together?

***

That evening, I escape to my room after supper, leaving Mum, Dad and Troy in the kitchen. As I lie on my bed, my thoughts circle around Mum, making me yearn for our former closeness. Will we ever find our connection again, or has it gone for good, decayed like rotting rope? My brain trails around in circles. If I don't tell her, the gulf between us will inch ever wider. If I do, her disappointment in my gullibility will produce the same result. Impossible to admit I allowed a man I barely knew to hoodwink me.

Besides, Mum will insist on the police getting involved. How can I explain to some hatchet-faced inspector that I went willingly with Dominic? There'll be a court case, with sharp-tongued lawyers tearing me to shreds. Not to mention the media coverage, the shame of everyone knowing. Impossible, all of it.

My mind drifts back to the women about whom I've heard, the ones who finally broke free after years in captivity. Those with that strange psychological condition, the name of which eludes me, although I can't bring myself to research the subject. I remember they had to assume new identities, a necessity if they were to live a normal life, or what passes as such after an abduction. No, hell no. I need to reconnect with Mum, and how can I do that if I move away, change my name?

I'm overlooking the obvious, though. With no Dominic to put on trial, the whole thing's impossible. Although the slim chance exists that he's alive and back at the cottage. A terrible thought strikes me. He knows where I live. Is he capable of coming to get me? Punish me for leaving, kill me the way he murdered the woman he called Julia, but who I knew as Amy?

Perhaps he's already watching the house. The thought of how he'd react to me visiting Marcus chills me.

Troy's voice reaches me though the floorboards. I can't catch what he's saying. My brother still ignores me most of the time, speaking only when necessary. When he does say anything, he doesn't look me in the eye. I'm certain he never said a word about Dominic, despite being in possession of facts that might have released me from my prison in two days instead of two years. I consider tackling him, forcing him to admit why he did nothing to help me, but I'm scared of what I'll hear.

'Mum,' I say, the next day after breakfast, after Dad and Troy have left and we're alone in the kitchen. She's stacking plates in the dishwasher. 'Can I ask you something?'

'Anything.' Mum straightens up, faces me.

'After I went missing. You said the police were involved.'

'Yes. I had to call them. We were frantic.' Her voice shakes. My stomach clenches at the pain in her face.

'What about Troy?'

Puzzlement clouds Mum's eyes. 'What about him?'

'Did the police question him?'

'Yes. They talked to all of us. We went through everything. Over and over, until I couldn't think straight anymore, until it all jumbled together in my head.' She sighs. 'None of it led anywhere.'

'Troy didn't say anything specific about that evening?'

'No. What could he say, Beth? He didn't know any more than we did.'

I nod. I'm right. Troy kept silent about seeing me with Dominic that night. Why, though, I have no idea.

***

I'm in my bedroom, lying on my bed, when I hear someone at the front door. Minutes later, Mum's calling up the stairs. Jake's here.

I'm reluctant to face him, aware he's come to lecture me. We sit opposite each other in my bedroom, awkward as new-born fawns. He doesn't waste time in small talk.

'Why him? Why my father?'

I take refuge in flippancy. 'Why not him?'

Anger clouds gather in Jake's face. 'For fuck's sake, Beth! What the hell do you think it's like for me, in bed at night, hearing you screw Dad in the next room?'

Blood rushes to my cheeks. I'm praying it's just the sound of the bed squeaking that he means.

'Is it his money?'

I bristle. Yes, Marcus is well-heeled, but that doesn't interest me. My next words aim to injure. 'No. It's purely sexual.'

Disgust crosses Jake's face. 'Then it won't last. None of his girlfriends ever do.'

Anger makes me sarcastic. 'Thanks for the heads up.'

'He's old enough to be your father, for God's sake.'

'I've already heard that line. Several times over from Mum and Dad. I don't need it from you too.'

'We can't be friends, not while you're fucking him.'

'Fine.' Part of me is breaking inside, but I shove it firmly away. Jake stands up. 'I'll see myself out.'

He pauses in the doorway. 'It should have been me, Beth. Not him.' Then he's gone.

***

It's eleven o'clock on a Saturday morning, and I'm wondering whether to surprise Marcus with a visit tonight. Sod the twice-a-week rule. I've already broken it by turning up unannounced after Dad pissed me off. Marcus was annoyed, but let me stay anyway. I'm desperate to be with him, despite my rational brain warning me to back off. He's tiring of me. Perhaps I'm too young, too inexperienced sexually.

My stomach growls. Keen to avoid a lecture from my father, I've not had breakfast yet. As I go downstairs, still in pyjamas, Troy's the last person on my mind. When I enter the kitchen, he's there, swigging milk straight from the fridge.

'Where's Dad?'

He shrugs. 'Dunno.' He attempts to push past me, but I block his way. I'm unaware of my intention to confront my brother until the words emerge.

'Did you tell anyone about me?' We stare at each other, the eye contact uncomfortable. He doesn't reply, not at first.

'Why didn't you say something?'

'No idea what you're talking about.'

I'm not having any of it. 'That evening I went missing,' I say. My mouth is dry, my heart hammering in my chest. 'Mum says you didn't tell the police anything.'

'Nothing to tell.' He tries to push past me again, but I hold firm.

'You saw me.' Do I spot panic in his expression? If so, it's extinguished in a millisecond. Troy's face resumes its usual bored, can't be arsed, mien.

'It's a long time ago.' He huffs out a breath. 'How the hell am I supposed to remember what I did or didn't say?'

'You could have saved me.' I spit out the accusation as though it's venom. 'Two years, Troy. Two long, awful years.'

Do I imagine it, or does guilt creep across his face?

'No idea what you're banging on about,' he says.

'You saw me. With a man.' Impossible to say Dominic's name. 'By his car. And you didn't say a word about it. You bastard.'

'Jesus, Beth. Like I said, I don't remember.'

'Of course you do.' My anger is rising, hot and molten. 'I was listed as a missing person, remember? The police were involved. You were questioned.'

He's silent. 'You never said anything. Didn't mention the man, the car.'

Still no response. 'If you had, maybe I'd have been found.'

My brother bites his lip, and shame steals into his expression, belying his words. Not that he seems able to admit it. Instead, his hands push me out of his path as he leaves the kitchen. Round one to Troy, it seems.

***

When she makes us coffee after lunch, Mum discovers we're almost out of milk.

'Can you go to the corner shop and buy some, please, Beth?' she asks. She wants more than milk, of course; her previous comment about moping all day in my bedroom hangs between us. She's keen to get me out of the house, even for a short while, and I can't refuse her, not for something so trivial.

I buy the milk and return home, my thoughts on Marcus. As I step into the porch, something catches my eye. A dead rose, once a vibrant red, its petals now blackened and shrivelled. It's lying on the shelf in the small alcove to my right, as though placed there deliberately.

With one hand I place the milk on the porch floor. My fingers reach out, pick up the rose, caress the tip of the stalk. It's been cut, not plucked, its straight neat end testament to that, and at about the same length as the red roses Dominic used to give me. I'm frozen to the spot, incapable of movement, while I consider the possibilities. Our neighbours next door have rose bushes, red ones too, but they're not in bloom at this time of year. Maybe it's from a bouquet sent to them, or someone else in the street, disposed of when dead and blown into our porch on the wind. The weather this morning and yesterday was calm, though; no gales with enough force to pick up a stray rose and transport it into our doorway.

A few fragments of withered petal break off under my fingers, emphasising the rose's deadness. A terrible suspicion arises within me. Has Dominic been to the house? At night, perhaps, under cover of darkness, to place the rose in our porch, its deadness a warning?

For a second, the memory of the man I saw a while ago who looked like Dominic flashes into my mind. The tightness in my chest reminds me I've stopped breathing, and I drag air into my lungs, all the while telling myself I'm imagining things. The man wasn't Dominic. How could it be? If he's still alive, fury would have driven him to seek me out long before now. The dead rose means nothing. I convince myself it must have blown into our porch. Perhaps it was windy during the night while I was asleep.

I tell myself I'm being ridiculous. Then I take the rose and dump it in the rubbish bin, before picking up the milk and going inside.

***

That afternoon, Jake surprises me with another visit. Mum shows him up to my room. The memory of his words hits me again. *We can't be friends, not while you're fucking him.* I'm bruised after the scene with Troy and in need of Marcus, so I'm brusque with Jake.

'Why are you here? You made it clear you didn't want anything more to do with me.'

'Didn't mean what I said.'

A small corner of me registers relief, happiness even. We've been mates a long time, after all.

'That's good,' I say.

He shuffles his feet awkwardly. 'It's hard for me, seeing you with him.'

His words hang between us. *It should have been me, Beth. Not him.* Shame on me, I think. How did I not realise how he felt?

'I get that.'

'He's an arsehole. You realise that, don't you?'

I do, but I'm unwilling to give Jake the satisfaction of agreeing with him.

'You don't see him much these days, though.'

I resent the hint of triumph in his voice. 'None of your business.'

Jake doesn't reply. Instead, I follow his gaze, and he's looking into the open drawer of my bedside cabinet. It takes me a minute before I register what's caught his attention. Inside lies the small silver charm, my memento of Amy. He stares at it, his expression unreadable, and then stretches out his hand. Before I can stop him, he's picked up the charm, passing the tiny boot between his fingers.

'Where'd you get this?' he asks.

The urge to snatch the charm back rises in me, but I suppress it. Our truce is too fresh, too fragile. 'I found it.'

'Where?'

I shrug. 'Does it matter?'

Jake's gaze on the silver boot is intense. 'Just curious, that's all.'

'Thought I'd make it into a necklace.'

'Looks like it's from a charm bracelet.' Jake's comment surprises me. He's a bloke, for Christ's sake. They don't usually know about such things.

We're in dangerous territory here. I reach out, take the charm from him, depositing it back in the drawer, before moving to hug him. At first, he stiffens, but then he relaxes, his arms around me, holding me to him. I take comfort in the embrace, resting my head on his shoulder.

'I'm glad we're friends again,' I say.

***

After Jake leaves, I take the tiny silver boot from my bedside cabinet, running my fingers over it. I call on Amy in my head, but she's not there. I'm slipping back into the black hole of negativity that stalked me as Dominic's captive. Every morning when I wake up, part of me yearns to slide once more into the oblivion of sleep. Taking a shower is too much effort. So is getting dressed, brushing my hair, cleaning my teeth. Why should I? It's not as though I have a life anymore, apart from Marcus. My world has contracted to the size of my bedroom, and I've no idea how to break free.

I toy with the idea of calling him, but reject it. He's forbidden me, in harsh unyielding tones, to phone him. If he wants sex, he texts me.

Sometimes, I awake at night, and as I ease into consciousness, the unfamiliarity of my bedroom bewilders me. In my head, I'm back in the basement, the mattress hard beneath my bones. Memories flood through me. Eating meals with Dominic, his mismatched eyes staring into mine. Everything's so tangible, as though I can stretch out my hand and touch solid flesh. Then reality intrudes, and I recognise my wardrobe, my dressing gown hanging on the back of the door, my swimming certificates on the wall. The contrast is jarring, shocking. I bury my head into my pillow, tears dampening the fabric, confused by my yearning for Dominic Perdue. The man abducted me, stole my adult life from me before it had barely begun. I shouldn't yearn for him, but I do. Without him, my mind is disintegrating, and I'm scared. If he's dead, then what happened to him? If he's alive, where is he? The need to find out is becoming an obsession, fuelled by my discovery of the dead rose.

I stroke my fingers over the silver boot, remembering Amy, or Julia as she really was. Dominic Perdue's a man capable of murder. If he ever made it home, my escape will have enraged him. Fear creeps over me as I remember he knows where I live. Is he planning to snatch me back? He might be watching the house, waiting to make his move. Will I spend my last seconds on earth staring into those weird eyes as he squeezes the life from me?

I'm being dense. A simple way exists to discover if Dominic ever returned home. I'll do it. In a few days, perhaps, when I've summoned up the courage.

CHAPTER 23 – *Ursula*

I t's a new experience for me, having to knock on Beth's door, accustomed as I am to our old, easy familiarity. These days, I tread carefully around my daughter, my awareness of her fragility growing daily. When did I need an excuse before to talk with her, walk into her room? The laundry basket under my arm reminds me I still have a place in Beth's life, even if only to wash her clothes. I raise my hand and rap. When a second knock produces no results, I push on the handle and enter.

Beth is perched on her bed, rocking back and forth, hugging her knees, her head bowed. She's sobbing; distressed sounds, those of a trapped animal, escape her, and my heart splinters in two. I throw the laundry basket to the floor and go to her, wrapping my arms around her shaking body. No words, just mother and daughter, one providing comfort to the other. In my brain, savagery rears its head, and I make a vow. I'll kill whoever's hurt my baby girl.

At last, Beth's sobs ease. I squeeze her tighter.

'Talk to me, sweetheart,' I say. 'What's wrong?'

A snuffle escapes her. 'Nothing.'

I press a kiss on top of her head. 'Tell me.'

'I can't.' She's crying again.

'Why not? You've always been able to talk to me. Remember when you spilt paint on the carpet when you were little? Did I shout? Was I mad?'

'No.'

'Exactly. What could be so bad you're afraid to tell me? I won't be angry. Promise.'

Beth's voice holds a world of sadness. 'It's not you being angry that concerns me.'

'Then what?'

'Told you already. I'm scared you'll be disappointed in me.'

My world stops as I take in what my girl said. If Beth's been with a violent man, why would I be disappointed in her? My daughter should know I'd be there a thousand per cent for her, should anyone hurt her.

'Why would I be?' All I get is a shake of her head.

'Please tell me.' I stress the word 'please' so hard it almost cracks in two.

Beth raises her head, her eyes meeting mine. I'm shocked by the blankness in their dark depths. Her expression is equally empty. When she speaks, her voice is flat.

'I can't tell you. He'll shut me back in the basement if I do. For good.'

I'm too stunned to reply. Fear wraps around my heart. What Donna said about Stockholm syndrome forces its way into my head. Does this go beyond domestic abuse, into something far darker? Brutality I can't begin to fathom?

I won't press Beth further, not after looking into those vacant eyes. I'm afraid for her mental health, though. I'll talk to Donna as soon as possible. First, Beth needs to understand something.

'Sweetheart,' I say. 'Under no circumstances will I ever be disappointed in you.'

***

Mid-afternoon, and I'm sitting on one of the lounge sofas, my thoughts dark. I've left a message for Donna on her mobile. Beth's upstairs, not a sound reaching me from her room.

The chimes of the doorbell startle me. When I open the door, Jake's there.

'Is Beth in?' His stance is awkward, his shoulders hunched. He must be as pissed off over the situation with Marcus as I am, possibly more. Unless he stays out at night, he's around when his father takes his childhood friend to bed. At the thought of Marcus Wilding having sex with my daughter, I shudder.

'She's not well,' I say.

Jake hesitates, his expression uncertain. 'Can I talk to you, Mrs Sutton? Please?'

'Of course.' I hold the door open for him. Jake strides into the lounge, plumping himself in one of the armchairs.

'Coffee?' I ask. He shakes his head. 'I'm worried about Beth,' he says.

I sigh. 'You and me both.' Then alarm pierces me. 'Has something happened?'

'Nothing specific. But she's changed.' He plays with the zip on his jacket, clearly ill at ease. Don't rush him, I tell myself.

'I need to ask you something,' he says.

'Go ahead.'

'Did you know my father is screwing Beth?' He studies me for signs of shock. I nod. Jake's face is pale, angry. Jealous. Part of me recoils from discussing Beth and Marcus with him. He's too young, this serious lad who I've known ever since Anna Wilding, flushed with love for her new-born, first showed him to me. Then I reconsider. Don't patronise him, I tell myself. He's an adult now. Besides, I might learn something useful.

'It's disgusting,' he says. 'He's over thirty years older than her, for Christ's sake. What's the attraction?'

'I don't know.' Nevertheless, Donna's words surface in my head. Chances are she's right. Stockholm syndrome might explain why Beth's turned to Marcus.

'He controls her. She's different with him.' Jake scuffs at the carpet with the toe of one trainer, anger darkening his voice.

I force myself to be calm. 'In what way?'

'It's as if she's a robot. Like she's going through the motions.'

'You said he controls her.'

'Yeah. He's like that with everybody.'

Memories crowd into my brain, of Anna Wilding long ago, her complaints bitter and numerous. Marcus's affairs. The way he ordered her about. How she chose every word carefully when speaking to him, terrified she'd ignite his anger. He never hurt her physically, at least not that she admitted to, but the bastard was abusive all right. Small wonder he pushed her into mental illness.

'Your father's not a good man.'

'He's a fucking arsehole.' Jake's foot stops scuffing the carpet. He glances at me, his expression sheepish. 'Sorry, Mrs Sutton.'

'Don't be. You're right.'

'She doesn't have a mind of her own anymore. It's all "Yes, Marcus, whatever you say, Marcus," all the time. She doesn't seem happy, though.'

Hope flickers within me. 'No?'

'He's already tiring of her.'

His words drive my hope higher. 'Really?'

'Yes. At first, he was all over her. Sickening, it was. Couldn't bear to be around them. But now…' He shrugs. 'It's as if she's too much effort. As though she's a toy he's bored with.'

Jake's right, I'm sure. He's perceptive, in spite of his youth.

I choose my words carefully. 'We may need to stand back, let matters run their course. I've spoken with Beth about this.'

'You have? What did she say?'

'Not much. She's defensive, puts up barriers. If we push her, it'll only alienate her further.'

'I guess.' Moodiness clouds Jake's voice. 'I should go.' He doesn't, though.

I sense he's holding something back. 'You care about her as more than just a friend, don't you?'

An unhappy sigh. 'She's not interested in me that way.'

'Must make it worse when you see her with your father.'

'It's hell. On all sorts of levels.' He runs his fingers through his hair, his gesture jerky and irritated. 'I've been pretty wound up recently.'

'Listen, Jake. Odds are he'll either dump Beth, or else the relationship will fizzle out. Either way, we need to help her. She's… she's not in a good place right now.' I don't elaborate.

Words can't convey the emptiness I saw in my child's eyes. 'We'll look out for her, OK? Pick up the pieces if we have to.'

***

'You'll feel better once you've got that down you.'

The evening after Jake's visit, and I'm at Donna's place. I take a gulp of the wine she's handed me. A smooth Merlot, my favourite. My head sinks back against the sofa, the alcohol warming my stomach. Beth is why I'm here, in the messy, overfilled room Donna calls her den. I drink more wine, anticipating the moment when the effect will kick in, sanding the rough edges off my thoughts. They're dark. Beth's been even more withdrawn today, spending her time alone in her room. Not over at Marcus's house, though, and for that I'm thankful.

Donna sits cross-legged on the floor in front of me. She stretches out her wine glass and chinks it against mine. 'Here's looking at you, kid.'

'You make a crap Humphrey Bogart.'

'Who cares? Tell me what's going on with Beth.'

I do, holding nothing back. When I've finished, Donna's uncharacteristically quiet.

'So.' She twists the stem of her empty wine glass through her fingers. 'You reckon it's more than domestic abuse.'

'Yes. Why else would she mention being shut in a basement by a man? For good, she said.' I shudder. 'She looks like hell, too. I'm worried about her mental state.'

'Is her fling with Marcus Wilding still going on?'

'No idea. She's not been over there the last few nights, though. Jake reckons his father's tiring of Beth. Thinks it won't be long before he dumps her.'

'Will she take it hard, do you think? If he does?'

'I don't know. I haven't a clue what's going on with her anymore.' The admission hurts. I've failed my child.

'What she said about the basement. She's afraid her abuser will find her again.' Donna's words shock the hell out of me.

A possibility I've not considered. Whoever took Beth might be capable of tracking her, may know where she lives.

'I'll go to the police.' I scramble to my feet, my eagerness to protect my daughter fierce and hot. 'So we can nail the bastard who did this.'

'Sit down, Ursula.' Donna's voice drags me back to earth.

'What?'

'You have no solid evidence.'

'But what she said. About the basement. Isn't that enough?'

'Not for the police.'

'Then I'll get her to tell me what happened.'

'Will you? You've not managed it so far. For whatever reason, Beth won't talk. If she refuses to tell you what happened, what chance is there she'll be more forthcoming in a police interview room?'

Donna's right; reluctant as I am to admit it. I sit back down. 'Someone's held her captive, though. I'm certain of it.'

'Are you? She packed a bag, remember. The evening she disappeared. Doesn't fit with her being abducted.'

'Maybe it does. Let's say she was planning to stay with a friend, like she said, but it all goes wrong. Somebody snatches her.'

'You think that's likely?'

'No. But these things do happen.'

'It's more probable she left to be with a guy. He turned into Mr Control Freak, wouldn't let her leave. Locked her in this basement she mentioned.'

'Still a crime.' My voice rises high, my breath faltering. I'm on to something, although how deep, how dark, I can't fathom. 'Help me, Donna.'

'I will. I'm here for you, babe. But you need a clear head. You can't go rushing off to the police, not yet.'

'How do I protect her, though? Suppose he's on a mission to snatch her back?' A sob chokes my throat.

Donna sets down her wine glass, reaching over to squeeze my arm. 'You say she spends her days in her room?'

'Yes. She only leaves the house when she's off to see… *him.*' Years of loathing of Marcus Wilding fill my voice.

'Make sure someone's always with her. If she goes to Marcus's, ask her to text you when she arrives. Same when she leaves. Pay for a taxi for her either way.'

'You think she'll agree? She's twenty, Donna. Not fifteen any longer.'

'If she's scared her abuser will find her, then yes, she'll play ball.'

'And in the meantime?'

'You hang back. Make sure she knows you're there for her.'

I realise I've not told Donna a certain detail. 'She said something else. How I'd be disappointed in her, if she told me what happened.'

Donna lets out a soft whistle. 'Any idea what she meant?'

'None.'

'Have you spoken with Chris?'

'No. Well, only to argue, as usual. I've not mentioned what she said about the basement.'

'Get him on side. Ask him to tackle bloody Marcus Wilding again, make him see sense. If the bastard's going to dump her, better he does it sooner rather than later.'

'I'll speak to him tomorrow.'

'What you've said sheds light on why Beth's so hung up on a man thirty years her senior.'

'How?'

'Let's suppose you're right, and she's been kept locked in a basement by some guy. Remember what I told you about Stockholm syndrome? She was missing for two years. More than enough time to develop an emotional dependency on whoever took her.'

'And Marcus Wilding is her solution.' Donna's words align with my own suspicions. 'Jake said something the other day. How controlling Marcus is with her, how she does whatever he tells her.'

'Makes sense. She's adrift, unused to thinking, acting for herself. So she seeks someone who'll give that to her. And they don't come much more domineering than Marcus Wilding.'

'So he's a replacement authority figure.'

'Yes. Meanwhile, do what I say. Back off with the questions. And get that husband of yours on board. If ever Beth needed a father, it's now. Time Chris took his head out of his arse.'

CHAPTER 24 – *Ursula*

Beth's not been to see Marcus Wilding for a week now. That's good, but I'm beside myself with worry. *He'll shut me back in the basement if I do. For good.* Despite what Donna said about not pressing Beth, I'm finding it increasingly difficult not to act. She came from my body; we're the same flesh. I'd kill for my daughter, my anger white-hot towards the man who bruised both her wrists and her soul.

I've cancelled my language clients so I can keep an eye on her. Not that it takes much. She's in her room most of the time. Most days she skips showering, appearing at meals in her pyjamas, her eyes blank. I'm no doctor, but I reckon she's depressed. Eggshells surround my child, and it's as though I'm cracking them under my feet every time I attempt to talk with her.

Today, I'm in the kitchen, chopping vegetables for soup, when I hear Beth descending the stairs. A good sign, I decide. We'll eat, spend the afternoon together, and with any luck, she won't be so brittle. The open doorway allows me a clear view of the hallway. What I see unnerves me, because I'm not sure what it signifies. In a strange about-face, Beth's at the coat rack, putting on her jacket, her handbag on the floor. She doesn't see me, or pretends she doesn't.

'Going somewhere?' I keep my tone artificially light.

Beth shrugs. 'Just out,' she says. 'Can I borrow some money?'

Before I can stop myself, the words issue from my mouth. 'What for?' Way to go, Ursula, I chide myself. Alienate her, why don't you?

Beth doesn't react, though. 'Bus fare.'

'OK.' I go into the lounge, grab my purse and hand her some cash, my mind racing all the while. Beth, out, alone, vulnerable to her abuser snatching her again. Just as I'm wondering how to handle this, my mobile rings.

It's Chris, phoning to ask whether I need him to buy groceries on his way home. He rambles on, while my daughter leaves the house before I can stop her. I peel back the lounge curtains and watch as she walks towards the bus stop. When she reaches it, she halts. Only one route, the 319 to Bath, services our road. Window-shopping then, for clothes at the Southgate centre. I'm reassured. A sign she's easing back into normality, overcoming whatever demons have been stalking her.

By the time I get off the phone with Chris, Beth's boarded the bus. Two hours pass, then three. Panic mounts within me, awful visions of having to report her missing a second time. I stare out of the lounge window throughout the afternoon. Just after four o'clock, a bus pulls up, depositing Beth at the stop.

When she walks through the door, I'm there in the hallway, and my arms go round her, hugging her so tight I don't think I'll ever let go.

'What was that for?' she asks, when I release her. My hand strokes her hair away from her forehead, and for a second the old connection between us returns.

'Just because,' I reply.

The next day is Groundhog Day. At the same time, Beth comes downstairs, reaching for her jacket, only this time I'm waiting in the hallway.

'Need bus fare?' I ask.

She nods. I hand her some notes from my purse. 'Treat yourself to something nice while you're out.' Play it cool, I remind myself. Once she's gone, I grab my car keys. I intend to find out where Beth's going. Check if any man is shadowing her. I did plenty of thinking last night, during the long hours when I couldn't sleep. I'm not proud of violating her privacy, but if it keeps Beth from harm, I'll do it and not think twice.

From behind the lounge curtains, I watch the bus stop. When Beth steps onto the 319 to Bath again, I leave the house, start my car and follow the bus. It's hard going. I have to pull in at every stop to check whether Beth's got off, attracting angry horn blasts from other drivers. Progress is slow. My mind races ahead. Once my girl's reached her destination, I'll park up, then track her until I get a handle on what she's up to.

My plans disintegrate when she gets off the bus along the A420 in Warmley. I swing the car round, desperate to find somewhere to park. By the time I've done so, Beth is well ahead of me, her gait determined. I hurry to catch up, falling in behind her a hundred yards or so back. She turns left, heading along the Siston turn-off.

Although we're close to the city, it's rural here, the narrow road winding through fields, a few houses dotted either side. Conviction that I'm onto something swamps me. Beth never knew anyone who lived at Siston, of that I'm sure. I'm gaining on her now, and I force myself to slow my pace, realising that Beth's walk is no longer purposeful or determined. Her head moves from side to side, as though she's searching for something. Or someone. Then she crosses the road, turning into a small lane, and I speed up, anxious to keep her in view. After fifty yards or so, Beth stops between a large oak and a hedge near the driveway to a house, her body concealed by the trunk of the tree. There she stays.

At the top of the lane, I duck behind the hedgerow on the main road. I've a good view of Beth if I stick my head out. I'm forced to crouch, my knees protesting, but I'm past caring.

Not that there's much to see. Beth remains where she is, facing the house, staring at it. The hedge I'm behind obscures much of it, although I discern the shape of a car in the driveway. Someone's home, then.

Time ticks by while I wait for Beth to approach the house, do anything other than stand, immobile, behind the oak. She doesn't, though. I'm at a loss to explain her behaviour. She raises her hand to her face, and I realise she's wiping away tears.

After half an hour, she moves from under the tree, towards where I'm standing. I sprint back along the Siston road, to a wall behind which I can tuck myself. She passes by, and although she's no longer crying, her expression is so unhappy I yearn to comfort her, before I restrain myself.

Back on the main road, Beth heads for the bus stop, forcing me to walk in the other direction so she doesn't spot me. I duck into a bakery, buying cakes as a cover; as I hand over the money, the 319 passes the window. By the time I leave the shop, Beth's boarded the bus.

***

The next day, mid-morning, I decide on a strategy. First, I call Jake. I don't have his mobile number, so I'm forced to call the landline, praying Marcus Wilding isn't taking a day off work. Luckily, his son answers.

I don't bother with preamble. 'Could you come over? Spend time with Beth?'

'I guess so. My shift at the gym doesn't start until later. Any particular reason?'

'I have to go out. Thing is, I'm worried about her, Jake. She's so unhappy. I'd be grateful if you'd keep her company.' A lie; I need to make sure she doesn't go to Siston today. Because that's where I'm heading.

We agree a time. Then I go upstairs and knock on Beth's door. I have no qualms about using my daughter's gastronomic preferences as ammunition.

'Sweetheart? I'm making blueberry pancakes for breakfast. Drizzled with maple syrup.'

Beth pulls open the door. Still in her pyjamas, but at least she's out of bed.

'If you're downstairs in half an hour, they'll be hot and fresh out of the pan.' To my relief, she manages a small smile.

'I'll grab a quick shower, then,' she says.

I'm sliding the first pancake onto Beth's plate when Jake arrives. I've made double portions with him in mind.

I'm heading into the hallway, nodding thanks to him, when Beth calls after me. 'Aren't you joining us, Mum?'

'Already had breakfast,' I shout over my shoulder. Before she can answer, I'm out of the door.

My drive this morning is much smoother. Before long, I'm back in Siston, my car parked up on a grass verge, and I head along the lane. At the top, I spot something I missed on my previous visit. A sign, overgrown by brambles. Heath Lane, it says. I position myself under the same tree as Beth did yesterday, my eyes taking in what's before me. I have a far better view of the house here. The place is old, clearly two cottages knocked into one, a silver BMW on the driveway. A plaque is fixed above the door, a name for the house, although I can't make it out. From my bag, I extract my mobile, tapping on the camera function. The zoom lens zeroes in on the sign before I capture it with a photo. When I stare at my phone, I have the missing part of the cottage's address. This place is called Hirondale.

Nothing else offers any clues. The BMW suggests money, and a fair bit of it. Whoever the occupant is, I'm guessing they value peace, quiet and seclusion. The nearest house must be a good couple of hundred yards away.

Not a bad place to hold a young woman captive.

When I'm done scrutinising the cottage, a detail at the side catches my attention. A window, tiny and set at ground level. One that can only be from a basement.

Beth's words fly back to me. Icy certainty clutches my gut. I reckon I've found where Beth spent the missing two years of her life.

Then the front door opens. A man comes out. Age? Hard to tell. Perhaps twenty-eight, thirty. Tall, lean. Dark curly hair. Moving with difficulty, a crutch under each arm. He has an air-cast walking boot on his right foot. The man is clutching a rubbish sack. He leans, panting, on the refuse bin, before transferring the bag into it with one hand while steadying himself with the other. Then he hobbles back into the cottage.

With a start, I realise where I've seen him before. He was the man I saw staring at our house a while ago.

***

Jake's still with Beth by the time I arrive home. They're watching television in the lounge, so I head upstairs. I need to examine my options. As usual, I turn to Donna. I pick up my mobile.

'Hey, babe. What's up?' The sound of her voice cheers me, as it always does. I outline this new twist of events for her.

'What the hell can I do, Donna? Short of knocking on the bastard's door, how do I find out who he is?'

'Where's that going to get you?'

'Maybe nowhere. But whoever lives at that cottage, he held my daughter prisoner for two years. I need his name. For my own satisfaction.'

'I assume you got the address?'

'Yes. Can I use that?'

'Do an online search. Land registry. Check the title deeds.'

We wrap up the call. I switch on my computer. First, I type Hirondale, Heath Lane, into a postcode finder, and then I bring up the land registry site. Donna's right. For a fee, I can get a copy of the cottage's title deeds. I enter the address and pay the money. Before long, I'm looking at a name. Dominic Perdue.

Perdue. The surname's vaguely familiar, but I can't place it. I turn it over in my head, the syllables bumping and clashing against each other as my frustration mounts, but where I've heard it before eludes me. Might have been one of Chris's business associates, I decide. I'll ask him tonight.

***

That evening, Chris and I are in the lounge. Troy's out; Beth's in her room. We're watching the news. I'm sitting opposite him, biding my time, waiting for the right opportunity to broach Dominic Perdue.

It comes in the form of the Middle East. My husband is an insular man, uninterested in events beyond the English Channel. As the newscaster relates a story concerning the Golan Heights, I sense Chris's withdrawal. I grab the remote and mute the TV.

'Does the surname Perdue sound familiar?' My voice is deliberately casual.

Chris glances at me. 'What name did you say? Purview?'

'Perdue.'

'Once knew someone with that name, yeah. Guy called Lincoln Perdue. Attended Rotary Club meetings, years back. Ran his own building firm.'

'How old?' The name on the title deeds was Dominic, not Lincoln. His father, perhaps?

Chris shrugs. 'I'm not sure, but he was middle-aged when I first met him. Fat bloke, always looked like he was about to have a heart attack.' He sets his coffee on the table. 'He's dead now. Why do you ask?'

I mirror his shrug. 'Came across the name today. Thought it sounded familiar, couldn't place it. Must have heard you mention him, way back when.'

'I probably did. He was a bit of a dick. Not exactly Mr Popular.'

'Did he have any children, do you remember?'

'I think he had a son. Darren, David, something like that.'

'Not Dominic?'

'Might have been. Yes, it was Dominic, I'm sure. What's this about, Ursula?'

'Just curious.' I turn the sound back up on the television, ending our conversation. Something's bugging me. I've heard the name Perdue other than as one of Chris's business associates, but the details elude me.

CHAPTER 25 – *Beth*

Eleven a.m., and I can't face getting out of bed, even though my stomach is growling. Instead, I lie under my duvet, my brain churning. I've returned to the cottage twice now. Dominic's there, because his car's been in the driveway both times. None of it makes any sense. He abducted me, shut me in a basement, shaped me into his companion, and yet when I escape, he does nothing. Why?

As always when I'm confused about Dominic, I turn to Marcus. Tonight I'll go to his house, I decide.

We've not planned this. The memory of our last conversation mocks me, hurts me.

'Shall I come over tomorrow?' The question posed after we'd just had sex. Emboldened, I decided to risk his anger.

'No. For God's sake, Beth, didn't I make it clear? I don't want to see you again this week.'

I didn't challenge him, because that's not how it works between us. Today, though, the emotional hole within me needs Marcus Wilding. Decision made. I'll go there tonight. Now that's sorted, the impetus to get out of bed, shower myself back to normality, sweeps over me. I swing my feet to the floor, stand up and tug open the curtains.

For a moment, the world stops turning. The breath stills in my lungs.

Across the road, fifty yards or so towards the bus stop, stands a man, partly concealed by a lamppost. He's tall, dark, his gaze directed at our house. His weight is supported by metal crutches, his right foot encased in one of those air boots. I can't see his face properly, not at that distance.

A flash of certainty deep within tells me it's Dominic. As it must have been the evening I walked home from Jake's after meeting his father again.

For a second, I stare at him, rabbit to snake. The nets at the window conceal me. But he's seen the main curtains being pulled back, knows someone's at the window, even if he can't identify whom it is.

The deadlock between us breaks as he hobbles away. I peel back my duvet, crawling into the cocoon it offers.

The crutches. An accident, then. His disappearance explained. So simple. I should have waited, stayed in the basement. He'd have come home eventually.

I remain in bed the rest of the day, ignoring Mum's pleas for me to come downstairs, eat something. A scenario runs through my head. Me telling her about Dominic, the basement. Her hugging me, telling me she'll make everything all right. Instead, I huddle under my duvet. Suspended, hanging in time, a mantra hammering through my brain. *He's found me. He's found me. He's found me.*

Followed by: *He'll kill me. He'll kill me. He'll kill me.*

My chest constricts with terror. I'm not so naive to believe Dominic intends to return me to the basement as his companion. Not when I've broken the rules so completely. I've experienced his hands around my neck twice. Once they almost killed me. Next time, they won't stop squeezing, no matter how much I wet myself. He'll strangle me, then entomb my corpse along with Amy's. I still can't think of her as Julia.

I force myself to breathe deeply. At least he can't abduct me with a broken leg. While he's on crutches, I'm safe. I can't stay here, though. Not now that he's found me again. I have to leave, but where can I go, without money or a job?

***

Mum realises I'm going to Marcus's when I come downstairs that night. Her mouth tightens, but she makes no comment.

Instead, she hands me a couple of notes from her purse. 'Here.' She thrusts the money into my palm. 'Call a taxi. Make sure you get one home, too.' Something she's not saying lurks behind her eyes, but I don't question it. The memory of Dominic, his body masked by the lamppost, is too recent, too potent.

Jake's car isn't there when the taxi drops me off. That's good.

Marcus's face, when he opens the door, displays his annoyance. 'I thought we'd agreed not to meet up this week.'

'You said that. Not me.' Greatly daring, to challenge Marcus. He huffs with impatience.

'Now's not convenient.' He hasn't asked me in. Desperation makes me bold.

'I need to ask you something.'

He's clearly reluctant, but unwilling to have me create a scene on his doorstep. As he stands aside, I walk past, our bodies touching for a second, before he pulls back.

Once in his lounge, I spot a bottle of bourbon on the table, alongside a glass. In it sits an enticing finger of alcohol. With one gulp, I drain it. I've never drunk bourbon before; the liquid burns a fiery trail into my stomach. Marcus stares at me.

'I needed that,' I say. The heat in my belly emboldens me. I walk towards him, pressing my body against his, my fingers unbuttoning his shirt. Sex has always been how we communicate. Time to turn it to my advantage.

'Take me to bed.' My voice is low and sexy. I'm shocked when Marcus shoves me away. For a moment, we stare at each other. Dislike contracts his pupils.

'What game are you playing?' he demands.

I need more bourbon. My hand moves towards the bottle, but before I reach it, he grabs my wrist, the pressure of his grip causing me to wince.

'Don't. I didn't offer you a drink. What the fuck's going on?'

My eyes plead with the flint in his. When I speak, the child in my voice embarrasses me.

'Can I stay here? Please?'

'No. Not tonight, Beth. I need to be up early tomorrow. You'll have to leave.'

'I didn't mean tonight.'

'Then what the hell did you mean?'

'I want to move in with you.' There, I've said it.

'*What?*'

'You heard me.' I close the gap between us, not daring to press myself against him for a second time. 'Can we give it a go? Me, here, with you? Please?'

Marcus's retreat is swift, determined. He steps backward, his expression set. 'No. What the hell's got into you? I thought we'd established the ground rules. Sex, nothing more, remember? Then why ask to move in?'

'It's good between us, isn't it? The sex, I mean.' The whine is back in my voice.

'It's OK. Nothing special.'

For a second, I hate him, I truly do. Nevertheless, I press ahead.

'A trial period. To see how it goes. Why not?'

'Out of the question.' Marcus's expression is frantic; he's a caged animal seeking escape. The reality of living with this man smacks me in the face. I've been so caught up in the need to keep myself safe from Dominic I've not stopped to consider how Marcus would be, twenty-four seven. The answer is, he'd be hell, but preferable to death at the hands of Dominic Perdue.

Marcus draws in a breath, eyeballing me at last. 'Pull yourself together, can't you? I've no idea what I was thinking, getting involved with you. You're too screwed-up, Beth. It's over between us. Get the hell out of my house.'

*　　　*　　　*

Once I'm home, my humiliation is complete. Mum spots me as soon as I walk through the door, my skin tear-stained and blotchy.

Concern floods her face, along with something else. Satisfaction, and the realisation makes me bristle. She'll have sussed Marcus and I have argued, that he's sent me away like a naughty school kid, so she's gloating. Her smugness angers me, pours salt into my wounds.

Behind her, tempting me from the wine rack in the kitchen, is the solution. I grab a bottle of French red, thrusting it under my jacket. She calls after me as I run upstairs, but I ignore her. Alcohol will wash away my resentment, erase my humiliation.

Less than an hour later, the bottle is empty.

***

I'm severely hungover the next morning, and my mouth tastes vile. I don't get up, not even to use the toilet. Moving requires energy, motivation, and I have neither. I'll stay here, under my duvet, where it's snug and safe. Where Dominic can't intrude and Marcus is merely an unwelcome memory. The blackness I fought so hard to keep at bay in the basement descends on me, its tentacles probing, testing my response. I allow myself to sink into it, bathe in its dark depths. So peaceful, allowing my mind to bob up and down in its warm waters. The idea of showering, getting breakfast, facing my mother, is inconceivable. Ridiculous, even. Why bother?

I curl myself tighter into my duvet's embrace, and drift into the blackness.

When I awake, I can't ignore the fullness of my bladder. Reluctantly, I haul myself from my cocoon. On my return, I pull back my bedroom curtains a fraction. No Dominic. I retreat to the womb of my bed, but every time I need the toilet, I check whether he's returned to watch the house. It becomes a compulsion. Mum knocks on my door, more than once, asking if I want food, but each time I tell her I'm not hungry.

The next day, I manage breakfast, and then position myself by my bedroom window, staring out. The day crawls by. By the time Mum calls me for supper, he hasn't appeared. On the way out of the kitchen afterwards, I grab another bottle from the wine rack. Back upstairs, I down it in record time, then slide into an alcohol-fuelled stupor, fully clothed, on my bed. I don't surface until eleven the next day.

Once I do, I resume my vigil, despite the pounding between my temples. Marcus Wilding doesn't enter my mind, not once. He was a stopgap, nothing more; right now, Dominic Perdue fills my head. Bathroom visits are the only things that tempt me away from my post.

He appears at five past twelve. His gaze is fixed in my direction, and although the net curtains obscure me somewhat, they won't conceal me altogether. He'll realise someone's at the window. We stare at each other, cat and mouse. Again, I can't see him too well thanks to the distance, but my eyes sweep over every detail of him. Hair, height, clothes. His leather jacket. The air boot and crutches. It's him, all right. I'm still his prisoner. I've merely swapped the basement for my bedroom.

Then he raises his hand, palm forward, in a gesture of acknowledgement. He gives me a brief wave, before he hobbles away.

In that moment, the blackness descends, winding coils tight around my soul, as my mind spirals downwards. Bed is my only option. Under the covers, it's warm and safe and my brain can switch off. For the rest of the day, I sleep, waking only when my bladder's too full to ignore, or when Mum's worried voice, urging me downstairs for food, wakes me.

***

The next day, just before midday, Mum knocks on my door. 'Beth? A parcel's arrived for you.'

I sit up, still drowsy with morning sleep, swinging my feet to the floor. When I open the door, Mum thrusts a package into my hands.

'You getting up for lunch?' she enquires, her expression concerned. Not without reason, I'm sure. I must look a mess, with a bad case of bed hair. I shake my head, and she leaves it at that, although not without a long backward glance as she walks away.

I sit on my bed, staring at the parcel. The label is printed rather than handwritten, and the sender's not put a return address on the back. It's oblong, and heavy, and I'm at a loss as to what it could be. Only one way to find out. My fingers rip open the packaging, revealing a layer of bubble wrap. Underneath is something encased in silver paper, but no card or note. I remove the bubble wrap, stroking the shiny paper before I tear it off. And see what's inside.

When I do, I slide off the bed onto the floor, stifling the howl rising within my throat. The words *Oh God, oh God, Oh God* issue from my mouth in an endless chant, as panic grips my chest. I huddle into a foetal ball, my eyes on the contents of the parcel.

It's the wooden box Dominic gave me last Christmas.

My eyes roam over the birds, the trees, the flowers, on its lid. All the while I continue my relentless chanting, and I hug myself into a tighter ball. How long I stay that way, I'm not sure. At some point I cease reciting my mantra and reach out my hand. My fingertips glide over the smooth wood. Then I flip open the lid.

Inside is a withered red rose.

A moan of despair escapes my mouth as I grasp its significance. The rose is a warning.

My only option is never to leave the house again. If I do, he'll snatch me, and he'll take me back to the cottage, and once he's got me there, he'll kill me, I know he will.

I crumple up the packaging, thrusting it deep into my waste bin. I pick up the box, opening my wardrobe and burying Dominic's death threat deep under the spare duvet, where it's hidden from view. Then I climb back into bed and pull the covers over my head.

I can't see my way forward anymore.

***

I've reckoned without Mum.

The next day, she swings into action. I'm woken at seven by her knock on the door, followed by her marching into my room. She's holding a tray of food. I stare at her, bewildered.

'Sit up, Beth.' Not a request. Groggy, my brain still full of sleep, I don't respond.

'I said sit up.' She sets the tray down on the floor. 'I've brought you breakfast.'

'Not hungry.'

'You'll eat.' She reaches over me, grabs my pillow and jams it behind my back, pulling me upright as she does so. Her mouth is a tight line, her expression unyielding. I stay where she's positioned me. She plonks the tray firmly across my thighs.

'Eat.' Again, not a request. It's not a battle I stand any chance of winning.

Once I start, I realise how hungry I am. Bacon, egg, toast and tomatoes disappear into my stomach while my mother watches. When I've finished, she takes the tray off my lap. 'Take a shower,' she commands. When I don't move, she yanks the duvet off me.

'I'll get your clothes ready while you're in there.' She inclines her head towards the bathroom. 'Do it, Beth. Now.'

When Mum gets this way, she doesn't tolerate any shit. Besides, the new me likes being told what to do. So I shower. Once dry, a towel around me, I lean my hands on the washbasin. My mouth is as rough as a coconut shell; I can't remember when I last brushed my teeth. The backs of them are tacky. I grab my toothbrush, but can't find my toothpaste, the kind for sensitive teeth that only I use.

Mum raps on the door. 'You OK in there?'

'Yeah.' Weariness, despite the sleep I've had, is overwhelming me. 'Do you know where my toothpaste is?'

'Been tidying up. I probably put it in the cabinet. Don't be long, will you?'

I tug open the bathroom cabinet door. Inside is my toothpaste. As I reach for it, I spot something. On the top shelf, tucked behind Dad's electric razor, is a brown plastic bottle, clearly from a pharmacy. Puzzled, I take it out.

It's a prescription for sleeping pills. The name on the label says Ursula Sutton. It's dated a week ago.

I remember her mentioning once not being able to sleep after I disappeared, how Dad made her go to the doctor. My fingers caress the smooth surface of the bottle, turning it upside down and back again, the pills edging from top to bottom as I do so. The bottle is nearly full.

'Beth? You done?'

'Almost.' I replace the bottle and do a perfunctory scrub of my teeth. Mum's waiting for me when I emerge. She escorts me back to my bedroom, the odour of which reminds me of one of Jake's pet sayings: stinky as a badger's arse. On the bed lie jeans, a sweatshirt, and clean underwear. On the floor, a laundry basket. In it is my bedding.

'Get dressed, Beth. Then you're coming downstairs.'

'You going to give me a little privacy?'

'No. Just do it.'

Once we're downstairs, I curl up in one of the lounge armchairs. I don't check whether Dominic is watching the house. The seductive blackness claims me once more, but with my belly full of bacon and egg, my hair clean, my breath fresh with spearmint, it's not so all-encompassing as before. I stay that way throughout the day, my mind blank. Mum leaves me alone, as though she realises she's pushed as far as she can for one day.

Did I say my mind's a blank? Not totally. The odd thought drifts, like tumbleweed, across its surface. The sleeping pills. The way they chinked against each other as they tumbled through the brown plastic depths of their prison. For now, my thoughts don't extend further than that. Just my hands, tilting the bottle, knowing I hold the power to liberate the pills from their cell.

Mum repeats her regime every day. I comply, but inside I'm dead. She doesn't press me to talk, for which I'm grateful. She will, given time, but for now, she's content to structure my day for me.

I spend the hours downstairs, pretending to watch television. I do my best to act normally around Dad, although sometimes I catch him staring at me, his expression one of concern. Troy, too. Occasionally my mind bumps up against memories, or regrets, but mostly it's blank. Only two things break the surface: Dominic Perdue and the bottle of sleeping pills. I sense they're intertwined; how is another matter. Right now it's too much effort to fathom.

At least she hasn't, as yet, asked me to run any errands for her. So far I've been able to stay inside, where it's safe. Jake has visited, for which I'm grateful, and we chat, but he realises something's wrong, although I dismiss his carefully worded enquiries with a brief, 'I'm fine.' Hurt sparks in his eyes each time, and for that I'm sorry.

Each morning, the first thing I do before I shower is take the bottle from the bathroom cabinet. It's less full every time I check. Mum's still using them, then. As I curl up each day in the armchair, the brown plastic bottle often sneaks into my mind, seductive, inviting. It stretches out a hand, willing me to take it, to walk with the pills to sweet oblivion, a place I can sleep forever, where Dominic will never find me.

The growing gap between the pills and the cap, the way they now slide rather than edge up and down as I tilt the bottle back and forth, nudges despair into me. With every pill Mum takes, my chance to reach the nirvana they offer diminishes. I've been such a disappointment to everyone. My parents, Jake, Marcus. In particular, to Dominic. They'll all benefit if I'm dead.

I picture myself going to bed one night, a glass of water in my hand. Waiting until I hear Mum exit the bathroom and go into her bedroom. Then, in my head, my feet pad across the landing. When I return to the bedroom, the brown plastic bottle comes with me. After that, it's easy. I climb into the warm cocoon of my bed. I unscrew the cap from the bottle and tilt a few pills into my mouth. A gulp of water. The tablets slide down my throat. I repeat until the bottle is empty. Then I ease myself under the duvet, pulling it over my head as I wait for oblivion to claim me.

I'm aware I can't do it, though. I'm not so selfish that I'd allow Mum to find me dead in bed, her own sleeping pills the instrument.

My mind seizes on a better idea. I'll steal the pills, then get a bus to the coast, armed with a bottle of wine to ease my exit from this world. After I've swallowed the last pill and drained the booze, I'll walk into the sea, allowing the waves to close over my head, my pockets weighted with rocks. As my lungs fill with water, I'll drift downwards towards the seabed, my arms outstretched, my hair a dark mantilla around my head. A note left on my dressing table will tell everyone I'm sorry for disappointing them.

I'll do it. Now I've decided to die, my mind is calm, settled. I even smile at Mum when she brings me a mug of coffee. I'll steal the pills when I go for my morning shower tomorrow. It's for the best, it really is.

***

In the bathroom the next day, my first move is to open the cabinet. My hands take the bottle, still three-quarters full. I twist off the cap and pour half the tablets into my palm, my fingers caressing their oval whiteness.

'Beth? I forgot the clean towels. Here you go—' Shock silences Mum's voice as she stands in the doorway, a bath towel draped over her arm. Her eyes switch between the pills and me. Neither of us speaks. Understanding, denial, horror, troop across her expression. Any attempt at subterfuge, persuading her that this isn't what it seems, would be futile. She takes the pills from me, replacing them in the bottle, which she thrusts into her pocket. Then she steers me back to my room.

The pain in Mum's eyes sears through me as we sit on my bed. Ashamed, I stare at my feet. She deserves a better daughter than me.

'Why, Beth?' Exhaustion haunts her voice. 'I need to understand. What could be so terrible you'd think of…?' She clears her throat. 'We've always been so close. Why can't you tell me? Let me help?'

What can I say?

'Is it him? The man you're afraid of? You're frightened he'll shut you back in the basement again?'

My breath halts in my throat. How the hell—?

'You told me, remember.'

I don't. The blackness must have claimed me more than I've realised.

'Tell me, and I'll protect you. Stop him from hurting you again.'

You can't. I don't say the words, but they're true. Dominic won't give up until he has me in his possession again. Impossible for Mum to watch me twenty-four hours a day. My alternatives? Death, or never leave the house again. In which case, I'm still his captive.

'We'll go to the police, file charges—'

'No. No police. Not ever.'

'Why not? This man can't hurt you if he's in prison.'

The inside of my lip grows ragged where I've been biting it. I shake my head. 'I can't.'

Mum takes my hands in hers. Her touch is soft, comforting. If I could, I'd stay here forever, with her, just the two of us, despite the fact I'm a bad daughter, undeserving of her love.

'Then will you go to counselling? Or at least think about it?'

I'm silent, contemplating the idea of unburdening myself.

'What would I tell them?'

'The truth, Beth. Or whatever you're comfortable with.'

'They'll inform the police.'

'No. Remember, they're bound by confidentiality rules.'

I shake my head. How could a counsellor help me? Unless you've been held captive yourself, it's impossible to understand what it's like to lose one's freedom.

'I can't,' I repeat.

'It'll be OK. I'll go with you.'

'No.'

'You have to do something. This can't continue.' Mum sits up straight, her back rigid with purpose. A chink echoes from under the bed as her foot strikes an empty wine bottle. She stoops to draw it out. Despair creeps across her face. At least she doesn't ask the obvious: *Have you been drinking*? Or deliver a lecture.

'Oh, Beth,' she whispers.

CHAPTER 26 – *Ursula*

When I first held Beth after she was born, I swore I'd protect the tiny scrap in my arms, to the death if need be. I meant it, too; my maternal flame burned bright and high. Now I'm powerless to help my child. I have failed her as a mother.

I've hidden the sleeping pills. I spy on her when she's in the kitchen, fearful she'll steal a sharp knife to use on her wrists. She's eating very little. Her eyes still hold that blank look, the one that plays a funeral march with icy fingers on my spine. Every morning, I force her to shower, eat breakfast, but beyond that, I'm helpless if she won't go to the police or counselling. I consider the alternatives. Psychiatrists, an enforced stay in a mental hospital? On what grounds? That I found her with a bottle of my sleeping pills in her hand? Impossible to convince a psychiatric professional she's a suicide risk with such meagre evidence.

'Talk to her,' Donna tells me when I phone her.

'I can't,' I say. 'She won't let me in.' Our conversations go round in circles.

Right now, Beth's upstairs in her room. I'm too exhausted mentally to insist she comes downstairs. Instead, I traverse the lounge carpet, trawling my brain for ideas.

My pacing halts in front of the window. My hand, on its way to smooth my hair, freezes in mid-air.

On the opposite pavement, fifty yards or so along the road, partly obscured by a lamppost, stands a man. Dominic Perdue. He's too far away for me to see his face, but the height and build are the same. As is the air boot over his right trouser leg, the crutches. His gaze is fixed on the upstairs part of our house.

At Beth's bedroom. My maternal flame bursts into a pit of fire, hatred its accelerant, the urge to protect my child all-consuming. The bastard abducts my daughter, locks her in a basement for two years, abuses her, but is that enough? Hell, no. Now he has the audacity to stalk her. Worse, he means to snatch her back. Why else would he watch the house?

I'm wrapped in my thoughts, oblivious to all else. When I return my gaze to the pavement, the bastard has gone.

I realise I've no idea what I'm dealing with here. Whoever Dominic Perdue is, I need to find out more. Fast, too. Impossible to talk with him. A man capable of abuse, of holding a woman captive, won't be amenable to reason. If I go to the cottage, I'll be in danger, even if his leg's injured.

He'll shut me back in the basement. For good. The tiny window, at ground level at the side of the house, comes into my head.

An idea forms in my mind.

Dominic Perdue's obviously the sole occupant of the cottage; how else could he keep a young woman captive? More to the point, he's not always there, despite the crippled leg. While he's out, I have an opportunity. I'll go back, wait until he leaves, then check out the place. Find out everything I can about the bastard. The fact I'll be breaking into someone's house doesn't concern me. Where Beth's concerned, I'll tear down the doors of hell if need be.

***

The next day, I aim to get to the cottage around eleven a.m., the same time I spotted Dominic Perdue watching our house. Troy is off school with a stomach bug and Beth has gone back to bed after breakfast, so she's safe for now. I slip an apple and a snack bar into my bag before grabbing my car keys.

The morning is damp and drizzly. I wait outside the cottage until mid-afternoon, my body stiffening with the enforced rigidity as the hours tick past. His car's here, but he won't be driving, not with that air boot. He must be using taxis or buses to get to our house. Once I see motion behind the net curtains, upstairs in one of the bedrooms, but whoever it is disappears within a second. The rain penetrates my thin jacket, and I shiver, the wind whipping my hair from its pins as I stamp my feet to stay warm. At three o'clock, I concede defeat. Either he doesn't spy on her every day, or else the weather's too wet for him. I promise myself I'll come earlier tomorrow.

I'm back in position at ten the next morning. Back home, I left Beth in bed again, and Troy is still off school. I stand and I wait. My body presses against the tree, its rough bark digging into my flesh through my jacket. No rain today. My gaze remains fixed on the front of the cottage; I shift my weight from side to side, praying he'll emerge soon.

I'm rewarded shortly before ten forty-five. The occasional sounds from passing vehicles reach me from the road, but this one's different. I hear a car drive along the lane, branches swiping its roof as it approaches the cottage. A blue saloon, a sign proclaiming it's from Downend Cabs, skirts past the BMW and stops in front of the cottage, tooting its horn. The front door opens. Dominic Perdue hobbles out and gets into the taxi.

Once he's gone, I approach the basement window, kneeling on the gravel, twisting my head to see through it. It's grimy, but the glass is clear, not opaque, offering me a decent enough view of the basement's contents. A bed, one of those guest ones, stands folded-up against the back wall. On the right, a metal filing cabinet. On the left, stairs leading upwards. Nothing else. If anything is below the window, it's impossible to tell from my angle. No obvious signs of habitation, which doesn't surprise me. He'll have cleared the cottage of all evidence once he discovered her missing. The bed interests me, though. No way to drag it up those stairs with a broken leg. It fuels my certainty Beth's been here. By itself, it's merely an old bed in a basement, but my gut tells me I'm onto something.

I need to get inside the cottage. I circle the place, checking for open windows without success. The front and back doors are both locked. My fingers stretch up, testing the top of the main doorway for a spare key, but find nothing. Ditto for under the stone planters set either side of the door. My hand reaches through the letterbox, searching for a key on a string, but draws a blank.

I stand back and survey the cottage. My attention is drawn to the old-fashioned bell, the shoulders of which are coated with a green patina, its age in keeping with that of the cottage. To sound the clapper, there's a chain. I position myself under the bell and peer upwards. Taped inside are two keys, a Yale and a Chubb. Bingo.

I drag one of the stone planters across, its weight pulling against my own, sweat breaking out on my face. The planter is square, stout, its occupant a sickly bush. One that leaves enough room for me to stand, a foot on each side, enabling me to reach into the bell and remove the keys. The tape is old, dirty, signalling the keys haven't been used in a long time. I'd bet good money Perdue forgot they were there.

Once inside the cottage, I head straight for the basement. The key's in the lock. I twist it and pull open the door.

***

I'm struck by the cleanliness in here. The majority of basements are dirty, dusty, forgotten places, but this one isn't. The floor is free from dirt, the wooden bed head sporting only a light coating of dust. As does the metal filing cabinet. Beneath the window, a strange square plastic contraption sits. As I raise the lid, the object's purpose reveals itself. It's a chemical toilet.

Beth's been here, I'm certain. My hands clench with anger.

It makes sense. The bed, the toilet, taking care of sleep and bodily functions. The filing cabinet a place to store whatever possessions he allowed her. Everything's easy enough to justify if the police come knocking. The prick will have considered all angles, both before seizing my girl and after he discovered her gone.

'Fuck you!' I scream into the empty bowels of the cottage. In my rage, I shove the filing cabinet hard. The castors squeal as its metal bulk shifts, its body moving several inches away from the wall. I lean against it, panting, before I remind myself my time here is limited. I can't allow rage to cloud my judgement. I press my shoulder against the filing cabinet, intending to heave it back into place, but I don't. Instead, I stare at the wall, near where it meets the floor.

Beth Sutton. Abducted by Dominic Perdue. She's even added the date that's burned into my memory.

Concrete proof at last. Evidence with which to convince the police, if I can ever persuade Beth to press charges against her abuser. My anger slides away, dissipating into the damp air of the basement like a blown dandelion clock. Icy determination replaces it. I make her a promise in my head. One way or another, I'll nail this prick's arse to the wall. Nobody hurts my daughter and gets away with it. Nobody.

***

I glance at my watch. I've only been here half an hour, but it's time to go. If Perdue returns while I'm here, my rage will flare up again and I'll kill the bastard, or at least try.

Outside the cottage, I tape the keys back under the bell, before dragging the planter back where it was. In the basement, the filing cabinet stands in its original position. No clues to indicate I've ever been here.

On the way home, I contemplate whether to tell Chris what I've found. Despite our issues, he's my husband, Beth's father, and he has a right to know. I reject the idea, though. He'd insist on going to the police, against Beth's express wishes, a betrayal that might break my fragile girl for ever.

I hatch plans. What Donna said about Stockholm syndrome makes perfect sense. I suspect my daughter harbours feelings for this man. Maybe even loves him, explaining why she won't go to the police. Why she came to stare at the cottage. If I'm right, her confused feelings pose a problem. My intention is to confront Beth; tell her I know the truth. How she'll react, though, is a concern. From what Donna told me, victims of Stockholm syndrome defend their abusers. If I'm not careful, Beth might turn against me. I may lose my daughter for a second time.

Haven't I already, though? I recall her vacant eyes, and shudder.

CHAPTER 27 – *Beth*

Ten thirty in the morning. The shroud of blackness hugs me tight today; I pull the duvet over my head, enveloping myself in its warmth. Mum's coerced me into showering and having breakfast, but no more. She didn't insist I go downstairs, for which I'm grateful; I'm aware she's itching to say something, though. Obvious from the way she hesitates before taking my empty tray, her eyes weighing up my mood. Then Troy calls her from below, and the moment is lost. Half an hour later, I hear him leave for school. Dad is already at work.

Footsteps sound on the stairs, then a knock at my door. Mum doesn't wait for me to reply before she comes in. I curl tighter into my cocoon.

'Beth.' When she doesn't get an answer, she places her hand on my shoulder, shaking it. Impossible to feign sleep any longer. I push back the duvet. Our eyes meet.

Mum sits on the bed. Her expression is tender, loving; I can hardly bear to look at her. Such a failure I've been as a daughter. I sit up, preparing myself for what's to come. She's about to badger me again about what happened to me, I'm sure. I'll repeat the same old lie, about staying with a friend called Dominique. It's not so far from the truth, after all.

She doesn't, though.

'I know what you've been through, my love. Some of it, anyway.'

I stare at her. Whatever I've been expecting, it's not this. Impossible for her to know. Isn't it?

'Dominic Perdue.' I'm unable to repress a start on hearing Mum say my abductor's name. 'He's the one who took you. Kept you prisoner. Hurt you.'

I shake my head, even though I'm aware it's useless. 'You're wrong. I already told you. I stayed with friends. A girl called Dominique. You're confused.'

'And you're lying.' Mum smiles. 'You're not very good at it, my love.'

My mouth is dry. 'Why are you saying these things? What is it you think you know?'

'I've been to the cottage, Beth. I've seen the basement where he kept you.'

Her words floor me. Alarm surges through me; panic that she knows, mixed with terror. If she's visited the cottage, she's in danger, if Dominic ever finds out. How to protect her, when she's no idea what she's up against?

'He's been watching the house, Beth. Did you realise that?'

I swallow hard.

'I followed you.' Another wave of alarm shoots up my spine. 'When you went there on the bus. I returned later. That's when I saw Dominic Perdue.'

'You saw him? Really?'

'Briefly. On crutches, his right leg in an air boot. Then I did some digging. Turns out he's the son of one of your father's business associates.'

'*What?*' Something Dominic omitted to tell me. Perhaps he didn't realise there was a connection.

'The man's dead now, though.'

'You're barking up the wrong tree. Why are you saying all this?'

'Did he talk much about his father?'

'Not a lot, no.' Too late, I realise what I've said. Impossible now to shelter behind the fictional Dominique.

'So you admit you were there.'

I nod.

'That he took you.'

'Yes.'

'Did he—' The expression in Mum's eyes warns me whatever's coming is hard to say. 'Did he rape you?'

'No.' The pain in her face recedes. I elaborate. 'He told me he wanted a companion. Didn't seem interested in sex.'

'Thank God.' Mum releases the breath she's been holding. 'How did you get away from him?'

'He didn't come home one day. I managed to escape from the basement. Then I broke a window.' I'm crying now at the memory of my hunger, my exhaustion, the sheer bloody desperation I felt before I smashed my way to freedom. Mum moves to hug me, but I pull back. I'm too raw, too stunned by her revelation. Unable to deal with it, I opt for deflection.

'You followed me?' I inject righteous anger into my voice. 'You had no right to do that. I'm not a child.'

'I'll follow you to hell and back if it keeps you from harm. For Christ's sake! What did you expect me to do? You won't talk to me.'

'Nothing to say.'

'If I didn't make you, you wouldn't wash, wouldn't eat. Don't forget I found you with my sleeping pills in your hand.' Mum grabs my chin, forcing it up so I can't avoid her eyes. 'So don't get pissy with me because I do whatever it takes to help you, because you sure as hell aren't helping yourself.'

Impossible to deny that. Instead, I divert the conversation.

'You said you'd seen the basement.'

'Yes.'

'You mean from outside, right? Through the window?'

'No. I found spare keys taped under the doorbell. Went inside.'

Terror grips me. Part of me, the half I don't understand, reacts on Dominic's behalf. 'You shouldn't have done that. He's a very private person.'

'Yeah, well, men who abduct young women tend to be, oddly enough.'

'You shouldn't have done it,' I repeat.

'I saw your message.'

'What message?' Then it comes back to me. My earring. 'You mean what I carved onto the wall. Behind the filing cabinet.'

'Yes. We can use it as proof he took you. For the police.'

How do I convince her that's not an option? 'What I wrote – it doesn't mean anything. I was angry with him, that's all.'

'You're lying again. Did he keep you in there all the time?'

'No. Not once I'd learned the rules.'

'Rules?' Mum snorts. 'Listen to yourself. You were an adult. You didn't need rules.'

I wipe a tear from my cheek. While I was in the basement, our relationship seemed so normal, so natural. Here, now, Dominic's regime appears twisted, aberrant.

'He's older,' I say. 'More experienced. I was eighteen when he took me. I needed guidance. He provided it.'

Another snort. 'Yeah. By force. I saw the bruises on your arms when you arrived home. Don't tell me he didn't abuse you.'

I don't deny it.

'He did, didn't he? The bastard. The vile—'

'It wasn't like that. Like I said, he had rules. Sometimes I misbehaved, didn't follow them.'

'You weren't a child. He had no right to punish you, to lock you away. Don't you get that?'

Panic swamps me. 'You shouldn't have interfered.'

'How can I not? Being a mother's a lifelong job. It doesn't stop when a child reaches adulthood.'

'Please. You have to let go of this.'

'I understand you're confused. Donna said—'

I'm angry again. 'You've spoken to her? About me?'

'Yes. I was worried about you, sweetheart. I don't ever switch off from being your mother.'

Despite the anger, I'm curious. 'What did Donna say?'

'Have you heard of Stockholm syndrome?'

'What's that?'

'It's when people become emotionally dependent on their abusers. Identify with them, make excuses for their behaviour.'

Recognition flickers deep within me. So that's what they call it.

'Tends to happen in hostage situations. Similar to what happened to you.'

I'm silent. This is too huge for me to grasp.

'You think you love him, don't you, Beth?'

Such a loaded question; I'm not ready to respond. My mind swirls back in time. Dominic's in my head.

'Do you love me?' he asks. In my mind, I smile at him.

'Yes,' I say. 'I love you, Dominic.'

Mum grabs my hand. 'It's understandable if you feel that way, sweetheart. But it's not real, don't you see? It's what people do to survive in terrible situations.'

'I've thought I must be going mad,' I say. 'He was good to me. Most of the time, anyway. When I did what he wanted. Somehow, I lost touch with how things really were. He'd make me tell him I loved him, and sometimes it felt like I really did.'

Mum nods. She gets it, I know she does. In my head, I thank Donna.

'When I came home, everything seemed weird, unreal. Before, he ruled every minute of my day. Then I had the freedom to make my own decisions. Only I couldn't. I'd lost the ability.'

'Is that the reason...?' Mum pauses, swallows. 'Marcus Wilding. Why you turned to him.'

'Yes. I didn't want him, not really.'

'The man's a control freak. Always has been.'

'He offered what I needed.'

'Trust me. You don't need anything from that bastard.'

Desperation overwhelms me and I move towards Mum. Her arms squeeze me tight, my cheek resting over her heart, as the scent of Chanel drifts into my nostrils. Safe in Mum's embrace, I own my greatest fear aloud.

'I'm terrified he'll snatch me again. If he does, he'll kill me.'

'That's why we must go to the police, sweetheart. Tell them everything.'

'No,' I say. 'I'll tell you. But not them.'

So I do. It pours from me, two years' worth of terror and abuse, the dam of my emotions now cracked open. I tell her about meeting Dominic at The Busy Bean, how I couldn't believe he'd be interested in little Beth Sutton, so much younger. How I'd felt adrift, rudderless, confused. The self-recriminations when I realised what he had in mind for me. Life in the basement. His hands around my throat. I don't mention how I pissed myself with terror. I tell her about hearing the radio appeal. My eventual escape.

I talk about Dominic. A lot.

'He's lonely,' I say. 'Like I said, he wanted a companion. Is that so very wrong? Isn't that what we all want?'

'That,' Mum says, 'is Stockholm syndrome in a nutshell.'

'How?'

'You, making excuses for what he did. Yes, we all need companionship. Normal people don't kidnap someone to find love, though. What he did was a crime. No excuses, Beth.'

'He's not all bad. He had a rough childhood.'

'So do many people. Doesn't turn them into kidnappers or abusers of women.'

She's right. Then I remember the books, the special meals he cooked, the red roses. The wooden box. Somewhere deep inside me, an emotion lingers that's akin to love, making it hard to tell the difference.

We're silent for a while. In my head, an old resentment resurfaces.

'I spent two years in that basement. Why wasn't I found?'

'You vanished, sweetheart. No clues, nothing that could help. Nobody came forward with information.'

'Troy.' My brother's betrayal still baffles me. 'Why didn't he say anything?'

Mum pushes me away, staring at me. 'What do you mean?'

'He saw Dominic collect me that night.'

Shock registers in Mum's expression. 'The police questioned him. He told them he didn't know anything.'

'He lied. He could have described him. The car, too.'

Mum's face is stricken. I'm her favourite, but Troy's still her baby boy, her little prince. She loves every atom of him.

'I'll get the truth out of him.' From the determination in her voice, I deduce the conversation won't go well for Troy. 'Later, though. First, we have to sort what to do about Dominic Perdue.'

'He's dangerous. He's already killed one woman.' The words escape me before I can rein them in.

'*What?* How do you know this?'

'He told me.'

'Who was it?'

'Someone called Julia. He didn't say much about it.'

'What exactly did he tell you?'

I breathe deeply, trying to suck courage into my lungs. The part of me terrified by Dominic is in control, and it's hard to prevent myself shaking, so great is my fear.

'That there was another woman, this Julia, before he abducted me. He said she was twenty when he took her. How she disappointed him, though, wasn't what he'd hoped for.'

'And he told you he killed her?'

'Yes. He said he strangled her, the same as he almost did with me one time.' I repress a shudder. For a second, Dominic's hands press against my throat, before I will them away in my head.

Mum's face is ashen. 'You're lucky to be alive, my love.'

I breathe a sigh of relief. She believes me. No need to show her the tiny silver shoe as proof.

'I wonder what he did with the body,' Mum says.

'She's in the other basement.'

'What do you mean?'

'The one next to mine. It's all sealed-up now.'

'Dominic Perdue told you this?'

'No.' Impossible to explain my conviction, born out of countless nights talking with Amy through the wall dividing us. 'But I'm sure that's where she is.'

Mum's face takes on her determined look. 'We have to inform the police. Someone, somewhere, is missing this Julia. They deserve answers.'

'No!' My fist pounds the duvet, my vehemence startling Mum. She stares at me as I labour to regain my breath, my heart thudding, tight laces of terror constricting it.

'I can't deal with going to the police,' I say.

'We have to. Don't you see? He's killed a woman. He'll murder you, too, if we don't get him arrested. Why else would he be watching the house?'

I don't mention the dead roses, the wooden box. 'It's all too much. The idea of everyone knowing, a court case, having it all made public.'

'Nobody will blame you. You're the victim here. As was the other woman.'

'I can't,' I repeat.

'We'll get psychiatric reports. About the Stockholm syndrome. You were kept prisoner in a basement, for Christ's sake. People will understand.'

'How can they? I don't understand it myself.'

'We have to, Beth.'

'No. Don't you see? I know what he's like. He'll have erased all traces of me.'

'Not all. Don't forget your message on the basement wall.'

'I can't handle the police. That's final, Mum.' My voice is firm now. My gaze on her is steady. It has to be, because it's vital she accepts what I'm saying. 'Don't you get it? I'm holding on by a thread here. A court case, reporters, having everyone find out – it'll tip me over the edge. For good.'

Our eyes do battle, but I don't waver. Accept this, I say to her silently. Because it's the only way possible. Resignation creeps across her face. She's not done yet, though.

'What, then? If you won't go to the police?'

'I need to rebuild my life.'

'How can you do that? When he's watching the house, waiting to pounce?'

'I'll move away. A different city, somewhere he won't find me.'

'How will you ever be sure you're safe? Do you want to spend the rest of your life wondering if he'll track you down?'

'I'll change my name.'

'Even if you do, he might manage to get to you somehow. People like Dominic Perdue don't give up easily.'

She's right. Again. 'It's all I can do,' I say, aware of how weak my words sound.

Silence for a while. 'I'll miss you,' Mum says when the tension between us almost snaps. 'I've only just got you back.'

'I'm sorry.'

'Can I ask you something?'

'What?'

'Why didn't you tell me? OK, so you've been confused. But you could have told me about Dominic Perdue. Even if you didn't want to involve the police.'

'I was frightened,' I say.

'Of him? Yes, but—'

'Not of him.'

'Then what?'

'I thought you'd be disappointed in me.' I can't bear eye contact, so great is my shame.

'What? Darling, why?'

'Because I was naive. Gullible. He tricked me, but I let him.'

'And you believed I'd blame you?' The sadness in her voice tortures me.

'Yes.'

Mum draws me back into her arms. 'Sweetheart.' Her hand strokes my hair. 'I told you before. Under no circumstances will I ever be disappointed in you.'

CHAPTER 28 – *Ursula*

Close as we are, I'm not always honest with Beth.

Yesterday she was too fragile for me to do more than hold her, once she'd admitted what happened. Twin emotions raged inside me, both of which I concealed from Beth. They're still warring within me today, as I linger over my morning coffee. Relief is the first one, the weight of my daughter denying her abduction now gone. So has my worry, in part. Her eyes aren't blank any longer. She's clearly confused and scared, but she's not a suicide risk anymore. Not from her talk about moving away, starting a new life.

The second emotion churning through my head? Rage. I'm mad as hell with Dominic Perdue, a fiery anger that begins deep in my gut before spreading to consume every part of me. The prick needs to be punished for what he's done. Beth's excuses about his father don't wash with me. I'm not one of these bleeding-heart lawyers who plead bad childhoods as the reason their clients do terrible things. I believe Beth when she says he didn't rape her, but both emotional and physical abuse featured in their relationship. Whatever warped feelings she harbours for this man, they'll best be helped by a court banging the bastard behind bars for twenty years. Screw his difficult upbringing.

I'm stymied, though. Beth's too fragile to endure the rigours of Dominic Perdue being put on trial. I picture her in the witness box, one of those bleeding-heart lawyers ripping her to shreds, and I concede she's right. Whether she'll change her mind, I can't say, but every day we don't go to the police, her case weakens. Apart from her message on the wall, precious little evidence exists to support her story.

***

Later, once I'm in bed, I decide on a strategy. In my anger, I've overlooked the fact the man's a murderer as well as a kidnapper. If I can't nail him for what he did to Beth, chances are I can get him banged up for the other woman's death. Impossible to betray my daughter by talking to the police. Instead, I'll dig deeper, which entails another visit to that damned cottage. I'll snoop around some more. Discover tangible evidence, if I can, about this Julia. Then I'll make an anonymous tip-off to the cops. A long shot, but worth the risk.

My thoughts turn to Troy. I'm at a loss to explain his behaviour. Why didn't he tell the police what he saw that night? I'll have to confront him, but right now, Beth's my priority. Once I've ensured she's safe, my son and I will have what I suspect will be a difficult conversation for him.

***

Later the next morning, I tell Beth I have an optician's appointment. Once I'm in Siston, I park the car, and then position myself under the oak, waiting, watching. It's a damp, drizzly day, one in which Dominic Perdue doesn't leave the cottage. He's there, all right; after a while, I spot a man moving behind the net curtain at the front of the house. After another hour, too stiff and soaked to continue, I give up. Tomorrow, I promise myself.

'You took a long time,' Beth comments when I get home.

'They were behind with the appointments.'

She runs her eyes over my damp clothes. 'How come you're so wet?'

I think fast. 'I forgot my umbrella.'

The next day I plead a dental check-up. Another fruitless trip. I'll go back when the weather's better, I promise myself. What with his injured leg, the bastard might not venture out when it's raining. The two wet days that follow, I talk with Beth. We bake cupcakes, practise her Italian, watch television, with me happy she's safe, at least for now. We never mention Dominic Perdue, or her plans to move away from Bristol. Every day, Beth becomes more her old self. The blankness has gone from her eyes; for that, I'm beyond grateful.

When I pull back my bedroom curtains the next morning, I'm greeted by a dry world. The sky is grey, but without rain clouds.

'Lunch with Donna,' I tell Beth, when she asks where I'm going.

***

An hour after I arrive at the cottage, a taxi pulls up at the door. It leaves with Dominic Perdue in the back. Within seconds, I'm pulling the stone planter into position under the bell, ready to retrieve the keys.

Once inside, I don't dawdle. I've decided to concentrate on the upstairs rooms. I'm not likely to find much in the lounge or kitchen, and the basement has already yielded its secrets.

I start in his bedroom. I'm careful to replace everything exactly as it was. The mail I find tells me he's deep in debt. In arrears with his mortgage, credit card balances mounting. He's one hell of a spender, evidenced by his wardrobe, crammed with designer shirts and leather jackets, their fabrics soft beneath my fingers. No pornography or sex toys. Whatever drives this man, it's not lust. I pull open the drawers of his bedside cabinet. In the top one, I discover herbal sleeping tablets, paracetamol, nail clippers. An old asthma inhaler. And, bizarrely, a bottle of Samsara perfume. That's weird. No signs he's a transvestite; no dresses in the wardrobe, no make-up that I've found. The leather jackets proclaim masculinity, loud and clear. So why the perfume?

Next, I enter the bathroom, which is immaculately clean, smelling of disinfectant and bleach. My prying reveals nothing, apart from his taste in toiletries. Once I've checked the contents of the cabinet, I move on to Dominic Perdue's home office. His computer is password protected, and I don't have the time or skills to crack it. The bookcases contain dull tomes about investment strategies and economic theories. Piles of magazines on the same topics. Files, each labelled with a different year, containing printouts, invoices and accounts information. There's nothing for me here. Disappointed, I enter the last bedroom, clearly used as a storeroom.

Boxes cover most of the floor. Once I start opening them, it becomes obvious this isn't Dominic Perdue's stuff. Everything I find is from Lincoln, the man who Beth described as a piss-poor father, the business associate Chris labelled a dick. Not Mr Popular, I recall him saying. I rifle through bank statements, letters, accounts files. His driving licence is in one of the boxes; I stare at the picture. Lincoln Perdue is overweight, his skin mottled and pitted, an unhealthy flush in his cheeks. A drinker's fleshy nose. The expression sour, cruel. Definitely a man unfamiliar with the more tender emotions.

I straighten up, rubbing my aching back. Underneath the window is an old suitcase, which I don't bother checking. It'll only contain more of Lincoln Perdue's life. Besides, his son could return at any minute, and I'm done with searching the cottage. I cast a glance over the boxes. Nothing out of place, no tell-tale signs I've been here. Time to leave.

***

On my way out, I pause by the basement, drawn to the dank place where my child was held prisoner. I stare into its depths, at the fold-up bed, the chemical toilet, the filing cabinet. Beth endured two years down there. I shudder.

Then sounds reach me. A car, presumably a taxi, arriving, its tyres crunching the gravel. Muffled voices as the fare is settled. Oh God, he's back. And he'll notice the planter has been dragged out of position, revealing my intrusion. The front door's unlocked, too. Pure instinct drives my reaction. Fight or flight is the choice, and I pick the latter. My feet pound into the kitchen, heading for the rear exit. It's locked, no key visible anywhere. I'm trapped. Think, Ursula, I urge myself, my brain in overdrive. To one side of the kitchen is a lobby. Upon investigation, I discover it leads to a small shower room. I slip inside, my breath held hostage in my chest. I'll hide in here, I decide, until I get a chance to make a run for it.

The main door to the cottage opens. Footsteps, supported by crutches, sound in the lounge. They pause, and then head towards the kitchen. Too late, I realise the shower room door, previously shut, is ajar a couple of inches. Impossible to close it without alerting him.

The door is pulled open. I find myself staring at my daughter's abductor.

'Who the hell are you?' Incredulity and anger jockey for position in his expression as Dominic Perdue fills the doorframe, blocking my exit. I weigh up our respective advantages. The man's minus one functioning leg. He's bigger than I am, though. His crutches are potential weapons. Not to mention the fact he's clearly mentally unbalanced. I'd put the odds in his favour. We stare at each other. The ice that's replaced the anger in his expression freezes my soul. If Beth encountered this on a daily basis, it's a miracle she's even halfway sane.

My instincts tell me he's sussed my identity. I doubt many middle-aged women commit burglaries. That only leaves one option.

'You're her mother,' he says.

'Yes.'

He nods. So calm, although what's going on behind those eyes is anyone's guess. With a shock, I register they're different colours. One brown, one blue. Weird, but nothing about this man strikes me as normal.

'How is she?'

'As you'd expect. Pretty messed-up in the head.'

A grin, vile in its smugness, tweaks the corners of his mouth. 'That doesn't surprise me,' he says. 'Otherwise you wouldn't be here today, poking your nose into my business. You'd have gone straight to the police. Looks like I trained my girl well.'

'You bastard.'

The grin disappears. 'The bitch left me,' he says. Like a five-year-old, whining because his favourite toy's been taken from him.

'She was never yours.'

'You're wrong. She belonged to me from the moment I saw her.'

'What happened to your leg?'

'Car accident. Not healing properly. Hence the air boot and crutches.'

'I hope it hurts like hell.'

He hobbles closer. 'How did you gain entry? The doors were locked. The windows don't open.'

'Spare keys. Inside the bell.'

Annoyance sparks in his weird eyes. 'Damn him. The old bastard keeps fucking up my life, even after he's dead.'

'Meaning?'

'My father kept a spare set hidden in the bell. I forgot they were there, after all these years.'

'Careless.'

He shrugs. 'So it seems. What are you doing here?'

'Call it a fact-finding mission.'

He grins. 'I'm right, aren't I? She won't give evidence against me. You're here hoping to find something. You won't.'

I shrug. 'Know thy enemy, as the saying goes. It's not been a pointless visit.' I'm amazed at how calm I sound. Then I cut to the chase.

'What happened to the other woman you murdered? The one called Julia?' For a moment, surprise creeps across his face. Then it's replaced by cunning.

'Wouldn't you like to know?' A smirk plays around his mouth.

'What the hell is wrong with you?' My abrupt change from calm to furious causes him to shift uneasily on his crutches. 'How can you abduct and kill women without caring? Without conscience?'

He doesn't reply, but stares at me with those odd eyes, and I realise he's weighing up a response to my question.

'It was different with Beth,' he says at last. 'She didn't die. Unlike the other woman.'

'Why not?'

'Because I cherry-picked her.'

'What the hell do you mean?'

'As restitution. Don't you get it? She had to live.'

I sense we're edging close to something important here. I wait.

'You asked what is wrong with me.'

I'm barely breathing now, my entire concentration fixed on the man in front of me.

'I'm damaged.'

I snort inwardly. Pathetic. 'I suppose you're going to plead a bad childhood.'

Anger flashes into his face. 'It wasn't exactly milk and honey.'

'Absent mummy? Abusive daddy?' Such pleasure in taunting this man, despite how dangerous he is.

'Spot on.' His voice is tight. 'My mother died when I was seven. Brain aneurysm.'

The bottle of Samsara in his bedside cabinet. The reason for it comes to me, confirmed by the sadness in Dominic Perdue's face. Part of him is still a small boy, missing his mother, worshipping her memory. The perfume is his comfort blanket.

'You loved her,' I say. He doesn't reply, but the way he drops his gaze tells me I'm right.

I decide to push deeper. 'And your father?'

Anger replaces the hurt. 'Like you said. He was abusive.'

'Really.'

'You think I'm bad. My father makes me seem like an angel. He was far worse than I've ever been.' His eyes flick away from me, as though he's recalling a distant memory. 'I saw him do something terrible once.'

I'm out of sympathy. 'You don't say.'

Dominic Perdue shifts his weight onto one crutch, lifting the other in the air, jabbing it at me, a gesture of accusation. 'You don't know the half of it.'

My patience snaps. I've had a bellyful of the man before me, the man who kidnapped my daughter, held her captive for two years, denying her food, showers, a proper toilet. Who almost strangled her. All done so he could wear her down, sand her soul paper-thin, before leading her into the dark realms of Stockholm syndrome. True, he never raped her, he didn't kill her, but he murdered something inside her, and for that, I'm mad as hell at Dominic Perdue. I don't hold back.

'You pathetic bastard. You've killed one woman. Kidnapped my daughter. And your excuse is that you had a less than perfect childhood. Clichéd or what? You're a sorry excuse for a man. The only way you can get a woman is to abduct her.' He doesn't respond, merely stands there as I hurl my fury at him. 'Beth's told me how you live. No friends, no family. Nobody to care about you. And I've seen the letters. You're drowning in debt. Your life isn't worth shit. Tell me, arsehole. What the hell do you have to live for?'

The silence crackles around us once I stop, my breath coming fast in my chest, my lungs aching from raw emotion. Dominic Perdue is still staring at me, and I realise my tirade has found his soft underbelly. A seven-year-old boy stands before me, concealed in the body of an adult male. He's hurting, he's vulnerable, and the satisfaction that delivers is priceless.

'I'm not as bad as you think,' he says.

'The hell you're not. One way or another, I'll bring you to justice. For murdering that woman. For keeping Beth captive.'

He shakes his head. 'I didn't murder—'

I'm no longer listening. Beth's face, tear-stained and tense, drives me on. 'The world would be better off without a prick like you.'

Dominic Perdue's silent for a few seconds. Then he sighs. 'At times, I've thought the same thing.'

'Shame you never did anything about it.'

'I've wanted to. In my teens, particularly. Hang myself from a rafter. Mum's death hit me hard. I've never got over it.'

I go for the kill shot. 'Your mother. What the hell would she think if she knew what you've become? You're a disgrace to her memory.'

I've found his Achilles' heel all right. My barb has penetrated deep. Sadness sweeps over his face, though, not anger, and the retaliation I expect never comes. Instead, he stands there, stricken, and I seize the moment. Before he has time to react, I lunge at him. My foot kicks at the crutch under his arm, on the same side as his air boot, while I shove him sideways with all the force I can muster. He fights to regain his balance, but his right leg's useless. The tips of his crutches skid off the floor as he hits the shower door. An enormous crack booms in my ears and the glass shatters. As he falls into the cubicle, I run into the kitchen, through the lounge, towards the front door. Thank God I didn't lock it after I entered. The bastard's quick to recover, I'll give him that. As I tug open the door, I hear his crutches connecting with the shower-room floor as he hauls himself upright, tinkles of falling glass accompanying the sound. I'm too fast for him, though. In a nanosecond, I'm running down the drive, towards my car, away from the monster that's Dominic Perdue.

CHAPTER 29 – *Ursula*

The house is silent. Beth's in her room, and Chris and Troy won't be home for several hours. Time to process the mess in my head, what encountering my daughter's kidnapper means. Because I intend to keep my promise to Dominic Perdue. *One way or another, I'll bring you to justice.*

I've overlooked something vital. The words Beth told me, that last time we spoke, are rattling around in my brain, knocking on the inside of my skull. *She's in the other basement.*

In my mind, I see the small dimensions of Beth's prison, realising only now that they aren't enough to stretch under the full length of the cottage. She's right. An identical room must be on the other side of the cottage. She mentioned it being sealed up; I sure as hell didn't see any door leading to a second basement. Doesn't rule out a window, though. If I go back to the cottage, will I find one?

I'm not so stupid as to think I'll locate the window, peer through it and see what remains of Dominic Perdue's first victim. Luck as nice, neat, and convenient as that isn't going to come my way, not with a ruthless bastard like Perdue involved. There's no murder weapon to find, not if he strangled this woman, and the cottage retains no signs of Beth's imprisonment apart from her message scratched into the wall. If he's taken that much care to expunge my daughter's presence, then he'll have been equally meticulous with disposing of evidence relating to the other woman's murder.

It's the one place I've not checked, though. The thought nags away at me, the worry I've not covered all angles where the cottage is concerned. If I return, I can locate the window of the second basement along with the sealed up entrance, break in if possible, search every inch, hunting for clues. What I'll do if I find anything, I'll decide later. My idea of an anonymous tip-off seems best. While I'm there, I'll chip Beth's message off the wall. With all evidence of my daughter scrubbed from the cottage, I'm not betraying her by setting the police onto Dominic Perdue.

I'll go back tomorrow, I tell myself.

Something else is nagging away at me. What I'll do if I don't find evidence of the other woman. Because then I'll be out of options. Except one.

I've wondered before whether I'm capable of killing the man who's harmed my daughter. I contemplate what the bastard's put her through, what she's still enduring. In my head, my hands grip an imaginary crowbar, heavy and lethal, smashing into his face, pulping it, slamming down repeatedly until he lies dead at my feet. The satisfaction that engulfs me is so sweet, so pure, that for a moment I'm back in Dominic Perdue's shower room, his blood spattered over my clothes.

I administer a mental head slap to myself. Impossible. Beth needs a mother who's here to support her, not one banged up in jail for murder. I don't give a shit about myself. I'd happily do time in exchange for ridding the world of that prick. I won't drag my daughter through hell to achieve it, though, or deprive my son of his mother.

Focus, Ursula, I tell myself. Don't dwell on killing the bastard. Check out the second basement first.

***

'Lunch with Donna again today,' I tell Beth the next morning. The clock on the lounge wall shows ten thirty.

Her eyes narrow. 'Isn't it a little early?'

I think fast. 'We're going shopping. At Cabot Circus. Then we'll do lunch.' I draw her close, kissing her cheek. She hasn't eaten much for breakfast, but at least she's showered and dressed, and my Italian grammar is beside her on the sofa. I'm reassured it's safe to leave her for a while.

'Stay in the house,' I warn her. 'And don't answer the door.'

***

Without having seen Dominic Perdue leave by taxi, I've no way of knowing if he's here or not. From my vantage point behind the trees, I gaze at his office window, hoping to see whether he's behind his computer, but the light's reflecting off the glass. I'll have to assume he's here, and carry on with checking the second basement from outside.

I skirt the back of the cottage. At the corner, I drop to my knees, listening for any sign he's in the kitchen, because I'm about to crawl under its window, and I don't want the sound of crunching gravel to alert Dominic Perdue.

My ears detect only silence from the other side of the wall.

After I've waited five minutes, and all I've heard has been a blackbird chirping in the trees, I make my move. Edging forward with caution, I crawl in front of the kitchen window, my senses on red alert. I reassure myself. If he hears me, he can't pursue me, not on his crutches. I'll have time to get back to my car. I pick up my pace, rounding the other side of the cottage, to where the window to the second basement should be.

And find nothing.

I stare at where it once was, spotting the signs where it's been bricked up. The edges of the newer stones are obvious against their older siblings, and I flatten myself against the cottage wall, releasing in one long breath the tension I've been holding. What I've seen corroborates Beth's story. The missing window would have been tiny, like its twin. Why go to the trouble of bricking it up if there wasn't something the other side he needed to keep hidden? Likewise with the entrance to the second basement inside the cottage. I'm guessing Dominic Perdue is one of those killers who get off on keeping their victims nearby. He could have disposed of the corpse elsewhere, but instead he chose to leave her where he killed her, saving the other basement for his second captive.

'Bastard,' I mutter. My hands grasp the imaginary crowbar again, before I suppress my anger. I'll wait, see if he leaves by taxi again, allowing me to search the cottage. I've plenty of time; I can't return home, not now I've told Beth I'm lunching with Donna. I'll return to my position under the trees, ready to strike if Perdue decides to go spy on my daughter again.

Back on my knees, I inch along the outside of the kitchen and round the corner, edging towards the basement window. Once I'm level with it, I can't resist peering in. For a second, I can't process what I'm seeing. Then I jerk backwards, an involuntary shriek emerging from my mouth before I stifle it with my fist. I lean against the cottage wall, my breath laboured, my eyes shut, the memory of what I've just seen burned onto my eyeballs.

It's a good thirty seconds or so before I can bring myself to peer through the window again. Dominic Perdue's body dangles from the rafter in the ceiling, suspended from a length of rope. The noose around his neck hangs from a hook he's hammered into the wood.

I rub my sleeve against the grimy window to get a better look. His eyes bulge; his tongue, swollen and purple, protrudes from his slack mouth. He's both pissed and shat himself, by what I can see of his trousers and the floor. Near him is an overturned stepladder, the one he must have stood on to attach the noose to the rafter. His crutches are scattered on the floor. On the fold-up bed is a piece of paper.

Think, Ursula, think, I tell myself. I need to find out what Dominic Perdue has written in what I presume is his suicide note, in case it mentions Beth. I head towards the front entrance while retrieving from my pocket the keys I took with me yesterday when I fled the cottage. As I enter, I note the basement door is open. The stench from below hits me immediately, a mix of shit, piss and early decomposition, causing me to gag and clamp one hand over my mouth. I hurry down the basement stairs, the smell intensifying as I snatch the note from the bed. It's short and to the point. A parody of my words yesterday. 'The world and I are better off without each other.'

I have my answer as to how far I'd go to protect Beth. Because I killed Dominic Perdue. Not directly, not the way I envisaged it with a crowbar, but I'm the reason he hangs in front of me, befouled with his own waste. He must have realised I'd make good on my promise to bring him to justice, one way or another. What drove him to the noose, the overturned stepladder, must have been my parting shot. *You're a disgrace to her memory.* A dirty tactic, to use his dead mother, but effective.

I search my conscience. It's entirely free from guilt.

Now I've found Dominic Perdue's body, I don't linger at the cottage. My priority is my daughter. She needs to know without further delay that her abuser is dead.

***

Beth's downstairs making coffee when I get back. 'Didn't expect you so early,' she says. 'What happened? Did Donna cancel on you?' My expression must have betrayed me, because she stops stirring her coffee. 'Mum? What's wrong?'

I'm silent. Dominic Perdue's bulging eyes haunt my brain.

'Mum? You're scaring me.'

'Let's go upstairs,' I say. I'm unwilling to risk either Chris or Troy returning unexpectedly, given what I need to tell Beth. 'Your bedroom.'

Beth doesn't ask why. Once we're in her room, I shut the door, leading her to the bed. She sits beside me, her face pale with concern.

I inhale deeply. 'I lied to you earlier.'

Beth frowns. 'What about?'

'I never intended meeting Donna for lunch.' Another deep breath. 'I went back to the cottage.'

She blanches. 'Mum! Why, for God's sake?'

'I went there yesterday too.' No need to mention how I taunted her abuser, hurling the words at him that drove him to suicide. 'Dominic Perdue walked in on me.'

Beth's fingers clutch my arm. 'Did he hurt you?'

'I'm fine.' I deliver an edited version of our encounter.

'You were lucky you managed to get away,' Beth says, when I finish, her voice shaky. 'You were mad to go there. After all I've told you about him.'

'I had to. Don't you see? The other woman, this Julia. I thought perhaps—' My hands grasp Beth's shoulders, willing her to understand. 'I might find evidence of her. So he could be convicted for her death, even if he never stands trial for your abduction.'

Silence from Beth. Does she resent me? View what I've done as interference?

'I didn't find anything, though. But, Beth…' I tighten my grip. 'There's something you should know.'

'You're shaking, Mum. What's the matter?'

'When I went there today, I found Dominic Perdue. He was dead.'

'*What?*' The word explodes from Beth like a bullet from a gun. Her body goes rigid. If I thought she was pale before, it's nothing to the chalk of her skin now. When she speaks again, her voice is strained, as though she's forcing it through gravel.

'How did he die?'

'Suicide, my love. He hanged himself. In the basement.'

Tears hover on Beth's eyelashes, waiting to fall. 'Oh my God. Why would he do that?'

'I guess…' I choose my words carefully, mindful that Beth doesn't need to know the part I played in Perdue's death. 'I snooped around a bit. Seems he had bad money troubles, sweetheart. He'd been contemplating suicide for a long time. Said he first thought about it in his teens. From what you've told me, he's led a sad life. His mother dying when he was young, an abusive father. Not that I'm excusing what he did.' I let go of her shoulders and pull her close.

'Part of me loved him,' Beth says into my sweater.

'I understand.' I don't, but then I've not endured what Beth has.

'I'm glad he's dead, though,' she says. 'Is that very wrong of me?'

'No.' Personally, I'm delighted he'll never harm her again. 'He hurt you, sweetheart. Don't ever forget that.'

Beth jerks her head up. 'What happens next? About Dominic?'

She has a point. Eager to erase the memory of his corpse dangling from the basement ceiling, I've not thought things through. I drag my brain into gear.

'I don't know. If we don't do anything, it might be a long time before he's found.'

'The message I wrote,' Beth says. For a minute, I don't understand what she means, and then I remember. The words scratched on the wall of the basement. Proof of her captivity. The evidence I neglected to erase.

'Think, Mum. It'll take time, but he'll be discovered. Eventually. Whoever finds him will call the police, won't they? Someone will spot my message, either when the cops investigate his death or when the cottage is cleared of his things. I can't risk anyone seeing what I wrote, especially not the police. Not with my missing person's record.'

She's right. I curse the fact I didn't remember this earlier on, but after the horror of Dominic Perdue's bulging eyes, his purple tongue, the stench of his evacuated bowels, leaving the cottage was my top priority.

'I'll go back,' I tell her. 'Don't worry, sweetheart. I'll sort it.' The thought nauseates me, but I don't see any other option. One more visit to scratch Beth's message off the wall, removing the last tangible trace she was ever in that basement. I'll leave the door open when I leave. With any luck, whoever delivers the next threatening debt letter to the cottage will be of an inquisitive turn of mind. The smell should flag up that something is amiss, leading the discovery of Dominic Perdue's body.

'I'll go with you,' Beth says.

I stare at her, unwilling to believe what I'm hearing. Is Stockholm syndrome raising its ugly head? Why does she want to return to that hellhole?

'I have to. Otherwise, I'll never be able to put it behind me.'

'You've spent enough time in that basement. No reason you should ever set foot in there again.'

Beth huffs out an exasperated breath. 'Don't you see? I need to know that it's over, that he'll never control me again. Sounds weird. But I have to do this.'

'You don't. I can sort everything—'

'I'm coming with you.' Never have I heard such steel in Beth's voice, and I surrender to it. For whatever reason, returning to the cottage is a catharsis for her, and if that's the case, then I need to support her.

'OK. But you're not going in that basement. Not with him hanging there.'

CHAPTER 30 – *Beth*

I t's the next day, and I'm in my bedroom, getting dressed. As soon as we've had breakfast, Mum and I are going back to the cottage.

I've not been completely honest with her. Yes, it'll provide closure for me to walk through where I was imprisoned, knowing I do so as a free woman, not a captive. But I can't miss out the basement. Even if Dominic's body is there. Or perhaps because it's there. Until I revisit my prison, see him hanging in it, I won't accept that he's dead. And until I do, I'm unable to move on.

***

An hour later, we're at the cottage, outside the front door. My mind flies back to two years ago, to an eighteen-year-old version of myself, the temptation of hot sex with Dominic thrusting common sense from my head. It seems a thousand years ago. I drag a breath into my lungs as Mum twists the keys in their locks and pushes open the door.

The smell hits me straight away. Naive, unused to the realities of death, I'd not expected that. A rank stench of shit and decay assaults my nose and I gag, barely able to restrain the vomit threatening to erupt from my stomach.

Mum puts her arm around me. 'Don't do this, sweetheart. Please. Wait for me in the car.'

'No.' I don't expect her to understand. I push past her, my hand over my mouth. My feet move towards the basement door; I stare at the slats of wood, so familiar. As I hesitate, Mum's hand yanks me back.

'We agreed, Beth. Don't go down there.'

I twist my arm from my mother's grip.

'Don't. I'm warning you, sweetheart. You shouldn't see his body. It's not a pretty sight.'

Too late. Before she can stop me, I'm through the open door, gazing into where I spent the most important two years of my life. I stop, transfixed, at the top of the basement stairs.

In death, as in life, Dominic Perdue fills my world. There he hangs, my abuser, the man I grew to love, if it can be called that, broken, his piss staining his trousers and the basement floor. The stench of his shit is rank in my nostrils. His eyes are swollen out of his head, his mouth slack, his tongue protruding. I get why Mum didn't want me to see this.

Something catches my eye. On the bed behind Dominic. A piece of paper.

'Don't go down there, Beth. Please.'

I have to, though. I need to read what Dominic wrote before he hung himself.

I walk, funeral-march slow, down the basement stairs, coming to stand in front of the bed. I pick up his suicide note. Its message is short. 'The world and I are better off without each other.'

An apology, for sure. Is it more, though? A voice inside my head wonders what Mum said to him when they met. I suspect she gave me a highly edited version of their conversation. I don't intend to challenge her, though. Some questions are best left unasked.

Then I'm snapped back to reality. The smell is too vile, too potent, the sight before me too terrible. I sprint up the stairs, barely reaching the kitchen sink before I vomit, long and loudly. Mum slips one arm around my waist, the other holding back my hair as I retch. It's a while before the spasms ease and I'm able to twist on the cold tap, rinsing my mouth with cool water. When I stand up, the tears come.

I remember I need to do something else. 'Can you give me a few minutes?'

'What for, sweetheart?'

'I spent two years in this cottage. I'd like to say goodbye.'

Judging by her expression, Mum doesn't understand my reasoning, but she stands aside anyway. From the kitchen, I head into the living area, past the sofa on which I spent so many hours. My fingers trail over the Chesterfield chairs, across the television. With a start, I notice my Italian grammars in the bookcase. I walk past the dining table, its memories of fish stew and wine still potent. Then up the stairs to the top floor.

In Dominic's bedroom, I inhale deeply, trying to regain a sense of him, but he's no longer here. I open his wardrobe, burying my face in his shirts, inhaling a faint whiff of the man. As I take in the sterile neatness around me, I'm saddened by the barrenness of his life.

Next is his spare room. In here, amid the neatly packaged boxes, any trace of Dominic is missing, for which I'm grateful. I lean against the windowsill, its edge hard under my bottom. I, Beth Sutton, am half an hour from being free of the cottage forever. Once Mum's scratched my message off the basement wall, nothing ties me to this place except my memories. Impossible to erase those.

'You OK up there?' Mum's voice shakes me from my thoughts.

'Fine. Won't be long.' As I ease myself off the windowsill, my foot scuffs against an old suitcase. I remember it from my previous exploration of the cottage. Now it strikes me as weird. The only other things in here are storage boxes, identical ones, neatly stacked in piles. The suitcase is an anomaly. So much of Dominic Perdue is a mystery, one I'll never know or understand. Curiosity gets the better of me. I flick open the clasps.

Shock draws in my breath, holding it captive in my chest. I struggle to comprehend what I'm seeing. So weird, yet fascinating. I ignore it, unable to process its meaning. Instead, I reach a hand into the suitcase, my fingers shaking as I extract the other item in there. A handbag. It's soft leather, purple, the handles long, tassels on the outer pockets. I twist open the gold fastening on top. Inside are tissues, keys, lip gloss, a purse. At the bottom, a silver charm bracelet.

I draw it out. I already know there'll be a gap in the row of houses, horseshoes, birds and such like. At the very end, near the clasp, where its absence isn't so noticeable, a charm is missing. A tiny boot.

This is Amy's bag, and with it her purse, probably containing some form of identification. I hesitate, part of me reluctant to shatter my mental image of the woman who helped me through the hell of Dominic Perdue's basement. I have to, though. For Amy's sake. Or that of Julia, as she was really called.

I open the purse, revealing a wad of credit cards. A name flies up at me from them, and it's not Julia. The tightness in my chest swells until my ribs threaten to burst from my body.

'Oh my God,' I whisper. I glide my fingers over the plastic of the cards, my brain refusing to take in what I've seen.

I've saved the final item in the suitcase until last. The one that won't let the breath leave my lungs. At first I can't bring myself to touch it; then I stroke its length, marvelling at its smoothness, its softness. How perfectly preserved it is.

I fight for control over my breath before I walk to the top of the stairs.

'Mum?' My voice, shaky with shock, echoes down the stairwell. 'Can you come up here, please? There's something you need to see.'

***

Mum comes upstairs to appear in the doorway. 'What's the matter, Beth?' Concern fills her face as she glances around the room. 'There's nothing in here but crap. Why did you call me?'

I gesture towards the suitcase. The purple handbag lies open, its owner's purse on top. I pick it up and hand it to Mum. 'Look inside. At the name on the cards.'

Mum draws out one of the credit cards. Straightaway she drops it, a gasp of disbelief escaping her. 'No,' she says. 'Dear God, no. It can't be.' She sinks to her knees beside the suitcase, and it's then her gaze falls on the other secret it's concealed for so many years. Her mouth sags open, her eyes widen, shock draining the colour from her face. She reaches into the suitcase, taking out the object that both repulsed and fascinated me a minute ago. A hank of hair, dark and thick, the plaiting at the top unravelled now. The end is held fast by an ornate silver clasp.

'I'm sorry, Mum,' I say.

I pick up the purse. I need to see the evidence again, otherwise I'll never convince myself it's real. I pull out a credit card and there, embossed along the bottom, is Amy's real name.

Anna Wilding, my mother's friend, who disappeared sixteen years ago. Not Julia, aged twenty when she died much later.

Tucked in the front of the purse are two photos. From the first, a young mother smiles at me, her right arm slung around a four-year-old boy, his features familiar although he's now a man. Jake. Anna's hair – long, thick and tightly plaited – is a dark snake against the white of her T-shirt. A silver charm bracelet hangs from her wrist. In the second photo, Jake and I stand in front of Mum and Anna, with Donna to our left. It's hard to distinguish which kid belongs to which parent.

Something's not right, though. The dates, the ages – they don't stack up.

'It can't be Anna who died in the basement,' I say.

'It's her. That's her hair. I'd know it anywhere. Besides, her name's on the credit cards.'

'But Anna disappeared sixteen years ago. Dominic was only a teenager then.'

'Not impossible for someone to commit murder at that age.'

I shake my head. 'With his father still alive? No way, surely.'

'You're right.' Mum says after a pause. 'He didn't murder Anna. She died too long ago. He told me as much, but I didn't listen.'

'What did he say?'

'That he wasn't as bad as I thought he was. He started to say something, but I cut him off. His words were: "I didn't murder..."

At the time, I presumed he meant the fact he didn't kill you. But I suspect he was about to tell me he didn't murder Anna Wilding.'

'Then who did?'

'His father. It must have been Lincoln Perdue who abducted and killed Anna. What's more, I don't believe this Julia he claimed to have murdered ever existed.'

I'm stunned by her words, but they make sense. What Mum's saying slots neatly into place in my head. 'He led me to believe he killed her, when he didn't. He played me.'

'Because your fear meant he could control you more effectively. I doubt he'd have cared about lying to you, if it got him what he wanted.'

'And all the time it was his father who was a murderer.'

'I remember something he said when I confronted him. "I saw him do something terrible once", he told me.'

So Dominic didn't abduct and kill a woman called Julia. Neither did he murder Amy, or Anna as I now know her to be. He must have witnessed her death, though. A fourteen-year-old boy, watching as his father strangles the life from my mother's friend, after hacking off her hair. Explains so much about the man who held me prisoner in the basement where his body now hangs. I was right. He may have been many things, but a killer wasn't one of them.

'With Lincoln Perdue as a parent, no wonder the bastard was so warped. Not that I'm making excuses for him.' Mum strokes the hank of hair. 'Poor Anna.'

I pick up the bracelet, holding it towards her.

'See where one of the charms is missing? She hid it in the mattress as proof of her abduction. Same as when I carved that message on the wall.'

'Is it still there?'

'No, I took it. It's in my bedside cabinet.'

Mum takes the bracelet from me, fingering the gap near the clasp. 'It's a shoe, right?'

'Yes. How did you—'

'Donna and I gave her that bracelet for her twenty-first birthday. She wore it constantly. It's as familiar to me as if it were mine.' She breaks down then, and I'm the one who holds her this time.

I point at the hank of hair. 'Anna wore it long in all her photos. When you and Donna talk about her, you often mention how beautiful it was.'

'Lincoln Perdue must have chopped it off.' Mum's face holds contempt. 'Your father described him as a dick. He didn't know the half of it.'

'Why did he cut off her hair?'

'To humiliate her. And to bag himself a trophy.' Hatred seethes in Mum's voice. Now she's done crying, her old self is back. She grips my arms tight. 'We have two problems. One is Dominic Perdue. The other is Anna Wilding. Jake deserves to know the truth.'

Jake. I picture him, knowing his mother died a brutal death, the hope she'll return one day crushed forever. 'Is that a good idea?'

'Yes. He's a man now, remember.'

'Even so. Not easy, finding out your mother was murdered. Probably raped as well.'

'Her body may never be found. If you're wrong and she's not in the other basement, that is. Besides, any evidence of rape will be long gone.'

I guess she's right. What's tormented Jake over the last sixteen years is the idea his mother deserted him, even if he believes mental illness the driving force. Better for him to discover the truth, no matter how late. In front of me, the contents of the suitcase are too grim to bear. I slam the lid shut.

'What now?' I ask.

'We need to crack on with what we came for. Removing your message from the basement wall. There's more, though. Listen. This is what we'll do.'

She outlines her plan. We'll leave the front door open, attracting attention from the postman the next time he calls. The police will get involved. They'll conduct a search; discover the suitcase and its contents. Anna Wilding is still listed as a missing person.

'I've remembered something,' Mum says. 'Why the surname Perdue sounded familiar.'

'You knew him?'

'Not me. Anna did, though. She once complained about a guy she ran into at a fundraiser. Drunk, he was. Made a nuisance of himself, she said, pestering her, even groping her. Marcus was there, but didn't give a shit. It's a long time ago, but I'm sure she said the man's name was Lincoln Perdue. Seems he didn't take rejection too well.'

'He must have targeted her. Marked her out as a victim. To get revenge.'

'We'll never know. But the police will zero in on Lincoln Perdue as a suspect in Anna's disappearance. Her hair will point to something bad having happened.'

'They'll find her body in the other basement. I'm sure of it.'

'Best we clean up a bit,' Mum says. 'Fingerprints, that kind of stuff. I don't doubt Dominic Perdue's death will be ruled a suicide. But it won't hurt to remove any traces we've been here.'

We go downstairs. Under the kitchen sink, Mum finds a couple of packets of rubber gloves. 'Put these on,' she instructs. She snaps a pair of yellow Marigolds over her hands before disappearing upstairs. When she returns, she holds two elastic bands in her hands. 'Found these in his office,' she says. Her hands loop her hair into a tight ponytail. 'Tie your hair up. We don't want to be shedding any.' She pulls out cleaning materials and rubbish sacks from under the sink, thrusting disinfectant and sponges towards me.

'I'll vacuum, you clean,' she instructs. 'Door handles, whatever you touched. Not the basement. I'll do down there.'

We get to work. From downstairs, I hear the hum of the hoover. Upstairs, I wipe everything in the spare room I've been in contact with, including the suitcase, before doing the same with its contents. Anna's purse, her cards, the photos.

Mum's feet sound on the stairs. Before long, she's vacuumed everywhere up here. Then she moves into Dominic's bedroom, where I've not yet cleaned. She wipes over his bedside cabinet, before pulling it open, removing a handful of letters, her fingers covered by her sleeve.

'I read these last time I was here. Seems Dominic Perdue had one hell of a lot of debts.' She taps the letters thoughtfully against the palm of one hand before laying them on the bed. She reaches into the drawer again, taking out an old asthma inhaler. 'You never mentioned he was asthmatic.'

I stare at the inhaler. 'He wasn't.'

'Strange he'd have this, then.' She drops it back into the cabinet, and then picks up the bundle of debt letters. 'Time for the basement. I left it to last.'

I follow her downstairs. At the entrance to my former prison, she turns to me, still holding the letters in her hands. 'Once was enough, Beth. You shouldn't go down there again.'

I don't. My time in the basement's done. Instead, I stay at the top of the stairs, my gaze fixed on my mother, deliberately blanking the body hanging from the rafter.

It doesn't take Mum long. She cleans and wipes wherever we've been, before returning up the stairs, pushing past me into the kitchen, rummaging under the sink. When she emerges, the cloths and spray are gone and she's holding a screwdriver in her hand.

'Best thing I could find to chip your message off the wall,' she says. She walks back into the basement, shoving the filing cabinet to one side. Once on her knees, she positions the screwdriver against the wall, pressing hard. A chip of plaster flies off, followed by another. Before long a raw wound scars the basement wall, all evidence of my message erased. Then she pushes the cabinet back into place. She gathers the debris into her palm, depositing it in the rubbish sack. Next she picks up the bundle of debt letters, stacking them on the bed beside his suicide note.

'Reinforces his final words,' she says. 'Let's go.'

***

We're outside the cottage now, my feet crunching against the gravel. Mum replaces the keys under the bell, having wiped them free from fingerprints. She slides the stone planter back into place, but leaves the front door open. In her hand she holds the rubbish sack containing the contents of the vacuum, our rubber gloves and the fragments of the basement wall. 'We'll ditch this on the way home,' she says. 'Make sure nobody's around to see us leave, Beth.'

I walk in the direction of the oak, the one under which I used to watch the cottage, this time reversing the focus of my surveillance. No one else is in sight. I turn towards Mum, who's walking towards me. My gaze isn't on her, though, but on the cottage. My eyes roam over the bricks, the windows, the front door, before resting on the small window at the side of the house.

Memories flood through me. Smashing the glass. Dominic's anger, the weeks spent without sunlight. Months spent earning privileges I deemed essential, when the only one worth having was freedom. Here I stand, my mother at my side, a breeze on my cheeks. Priceless.

'Sometimes I thought I loved him.' My voice shakes.

'It wasn't love, Beth.'

'No. But it felt like it.'

CHAPTER 31 – *Beth*

B y the time we get back, it's mid-afternoon. In my bedroom, I stand at the window, half expecting to see Dominic by the lamppost. I give myself a mental shake, recalling Mum's strength, how she held me together when I was falling apart. The least I can do is live up to the example she's set.

'Be strong, Beth,' I tell myself. I will, too. I'm emotionally battered but no longer blank. The blackness has gone. I don't sense my old adversary, depression, anywhere nearby.

***

Later, after supper, I'm reading in my room, when I hear Troy come up the stairs. Mum and Dad are in the lounge. I suck up my courage. Time to confront my brother.

Troy's eyes are hostile when I appear in his doorway. He's sprawled on his bed, a music magazine in one hand. I lean against his chest of drawers.

'You didn't think to knock?' A leave-me-alone vibe emanates from him.

I don't take the bait. 'We need to talk. This time you'll give me an answer.'

Realisation flashes across his face. He's aware of what I mean. Doesn't stop him trying a spot of deflection, though. 'No idea what you're banging on about.'

'I'm referring to the night I disappeared.'

Troy doesn't reply. Merely watches my face, his expression wary.

I take aim, then fire. 'I told Mum what you saw that evening.'

'Shit.' My brother shifts uneasily.

'I'm not leaving until you tell me why. If you won't talk to me, you'll have to deal with Mum.' That hit home, I can tell. 'She's going to tackle you about it. You do realise that?'

'Jesus.' Troy's magazine slips to the floor, unnoticed. 'Why the hell did you tell her?'

I'm not sensing anger from him, despite his words. Instead, I detect something akin to regret, or sadness, or both. 'You know what she's like. Only a matter of time before she wormed it out of me.'

'Yeah.' Troy swings his feet over the side of the bed, coming to a seated position, hands clasped under his chin. I sense we may be about to communicate properly for the first time ever.

My brother huffs out a breath. 'I should have said something. About what I saw.'

'Why didn't you?'

He doesn't answer. He stares at me, and although our eye contact is uncomfortable, I don't shirk it. Instead, I wait.

'Was it awful? What happened to you?' he asks.

Best to let him assume what Mum did at first. It's not so far from the truth. 'The man you saw. He was abusive. In the end, I left him.'

'I'm sorry.'

'So why didn't you speak up?'

My brother bites his lip. 'I was ashamed.'

'Of what?'

Troy's next words fire shock deep into my belly. 'That night I saw the two of you together. It wasn't the first time I'd seen the guy.'

I moisten dry lips. 'What do you mean?'

'He approached me one day a few weeks before you disappeared. Asked about you.'

'*What?*' Right when I think Dominic Perdue can't throw any more harm my way, he chucks another curve ball at me. No random encounter, then, meeting Dominic at The Busy Bean.

'I'd been skateboarding. Ran into you and Jake afterwards. Outside his house.'

'I don't remember.'

'Jake and I chatted about my skateboard for a bit. Then I made towards home.'

'And?'

'This guy came up to me, asking about you. Told me his name was Darren. Darren Price, he said. Mentioned he'd seen you around. How he fancied you. Told him he must need his eyes tested.' Troy laughs, and to my surprise I do too.

'And you said – what, exactly?'

'Not much. He said he'd like to ask you out.'

'What else?'

'I told him you were my sister. Your name. He wanted to know more, though. Stuff like did you have a job, and if so, where.'

'You told him I worked at Homeless Concern?'

'Yeah. I shouldn't have, I know, but he didn't come across as a nutter. Just a decent guy.'

'So why didn't you mention this to the police?'

Troy's expression is guilt-ridden. 'I was fourteen years old, Beth. I thought I'd get into trouble. Big time.'

'You thought the police would blame you?'

'Yes. Because I gave him the information he used to abduct you.'

'They wouldn't have. But I get why you'd assume that. You were still a kid. Not thinking straight.'

'When you went missing I was shitting bricks. Kept telling myself I should say something. As time went on, though, I couldn't. Because then I'd get into even more trouble. It was a crock of crap, and I hadn't a clue how to sort it.'

I guess I can understand Troy's position. Seems my brother's been yet another strand in Dominic Perdue's web, albeit not as close to the centre as I've been.

'I persuaded myself you were fine. Safe. Even though I knew you'd have called Mum if you were.' His voice is thick, choked with what I suspect is remorse.

'It doesn't matter now. Don't worry. I'll make it OK with Mum.'

Relief flits across Troy's face. Then guilt. 'That guy, whoever he was – he hurt you badly, didn't he?'

'Yes,' I say. 'More than you can imagine.'

'Do you hate me?'

I shake my head. 'Come here. Give your big sister a hug.' Our embrace is awkward, and brief, but it's a start.

***

I tell Mum next morning, when we're alone after breakfast. 'I talked with Troy last night.'

Mum's expression turns angry. 'Been meaning to do that myself.'

'Don't. Please, Mum. Just leave it, will you?'

'Did he tell you why he didn't say anything to the police?'

'Yes.' I give her a brief rundown of what Troy told me. In particular, how Dominic approached him, seeking information about me.

'That makes sense,' Mum says.

'It does? How?'

'I've been bothered about something Dominic Perdue said. It seemed too much of a coincidence. First his father kills Anna Wilding. Then his son takes you. OK, so you're not related to the Wildings, but there's a connection there, of sorts. Why you?'

I shake my head. 'No idea. Tell me what he said.'

'That he cherry-picked you. As restitution.'

Something Dominic once said stirs in my brain. When I asked whether Julia had looked like me. Him, confirming that she did. Said with Anna in mind, though.

'I'm guessing he'd been watching the Wilding house,' Mum continued. 'Anna's address was in her purse, remember. Along with those photos.'

I remember how my four-year-old self stands in front of Mum and Anna, so it's hard to tell which child belongs to which mother. 'He thought I might be Anna's daughter.'

'Yes. He targeted you. Watched you come and go with Jake from his house. Spotted the two of you talking with Troy, so he quizzed him when he got the chance. Found out you weren't Anna's daughter after all.'

'He told me I looked like her.'

'You do. Because of that, you fitted his plans for restitution, even though you weren't her child. So he decided to abduct you to put right his father's crime. In his weird way, he recreated Anna's disappearance, intending to rewrite it with a happy conclusion. One in which you became his companion. Cherry-picked, like he said. If Jake had been female—'

'My God.' The pieces slot into place. 'He'd have been taken, not me.'

***

Two evenings later, I'm watching the evening news on television with Mum. Both of us have become obsessive that way, the radio in the kitchen constantly tuned to a local station. Troy's in the lounge with us, but he's texting, his attention on his mobile. Dad will be home later; a business meeting with Marcus Wilding, Mum said. I must be making progress, because I don't flinch when she says his name.

The national news ends, and the programme switches to *Points West* for the local stuff. Dominic's death is headline news tonight. The photo they show is old, clearly from his driving licence, his hair longer, his face younger and unsmiling, but seeing him is still a shock. Mum grasps my hand. Keep it together, Beth, I tell myself. Troy doesn't glance up from his mobile, but I doubt he'd recognise the face on the TV screen, not when Dominic looks so different. Besides, he knew my abductor as Darren Price.

'Police called to the scene say they found items of a personal nature belonging to a local woman, Anna Wilding. Mrs Wilding was reported missing from her home in Downend sixteen years ago. It is not known how they came to be at the cottage owned and lived in by Dominic Perdue.'

Even though we've been expecting this, it still comes as a shock. Mum's hand flies to her mouth, freezing there. A loud intake of breath escapes her.

'Oh, God,' she says.

Troy glances up, before his attention flicks to the television. A picture of Anna, the same one we found in her purse, fills the screen. The television presenter drones on.

'Shown here shortly before her disappearance, with her young son, Jake…'

Troy's attention is fully engaged now. He'll have recognised Anna from the photos on the sideboard. 'Mum, is that your friend? The one who disappeared?'

'Yes. It's Anna Wilding.'

At sixteen, Troy's clearly struggling with the right thing to say. 'Has she been found?'

'Not yet. But it's looking likely she will be. Not alive, though.'

The news ends, and a sense of normality creeps back into the room. Not long afterwards a key sounds in the front door. Dad is home.

He looks serious as he comes into the lounge, his eyes on Mum. 'I need to talk to you, Ursula.'

'About Anna? You've been with Marcus Wilding, right?'

'No. That's why I'm back early. He cancelled our meeting, phoned to tell me the police want to speak with him. Listen, there's something you need to know—'

'I already do. It's been on the news. They've found her things. Not her, though. But they will. Soon.'

My father sits beside Mum, the sofa sagging with the extra weight. 'What did they say?'

She gives him a summary of the newscast. 'That's the weird thing,' Dad says. 'This place where her stuff was found. Used to belong to someone I knew years back, an old business associate. Hell, we were only talking about him the other day. Guy by the name of Lincoln Perdue.'

Mum nods. 'I remember. A bit of a dick, you said.'

'Worse than that, I suspect. Why else would Anna's stuff be in his house?'

***

A day later, the police discover Anna's body. Her corpse is where I knew it would be, in the sealed-up basement next to mine. We're watching the evening news again, Mum and I, alone this time. The same reporter is doing the broadcast.

'The area is now an official crime scene. Police are looking into the background of the former owner of the cottage, now deceased, local businessman Lincoln Perdue…'

'You were right,' Mum says.

'I wish I weren't.'

In front of us, the reporter carries on. 'According to his death certificate, Lincoln Perdue died from a fatal asthma attack…'

'Oh, my God,' Mum says. 'That explains it.'

'What?'

'The reporter said Dominic's father died from an asthma attack. That's who the inhaler in his bedside cabinet belonged to.'

'I don't follow.'

'Dominic Perdue wasn't lying when he told you he'd murdered someone. It wasn't a woman; it was his father. If my guess is correct, he didn't strangle him, though.'

I'm silent, chewing over her words. She might well be right. 'He obviously hated his dad.'

'Yes. For being an abusive parent and an all-round dick, as your father called him. That's why the inhaler was in his bedside cabinet and not with the rest of Lincoln's stuff.'

'What do you mean?'

'It's like Anna's hair. A trophy. I'd bet a truckload of money Dominic Perdue killed his father by withholding his asthma medication.'

So Dominic had been a murderer after all. Mum was right when she told me I was lucky to be alive.

***

283

I go to Anna's funeral. We all do. Marcus Wilding's there, but I ignore him. From my seat at the crematorium, I watch as the coffin descends to its final destination. Closure for Mum, Donna and Jake. For me, too.

After the funeral life returns to normal. If the police haven't come knocking on our door by now, connecting us with what happened in the cottage, it's odds on they never will. As we expected, Dominic's death has been ruled a suicide, attributed to his mounting debts. As for Anna, the police don't have much evidence to go on, what with Lincoln Perdue being dead. He's the main suspect, so I hear, which is about as much justice as Anna will get.

Jake called me this morning. 'The police say we can get Mum's stuff back.'

'When?'

'Soon. The investigation is running out of juice. Dad doesn't give a shit, of course.'

'No surprise there.'

'I'd like her charm bracelet. As a memento of her. I don't remember it, but it's so familiar, what with her wearing it in all her photos.'

'She'd want you to have it,' I say.

Two days later, he calls again.

'The police are releasing her stuff today. Said I can pick everything up this afternoon.'

I'm glad. Since Jake discovered what happened to his mother, he's been more settled, more grounded. I believe he always knew she was dead but refused to admit it, keeping hope alive along with her memory. Now the truth is out, he's able to move on.

'Can you come over? Once I've collected it?' Hesitation in his voice, as though he's embarrassed to ask. 'Thing is…' He clears his throat. 'I don't want to do it on my own.'

***

Later, after I arrive at his house, Jake waves me upstairs. 'Everything's in an old suitcase in my room. I've not yet opened it. I've been warned her hair is in there.'

'We'll look through it together.'

'I'll make coffee. Go on up.'

In Jake's bedroom, the suitcase sits on the floor. Noises from the kitchen reach me as Jake collects mugs, spoons, fills the coffee machine. I don't have much time.

My fingers flick open the clasps to the suitcase. Inside is Anna's hank of hair, along with her handbag. I rummage in it, locating her charm bracelet. From my pocket, I fish out the tiny silver boot and attach it to the vacant link. Jake will never know it was missing. He might have made the connection with the charm he saw in my bedside cabinet if he received the bracelet back without it, but now he never will. My secret is safe from him.

***

'He cut off her hair.' Jake's voice is loaded with anger, as well as laced with sorrow. We're sprawled on his bedroom floor, drinking Marcus's whisky, an illicit act that flicks him the finger. 'Why did the bastard do something so weird?'

To humiliate her, but the words don't get farther than my brain. Some things are best left unsaid, and Jake already knows the answer. At least he doesn't ask whether she suffered before she died.

'Lincoln bloody Perdue.' He spits the name out like poison. 'What a fucking arsehole. Warped to the core, obviously.'

I stay silent.

'Sad, his son killing himself, but for me, it's good. Because if he hadn't, we'd never have discovered what happened to Mum. He couldn't have known what his scumbag father did, of course.'

'I guess not. After all, he was still a teenager when his father murdered Anna, wasn't he?' I'm amazed how well I play my part. Beth Sutton, uninvolved in any way with the Perdues.

'Yes. He obviously never looked in that suitcase after his father's death. Just dumped it in his spare room along with the rest of his father's stuff, and didn't look inside.'

'That's how it must have been.'

'I wonder how long Lincoln Perdue kept her there,' he says. 'In that basement. Before he killed her.'

I bite my lip, uncertain how to reply.

'It only had a tiny window. Can you imagine how terrified she must have been?'

'Yes,' I say. 'I can.'

'No, you can't. Not really. Unless you've been through something that awful, none of us have any idea.'

I nod. 'You were right all along,' I tell him. 'She didn't abandon you.'

Jake will never realise how much I empathise with Anna Wilding, but that's good. Some things are better left unknown. He's found his mother at last, or the memory of her, and that's what matters. No need for him to know I was the basement's second captive.

EPILOGUE – *Beth*

L ife is slotting back together for me. I thought I'd be free after I escaped the basement, but things didn't turn out that simple. Back with my family, I remained a captive. It took Dominic Perdue hanging himself before my prison door finally opened. Now I can start to heal.

The process is slow, though. That's to be expected; people don't recover overnight from experiences such as mine. It's not linear, either. In my naiveté, I expect my mood to lighten more every day. It doesn't. Some days I wake up and I can't wait to practise my Italian or chat with Mum. Other times a fog descends into my brain during the night, making me aware the blackness of depression is lurking, waiting to claim me if I allow it.

I tell Mum. These days we have no secrets from each other.

'Exercise might help,' she suggests. 'Maybe you should start swimming again.'

This morning I'm taking her advice at our nearest pool. Piling up the lengths, allowing the chlorinated coolness to wash away the blackness. As I pause at the shallow end, the sun streams through the large windows, filling me with hope. So much light and space, along with room to move, other people. Everything Dominic deprived me of in the basement.

Donna's helped as well. Mum and I allow her to believe I was in an abusive relationship, one I managed to escape. The truth, but a watered-down version. I go to her house once a week. She regrets not finishing her psychotherapy qualification, so she practises on me, unofficially, as we chat. She dispenses common sense, humour and wisdom.

'Live, Beth,' she tells me one day. 'That's the best advice anyone can ever give. Live your life, the whole length and breadth of it.'

'I will.' For Anna. Or Amy, as I remember her. For myself, too.

Things are better at home these days. Troy and I talk more than we've ever done, although, at sixteen, he's yet to emerge from teenage self-absorption. That's OK. We have time. We don't discuss him not telling the police about the night I went missing. He regrets his omission, he's made that plain, and besides it's now lost amongst stuff that's more important. Our conversations never go very deep. Instead, I ask whether he's going skateboarding at the weekend or if he plans to see the latest sci-fi movie. Troy's aware these things mean little to me, but he's savvy enough to realise we're forging new connections. In turn, he feigns interest in my Italian studies and his tone is warmer towards me now. We're getting there.

Dad's not so hard on me anymore. No more nagging me about university or getting a job. Like Donna, he's now convinced I'm a victim of domestic abuse. I sat him down one day, Mum at my side, to deliver a highly edited version of events. Our conversation ended with my father believing I endured two years with an abusive boyfriend.

'So now you know,' I said once I'd finished.

'I'm sorry I doubted you, sweetheart.' His face is stricken with guilt and remorse.

'I couldn't tell you before. You understand, don't you?'

He nodded. 'Can you forgive me for the way I behaved after you came home?'

'Oh, Dad.' I smiled my answer at him, before holding out my arms. We hugged for a long sweet moment, turning me into his little girl again, his Beth. Beside me, Mum smiles.

'Your mother's still devastated about Anna,' Dad told me yesterday. 'Even after so long, it's been a shock.'

'A relief, though, surely? To know for definite, one way or another.'

Dad's expression turned solemn. His hands grasped my shoulders.

'She needs our support. Can you do that, Beth? Be there for her?'

'Yes.' I owe it to the woman who's done so much for me. Besides, when my father smiled in reply, I realised it'll help us to grow closer. We're a team now, united by our love for Ursula Sutton. Last night, I heard her voice, low and with a laugh in it, coming from Dad's bedroom. Chances are they'll knit back together as well. Everything's looking good.

As for my relationship with my mother, our former closeness has returned. Except now we're bound together so tightly I doubt anything will ever unravel us. We hug more than ever, and there's no finer therapy, not even Donna's wise words. Mum laughs more these days; we even joke in Italian together. We never mention my abduction, the cottage, or the body hanging from its rafters. Instead, we agree, without words, to lock the past in a metaphorical basement, never to be disturbed.

Twenty lengths of the pool completed. I stop, panting, at the shallow end. The sunlight is streaming full pelt through the windows now. Two years I spent away from its warmth. I make a decision. Whatever my future holds, I have to find the sun.

An idea pops into my head and the minute it does, it feels right. Ticks every box.

Italy. I'll go to Italy. Improve my language skills. Get an au pair job, work with kids, the way I've always dreamed of. Discover what I want to do long-term. Crushed by my abductor, my decision-making skills are rusty; the heat and noise of Rome will tease them back to life. For nearly two years, a view of the Colosseum brightened up the basement where Dominic held me captive. Before long I'll stand on the same spot from where the photo was taken, the Italian sunshine caressing my skin. Donna will be pleased. It's what she means by me living the length and breadth of my life. A start, anyway. Mum will understand, if I tell her it's my way of escaping Dominic Perdue. Forever.

I think about him often. How could I not? For two years, he controlled me to the extent my entire being dissolved into his. He intrudes less and less into my head these days, though. Every day of freedom strengthens my mental barriers against him. I've read up on Stockholm syndrome, how its tentacles can grasp victims for years afterwards; I'm determined not to let that happen. A tiny part of me may always have feelings for him, but I keep it, and them, firmly suppressed.

'There's a lesson to be learned in every situation,' Donna tells me one day.

She notices my sceptical expression. 'Believe me, Beth. You just have to find it.' She smiles. 'Search hard enough, and you might discover gold in what happened to you.'

Since that day, her words have echoed in my head, and I've decided she's right. Class is in session and Dominic's my teacher, the lesson being the value of freedom. Not something I'll ever take for granted again. I'm a different person now; stronger, more confident, determined to savour everything good this world can offer. As each day passes, I'm reassembling the soul I surrendered to Dominic Perdue. The real Beth Sutton is emerging, a butterfly crawling from the chrysalis of the basement. The Italian sun will dry my wings, harden them, ready for me to take flight.

Into the rest of my life.

A Note from Bloodhound Books

Thanks for reading The Second Captive. We hope you enjoyed it as much as we did. Please consider leaving a review on Amazon or Goodreads to help others find and enjoy this book too.

We make every effort to ensure that books are carefully edited and proofread, however occasionally mistakes do slip through. If you spot something, please do send details to info bloodhoundbooks.com and we can amend it.

Bloodhound Books specialise in crime and thriller fiction. We regularly have special offers including free and discounted eBooks. To be the first to hear about these special offers, why not join our mailing list here? We won't send you more than two emails per month and we'll never pass your details on to anybody else.

Readers who enjoyed The Second Captive will also enjoy

Guilty Innocence also by Maggie James

Baby Dear by Linda Huber

Acknowledgements

Thanks to:

Lucy Davies, Kim Feasey, Maxine Groves, Karen Harris, Derrian Ireland, Hannah Millar, Mary Moss and Magdalena Vidgen, for their invaluable help and feedback.

This book is dedicated to Maxine Groves, a wonderful friend who has been very supportive of my writing endeavours. Love and hugs to you.

All the places in and around Bristol featured in The Second Captive, such as Kingswood's Clock Tower and Hanham's Troopers Hill, are real. The Grade 2 listed chimney on top of the hill, with its characteristic lean to the west, was used for copper smelting and may date from the eighteenth century.

Free Books!

Why not sign up for my newsletter? I send the latest edition to my subscribers every two months and whenever I release a new title, so you won't get bombarded with emails. I often include free copies of novels from other authors (with their permission, of course!), book recommendations, news about my latest titles, and discounts on my novels.

To be added to my newsletter, click this link: http://eepurl. com/cn7Jb5. I respect your privacy and will never sell your details to any third parties. Thank you!

About The Author

Maggie James is a British author who lives in Bristol. The Second Captive is her fourth novel.

Visit my website and sign up for my newsletter! An occasional email with details of new novel releases. My blog is also on my website - I post regularly on all topics of interest to readers, including author interviews and book reviews. You can find it here: www.maggiejamesfiction.com

Other Books by Maggie James

Blackwater Lake (A Free Novella)
Matthew Stanyer fears the worst when he reports his parents missing. His father, Joseph Stanyer, has been struggling to cope with his wife Evie, whose dementia is rapidly worsening. When their bodies are found close to Blackwater Lake, a local beauty spot, the inquest rules the deaths as a murder-suicide. A conclusion that's supported by the note Joseph leaves for his son.

Grief-stricken, Matthew begins to clear his parents' house of decades of compulsive hoarding, only to discover the dark enigmas hidden within its walls. Ones that lead Matthew to ask: why did his father choose Blackwater Lake to end his life? What other secrets do its waters conceal?

A short (25,000 words) novella, Blackwater Lake examines one man's determination to uncover his family's troubled past.

Available free in e-book format from the following retailers: Amazon, Apple, Barnes and Noble, Google Play, Kobo, Scribd and Inktera.

After She's Gone
Lori Golden's family has had more than its fair share of troubles. But through it all, Lori and her sister, Jessie, have always supported each other. Then Jessie is killed. And Lori's world turns upside down.

Devastated, Lori struggles to cope with her loss, and to learn to live in a world without her bright, bubbly sister by her side. Around her, her already fractured family starts to fall apart. And as Lori and her mother try to pick up the pieces of their shattered lives, secrets long thought buried are coming painfully to light.

Faced with the unthinkable, Lori is forced to ask herself how well she really knows those who are left behind…

A tense novel about murder, arson and a family falling apart.

Available from Amazon in Kindle, audio and paperback formats here.

Guilty Innocence
A letter that reveals a horrifying truth…

Natalie Richards finds more than she bargained for when she snoops through her boyfriend's possessions: evidence that Mark Slater was once convicted of a brutal killing. Heartbroken by what she's discovered, Natalie's dreams of a future with him collapse.

Only the other person jointly sentenced for Abby Morgan's murder, the twisted and violent Adam Campbell, knows the truth. That Mark played no part in Abby's death.

Meanwhile, circumstances have thrust Mark back in contact with Adam, who, aged twenty-five, is more domineering and chilling than ever. Can Mark rewrite history and confront his nemesis?

A gritty novel examining child murder and dysfunctional families, Guilty Innocence tells of one man's struggle to break free from his past.

Available from Amazon in Kindle and paperback formats here.

Sister, Psychopath
When they were children, Megan Copeland adored her younger sister Chloe. Now she can't bear to be in the same room as her.

Megan believes Chloe to be a psychopath. After all, her sister's a textbook case: cold, cruel and lacking in empathy. Chloe loves to taunt Megan at every opportunity, as well as manipulating their mentally ill mother, Tilly.

When Tilly, under Chloe's malignant influence, becomes dangerously unstable, the consequences turn ugly for everyone. Megan's world falls apart, allowing long-buried truths to rise to the surface. Her sister's out of control, it seems, and there's little she can do about it. Until Chloe's actions threaten the safety of Megan's former lover. A man from whom she has withheld an important secret…

A study of sibling rivalry and dysfunctional relationships, Sister, Psychopath tells the story of one woman's struggle to survive the damage inflicted by her sociopathic sister.

Available from Amazon in Kindle and paperback formats here.

His Kidnapper's Shoes

On some level deep inside, Laura Bateman knows something is wrong. That her relationship with her son is not what it should be. That it is based on lies.

But bad things have happened to Laura. Things that change a person. Forever.

For twenty-six-year-old Daniel, the discovery that his mother is not who he thought comes close to destroying him. As his world turns upside down, he searches for sanity in the madness that has become his life. Daniel is left with nothing but questions. Why did Laura do something so terrible? Can he move past the demons of his childhood?

And the biggest question of all: can he ever forgive Laura?

A tense novel of psychological suspense, His Kidnapper's Shoes weaves one man's quest for his identity with one woman's need to heal her troubled past.

Available from Amazon in Kindle and paperback formats here.

Non-Fiction: Write Your Novel! From Getting Started To First Draft

Have you always longed to write a novel? In Write Your Novel! From Getting Started to First Draft, I aim to inspire you with the confidence to do just that. With this book, I'll be your cheerleader, your hand-holder. We'll work on your mind-set, find sources of support, and deal with procrastination issues. I'll help you carve out the time to write and together we'll smash through the excuses that are holding you back.

What else? Do you need help in finding ideas? Worried where to start? Unsure whether writing software is right for you? Confused how to plan your novel? No problem! We cover all these issues and more. Every section ends with an action plan so you're raring to go!

I've included two chapters on plotting and another with writing advice. That way, once you've finished Write Your Novel!, you'll have an outline in place, one that will inspire you to get going, and you'll know how to start. My aim is to prepare you to write your novel as soon as you've completed the exercises in this book.

So if you've always yearned to be a novelist but you're unsure how to begin... why not buy Write Your Novel! and get started?

Available from Amazon in Kindle format here.

Lightning Source UK Ltd.
Milton Keynes UK
UKHW011809070419
340625UK00001B/157/P